Sill[illegible] born [illegible] [illegible] factories until becoming an [illegible] control assistant with the Ministry of Aircraft Production in 1945.

He enlisted in May 1946 into the RAFVR, and spent two years on active service in Malaya as a wireless operator. At the end of 1949 he was invalided out of the service with a hundred per cent disability pension.

He began writing, and lived for six years in France and Spain. His first stories were published in the *Nottinghamshire Weekly Guardian*. In 1958 *Saturday Night and Sunday Morning* was published, and *The Loneliness of the Long Distance Runner*, which won the Hawthornden Prize for literature, came out the following year. Both these books were made into films.

Further works include *The Ragman's Daughter* and *The General* (both also filmed), the *William Posters* trilogy, *A Start in Life*, *Raw Material*, *The Widower's Son*, *The Second Chance* – as well as six volumes of poetry. His latest books include *The Open Door* and *Last Loves*. With his wife, Ruth Fainlight, he divides his time between London and a house in France.

Fiction

Saturday Night and Sunday Morning
The Loneliness of the Long Distance Runner
The General
The Ragman's Daughter
The Death of William Posters
A Tree on Fire
Guzman, Go Home
A Start in Life
Travels in Nihilon
Raw Material
Men, Women and Children
The Flame of Life
The Widower's Son
The Storyteller
The Second Chance and Other Stories
Her Victory
The Lost Flying Boat
Down from the Hill
Life Goes On
Out of the Whirlpool
The Open Door
Last Loves

Poetry

The Rats and Other Poems
A Falling Out of Love and Other Poems
Love in the Environs of Voronezh
Storm and Other Poems
Snow on the North Side of Lucifer
Sun Before Departure: Collected Poems 1974–1982
Tides and Stone Walls

Plays

All Citizens Are Soldiers (with Ruth Fainlight)
Three Plays

Non-Fiction

Road to Volgograd

Essays

Mountains and Caverns

For children

The City Adventures of Marmalade Jim
Big John and the Stars
The Incredible Fencing Fleas
Marmalade Jim on the Farm
Marmalade Jim and the Fox

ALAN SILLITOE

Key to the Door

PALADIN
GRAFTON BOOKS
A Division of the Collins Publishing Group

LONDON GLASGOW
TORONTO SYDNEY AUCKLAND

Paladin
Grafton Books
A Division of the Collins Publishing Group
8 Grafton Street, London W1X 3LA

Published in Paladin Books 1990

Previously published by Grafton Books 1986

First published in Great Britain by
W. H. Allen & Co. Ltd 1961

ISBN 0-586-09006-1

Printed and bound in Great Britain by
Collins, Glasgow

Set in Garamond

Preface

This preface tells how *Key to the Door* came to be written, and gives my observations on re-reading it since it was first published in 1961. It was 'in progress' during the same years as *Saturday Night and Sunday Morning*, *The Loneliness of the Long Distance Runner* and *The General.*

Key to the Door, however, was started before any of them, because the first dozen pages I ever did, at the age of twenty, formed a nucleus around which the rest of the novel grew.

An author's work is like a vast conglomeration of statuary that is hewn out of his life but bears no resemblance to the design of his own soul. I remind myself of this fundamental law so as to emphasize that while *Key to the Door* might in superficial ways appear to be autobiographical, it is an imaginary work, and I shall explain why it could never have reflected the state of my own soul at the time it was being written.

It's true that I used all the ramified energy of my soul in an attempt to create one that belonged to somebody else. That is a different matter. The distinction is a thin one, but it is definitive nevertheless. While the details of one's life are occasionally used in a novel, they are transmuted by the imagination, and are employed only as stable and convenient points from which to advance through more emotional and fictional zones.

Having started the novel thirty years ago, it is hard to say where truth ended and invention began, though it is certain that there was no dividing line by the time it was finished, when all was fiction. Although many incidents in the early stages were familiar on one level, and a fair number of the characters loosely based on recollected faces, the fundamental attitudes of 'our hero' (if such he can be called: why it was intended that he never should be is revealed in the course of the book) can in no way be applied to me at any stage. It should not be regarded as other than a work of fiction whose origins may be interesting, but are finally irrelevant as far as following the actual narrative is concerned.

On 8 May 1948, after twelve months' training as a wireless-operator in the Royal Air Force, I embarked on a troopship for Singapore. In June the following year, while stationed at Butterworth Airstrip in north Malaya, I went on a week's Jungle Rescue Exercise, an attempt to ascend Gunong Jerai (in Kedah State) from the south. It was a backpacking stint of the most strenuous sort, with rifle and bayonet, into tropical rain forest.

Towards the end of that year, back in England, being treated in an RAF Hospital at Wroughton for tuberculosis, I got out my rain-and-soil stained diary of the jungle climb and wrote what was to become the first dozen pages of *Key to the Door*. I called it 'Kedah Peak'. The substance of it was broadcast by me on the BBC early in 1957 during a short visit to England.

In Nottingham, towards the end of 1949, I got hold of three or four limp-covered folio cash-books and expanded 'Kedah Peak' to take in the whole of my time in the Far East, calling it 'Adventures in Malaya'. It was a first-person chronological account which drew the honest comment from a friend who read it that: 'It's interesting, but doesn't read like a real book.' I did however re-write one of the chapters, which then appeared as my first published story in the *Nottinghamshire Weekly Guardian* called 'No Shot in the Dark'.

I went on to turn out three more (unpublished) novels. What was to become the second part of *Key to the Door* was written in Majorca in 1953, a narrative about my childhood which I called 'Nimrod' – a nickname given to me in infancy by my grandfather. I typed it, but did nothing with the two hundred or so pages except revise them from time to time.

I also continued to work on 'Adventures in Malaya', so that from May 1950 to March 1955 it went through six drafts, and the expanded version became 'Letters From Malaya' – a label rather than a title. More invented episodes had been put in with each fresh revision, and the novel ended with the fighting during the Malayan Emergency. The main character was called Brian Seaton, but the novel contained nothing about his early life. My agent sent it to one or two publishers, who turned it down. I kept no copies, though an old notebook has turned up in which there are some references to it.

During the next two years I wrote three other novels (also unpublished) and one travel book about the island of Majorca called 'A Stay of Some Time' – a stay which ran into years, in fact, for I was able to live there on my RAF pension.

In 'Letters From Malaya' Brian Seaton's encounter with the communist bandit in the last section of the book ends in a quite opposite way to what was made to occur later in the completed *Key to the Door*. Seaton, after all, belonged to the RAF; his enlistment oath and conditioning, as well as a great part of his temperament, would lead him to act only in a certain and predictable way, and so – in those early drafts – I caused him to act.

From the age of fourteen I had been in a cadet organization (during the War), knew what attachment to a corps or uniform meant, and was incapable of any moral judgement that implied disloyalty to it. So I felt that Brian Seaton would never allow himself the luxury of such judgement while wearing a uniform, a possible lack of imagination on my part because the whole problem was still too close to my own experience. However much that fact might embarrass me now, such was the case.

It took a long time to achieve a respectable distance and thereby turn it into fiction. It may simply have been my inability (as much as unwillingness) to take a risk – a lack of confidence. However, the following uncorrected quotation from the final chapter of 'Letters From Malaya' shows that cracks in Brian Seaton's armour of rectitude, and in my own rigidity, were beginning to appear:

'I know now that I had no part in the war. I wanted to withdraw myself from Malaya, to anywhere else in the world, mainly to another climate, probably most of all to England. I was horrified to know that I had killed a man, and it seemed now that I was to pay for what I had done. I have killed a man, I kept saying to myself, I have killed a man. By way of hasty judgement I said to myself that I had been tricked into killing the man; I did not know at the moment how the trick had worked, when it began, or the mechanism of it, or how its progress had been marked. But I was sure that the trick had started working as soon as I was born, for I was not a person given to killing. I asked myself who it was that had played this trick on me, but – after hours of wild thought that had kept me awake half the night, I could not reach a conclusion. Perhaps I did not want to reach a conclusion, because it might have told me that I could after all blame no one for the trick that had been played on me except myself.'

This paragraph, by chance preserved, is a vital part of the transition machinery that led to Brian Seaton's more unusual, though politically meaningful, action. After *Saturday Night and Sunday Morning* was published in 1958 (I returned that year to England, having been six years abroad) and *The Loneliness of the Long Distance Runner* (1959), and while I was preparing *The General* for publication, I began the final gathering of material for *Key to the Door* – with the problem as to how it should be presented as a story and a theme.

I decided that what transpired between Brian Seaton and the communist bandit who was at his mercy during a pre-battle skirmish in the jungle, was to be more logically explained in terms of his upbringing during the Thirties – and of his factory life in the early Forties, which chapters I now wrote in order to bring the emotional and cultural pattern into shape.

While doing so I recalled a novel read in Wroughton Hospital called *Tell England*, by Ernest Raymond. It described the lives of two boys at public school who were eventually commissioned in the Great War and killed at the Dardanelles. I enjoyed the book, which seemed remarkably well-written at the time, and the sentimental patriotism, being beautifully underplayed, was quite affecting. It told of a world I knew nothing about, though I thought I understood it rather better after reading the book.

I was filled with pity for those who exposed themselves to be killed when it appeared they had so much to live for, though I knew they couldn't have done anything else, considering their education and the philosophy that went with having the good things of the world. The message of the book was for those who had survived the Great War, and even more of these two young and precious boys who had selflessly gone to die for them. The young men valued what they were giving up at the age of twenty, and knowing this, and having been tolerably well-educated, they had had the key to the door for quite some time. The rationale for their going was 'adventure', and the further pity of it was that it was not *their* rationale, but a camouflage put on it by fate or destiny.

I found a copy and re-read it, and thought about the possibility of writing of someone whose life had been the antithesis of the kind they had led: a young man who, when called on to fight, did not automatically accept the fact that his country was worth dying for. To say that the harder a person's life has been, the more reluctant he is to give it up, is no mere exercise in subversion, but an attempt at a reality which I knew to be common enough. Tell England this, as well, I thought.

The 'form' of the book was not easy to organize. I was against a plain progression of step-by-step events from the marriage of Seaton's parents to his twenty-first birthday, which would make it one more family saga. It wasn't that I wanted a scheme for a scheme's sake, but it seemed that the most likely time to plant the adolescent and factory chapters, given the way I had decided to conclude the book, would be during Brian Seaton's time on active service in Malaya when, while keeping his solitary watches as a wireless operator, he had many hours to mull on these significant years.

Real life began for Brian Seaton as soon as he was born, and was intensified by going to school. But his position in the world only became plain to him on starting work in a factory at the age of fourteen. While he was in Malaya the period of his childhood receded, whereas the youth and factory years he had just lived through seemed like a decade each (as every year can at that age), and retained what turned out to be an overpowering influence at the vital moment of confrontation with the communist bandit in the jungle.

The three parts of *Key to the Door*, drawn together for the first time in 1960, totalled more than 750 pages. In order to shape it, give it body and soul, and replace some of the early dross which has been excised, I stitched in many stories that I had thought to save for another volume after *The Loneliness of the Long Distance Runner*. It reminded me of Benvenuto Cellini who, faced with the Pope's threat to have him hanged because of non-delivery of a commissioned statue, throws into the cauldron all his priceless but smaller statuary to have enough metal in the mould to complete his work.

Thus I meshed into *Key to the Door* a novella about a wireless operator, several factory stories, a few Malayan tales, a couple of troopship episodes, as well as a childhood piece or two. The frantic months before the deadline, which I had contrived in order to force my tardy hand, kept me at it night and day. I knew that I must soon write 'the end' under the last line of the book, or throw the whole long project into the old tea-chest of unpublished novels.

The finished book was given to the printer twelve years after the first 'seminal' pages of 'Kedah Peak' were written. The reviews were generally more favourable than I had anticipated, though some of the critics had difficulty (not surprisingly) with its political implications. My book showed a comparatively sensitive young man from what was called 'the working classes' who instead of walking in the fields clutching an anthology of romantic poetry (misunderstood by an uncouth father and seared by an overloving mother, much as if he were still kicking and screaming to get out of *Sons and Lovers*) puts the experience of his life into political terms because they were the only ones he could dimly perceive at that time.

It is the story of a life which ended at twenty-two. From then on he would become a family man, a factory worker and trade union member. His great action had already been performed. He was not destined to become the proletarian hero of communist literature – nor was he during his first twenty-one years. The 'key to the door' which he obtained by bitter experience was meant to be more diverse and subtle than that.

The book went into many editions, both in England and abroad, and has been translated into twelve languages. In Russia it was published in a vast edition of one million hardbacked copies, but during the process of what they called 'translation' it was so severely mangled that nearly a third of it was cut. Much of the omitted matter was that which showed Brian Seaton to be no simple lover of Socialism; neither he nor his mates quite lived up to the ideal the Russians had in mind; certain sections were cut out because they did not sufficiently indicate that England was the inhuman capitalist scrap-heap they liked their purblind readers to believe.

It was knife-censorship, not deliberate distortion or actual re-writing, but judicious hacking, so that the finished work, as presented to Russian readers, was nothing like the one I had written with so much care. The censors, concerned that the book contain nothing emotionally or politically disturbing, distorted it beyond recognition. I understand that many works translated from 'the West' go through a similar mincing-machine of falsification.

To admit that a piece of work is cherished after so much love has been put into it may seem out of place in this preface to its unabridged printing, but I take the opportunity of telling those anonymous Soviet 'cultural workers' who butchered my novel that I shall never forgive them for what they did – though in some ways I feel sorry for them at having had to do it. If I had been one of their own writers, with no other edition possible, I would have exiled myself forever or till conditions changed beyond recognition.

And yet, on second thoughts, cool down, I tell myself. My last and I hope more dignified opinion on the matter is that to have had my novel so used in this way by the Russians is surely a distinction of great value and meaning. If they had printed it as it stood I would indeed have needed to worry about the state of my soul. A philosophy of writing which does not have as its basis the idea of pity for *everyone* paves a way to hell, both for its practitioners and for all those about whom they write.

Alan Sillitoe
5 December 1977

PART ONE
Prologue

1

Brian, watched by his mother, stood in the paddling-pool without becoming part of the fray. His vacant blue eyes were caught by the broad elbow of the river, though he couldn't be entirely captivated by its movement, for he clutched a mouth-organ as knuckleduster in case the flying bolts of screamed-up kids should on purpose or accidentally jolt him face-down into the gritty water.

Thinking he needed fresh air from the bug-eaten back-to-backs of Albion Yard, Vera had put on their coats and led him up Wilford Road, meaning to save threeha'pence by walking in order to buy him an ice-cream cornet on the way. Maybe she'd even get a free ride back on a tram by saying Brian was under five and winking at the conductor. Harold would paste her if he knew, but then, what the eye don't see the heart don't grieve, and that was the end of that by the time they'd reached the railway bridge and Brian clamoured to see a train drive underneath. Satisfied only when coughing smoke back at the loco-funnel, they walked as far as a boat on the Trent and cows by the far bank chewing beneath tree umbrellas, then turned into the compound of a grass-lawned paddling-pool already full of other kids and mams. Vera picked up a yesterday's *Post* from the bench, to read while Brian with rolled-up leggings stepped cautiously into the water.

The mouth-organ stuck from a pocket, and he played at a recently discovered trick of pressing both hands on his ears, half-blocking the immediate wild yells of spinning kids to hear instead a far-off echo or reflection of it. He completed the illusion by closing his eyes, and the noises of this distant eldorado, though appearing to come from a similar paddling-pool and river, seemed a haven of enjoyment compared to the brickbat yells that assailed him when he took his hands down to test out a hope that they had been magically replaced by those of the more agreeable playground.

'Don't push your 'ands in your tabs like that,' his mother called, 'or you'll get canker.' But he was still tuned to the crystal set of that muted unattainable land somewhere beyond the river, wondered where it was and whether his mam would ever take him to where children of another world sounded so much happier than anyone could at the pool wherein his excalibur feet were planted now.

Women paddled as well – anything for a laugh – white feet dipping into watered sludge, and Vera remembered wading not in a shallow corporation pool on a sunny day, but in two feet of cold and swirling water from the ancient New Bridge house to the firm ground of Peter's Street. She and Seaton had wakened from a night of thunderstorms, a deluge of water still splashing and ricochetting in luminous flakes against the windows as they descended in the half-dark of morning to see furniture and belongings floating around the darkened room like ducks that had strayed into a trap. Vera paddled out when the rain stopped, followed by Seaton with an arm-chair on his head.

'We'll get consumption if we stay here,' he called. She turned on him: 'Where do you think we're going to live then? Under the canal bridge?' 'No,' he answered, 'we'll get a house.' He stacked each piece of furniture on dry ground, leaving Vera as guard while he went back a dozen times for more chairs, sofa, a bed – planted on his hard head and beefy shoulders as he emerged from the isolated lane on which only a pair of cottages stood. Abb Fowler, cloth-capped and jaunty at the door of the other, helped him after his own was done, while Vera was told, by a passer-by, of vacant houses in Albion Yard on the opposite side of town, flea-ridden but dry, that they could be in by teatime if they looked nippy.

Harold and Abb co-operated in the move, spent sixteen hours pushing a handcart back and forth to shift the happy homes, dead on their feet by eight that night. Harold had been a bloody rotter anyway, and I suppose he allus will be, Vera thought to herself, half an eye on Brian in the pool. I'll never forget the swine – what he did over my red coat. I said to Abb's missis after he'd gone to work: 'What does this smell like on my coat, Lilly?' 'Why,' she says, 'it's paraffin.' 'That's what 'Arold done,' I told her. 'He got mad at summat before he went out this morning, though I don't know what, and this is what he went and done.'Lilly turned white with rage, somehow making up for Vera's feeling of apathy, who nevertheless had to hold her heart in check for fear it would burst. 'You know what I'd do if it was my coat?' Lilly said. 'I'd wait for him coming in that gate, then I'd put a match to it and throw it over him in flames. I would, by bleeding Christ, I would an' all. No bleeding man 'ud do that to me.' 'Well, I daren't. I couldn't,' Vera said, easier now, as if in some way Lilly's outburst and suggested punishment had gone into Seaton's skin while he was at work and let him know what the world thought of such a trick: the bleddy blackclock.

She opened her eyes from the blank-stared reminiscence to hear Brian say: 'Mam, let's go to the other paddling-pool.'

'What other paddling-pool?'

'The other one, over there,' and he pointed across the wide river, south into the country.

'There's only one, you daft lad, and we're in it now.' He didn't believe it, thought she couldn't be bothered to take him, and wondered whether he'd ever find it if he went off by his blue-eyed well-legginged self. Though Albion Yard was no playground or paddling-pool, he still, on standing in the common yard of a comparatively quiet afternoon, thought he heard – even without putting hands to his ears – the sound of a thousand children joyfully playing by some sunlit storybook river that would need a long bus ride to get there.

But nine lives were his rock-bottom minimum, and out in the rain-puddled wasteland of Albion Yard he scooped trenches with broken bottles and built his walls with sludge-cement, watching the former silt up when they became too deep and the latter topple to earth on reaching too high towards duck-white clouds above often capsizing chimney-pots of the condemned houses. They'd been ordered to leave and several boarded-up dwellings turned their blind eyes on others still lived in. A two-foot piece of wood was fixed into a slot across the open doorway of some, to hold a stick-brandishing two-year-old from prematurely getting at half-bricks and broken bottles, and over which visitors had to step before asking in private to be lent a cup of sugar or a mashing of tea until Thursday. And on that day, when Mr Mather the next-door neighbour slept on the sofa after the exertion of walking to the dole office, Mrs Mather would silently lift the pound note from his pocket and stalk to the street-end in her shawl with a white washstand jug in her hand, and make her way to the Frontier, from which post she returned, treading delirious footsteps with a devalued pound and a swimming jug, still singing 'I want to be happy' as she advanced into a black eye and cut lip from Mather waiting behind the door. She would complain to Vera: 'I told him it was all right because we'd leave the rent that week, but he said we wouldn't have paid it anyway and that we'd still be four and a tanner down. Then I offered to make up for it by wangling some grub on tick from Mr Coutts's shop, but he swore I'd still done him out of the money he was going to buy a budgie with. So what can I do, Vera? If you could see your way to lending me a loaf till next week I'd be ever so grateful, I would and all.'

A rusting motor-bike leaned forgotten against the end wall, bought in the roaring twenties and left to rot in the dirty thirties after the means-test men had valued it at more than it was worth to the bloke who owned it; but Brian drove it from one land to another, pulling levers as the engine in his mouth revved-up to take in mountains whose steep sides he had seen in picture-books, and run down witches shown him in magazines by his girl-friend, Amy Tyre. On actual legs he went to the street-end that debouched into the rowdy bonfire-night of the quarter-million town, into the flaming shell-filled no-man's-land of Orchard Street where crackers barked beneath your legs and the smell of roasting bugbound mattresses choked you as you flattened yourself against a wall to get farther up the street, running only into another bonfire at the next explosive corner. A warehouse window cracked from the heat, and bales of lace were liberated by fire from their artistic patterns so that fire-engines more fearful than any Little Demon or Australian Gun filled the street with steam and water, driving Brian back to the refuge of his two-roomed house.

The flat world was only real within the radius of his too-choosing sight, missing everything that did not tally with the damp rarely ignited soil of his brain. He woke up one day to find he had a sister, but this meant nothing until she was able to crawl up to his paper aeroplane and tear it to pieces. He did not know he had a father, only that a man (what was a man?) sat always humped before a firegrate and was liable to throw out a fist like lightning if he went too close; until he came in one day and found his wailing mother bending over a bucket so that blood could drip into it from her forehead. 'Your dad,' she shouted. 'That's what your dad's gone and done with a shoe.' And so amid the weeping and blood-bucket he came to know what a dad was. He was something else also; a blackclock killer. Dad sat on the stone floor with rug pulled back, holding a hammer and staring at the skirting board, bringing the hammer down with a ringing crash whenever a blackclock thought to run the gauntlet of his keen maniacal sight. The floor was already strewn with corpses, but the killing went on for a long time more, until dad put the brown-juiced hammer back in his toolbox, having grown tired of the game which Brian took up with the same intent perseverance next day while his mother was washing clothes under the yard-end tap.

The living-room ceiling of the house next door collapsed at four o'clock one morning, fell with an earthquake thump into the room below, breaking an arm and cutting a face of those still dead upon the brass-bed raft of sleep. Dole-day came quickly, and Seaton, who didn't want his family to be buried under a ton of rubble, paid six bob down on an equally decrepit but not yet condemned house on Mount Street, after Abb Fowler had forged the Albion Yard rent-book as paid up to date. That evening, when the keys were in his pocket, Seaton called Brian over from his floor-game of dominoes.

'See this, son? Do you know what it is? No? Well, it's a rent-book.' He held it outstretched in his Woodbined hand.

'Yes, dad.'

'Well, take it. Got it? Don't drop it, you silly bogger. Now carry it over to the fire and drop it on. An accident, like.'

Brian threw it from a yard away, saw it devoured. 'Ah! There's a good lad as does what he's towd,' Seaton said. 'Now I'll give you a cigarette-card.'

'You are a sod,' Vera put in. 'You'll get copped one of these days.'

'Well,' Seaton smiled, made happy by his audacity, 'they know where to find me.'

A moonlight-flit had been arranged for the darkest night of the month according to Old Moore. Seaton struck up an everlasting alliance with Abb Fowler, who also had a dole-stricken family and would push one of Seaton's handcarts if Seaton would do the same whenever he needed to flit. Through a certain handicap Seaton could not reciprocate regarding the rent-book, but Fowler was enough of a jaunty cap-wearing scholar to forge his own.

Two handcarts were loaded, each the platform for a sky-scraper of furniture, with clothes-lines for cement. Fowler gave a grunt and a jerk, pushed his cart away from the kerb so that its wheels rolled forward on to the cobblestones and rattled smoothly up the street. Seaton told Vera to start pushing the pram, then got his own cart into motion with a similar grunt and jerk.

Wideawake Brian walked, pulled his mother to the middle of the road, eyes riveted to swaying bedroll and sofa tilted against rooftops and eavings, afraid to leave her side and go too close for fear the heap would move into a capsizing frenzy and fall on him no matter how far the frog leap took him clear.

'You'd think the Jerries was after us,' Abb shouted from up front, to which Seaton called out: 'The rent man is, and that's worse,' turning them from refugees into a jovial convoy marching its belongings to the bonfires. He clung tighter to his mother's hand in the dark troughs between gas-light heads and eyes, in the valleys of fearful dragons skulking for a meal of cats and moonlight-flitting children. 'I'll gi' you a game of draughts when we get there, Harold,' came Abb's next sally. 'You're gonna lose it, then,' Seaton boasted. They crossed the main road to a maze of narrow lanes. 'We'll gi' Slab Square a miss,' Abb decided.

Brian felt himself lifted by the waist and set on top of a barrow, wedged between an arm-chair and a mattress. Stuck in the crow's-nest of the moonlight-flit, he saw blue peep-holes of stars when he dared open his eyes. He clung hard at the extra peril as a corner was turned, a public house exploding like a tiger, lights and noise around the door scratching at his closed eyelids. The rocking was gentle as they went uphill.

'You flitting, mate?' a voice called from the pavement.

'Ar.'

'Where from?'

'Albion Yard' – in a lower tone.

'What number? I could do wi' a place myself.'

'Yer welcome to it,' Seaton told him. 'It's condemned though. Ain't woth a light.'

Brian's mouth was jammed with a piece of bread passed up by Vera, and he woke with it still uneaten when shaken down by his father and told that here was his brand new house. He finished his night's sleep in a corner on two coats.

Next morning the world was new: it had even rained to cover up the tracks of the old. A neighbour's girl liked taking Brian out because it made her feel important. She called every day, cajoled him from a game on the pavement with Billy French by a handful of blackened dolly mixtures and a promise to take him somewhere he'd never been before. 'I'll let you come to our 'ouse after for some bread and tea.'

'What's 'ospital?' he asked her one day. His mother said to dad that morning that Mrs Mather had been carted off to the General after falling into a midnight gutter. It was a knock-out collapse, and the only thing retained – discovered by nurses on a pre-entry wash – was the white handle of a jug gripped in one hand like it was a silver purse.

Mavis didn't know, but: 'I'll take you and show you one of these days.'

He grunted: 'Tell me now what it is.'

'No,' she was adamant, 'but I'll *tek* yer soon. So come on, or we'll be too late to see one.' A pair of streets joined hands at an acute angle and the arrowhead was a boarded-up sandtip. Heavy supports to timber ran between ground and house-side to stop the wonky edifice sprawling flat on its exposed wound. Running beneath the timber Mavis sang about London Bridge falling down, while Brian with a glum face built sandcastles and bored tunnels with clenched fists. Damp sand stayed easily in place and shape, but tunnels collapsed when buildings grew above. He worked a long time, cupping hands for towers, holding them rigid and face to face for walls, but the crash was inevitable, a rift through the outworks and a crater opening from underneath when the sand, drier below, was sucked downwards as though through one of his grandma's egg-timers. No tunnel could bear such weight. Around the tip's edge he found laths of wood, and reinforced the tunnel so that his castle stayed up: until Mavis's foot sank through it because he wouldn't come to another place. At which he kicked her on the leg and made it bleed.

Her dad was a hawker and they lived in two rooms of a cellar. From drinking tea at her table Brian had only to look up at the grating to see the wheelspokes of her father's barrow stationed by the kerb. She fed him toasted bread and apple while her mother read the paper in a rocking-chair. A pustule of white light flared and went out. Grey flakes of mantle fell from the gas-bracket on the wall and Brian ran with Mavis through the rain to buy a new one. 'Mam said it cost tuppence,' she said when they came out of the shop, 'but it on'y cost threeha'pence. I'll not tell her, and buy a ha'porth o' tuffeys. And I'll gi' you one if you don't say owt about it.'

On a hot dry day they came to a factory whose coal cellar was close to the pavement. Bending down he saw a row of oven doors, from which flames bellowed when they were pulled open with long-handled rakes. Gusts of heat forced him back, and a shovel-armed man told him to scram. Brian stood by a hillock of black cobbles, watched the shovel singing them into the coal-hole. Mavis came close, led him forward to see the fires again. He was hypnotized by the round holes of flame.

'That's 'ospital,' she said into his ear, and the three dreadful syllables reached his brain, bringing back to him the drunken image of old shrill Mrs Mather who, so mam had told dad, had been shovelled in there like coal after they had taken the white jug handle from her clenched hand. Mavis pulled him quickly away.

The moonlight barrows moved once more, a pair of collapsible life-boats swaying down Mount Street towards Chapel Bar, Abb Fowler in front and Vera pushing the pram behind. When a copper stopped Abb to ask where he thought he was going with all that stuff, he said he was changing houses at night because he didn't want to lose a day's work. Shuttlecocked Seaton and battledored Vera were gamed from one house to another, because Mount Street also was about to fall before the mangonels of a demolishing council. Need for a bus-station gave slum-dwellers the benefit of new housing estates, though Seaton was having none of this, clung to the town centre because its burrow was familiar and therefore comfortable, and because no long walk was involved to reach the labour exchange on Thursday to draw his dole. Sometimes he was able to get a job, and there would be bacon and tomatoes for dinner (Yorkshire pudding and meat on Sunday) but though he woodbound his muscles to show willing at the hardest labour, the work never lasted and he was back on the eternal life-saving dole, running up bills at food shops that he would never be able to pay, and playing Abb Fowler at draughts, swilling mugs of reboiled tea in move and counter-move until neither had a penny left to put in the gas for light.

In every staging-post of a house they found bugs, tiny oxblood buttons that hid within the interstices of bedticks, or secreted themselves below the saddles of their toes. Cockroaches also fought: black advance guards of the demolition squads came out in silent, scuttling platoons over the kitchen floor after dark, often encountering lethal powders sprinkled by Vera, and those that succumbed would be swept up by Seaton before he mashed tea in the morning; or they would run into Seaton's equally fatal hammer-blows and be washed up by his wife when she lifted the rug on the unequal battlefield next day.

The demolition of one condemned block took a novel turn: the Albion Yard area, deserted and cordoned off, was to be the target of bombs from buzzing two-winged aeroplanes, the sideshow of a military tattoo whose full glory lay on the city's outskirts. The bombing was to be on a Sunday afternoon, and Seaton hoisted Brian on to his stocky shoulders so that he felt one with the trams that swayed like pleasure-ships before the council house, ferrying crowds to the bombing; he rocked on his father's shoulders, gripping the neck of a dad he hated when he did or said something to make his mam cry. But the grim and miserable emotion was kept to the ground as dad swung him up high, an action that split his hate in two upon such kindness. The first intimation of a good deed to him by dad only brought back his mam's agonized cries as the blood streamed from her face, but his turning head beheld his mother at this moment happy and saying he would be taken to see the bombing if he was a good lad, passing his father a packet of fags from the mantelpiece for a smoke in case they had to wait long before the aircraft played Punch-and-Judy with the enclave of slums in which they used to live.

Seaton's body swung as he walked and Brian was often in danger of falling overboard, pitching head first from his life-boat-dad into the boiling sea of other heads around. Peril came at the quick switch into an unexpected short-cut, and his flailing arms, finding nothing closer, grabbed the black tufts of dad's short, strong hair. When dad cried out he'd get a pasting if he didn't stop that bleddy lark, Brian's instinct was to go forward and bind himself on to dad's bull neck, a tightened grip that brought forth a half-throttled exclamation from dad below saying that he could bloody-well walk if that was going to be his game; at which a shirt-sleeved tentacle reached up and tried to lift him outwards; but Brian reacted to the danger of his imminent slingdown by clinging tighter in every way so that the well-muscled arm dragged at him in vain. 'Come on, my lad, let's have you down.' And again: 'Are you goin' ter get down or aren't you?'

'I'll fall' – his arms bare and the neck slippery with sweat.

'No you won't.'

'I will, dad, honest.' They were near the lassoed bomb-target, bustled to the kerb by those who wanted to get near the rope, maybe feel the actual blast and pick up a fallen brick for a souvenir. Mounted policemen pushed those back who infiltrated into the brick-strewn neutral ground, and Brian, forgetting to struggle, saw white foam around a horse's mouth. He asked dad if it were soap.

'Yes,' Seaton told him. Brian bent his head and inquired of the nearest ear: 'What do they give it soap for?'

'So's it'll bite anybody who tries to get past the coppers.'

'Why does anybody want to get past the coppers?' he whispered.

'Because they want to see the bombs closer.'

'But they'll get blown up.'

''Appen they want to. Now come down for a bit, my owd duck, because my showders is aching.'

'Not yet, our dad. Let me stay up some more.'

'No, come down now, then you can go up again when the bombs start dropping.'

'But I want to see the horses bite somebody first.'

'They won't bite anybody today,' Seaton said. So down he came, jammed among the shoes and trousers of a surging jungle, evading a tiger boot or a lion fist, a random matchstick or hot fag-end. Three biplanes dipped their wings from the Trent direction. Brian climbed up to his dad's shoulders to spot from his fickle control tower, his hand an unnecessary eyeshade because the sun was behind a snow-mountain cloud silhouetting the yellow planes.

They swung back, flying low in silence, like gliders because of noise from the mass of people. 'They aren't going very fast, dad,' he complained. 'They're slower than motor-cars.'

'That's because they're high up, kid,' someone told him.

'They'll come lower soon,' dad said.

'Will they crash?' Brian asked. 'I've never seen an aeroplane crash.'

'You will one day,' somebody laughed.

Each plane purred loudly along the rooftops, like a cat at first, then growling like a dog when you try to take its bone away, finally as if a roadmender's drill were going straight to the heart, so that he felt pinned to the ground. Two black specks, then two more, slid from the rounded belly of each. The gloved wheels beneath seemed to have been put down specially to catch them, but the dots fell through and disappeared into the group of ruined houses.

'Now for it,' somebody announced, and an enormous cracking sound, a million twig-power went six times into the sky – followed by the muffled noise of collapsing walls somewhere in the broken and derelict maze.

A policeman's horse reared up, tried to climb an invisible stairway leading from the explosions, then saw sense and merely stood nodding its head and foaming. A bleak scream came from some woman at the back of the crowd and Brian saw her led away by men in black and white uniforms. 'Is she frightened, dad?'

'Yes.'

'Well, I'm not, are you?'

'No.' But Seaton lifted him down, dragged him roughly out of the crush.

'Is that the end, dad?'

'Stop asking bleddy questions, will yer?' Brian caught his mood, and the bomb that had lodged itself inside his chest suddenly burst, scattering more blind havoc in him than the actual grenades sent from the flight of planes. 'Stop cryin', will yer?' Seaton tugged at him angrily. 'Come on, if you stop cryin' I'll buy you an ice-cream cornet.'

'I don't want one,' he roared, thereby creating a big puzzle, its depth measurable only by Seaton's inability to solve it. 'Then what *do* you want?'

And without giving the question any thought he answered: 'Nowt' – and went on crying till he stopped.

On a wet afternoon two tall men wearing raincoats and nicky hats knocked on the front door. Vera led them into the room where Seaton sat. Brian, sprawled on the floor playing with a box of dominoes, noticed that she was almost in tears, something that never failed to touch off the sea-controlling springs at the back of his own heart. She stood with folded arms, and the two men stayed by the door. 'They've come for you, Harold,' she said. He turned his head and looked up from the fireplace.

'We don't want any trouble,' one of the men said, seeing desperation in his ashy face.

He looked at them for some time. 'You'll have to keep me,' he remarked at last, forcing a smile.

'We know all about that.'

Seaton hadn't moved from his chair. 'And my family as well you'll have to keep.'

'That's nothing to do with us,' he was told.

Vera unfolded her arms, ran a finger along one of her eyes. 'Shall I get you your coat, duck?'

'Aye, you might as well,' he answered, standing up. 'I'm going on holiday, and I suppose I'll see a lot of my pals there as well.' This witticism amused him, and he laughed, his face relaxed. The two men said nothing. 'Got a car?' Seaton asked them.

'No,' one said, 'it's not far; we'll walk you down.'

'Well, I don't suppose it matters if the neighbours guess what's going on. It might 'ave been them if they did but know it. If I'd 'ad a job to wok at I wouldn't a done this. But when yer kids ain't got no grub what else can you do?' He'd run up too many food bills at too many shops. It's a big country, he thought. There's grub in the shops for everybody, so why ain't there wok? I don't know, it beats me it does.

Vera came back with his coat. 'Will you want your mac as well?'

'No,' he said, 'keep it. You'll have to pawn it when you get short.' Brian felt himself lifted from the dominoes and kissed; then quickly put down. 'Don't let the kids get at my tools, Vera, will you?'

'No,' she said, 'they'll be all right.'

A watch was looked at, and Seaton realized aloud that he'd better go. 'I'll see you in a couple o' months then. It's nowt to worry about, duck. I'll be all right, and you'll be all right. They've got to keep you all, so they'll be the losers in the end.'

'Come on, young man,' the eldest said. 'We haven't got all day. We're busy.'

'I expect you are,' Seaton said.

Brian was too involved in his collapsing line of dominoes to wonder what was going on, and his mother must have been crying for some time before he joined in, without knowing why. Not that she knew why she was crying, because, as Seaton had truthfully said, none of them would starve while he was in Lincoln; and it would be as much of a holiday for her as it would be for him, and this thought lifted her from despair as she set the table and put on the kettle to boil and sat wondering however she'd come to marry a bloody fool who got himself sent to jail – and was a rotter to her in the bargain. She could hardly believe it had happened like it had, and that she was in such a fine bleddy mess; and it was impossible not to spend the next hour brooding on it, going back over the last few years and picking them to pieces as if they were the components of a complex lock that, once opened, might solve something.

2

Merton had scratched his head. He drew back at the sound of some far-flung twig or half-hearted gate rattling from outside, hoping to hear the door-latch lift and Vera make her way across the kitchen to say she was sorry for being late.

Which is too much to expect, he thought, from any man's daughter since the War. Leaves made a noise like the erratic beginning of a rainstorm: October: if she comes in wet she'll get my fist, he promised himself, turning back to the fire, and no mistake; I can't have her getting her death o' cold and then not being fit for work; she manages to get enough time off as it is. But he knew it wouldn't rain because he hadn't yet noticed the pause between the end of leaves falling and the commencing tread of mute cats running light-foot through them; so swung a watch from his waistcoat pocket in pursuance of another reason to be angry, and saw with satisfying indignation that it was eleven o'clock. What a bloody time to be coming home, and me having to get up at five in the morning because they're bringing a dozen ponies up from the Deep Main. They'll be hell to pay getting 'em out of the skips – and all of 'em to be shod before they're turned loose by the tip-field. Allus the same when you want an early night.

He spat forcefully at the fire-bars and his spit didn't sizzle with the alacrity to which he was accustomed, thereby reinforcing his often-said conviction that nothing in life could be relied on. By God she'll get the stick when she comes in for keeping me up like this. Yellow flames from a darkening unstable fire-bed blazed full-tilt upwards, and with the self-made poker he pushed a lump of prime pit coal into the last effort of the inferno. God bugger it, there was no doubt about using the stick, and he turned, while thrusting back his watch, to make sure it still leaned by the pantry door. It was bad luck for Vera – the last of Merton's brood young enough to be disciplined in this way – because she shared his anger with the dogs now barking in the yard, was the wall to his violent and frequent upstarts of passion which usually – though not always – coincided with signs of defiance in what animals or humans happened to be under his control; and whereas the dogs would lick his hand a few hours after one of his uncouth godlike flings of rage, Vera took days before she could force herself into the kitchen for a meal. Such domineering reached beyond the borderline of family, for Merton was recognized as the main-staying blacksmith of the pit he worked at, where no matter how obstinate or too-happy the horses and ponies became they were soon broken into docility by his strong will; hence shoes hammered on to tranquil hoofs by Merton only loosened when nails could no longer support the thinning metal. A lit pipe signalled a good job done, and no chafing butty or gaffer begrudged him the loud smack their horses got on the arse as an indication that it should be taken clip-clop back to its shafts outside the shed door; they'd better not, either, because that was the on'y way to deal with 'em; a clout for the hoss so's the rest on 'em would do as they was towd.

Vera's footsteps came quickly up the path, crunching lightly on cinders as she crossed the yard. By God, he told himself, straightening up against the chair-back to make sure he was hearing right, if she brings trouble to this house by her running around with lads, she'll be out of that front gate and on the road for good and all with every tat she's got. The leaves had stopped racing, and both dogs whined in a duet as she passed the kennel: about time, he muttered, but I'll teach her to stay out so long at the tuppenny hop, when she should a bin in at half-past nine. I'll put a bloody stop to this – his mental peroration cut off by the rattling door-latch.

She had been to the Empire, was still happy at remembering the antic-clowns and unclean jokes and the pink ribald heads shaking with laughter as seen from a front seat of the fourpenny gods. Her new scarf had slid from the rail, and after the last curtains had dropped and closed (she was half sick from the heat and cigar smoke that rose through the show from pit to sweating ceiling) she had wheeled down the slippery steps with Beatty and Ben and Jack and invaded the deserted dress-circle to get it back. A tripe-and-onion supper revived all four, piled them, after custard pies to follow, on to the last tram that rattled its way towards Radford. Beatty and Jack were jettisoned into the darkness of Salisbury Street, and Vera began to wonder whatever in the world her father would say at her getting home so late. She already pictured herself trying to borrow the fare to Skegness so as to find a living-in job at some boarding-house, chucked out of the Nook with a heavy heart and a light bag holding her belongings, with Merton's words that she could bloody-well stay out for good stinging one ear, while the fact that she wouldn't be able to get a job now at Skeggy because the season had long since finished made an ironic tune in the other. Well, perhaps he would already have gone to bed and locked the door on her. She hoped so, for then enough sleep could be had in the wash-house curled up on sacks next to a still warm copper, and by tomorrow he may have forgotten how mad he'd been. Ructions, she thought, that's what I'm sure it'll be; even though I've been working seven years I can't do a thing right as far as the old man's concerned. One bleddy row after another just because I come home late; and I don't suppose it'll alter a deal either until I'm married; and then I wain't be able to go out alone at night at all, with some big husband bullying at me for his supper.

She ignored the silent Ben beside her and ruminated on her previous runnings-away from home, and twice she came back because she'd lost her living-in job at the end of a season and couldn't earn enough at shop or factory to pay for her board. There wouldn't be a third time, her father had promised, which she knew to be true: 'And you wouldn't be sitting at this table now,' he bellowed, 'if your soft-hearted mother hadn't let you in last night when you called up to the bedroom winder and asked if she'd have you back. Next time it'll be ME you'll have to ask, and I'll say NO.'

Still, it might not be so late, she thought, Ben having set out for Wollaton – morosely because she'd refused to descend to the canal bank with him. Turning down the lane towards Engine Town, she was terrified at the twig-shadows, and leaves rustling like the thin pages of a hundred well-hidden Bibles caught in the wind, and stepped softly into the pitch-blackness wondering: Shall I be murdered? Is there a man behind that tree? as she did on every dark night coming back to the Nook. I'll run by it anyway, and walk when I come to the lit-up houses, because if anybody stops me there I can knock at a door for help. In the split-timing of terror she laughed, remembering the man dressed up as Charlie Chaplin, and imitating the leg-work of a dancer on reaching the long railway tunnel, hardly knowing she was under it until a goods train came out of the fields like a cannonade of Coronation guns and made her run with all speed to the other side with coat open and mud splashing her ankles, afraid the train might weigh too heavily on its sleepers and crash through underneath, or that some unknown evil would stifle her in the complete silence of its noise.

With no breath left she walked along the sunken lane, elderberry and privet hedges shaking softly above, black night split only by a melancholy old man's whistle from the distant train.

She patted the dogs before the kitchen door, as if thankful for the happiness they must feel for her safe return. The latch gave easily into a safe refuge, and the suspended oil-lamp in the corner dazzled as she took off her coat. She saw her father sitting by the fire, legs stretched out towards the hearth, his long lean body stiffening. 'Wheer yer bin?'

He's mad, right enough. So what shall I say? His 'wheer yer bin?' turned the first spoke of the same old wheel, with every question and answer fore-ordained towards some violent erratic blow. 'Out,' she replied, pouring a cup of tea at the table.

'If yer don't answer me you'll get a stick across yer back.'

She was unable to meet the glare of such grey eyes. His clipped white hair, lined and tanned face, and white moustache above thin lips, made up a visage from which all her misery emanated. 'I've been to the Empire,' she admitted.

He was unappeased:'What sort o' time do you call this, then? It's past eleven.'

'I had to walk from Nottingham.' The tea was cold, so she wasted no sugar and pushed the cup aside; an effort of kindness by her mother coming to nothing. 'I dare say you did,' he shouted, 'but you could a got 'ome earlier.'

From experience she knew that arguments in this house were too short; afterwards they were seen as illogical explosions from which reason had been excluded by their inborn force. It was impossible to say: All right, I should have been in earlier, so please don't hit me now; and just as out of the question to defy him by force, for he was the unassailable father of more than fifty years whom she couldn't dream of defeating. Only a craving for his extinction seemed possible and good enough, a hooked thunderbolt to lift him out of the house but leave her unharmed. The impossible was not on her side and she knew it, sensed rightly that it never would be. So she cried out in rage, which only made things worse, as she had known it would before the row began: 'I couldn't leave the show until it was finished, could I?' implying that he lacked sense to think so.

'You should a come out earlier, you cheeky young madam.'

'I did,' she conceded, beyond hope. 'But I had some supper wi' Jenny and Beatty.' She fell into a chair, choking on tears of hatred and bitterness. Who knows? Merton's temper often wavered with his own children, hid contrition and a peculiar gruff kindness that sometimes turned to their advantage at the last moment. But the reins of compassion were rarely in his hands, had to be hoped for by those who had broken his rules. He might have been softened up to this point by Vera, been satisfied merely to wave the stick from the corner where he now stood; but the verifiable boundary of this was passing – too well disguised for her to see it, too faint for her to take advantage of it in such confused distress. She saw what was coming and hurried towards it, her wish to escape thrust out of the way by an uncontrolled defiance that could bring nothing but defeat. 'Leave me alone, you rotten bogger. You aren't going to hit me like you hit your dogs!' She didn't move. He would hit her the same as he'd hit anything else. The weight of his hammer at the forge was heavy, and burning metal was moulded without trouble; he drank beer by the pint tankard on Friday night, but always woke from his stupor with an urge for more obedience, more work, more beer at the week-end, and to tame the defiance that sprang as much from him as anything else. All his blows seemed made for life and self-preservation, which afterwards he sometimes felt, mistaking his resentment of it for a pang of conscience.

He struck her fiercely across the shoulders: 'Let *that* teach you, you cheeky young bitch.'

'I wish you was dead,' she moaned. 'I wish everybody was dead.' The dogs outside whined at the noise, a pitying tune to her fit of dereliction. Silence between the last frantic rustling of leaves and the first onset of rain went unnoticed, and raindrops swept the yard like a square-mile sweeping brush.

I'll run away, was her first thought, as Merton threw down the stick and went up in his stockinged feet to bed. But how can I? I've got no money. But I must do summat because I can't stand this. I'm nearly twenty-three and wain't put up with the old man's bullyin' any more. If I can't run away I might as well chuck myself in the cut or under a train as go on puttin' up with a dog's life like this, because it'll go on and on, I know for a fact, if I stay here. I'll never be able to go out to the Empire and come in late after it. I've stood on the canal bank before, trying to chuck myself in the deep locks, but I never could do it; and I've waited for a train on the embankment to come fast out of Radford station but I've allus been frightened at the noise as it gets closer, and before it comes near me I run away, down the bank and back through the field because I was frightened to death. But then, I don't see why I should kill myself just for the old man, because I'm sure it wouldn't bother him a deal if I did. No, why should I? though it would be nice one day if I did get killed by a bus or tram so's he'd happen be sorry and think of all the times he's been a rotten bogger to me.

Looking around the too familiar room – a whitewashed cottage kitchen with a Sandeman sherry mirror by the door, a large home-made rug by the hearth, chairs and table under the window – she saw his case of horseshoes on the wall, brass and chromium-plated prizes that kept the girls polishing and cleaning all Saturday morning as if they were silver and gold. Supported behind glass on specially wrought nails, these horseshoes had been accumulated by Merton from apprenticeship to his becoming one of the finest craftsmen in the county. She took down a big shoe and held it, feeling its weight and knowing it would slip easily from her fingers if a fair grip wasn't kept on the bend. Two prongs pointed upwards and the grooved, smoothly polished side – meant to tread the soil on more workaday productions – was held facing her. A ray of red paint had been spilled into the groove from pronged tip around bulging curve to pronged tip – red because blood from the horse's foot wouldn't be noticed when the nails went in, she had always thought. On the left side were four holes and on the right side three. Beginning from left to right she muttered: Monday Tuesday Wednesday Thursday; and then looked at the three remaining holes on the right, completing the week: Friday Saturday Sunday; the first four were to be said quickly because you wanted them to go as fast as possible, thus bringing you sooner on to the last three which you spoke more slowly because they were enjoyable days – looking at the seven holes through blood-red paint and holding the prongs upwards so that no luck would run out.

She remembered Merton singing rhymes when they were children, holding each child on his knees in turn and chanting the words to them, again and again as rain poured down and thunder boomed. When they were afraid of black Sunday evenings in summer, the sing-song chant had gone in and stayed, seven nails for a nursery rhyme rough-edged into them who were disturbed at being so close and not knowing with what amount of ease to take his momentary kindness and good nature, so that the jingled forgeries had stayed there for good.

She saw herself taking a basket from the pantry, opening the door so that Merton would not hear and returning up the steps to fill it with all thirty horseshoes. Then the outer door would open and into the choking rain she'd go, hatless and without coat between the pigeon coop and the house side, her skirt soaking on long nettles and grass, shoes sogged and distorted on stones until she turned into the open and went towards the well. How would she find it? As easily as if it were a birth wart in the centre of her hand. And then I'll throw the horseshoes one by one into it, hear each splash as it hits bottom and sinks and laugh to think the old man will never see them again.

The impossible dream faded; her hand covered her ear and cheek, was hidden by long hair; leaning on her elbow she went on looking at the case of horseshoes until she grew too sleepy to stay awake.

She was just back from Engine Town with a box of buttons to sew on her blouse, dodging mud-puddles under the railway bridge and negotiating ice-ruts in the lane so as not to wet her shoes in the piled snow. Looking out of the bedroom window her desire to solve any problem was killed by the hard winter. Perhaps the year would break through. A long thick layer of cloud spearheading towards the Pennines was ghost-green on top and turning pink below, indicating a half-beaten-to-death sun lurking somewhere, licking its wounds after an agonizing Armageddon of autumn. Lines of snow lay in the furrows of the next field, and in the garden it gathered in uprooted cabbage hollows like deserted pools of unpalatable milk. Winter's juggernaut crushed everything except people, who still went to work, quarrelled, played football, got married and died.

She walked up the lane on Sunday afternoon when her father was sleeping off his dinner and beer, noticing black withered beads of elderberries clinging still to twigs contorted by icy cold. Three greyhounds flashed through a hedge into a hollow of Cherry Orchard, back legs skidding on frost-flowers when they tried to ascend and breach level ground. Off they went under the heavy lead of afternoon sky, across treeless humps and dips, each growl heard low from the distance they were suddenly at, the only sound from them as if caught in cupped hands and placed just outside her ears. And also Seaton's ears: he put two fingers into his mouth and knifed the dead man of silence, so that the three greyhounds came racing back, front legs and back legs machine-gunning the turf.

'Hello, duck,' he said, seeing her for the first time.

She asked a question: 'Are them whippets yourn?'

'They aren't whippets,' he told her, putting her right, 'they're greyhounds and they belong to my feyther.' He untangled the chain-leash. 'I bring 'em out every Sunday for a run.'

'They go fast.' They approached in line ahead, and she moved out of their way. 'You'll be all right, duck,' he said in a kind voice. 'I'll tie 'em up soon an' tek 'em back 'ome. This sort o' dog likes a good run, you know,' he explained, by way of breaking the silence when she showed no sign of speaking.

A further whistle sent the dogs across the mile-long roughs. 'They ain't had enough yet,' young dark-haired Seaton with the leash said. She gazed vacantly towards the three dogs, watching their mad mechanical legs careering almost out of sight, then bend head to tail by the wood and bear round again towards them. Framed by green hollows and a dark pack of jellied trees, they broke formation often, one to manoeuvre its long whippet head towards another, each in turn failing on the same trick, and devouring only the too vulnerable gap of much coveted dank air between the end of its muzzle and the flank of the one attacked. The best defence was to get slightly ahead, swing the head outwards and outflank the outflanker, showing a fierce growl and shine of teeth, make the other afraid to resist effectively by increasing the fierceness which would then be outdone by the other dog, and to surmount it still again until a final pure competitive speed would remain. They turned their elongated, gracefully swinging bodies about in the frolic, drum-tight pelts stretched over distinguishable ribs and bones, sometimes rolling in the grass so that the pursuer, unable to pull up for its victory, thundered by to return only when the fallen dog was back on its four legs belting away in another direction.

Wheep, wheep! A signal from Seaton, whom she had forgotten, wheeled them in his direction, and they came leaping three abreast up and down the dips and hollows, parted by a bush, then a disused well, until for no reason they swung away from Seaton's repeated whistle and stamped against Vera before she could break the stony paralysis into which the sight of their seemingly unnatural advance had fixed her. Neither had Seaton time to act: she was on the crisp frost-bitten grass before he could swing the leash into a circle and intimidate his animals to a halt.

'Well,' she said, as he fastened his dogs first, 'don't bother to pick me up, will yer?' Now he ran to do so, but it was too late. He pulled at the dogs and fastened the master-lead to a bush stump, laughing as he stood up. 'I'm sorry duck,' he said. 'I didn't know they'd bowl you over like that. You must be as light as a feather. What do they feed you on down yonder?' He pointed a tobacco-branded finger to the chimneys of the Nook. 'Pig-taters?'

She pulled her coat and wiped wet hands on the pockets. 'Don't be so nosy, sharpshit. I get fed all I want.' A scornful look was thrown at his dogs: 'Them whippets o' yourn don't get too much snap though, by the look on 'em.'

'Nay,' he said in a quiet tone, not willing to show even slight resentment to a stranger, 'they get fed plenty of stuff. Hoss meat and boiled taters. It looks so good I could eat it myself sometimes.'

He don't seem English to me, she thought, with them brown eyes and that black mop, though it's combed well and he's a smart-looking chap all right. He looks like an Italian, with his skin and all, though his talk is Radford enough, I will say that for him. 'My old man's got two dogs,' she said. 'Mongrels, but they're good house-dogs. He uses 'em for fetching the birds when he goes shootin' as well. And they allus know when a stranger's coming up the yard, even before they see 'em, because of the feet. They never make a murmur at any of the family.'

'They must be well trained,' he conceded. 'Let's walk down the lane a bit, duck. It's cowd standin' 'ere.'

The dogs pulled hard, and she noticed his strong arms tugging them back. When she agreed to walk they jerked forward and nearly sprawled him into an icy rut. 'Gerrr-er BACK,' he shouted.

'The old man trained our dogs right enough,' she said, hands in pockets, noticing Seaton's leather gloves. 'The poor boggers think themselves lucky if a day passes wi'-out 'im taking a stick to 'em.'

'It's like that, is it?' he said self-righteously. 'I don't like cruelty to animals. I mean, you can gi' 'em a kick now and again if you lose your temper and don't think what you're doing, or if they get in your way, but it ain't right to tek a stick to 'em.' He braced himself against the pull of the dogs and lit a crumpled cigarette from his raincoat pocket. On second thoughts: 'Shall you have one, duck?'

'If you've got another. I'd better be careful when I go past our gate in case the old man sees me.'

He took a new packet from his coat and lit one for her. 'Why? Has your old man tamed you as well as his dogs?'

'Don't be daft. He just don't like me to smoke, that's all.'

'I see nowt wrong wi' a woman smokin' a fag now and again,' he said, generous and liberal at the same time. He's a short-arse, she thought, but nice: only an inch bigger than me. 'What sort o' work do you do?'

'I wok for me feyther, 'polsterin'.'

Her cigarette went low as they passed the gate, though the old man would sleep for a while yet. 'What's 'polsterin'?'

'Repairin' sofys and chairs. The old man teks wok in from pubs and 'ouses. We've got a shop in Radford. I don't do much tackin' or cuttin' though. Mostly I fetch the stuff on a handcart and tek it back. I go for the leather and cloth as well from time to time. It's good work, but you've got to be as strong as a hoss, climbing up three flights o' stairs wi' a sofy on your back and getting nowt but threepence for your trouble when you get there.'

'Don't your old man pay you wages?'

'Ay,' he said, 'but it ain't a sight.'

They reached the bridge. 'I'll go no farther,' she said. 'The old man'll be mad if I don't get back in time for tea.' Which was as good an excuse as any to leave him at this point. Beyond the other side of the long bridge she saw the houses of Radford Woodhouse: colliers' houses, poachers' dens, shops and beer-offs.

He had expected her to walk to the main road. 'You don't want to be so terrified of your old man,' he said. 'He don't bite that bad, does he?'

'It's not that. I'm hungry, so I think I'll get back. I didn't bother wi' any dinner.'

'Come on wi' me, then, and I'll buy you some tea.'
'Another time I might. But not now.'
He jerked the leash so violently that he nearly throttled the dogs. They ambled back, subdued, to Vera, and she patted their heads. 'I'll pass again next week,' he said. 'Shall you wait for me?'
He's so quiet, except for them eyes. Half a pint o' mild and a couple of hot whiskies. 'If you like. I can be leaning on our gate.'
'All right then, duck. I'll be seeing you.'
Black hair, and teeth going to bad: he couldn't 'a bin a day over twenty-four. He walked off, with a slight swinging gait which might, as far as she could tell, have been the way he always walked; or it might have been caused by the predatory forward pull of his three strong dogs.

She kept telling herself that she didn't want to be married, that, even though it meant getting away from the threat of the old man's fist and stick, she didn't want to let herself in for something that as far as she knew might turn out to be worse. What did she know of Seaton? He was quiet, kind, and often charming in a simple sort of way; but he'd been barmy enough to ask her to marry him at the end of their second meeting, and she'd been just as barmy in saying all right. And now the three-month wait he'd agreed to was over and she sat by the window in her underwear, looking out at the garden and fields because she couldn't stand the sight of her wedding-dress spread out on the bed behind. In half an hour she would be off to Lenton Church, in a horse-drawn cab on which Seaton had seen fit to splash part of his wages earned at an outside labouring job – saved up for what he hadn't dared hope for when he'd 'popped the question'. Vera remembered his disappointment, a black look when she mentioned the three-month wait. So how do I know what being married to him'll be like? she wondered, nagged by the uneasy memory of their second meeting in the Cherry Orchard, a scrag-end of a field whose scrub-covered up-and-down surface matched well with her feelings at that time.
To get away from home for always was a good thing that

nobody could gainsay, though Merton had hinted after seeing Seaton for the first time that he didn't think he was much of a bargain for his gel, and that she'd realize (by God she would) what a good home she'd had when she'd lived with *him* a while in Nottingham. But this had only made her more anxious to escape, had cut her apprehension at the roots and made her look forward to starting a new life in a Nottingham house or flat, despite the needling of premonitions that soon came back.

There was no time left to deliberate. She closed her arms over her soft, well-shaped breasts and began to weep, the sound of it bursting upon her ears and cordoning her off from the noise of fussing in the kitchen below. She did not want to be married, was prepared to stay more months or years in peril of the old man rather than take a chance of living with someone she did not know, throw herself at a stranger after three months' acquaintance.

People were going and coming from the house, many of them unknown to the dogs, who hadn't stopped barking and dragging their chains since early morning, despite Merton going out twice to them with the stick. She stood in the middle of the room, dressed now, unable to go downstairs, knowing that this was expected of her yet unwilling to reconcile it with the fact that she had made up her mind not to get married. The stairfoot door opened: 'Vera!' came her mother's voice. 'Are you ready? Don't be too long, or we's'll keep Harold waiting at the church and that'd never do.' There was an intentional pause, giving her time to call out:

'I'm not coming.'

Another pause, from shock. Her mother ran up, and came into the bedroom with a worried end-of-the-world frown on her face. She leaned on the washstand to get her breath. 'What do you mean?' was all she could ask for the moment.

'I'm not getting married, mam. I don't want him. I want to stay single.' She was afraid of saying this, and afraid above all by the silence downstairs, as if the whole house had stopped breathing to listen to her argument, even the dogs quiet at last.

'I don't know what you mean,' her mother said. She had wanted no trouble, hadn't expected any after the tight-fitting locks of plans and arrangements had turned on her daughter's life. Now she trembled and was upset because there looked like being a row.

Vera's face set hard, though she knew her determination to be only a thing of the minute, a fluctuating protest to try and save herself. 'I mean what I say. I don't want to go to church.'

'But everything's ready.'

'Well let it be.'

'But don't you love him?'

'No,' Vera said, 'I never did either.'

Her mother felt a pain above the eyes. Merton also had thought she shouldn't marry Seaton, but even he would agree it was too late to turn back now. Vera maintained a deadly silence in which time passed quickly, and her mother couldn't stand such obstinacy. 'Don't you even like him then?' Vera began to say 'yes'. 'Well come on down and get married. They're waiting for you. Come on.'

'Oh I can't, mam,' she cried. 'I don't want to.'

Her mother's voice was harder now: 'For Jesus Christ's sake, come on. Everything's ready. If you let Harold down he'll kill you.' She went to the stair door: 'Ada, come up here a minute will you?'

Ada had travelled from Chesterfield especially for the wedding of her sister, and if it were called off, her disappointment would be almost as great as Seaton's. She was nearly thirty and already on her second husband, the first having stopped a bullet in Flanders. Brawling bombardier Doddoe had been fresh out of that fiasco when she met him. Ada was in her weeds at the time – she made a big laughable issue of her story now to Vera – going back into servant work to feed herself and the only child of her first quick set-to, taking a slow train to Chesterfield up through the black pimplescapes of the industrial Pennines. She was blonde and fair skinned, handsome and attractive with a tantalizing expression of cheek and sadness, so that Doddoe who got into the opposite seat of the empty carriage at Codnor Park was soon in conversation with her. At Chesterfield he carried her box to the tram stop, and when she was on the platform fifty yards away he bawled out through the bell and grinding wheels: 'Will you marry me, duck?' After a week of courting she said yes, and now she had another child and, to judge by her stomach, a third one was due in a month or two.

'How do you think most people get married?' she said to Vera. 'You don't want to bother that much about it. Just laugh and say yes and then the bad times you might 'ave now and again wain't seem so bad. Come on, duck.'

Vera was confused, pinned on to the flat spirit-level of indecision. Her mother pleaded and took her hand. Shall I go, or shan't I? she asked herself. It was like throwing a penny and seeing on which side it landed. Maybe Ada was right, and it didn't matter either way, because if it isn't Harold Seaton it'll be somebody else. She rubbed a handkerchief over her eyes, followed her mother and sister down the dark stairs, comforting noises from the kitchen once more filling up the desolate, companionless void of protest. She knew she wouldn't even be late at the church as the cab trotted under the long tunnel and emerged into the Radford Woodhouse sun.

3

Ascending stone steps to the railway bridge, a fine spring rain began to fall, hiding towers, wheels and sheds of the colliery below as Vera fastened her coat and hurried towards the first streets of the city. When Seaton left for the tannery that morning she had been unable to face the empty day and had gone to visit her mother at the Nook, short-cutting it there and back across the fields.

The novelty of decorating two unfurnished rooms had long since worn off, though it had been enjoyable while it lasted, had proved that Seaton who had seemed too much of a numskull to talk about anything (even his work had been described and forgotten in five minutes) had proved his worth by papering the walls and ceiling, painting doors and skirting boards, pinning down cheap lino from Sneinton Market. He set them both to making rugs from a pile of clippings and a couple of boiled-clean sackbags, using a sharpened piece of stick to thrust each sliver of coloured rag beneath and then pull it up above the rag-bag base. Plate-shelves and pot-shelves were plugged and bracketed on to the kitchen walls, covered with fancy paper and adorned with oddments unearthed from piles of penny junk. Even the tips yielded certain usable objects, such as screws and hinges, firebricks, and strips of wood that made a clumsy but effective clothes-horse.

Vera was next to useless in these slow constructions, sat on a chair and watched, looked through a newspaper or hummed a tune, mashed Seaton's tea and marvelled at what the black-clocked numskull was doing with his clever slow-moving fingers. When his hammer tried to take a bite out of his thumb he swore with such awful care and deliberation for five minutes that Vera went into the other room until his vocabulary gave under the passing of time. She looked across the road at the large windows of the lace factory, seeing the cheeky bedevilled girls working at looms and threading bobbins, slaving under the forewoman's eye when they weren't winking at the men-mechanics or cat-calling to each other above the noise of their machines. That was me, Vera thought, not so long ago, and now I'm married to Harold Seaton, though at times I can't believe it except when we're in bed together at night and he gets up to his dirty tricks, and often he don't even wait until then. Yet strangely, it seemed to her, there was a compensation in that she was on a higher plane of respect at the Nook. She had never seen more sense in her mother or more kindness and deference in her father, and it often occurred to her that had this been the case all her life she would never have got married, at least not so soon. But that's how it is, she said to herself. 'You've made your bed so lie on it,' her mother said when she first mentioned in a not complaining voice that Harold's temper wasn't all he had led her to believe it would be when they walked together over the Cherry Orchard. Her eyes were drawn out and back to the bobbinating girls, across the road that widened the more she thought how wide it was. I was earning a quid a week then, and now Harold's bringing thirty-eight bob home, so it's no wonder we can hardly manage.

They did for a while, because Seaton was never a boozer, though the tuppences doled out for fags made holes enough in what his wages came to. But he picked up a decrepit pair of shoes for next to nothing in the market and cobbled them into good enough condition for work. He sometimes spent an evening at his father's shop, pushed a loaded barrow to some pub or house and planted a half-crown in Vera's palm when he came home. Nevertheless, she thought, hurrying through the Hartley Road traffic, he's a sod to me when he loses his temper like he does. I wonder if he found the note I left telling him what to have for his tea? A red sky at evening settled over the fields behind as she walked into the house and climbed the stairs.

Seaton sat in his cap and coat, smoking a cigarette by the

empty fireplace. One hand shaded his eyes as if sun still shone into the room, and he held himself from looking up at her, which told her he must be angry about something. 'Where've you been?'

'Mam's,' she told him, hanging up her coat behind the door. 'I got fed up, so I went this morning. I've just got back.' He said nothing, and Vera, feeling his hateful silence, asked: 'What time did you come home?' He wouldn't answer 'What's the matter, then?'

'Nowt.'

She looked round the room. Clean. Tidy. Little to complain about there. The table had been set for the bare event of a meal since morning, and the note she'd left for him was still on the shelf, fastened down by the clock. 'What time did you come home?'

'Five,' he muttered.

She remained standing, intrigued by the reason for his unbending anger, yet also afraid of it. 'Why didn't you cook summat for your tea?'

'What tea?'

'It's all ready. In the cupboard. Bacon and potatoes. You only needed to fry 'em.'

His hand fell, and he looked up at last: 'How the bloody hell was I to know *that*? Are you tryin' to clamb me?' he shouted. 'Where've you bin all day?'

She was unable to counter such blind unreason with swift arguments of her own because it blamed her too much for something she couldn't quite prove was undeserved. 'I've been to my mother's. I've already towd you.'

'Well you should be at 'ome cooking my tea. If I work all day I want to come 'ome to some snap at night.'

'I didn't know you'd be in as early as this,' she countered, thinking he was angry because she'd been to the Nook. He wasn't fond of her parents, often referring to them as 'That bloody lot'.

'I'm not a prisoner, am I?' she exclaimed righteously.

'And I can't work if I've got no grub,' he contended.

'It was all ready for you.'

'How was I to know that then?' he went on.

'Because I left a note,' she protested, 'to tell you what to have.'

His voice became calmer. 'What note?' She took it from the shelf and handed it to him. 'Here it is, plain as black and white.'

He looked at it meaninglessly while Vera lit the stove and set the table. Seaton screwed the note into a pellet and threw it into the fireplace, stood to take off his cap and coat.

'Didn't you see it, then?' she said, in a pleasant voice.

'Yes, I did see it.'

'Then why didn't you cook the dinner?'

He looked to where he had thrown the note: 'I'm not much of a scholar, duck.'

'Neither am I,' she said, not quite understanding. 'Only I felt like going to the Nook for a change. You didn't mind that, did you?'

He burst into a vivid flower of swearing: 'No, but I like to fucking-well come home to a bleeding meal.'

He merely glared at her request that he use less dirty talk, seating himself again by the fireless grate. She detested him for making her miserable, though felt guilty at not having cooked his meal. 'I left everything for you,' she said with tears in her eyes, 'I left a note to tell you as well.'

But he'd had enough of quarrelling: 'You bloody fool,' he said calmly, almost laughing, yet a little ashamed that she hadn't quite understood, 'don't you know I'm not much of a scholar?'

It seemed at times she was still a girl of sixteen, single, back at the Nook helping Farmer Taylor with haymaking in the summer; and an hour later, involved with shopping or cleaning the rooms, she was married so firmly that she had never been anything else, had been so for a century, with the Nook (whose years she now looked on as wide with gaiety and freedom), a dream-house lingering in the sunlit outskirts of her mind. At times she wished she'd never set eyes on Seaton, often hoped he'd step out of the house one fine morning and never come back, that someone would rush to her from the skin-yard to say he'd been run over or crushed by some fatal weight of bales.

Many quarrels centred on cigarettes. He came home from work one day:

'Any fags?'

She'd been dreading this question. 'I ain't got one. Have you?'

Young, stocky and dark, he took off his coat, showing rolled-up sleeves and heavily muscled arms. 'What do you think I'm asking yo' for, then?'

'Can't you go without 'em for one day?' she reasoned. 'You get paid tomorrow.'

He couldn't, swore and spat into the fire. The coal flames killed his spit, almost threw it back, they killed it with such speed. She faced him with eyes averted, arms folded over her breasts, unable to look when he was like this. 'Can't you get any?' he asked after a long silence.

'How?' she cried. 'Shall I cadge some on the street? Pinch some?'

Such absolute logic could in no way stop the quarrel, made it worse in fact. 'What about the corner shop?'

'We owe them ten bob already.'

He cursed under his breath. She saw the shape of the well-formed words. 'You dirty beast. Why don't you stop swearing?'

It was finished in a second, as she had guessed it would be. He stood up, took his steaming dinner from the table, and threw it against the burning soot of the fire-back. 'That's what your effing dinner's worth.'

But the next day, all smiles and amiability with a wage-packet in his pocket and a Woodbine fresh between his lips, nothing could shake his happiness. 'Hello, Vera, my love,' he said as he came in, hoping she'd forgotten the previous evening. She knew he was sorry now, that he was trying to forget it and hoping hard that she'd already done so. He laughed as he sat down to his food. 'Well, my duck, come on, talk to me.'

She turned her head, almost weeping again, his exuberance bringing it back more than taking her mind from it. She had made the meal he had thrown away. The food she had collected and scraped for he had fed to the devil.

'Now then, duck, now then!' he entreated, leaning across to touch her face. She pushed his hand off: it's always the guilty who try to forget, she thought. But he looked into her eyes, and somehow it seemed foolish and unimportant to remember it, until she almost smiled at his clumsy attempt to reconcile her to his good humour, only wanting a few more endearing words and laughs to be won over. But:

'Take your hands off me.'

'Now then, Vera! Don't get like that!' It wasn't possible to rile him tonight. He drew back to begin his meal. 'It's pay-day,' he told her, in the same tone of endearment.

'What if it is?'

He laughed: 'You want some money, don't you?'

'You want your meals next week as well, don't you?' Her quick retort did as much as his gallantry to break down the memory of the burnt dinner.

'I do,' he admitted, pouring a cup of tea. 'Will you have one, duck?' The lure of peace was too attractive, and she relented. 'All right. Pour me one in here' – pushing her cup across.

'Have summat to eat, as well.'

'No, I had summat before you came in. I eat bits and bobs all day and don't feel like eating at dinner-time.' He pushed the empty plate aside and took out a cigarette, striking a match across the fender: 'I drew thirty-two bob this week.'

'Is that all?' she said, in an alarmed voice.

'I was on short time Monday and Tuesday, you know.'

'Oh.'

'Never mind,' he soothed, 'we'll get on all right.' The Nook returned to her in a sudden blaze of reality, and she thought that if there were no food or money remaining in the two rooms she occupied with Seaton, then she had only to pack her few things and go back to the Nook, take up life as she had left it before the last outburst from her father. The Nook stood behind her as a refuge, still regarded more as home than her rooms in the city that had been given life only by Seaton's ingenuity and a few bare promises in church, and therefore belonged more to him than to her. But the fatal phrase that she had made her bed and must lie on it sank the solid island of the Nook, left her feeling alone and hopeless in an empty sea, unable to commit herself entirely into the safekeeping of Seaton's capabilities. No one had ever been out of work at the Nook. Her father and brothers had been blacksmiths either at the pit or in private forges where there had always been labour enough, and besides their small but regular wages there were pigs and chickens and a large garden, tangible amounts of food to be seen from any of the bedroom windows, besides a ton or two of pit coal standing in the yard because the coal-house was packed to its gills already. And the house itself, one of Lord Middleton's cottages, cost practically nothing to rent. But Seaton, she told herself, was a duffer and a numskull – sometimes reminding him of it to his face – pitted inside a city at a mere labouring job when thousands of such men were being sent home day after day because there was nothing for them to do, often to be laid off altogether.

They owed rent, and Seaton decided it was time to leave. He found a house on a lonely lane near the city's edge, closer to the Nook by half a mile, and costing less than the two rooms. Vera was fearful of moving, wanted to stay fixed in the rut they had made for themselves, hating to change the tenuous routine and walls that were familiar and therefore comfortable. To sally out and live on a new lane or street meant exposure to different faces, traffic, trees, and turnings to reach the town centre. Yet she knew Harold was right and that they must go.

The flit was planned for a Saturday night, when Raglin the rent collector (who had a room off the entrance hall) would be boozing in his favourite pub at Canning Circus. Seaton looked on the prospect of a 'moonlight' with elation: days beforehand he was taking down shelves and dismantling the furniture, was ready to rent a handcart from a near-by woodyard half an hour before they were due to move, time enough to carry everything downstairs on his broad, long-accustomed shoulders and rope it firmly on.

Vera was nervous. 'You're sure it'll be all right?'

'Course,' he replied, scornful of her anxiety. 'Raglin'll be off to his pub soon, and then we'll get going.'

'I mean about the house.' He wrapped two pictures in brown paper, a wedding present from one of Vera's brothers. 'I told you before: everything's ready. The house is clean from top to bottom and I've got the rent-book and keys. All we've got to do is get the stuff there.'

A common peril – having other things to fight beside themselves – made them amiable. They were too busy to quarrel, warmed by the risk of a secret move. Yet Vera tormented herself by wondering how long this happiness would last. 'I hope we do better in the new place than we've done here.'

'We haven't done too bad, you know,' Seaton said, making a packet of knives and forks with tea-towel and white tape. He worked with a single-minded intensity, an undeflectable purpose in which action became an emotion and therefore was contentment for him. 'Think of it, duck, a house to oursens!'

'It'll be a lot better,' she admitted. 'There's too much noise here. And besides, the house is cheaper.'

Blankets and sheets were drawn into brown paper, became a parcel bulging between a squeezing network of thin string. 'Put your finger on here,' he said, twisting the first loop of the final knot and pulling it tight. She did so, exerting a gentle pressure where the string crossed. He looped the cord again in the half-dark room. 'Take it off now,' he said, and snapped the fixity tight as soon as she did so. 'There!' he exclaimed. 'That's done.' He sat on one of the chairs to rest. 'We can get going in a bit' – and lit a cigarette to wait.

Vera opened the window and rested her elbows on the cool ledge. It was autumn and the red-bricked factory wall glowed with light, turning a salmon-pink from the dying sun that could no longer be seen, making her think of the sun as she remembered it going down behind Wollaton Church whose spire split the glowing clouds suspended above Balloon House hill. And she thought of suppers at the Nook and the small bedroom shared with Ada and Lyddy, and being half asleep in the dim light in spite of stories told in the same or next bed and the grunt of ever restless pigs in the sty outside. Now the factory bricks were dull and a few dead-eyed stars came out above the roof. She heard the oven-door clang at the Nook and smelled new baked bread.

A voice was talking and she turned back to the dark room, in time to remember that she had somehow been landed in the middle of a moonlight-flit.

Back from work he glanced at her distrustfully, saying with unlimited concern: 'You ain't bin working too hard, have yer?'

Steak-potatoes-cabbage came from oven to table. 'I've got to work, you know.'

He patted her on the stomach: 'I don't want owt to 'appen to my little gel.'

'How do you know it'll be a gel?' she joked, sitting by the fire.

'It's sure to be,' he said, eating. 'If I want it to be a gel, it will be.'

'I want a boy. He can look after me then when he grows up.' Against you, she added under her breath.

'Whatever it is,' he grinned, 'it's bound to be a baby.'

He made her sit down while he mashed the tea. She couldn't help saying: 'I wonder how long this will last?'

'What?' – boiling water went into the pot.

'You being so nice.'

'For ever, my sweetheart. You know I'm a good lad to you,' he claimed, pressing the cosy down.

'I don't think so,' she said, almost as uneasy as if he were in one of his rages. But it was impossible to provoke him. He laughed off her taunts, fussed over her and squeezed her hand, got her to tell him what was in the newspaper while he cleared the table and washed the pots. Coming back from the scullery he seated himself opposite, took out a pair of old trousers to mend. 'You're a real Jack-of-all-trades,' she said.

'Aye,' he answered, looking for the thimble, 'and master of none. I should a bin a good upholsterer, but my feyther thought too much of his booze to bother learnin' me.'

'You're a sight cleverer than me, I will say.' It was one of two cottages they inhabited, living-room, scullery and a pair of small bedrooms set on a lane. Vera missed the sound of factory engines and traffic, found herself immersed again in silent afternoons as she waited for a reasonable time at which the kettle could be set on the fire, or sat with folded hands waiting for the tread of Seaton's shoes on the ash-laid path.

She liked to see him busy, for then he was less irritable. He turned his hand to many tasks, employing such slow-moving methods that she thought he would never be done, when suddenly there was a neat patch, a pair of refurbished shoes, a new latch on the gate. When a brother lent him tools he made cabinets, and ornamental shelves into which he fixed diamond-shaped mirrors, sold for five shillings to people met in Radford or at work. But his suit still went to the pawnshop on Monday morning, a hand-to-mouth loaning system on which they lived until Friday night.

Winter snowed its snow, created a masterpiece of arctic mist and rain until a vanguard convoy of warm days turned into Easter, with supplies of sun run surreptitiously through from warmer lands. Normally slim Vera felt her body growing to what seemed enormous size, which often made her half ashamed in spite of Seaton saying with a laugh that she looked no different from other women, and that was the truth. 'In fact you wouldn't know there was owt inside you at all unless you thought to tek a closer goz,' he argued. Well, she felt too sluggish to worry much.

She walked up the lane one afternoon, passing the sandtip where lorries sometimes came to empty their humped backs. Over the low sandstoned wall lay a stagnant stream, a green and still surface whose tadpoled water beneath seemed to have come from nowhere, a lost tributary of the Lean displaced by the machinations of the pit. She passed primroses and ripening elderberry bushes, and from the railway bridge looked down at the colliery working full tilt. Trucks jangled in the sidings, hooters sounded, and coal rushed into railway trucks from glistening steel chutemouths on the underside of enormous reservoirs that matched the free-wheeling pit shaft in height. Smells of dust and train smoke were in the air, but she enjoyed the sun, and the sight of buttercups growing out of the parapet wall. She told herself that, though Christmas had carried off her twenty-fourth birthday, she was still a girl, felt a girl at any rate, and was somehow distantly frightened that everyone should consider her a woman. And Harold isn't much more than a lad either, she thought.

It was hot and still, a world without wind. Looking in the direction of the Nook she wanted to leap down the bridge steps and go there, crossing the far ridge to where safety lay. Her mind slipped into the momentary refuge of this idea, saying that to run back would mean no more worry about the baby on its way. Once she had slammed the door (hearing the dogs chase off the few pursuing devils), her pregnancy would disappear and she would be a girl again. She stood a long time by the wall, various scenes arising from a well of forgotten relics. It must have been twenty years ago, on a Saturday night when she had been hours asleep with her sisters, that an arm lifted her up, out of bed and room. She huddled to what carried her, still trying to sleep in spite of movement and the sound of creaking stairs. 'Now then, Vera, wake up,' Merton said when the kitchen lamp blazed white upon them. He set her on the table and took a screwed-up fist from her eyes to show her a circle of collier pals, with grinning faces, done up in their week-end best, breathing beer and pipe-smoke when they laughed at what Merton had done. 'She's going to dance,' he said, drumming a rhythm on the table. 'I towd yer she was pretty, didn't I? Now you'll see her dance as well. Come on, Vera, my duck, cock yer legs up and do us a dance. Come on, and I'll gi' yer a penny.' A man's voice sang and she stepped around the table edge, feet lifting and falling to the tune, smiling at the long moustaches and laughing voices saying what a pretty little dancer she was.

Seaton entered the house whistling a song, cap in hand and coat half off; a minute later he left the house, his face a yellow white, and hurried in the direction of the nearest houses to get a midwife.

While waiting he set himself to clean the kitchen and scullery, but because of his nervousness this task lasted half an hour instead of a possible two or three. He sat by the fire smoking, his mind clouded by a numb unhappiness, a helplessness at what was going on upstairs. The groans and cries suggested only disaster, an unspectacular black ending of the world that kept him pinned like a moth to the fireside. His enforced quiescence released only a paltry feeling of rage, not strong enough to dispel the hypnotic grip in which each fresh cry caught him. A flame suddenly burned his fingers, its pain reminding him to strike another match and light up in earnest. He thrust a heavy brass-handled poker between the fire-bars, and glowing coal fell wastefully through into the tin beneath. 'How long will it be,' he wondered aloud, 'before it's all over?'

Eleven struck from some church. 'The first one's worse then waiting to go over the top at Gallipoli,' a workmate had assured him. For the woman it might be, Seaton thought, throwing more coal on, because sometimes they never got over it. No amount of thinking could take him further than that, and his face was ashen with the burden of pity. He wished some pub or picture-house was open, or that some pal would be glad to see him at such an hour, but it was black outside with only the odd bird trying to whistle and maybe a few rats scuttling through long grass in the field.

The coal-scuttle was empty: his searching hand rubbed among cobbles and dust on the bottom, so he went outside to the garden shed. He dislodged a ledge of coal in the light of an uprisen half moon, then set to breaking pieces off without spilling too much slack or making much noise. He used both the blunt and blade of the axe, spinning the smooth haft in his palm without once letting it fall, chipping a wedge into the coal grain with the blade, and knocking it apart with the back, until a pan of even lumps had been gathered. A handbrush hung on the wall and he swept the slack up to a corner, then stacked the coal into a more even arrangement as far from the door as possible, happy and content now that his mind was empty, whistling a tune from nowhere that no one had ever written as his stocky waistcoated figure stooped to his made-up work.

By the kitchen door he heard Vera cry. He had forgotten her, and the blinding cry of pain startled him so that he almost dropped the coal. He went in and loaded the fire, but couldn't stay by it. The clockhands had moved on ten minutes, and that was the only difference in his mood between now and before he had broken the coal. Another cry of pain brought a response of hatred and anger, and he leaned on the gate outside hearing the distant beat of colliery engines, and seeing occasional courting couples sauntering along the lane to vanish in darkness by hedges farther up, until he felt deathly cold and returned to the fire. He swore in a low voice, cursing no one in particular and nothing he could give words to, unless it was whatever made his lips whistle the unwritten tune in the coal-house, that he didn't even know he'd been whistling.

The midwife said it was a boy, and he went quickly up the stairs. 'Are you all right, duck?'

'Yes,' she told him, her face bleached with exhaustion. He stood a few moments not knowing what to say. She held something in her arms 'Can I see him?' The baby was shown. 'It's small, in't it?' was his opinion. 'Though I expect it'll get bigger. They all do.'

She looked at him looking at the baby. 'It will.'

'What shall we call it?'

'I ain't bothered about that yet,' she said, thinking: I don't want to go through that lot again.

'Call it Brian,' he ventured.

She closed her eyes. 'All right.'

'I'm going to work in the morning,' he told her. 'But I'll go to your mother's first and tell her to call and see you.' She was asleep; my young gel, he thought, walking down the stairs to make a bed on the sofa, my young gel's got over it at last and it's about time.

Rain beat in gusts against the bedroom window, an uneven rhythm singing with the wind, and Vera realized from her blissful half-sleep that Seaton was still in bed, that he had to be at work by half-past seven, that it must be late because the room was light already. Six-month bottle-fed Brian would cry his guts out from the crib for milk any minute, so she sat bolt upright, while Seaton grunted and turned over in his sleep at the disturbance. She glanced at the clock on the dressing-table, nudged him in fear and apprehension.

'What's a matter?' he yawned.

'Come on, 'Arold. It's gone eight-thirty.' Dressing quickly, she knew there'd be trouble, always the case when he overlaid like this. He acted as if it were the end of the world because he'd be an hour late at his job. She could never understand it; he seemed not to have much fear of losing it, or to be afraid of his foreman; but he became a maddened bull when jerked straight from sleep into something to worry about, a rush that wouldn't let him dawdle by the fire over a cup of tea and some bread-and-jam, then wander off briskly yet with a settled mind along the morning lane. With a glance at Brian she went downstairs, leaving Seaton looking sullenly for his trousers.

She poked ashes through the grate and screwed up a newspaper, shivering in the damp cold. Seaton came down: 'Get out of my bastard way' – pushing by and sitting in an arm-chair to pull on his boots. She spread sticks over the paper. 'Why don't you wash your foul mouth out?' she cried, knowing how true it was that their quarrels never began by a stray word and went by slow stages to a climax, but started immediately at the height of a wild destructive battle, persisting with violent intensity to blows, or degenerating to a morose energy-less condition often lasting for days. There seemed no half-way stage between a taunting fray, and a loving happiness. Vera could not switch her moods with Seaton's speed, and so detested his fussiness between quarrels, treating him at the best with brittle gaiety and reserve. She had tried controlling her retorts in the hope of finding some other man in Seaton who never quarrelled, who was kind all the time, who would love her in spite of them both, only to discover that no such breadth existed in him. For six months after Brian was born he had been near to this, but the novelty of a baby soon wore off.

A bootlace snapped and he snorted with rage, muttering inaudibly. Her heart beat wildly: 'Why didn't you wake up?' she implored.

'Because the bastard alarm clock didn't go off,' he shouted. 'Or you forgot to set the bleeding thing, one of the two.'

Sticks and paper flared in the grate, cracking and sparking. His continual swearing was the carrier of terrible hatred seen in his face; thus she attacked his swearing, as if his hatred – and therefore their troubles – would go could she cure him of that: 'For God's sake use less filthy talk.'

'You what?' he bellowed. 'You what?' She wanted to say something else, but no words were good enough. If only the minute-hand would race around the clock (that he had set on the shelf as an accusation against her) so that he would clear off to work; or if better still it would run back to seven o'clock and they were happily drinking tea. She was crying now. 'You can get into the factory at half-past nine, can't you?'

'Shut yer cryin', yer mardy bleeder.'

'I'm not cryin' for you.'

'I wouldn't want you to cry for me,' he shouted, dragging cups and saucers from the cupboard. 'I wouldn't want any bastard to cry for me.' She sat by the window, which was the farthest point she could get from him in the house without actually running away – which she felt powerless to do. 'I wish I'd never married you. And I wouldn't a done if Ada and my mother hadn't made me come downstairs on the day we got married.'

The kettle boiled and he was not deterred from making the tea. 'It's the worse turn they ever did me, then.'

'I wish I'd never married you,' she wept.

'Well you know what to do,' he roared. 'Go back to that dirty mother o' yourn, and that drunken old man, and that pack of poxetten brothers and sisters.'

She picked up a cup. 'Don't you call them, or you'll get this at your face. They're worth fifty of yo'.'

Seaton stood, head and shoulders bent towards her, eyes pierced with madness. 'You throw that bastard cup, that's all. Just you throw that cup.'

No thought, no caution. 'I will,' she cried. 'I will' – words of affirmation echoing through her memory back to the day she was married.

'Go on,' he hissed, 'go on, throw it. Just you throw it, and it'll be the last thing you ever do.' He stood by the wall, a loaf in one hand and a knife in the other.

The table was between. 'You think I daren't, don't you?' – her heart breaking in agony.

It flew for his eyes, all her might and aim behind it, smashing to pieces on the wall. He had not leaned out of its track; and then she felt his hand hitting at her face. Reeling back to the sofa, covering her head, she remembered the breadknife gripped in his fist before her letting fly with the cup. The stinging blows somehow hurt through to her cheeks despite the protection of her hands, until she felt no more stings because he must have stopped.

'You'll have your day to come,' she sobbed, shaking with misery, hands still over her eyes, 'when he grows up upstairs.'

His answer was a barrage of curses: no reasonable reply to her long-term threat, but simply a spring reaction to what could be countered in no other way.

'God will pay you out,' was all she could say to it.

'What bastard God?' he shouted with a sneer. 'There ain't no bastard God.' His sacrilege overwhelmed her and she looked blankly out of the window, at tree trunks showing dimly through sheets of rain. You'd think God would strike him dead, saying a thing like that; but happen he was right: there was no God. He was cutting bread and wrapping it in paper for his lunch, then drinking a cup of tea, and all the time she hoped he would put on his coat and leave her in peace.

''Ave some snap and fags ready for when I get back tonight.'

'You'll get nowt else from me,' she cried. 'I'm going home this morning, and I'm taking Brian with me. You wain't see me again, so don't try and come for me.'

He reached for his coat and cap. 'We'll bleeding well see about that.'

'You can't stop me from leaving,' she called out.

He spun round: 'Can't I?'

'No.'

'We'll see then,' he bellowed, and with one rush caught hold of the table rim, tipped it, and sent it spinning across the room. Dishes and cups flew towards the fireplace, and a pot of steaming tea sprayed over the rug. He was no one she knew, had never known anyone so wild as this, a stranger here with her, gone mad in a way she hadn't seen before. Her father had ruled the roost right enough, had wielded big stick and bony fist, but had never havocked and scattered his own goods in so blind a way. There was no man left in his unseeing eyes, and she waited, waited.

It's no good, she said when he'd gone out into the rain, it's no good not knowing what to do, not even crying any more, though the pain was sharper than knives. Can I really go back to my mother's? She decided she could not. It was as bad there as it is here, so either way it's a rotten lookout. What reasoning she did sprang from hatred, the hope that Seaton would be struck down by a lorry and killed on his way to work, or mangled to death when he arrived there. If only he'd injured me, came another burst of reason, and I'd had to be taken to hospital, then he'd happen have been frightened to death by the police, and have been good to me for a bit. She was startled by the baby crying. But how can I stop its rotten father from being such a rotter to me? A positive thought told her to visit one of his brothers, tell Ernest for instance what had happened, and ask if he couldn't talk to his batchy brother Harold and ask him to have more sense.

She levered the table back on to its legs and fed the baby. A cup of tea, and a resolution to see Ernest Seaton, made her feel better. It wasn't raining so heavily when she set out, pushing Brian in the pram.

Turning through street after street she wondered again why Harold was a numskull, while his five brothers stood apparently on another level, in the firm grip of good jobs. One was a shoemaker, two were upholsterers, the fourth a lace-designer. Ernest managed a draper's shop in town. Harold Seaton, a labouring numskull, earned thirty-eight bob a week, when he was lucky, at a tannery and skin-yard. The explanation had been pieced together that Harold, having had the bad luck to be the baby of the family, had been left behind by his upgrowing brothers, and half forgotten by his too-old parents. He had had rickets, from thoughtless neglect rather than lack of money, and the disease had prevented him going to school, caused him lifelong to walk with the swinging gait that Vera, on first seeing him, had mistaken for the pull of the three whippets. She suspected that the bad end of a bargain had come to her, and from wondering whether Seaton was more to be pitied than blamed, gave in to another fit of weeping as she turned on to the street of semi-detached houses where Ernest lived.

Ernest himself opened the door, and she was glad at finding him in. He'd got a good job right enough, able to go in when he liked: I wouldn't be here now if Harold had such a job. He greeted her in a friendly way. 'Hello, Vera. You are a stranger, aren't you?'

He was twelve years older than Harold, with the same dark eyes and complexion, similar stature going to roundness, afflicted with baldness blamed on his Army days in Mesopotamia. They've all got strange eyes though, Vera thought, leaving the pram by the window and following him into the living-room where a huge fire burned in the grate. He offered her some tea, as if, she divined, being polite to one of his customers. The sound of herself saying no brought all the events of the black morning bursting into her. Ernest was thinking how pretty and lively she was, that Harold, though backward, had known how to go for the women, that in his opinion he'd done better than the rest of them in this respect. He hardly knew what to say to her, though what could one ask one's sister-in-law, except how your own brother was?

'I don't know' – her tone was bitter – 'and I don't care.'

He'd thought something like this was in the offing. 'What's the matter then, Vera?' He was alarmed when she began to sob, yet also gratified because he had never known his own wife to shed a tear over anything. 'Sit down,' he said; 'that's right.'

She cried into her hands: 'It's your brother. He's a swine to me.'

Ernest sensed that some sort of blame was being thrown on to him. 'Harold? How?' and didn't like hearing his brother referred to in this way either.

'He hit me,' she accused, 'for nothing. He's a lunatic, that's what he is.'

Ernest stayed calm, reasoning: 'He couldn't have hit you without a reason.' Since he wouldn't dare strike his own wife he thought all that sort of thing had been stopped years ago, had gone out of fashion.

'He tipped the table up as well,' she told him, 'and smashed all the pots.'

'Whatever for?' – still unbelieving.

'I don't know. Because we overlaid. He's always using filthy talk. They'll cart him off to Mapperley one day, the hateful way he looks at you. I couldn't stand his dirty talk, and he hit me because I told him about it. I'm going back to my mother's. I daren't stay with him.'

Ernest caressed the top of his bald pate, looked at her sardonically, stood before the fire with his legs apart. He patted her on the shoulder. 'Calm down, Vera,' he said kindly. 'Beryl will be back soon with the shopping, and we'll have something to eat.'

But she wouldn't calm down, felt Seaton's blows once more and saw the table flying across the room, and she felt them again for tomorrow and the next day. 'Can't you talk to him?' she asked, a last desperate remedy that she didn't think would help.

He was cautious. 'I suppose I could, but I don't know anything about it.'

'I've told you already,' she protested.

'I haven't heard Harold's side yet, have I? I must be fair.'

'And you won't hear it,' she cried. 'He daren't tell you, don't worry.'

'I think he will. There's two sides to every story. People don't do things like that for nothing.' He hadn't meant her to take this in the way she did, but blood was thicker than quicksilver in the Seaton family.

'But *he* did,' she roared, 'because he's loony like the rest of the family.'

Well, this was the bloody limit. Now he could see how Harold had been provoked. They're all alike, these women. And on she went: 'He's a numskull who can't even read and write, so it's no wonder he does such rotten things. If he'd been to school he might a been a bit more civilized.'

The two things don't figure, he told himself. 'You must have asked for it,' he said sharply, 'that's all I can say.'

Yes, they're all alike, she thought. 'You're all the same,' she threw at him.

They must fight like demons, and I'll bet she does a good half of it. If me and Beryl did a bit as well, our lives would be a bloody sight livelier, but one word back from me and we'd be finished. And this no-good bloody girl complains of Harold, and then comes here to cheek me off as well. 'You should go back and look after him,' he exclaimed.

As thick as thieves, that's what they are. 'But won't you help me? Won't you talk to him for me?' she pleaded.

'No, I bleddy well won't; not until I've heard the full story.' She turned from him: 'I'm going. But *he* isn't going to swear at me and hit me any more. I'm going to do myself in,' she sobbed. 'I can't stand it, I tell you. I'll chuck myself under a bus.'

The door slammed, every window in the house tingling against its frame. She pushed the pram down the path and into the empty street, walking quickly along the semi-detached rent-collecting shop-managing pavement. Everybody hates me, and he's only the other side of the bad penny. I can't understand why I ever got married. Now why did I? And I didn't want to, no, never wanted to do any such thing, though if I'd stayed at home the old man would have gone on pasting me, because they're all rotters and if it ain't Harold it's the old man. Everybody hits me, and why? That's what I'd like to know, because it's no use living like this. I can't keep on with it. I'd be a sight better off dead, I'm sure. I wish I was dead, and I will be soon, quicker than anybody thinks, under a tram at where it'll be going fast, and then to have no more rowing and misery like I've allus had. The boulevard isn't far off and there'll be lots of traffic. Around two corners and up a bit of hill. Ernest is rotten like the rest. They hate everybody: and it's no good going back so's it'll happen again in a few more mornings. Why am I still crying? Because they made me? I wouldn't cry for them, the rotten lot. Thank God it'll soon be over, because never again. I'm out of breath, but here's the corner. They are all rotten. I'll wait here as if I'm going to cross the road. Nobody'll think to stop me.

As a tram came one way, footsteps ran up the street behind her, and stopped when they came close. A hand touched her shoulder.

'Come on, Vera,' Ernest said gently. 'I'm sorry about all this. I'll see Harold and make things right.'

She shook him off. 'I'm not frightened, so leave me alone. I'm fed up with everything.'

'Don't be daft,' he said. 'Come on, duck. Harold won't hit you again.'

A suggestion of Harold's kindness after a quarrel lurked in the tone of his voice. 'No,' she said, watching a tram gather speed at the crossroads.

'Come on back to the house and we'll have something to eat.' He took her arm firmly. 'You'll be all right. Things are never as bad as they seem.' His considerate inflexion so closely resembled Seaton's that for a moment she thought he was behind her too, as if by magic he had come out of the factory to find her and make up for the quarrel.

She turned. He pushed the pram. Brian woke up and she thought he was going to cry. Bending over she pulled the coverlet up to his neck. He did not cry. She let herself be led by Ernest, feeling bitterly cold, though the air was warm and Seaton had dashed out without a coat. She shivered on her way back to the house, and a drowsiness replaced or accompanied the cold, as if she had been a week without sleep.

When she left Ernest's a huge basket of groceries rested at the foot of the pram, and the small fortune of a pound note lay in her coat pocket. But she was indifferent to these gifts and all that Ernest had meant they should mean. Yes, he would meet Harold coming out of work. Yes, he would say he should control his temper and not lead her such a dance; yes he would say this and he would wag his head and nod his chin and tell Harold he should behave himself. Fine, fine, fine. But in the end it wouldn't mean a bleddy thing. You can say things to a reasonable man that he'd take notice of, but you can't tell a madman not to be mad any more. And so it would go on, though one day, she said, Brian would grow up, the proof of it being that he was beginning to cry.

PART TWO
Nimrod

4

Brian had just height and strength to wrench himself on to the parapet of New Bridge and see the free-wheeling bare spokes of the headstocks riding the empty air like upside-down bicycle wheels. Leaning on his elbows and booting a rhythm on the wall he saw the semaphore arm of a signal rise upwards, and settled himself in the hot sun to wait for a train.

When on an errand to his grandma Merton's, the couple of grandiose miles out from the last houses of Nottingham became an expedition. Across his route lay streams and lanes and stiles, while to the left stretched a green-banked railway line, rightwards an acre of allotment gardens whose shabby huts and stunted trees were often raided by roving kids from Radford – among them, he knew for a fact, Bert Doddoe and his elder brothers. Brian remembered, in the awesome silence before the advent of a train, how the whole family had descended on his house during the bitter blue snow of last winter. Ada, Doddoe her husband, and their four kids had done a bunk from Chesterfield with their bits of furniture because Doddoe had lost his job for cursing at the overseer down pit; and had spent his wages on booze before going home. Being two months behind in rent they'd come back to Nottingham without a penny in any pocket, had been given a lift all the way by a lorry driver who had lived next door – otherwise they'd have walked. It drew up outside the house one morning, and there was Ada calling to her sister Vera – crying at the same time she was – asking if they could come in for a warm because they were freezing to death. The look on her face forbade any questioning; to do so would mean going into the animal glare of uncivilized territories, as even Harold Seaton realized when the anger felt at their disturbing arrival had worn off. Ada tried to climb from the lorry-back, but her chapped fingers went aside – like cotton thread that misses the needle-hole when it don't seem possible it can – and she fell towards the pavement while Vera screamed a warning. The rest of the kids watched, except Bert who ran from under the lorry into his father's stinging fist, a quick hand that opened in time to catch his wife and stop her fall.

That afternoon Bert and Brian played on the recreation-ground roundabouts while their mothers walked to the convent at Lenton to ask the nuns for bread. They slid face downwards from the high apex of the slide, hoping to work up speed for a dive into soil at the bottom – impossible because the surface wasn't smooth enough. 'You want a candle to rub on it and mek it proper slippery,' Bert had said, and Brian was impressed with the useful know-how of his much-travelled cousin. Their mothers came back with two carrier bags of bread and a tin of corned beef, making a supper for the ten people who that night slept in three rooms. Next day Ada's half-dozen moved into a house up Sodom. Lucky Doddoe bluffed a quid out of his old man and got a six-week navvying job from the labour exchange – at which the unwieldy barge of the Doddoe family was once more afloat in its native Nottingham.

A signal passed from the wall to his fingers: train coming. The thunder of its warning grew louder behind, until a black engine burst into the open and shot a choking cloud up from its funnel. He had intended counting the carriages as they clicked one by one into sight, but heavy smoke threw him from the wall.

The fields were divided by a narrow sandy-bottomed brook, and he descended the steps towards it. White clouds climbed shoulder upon shoulder over the houses of Radford, while in front two horses tethered to a tree-stump meditated the clover like statues. He forced a branch back from an elderberry bush until it cracked, stripped it with a quiet, preoccupied ruthlessness, each leaf dropping to the path and taken into an unwilling dance by the wind. His stick was a sword, and he fenced with the shadow of a bush. Thistles were sabred, stinging-nettles laid low, flowers massacred, and he turned up a lonely lane where bordering thorn hedges were tall enough to hide everything from view but the blackening clouds.

A thunder-noise quickened his walk, a distant drumroll that seemed to single him out from everyone else in the world as its first victim. With thunder, fear had come before the word. At its first sound in a darkening house his mother had looked at the window and said: 'Thunder' and between both pronouncements he had run to hide himself. I'm frightened because it makes a noise like guns and bombs, and guns and bombs can kill you, he thought.

He stood in the silent field half-way between home and the Nook, and without thinking he walked on, knowing he would rather go to his grandma's than run back home, even though the storm might come smashing down any minute, chase him along the lane with each growl louder than that last, blue lightning like cats' tongues licking the hedgetops. His stick was brandished, as if it could be used as a weapon to wheel and fight the storm should it catch him up.

He leapt a stream with bursting heart, seeing reedgrass between scissor-legs as he went across. Green and blue thunder clouds rose like jungles over the uncannily lighted red of city buildings behind, and with the next burst of noise flat, heavy drops of rain fell against knees and forehead.

Still clutching his stick, he stood on tiptoe to reach the gate-latch, heard the ceaseless grunting of the pigs as he rushed up the yard. A blue sausage-like globule of lightning bounced from a too-close hedgetop and he was impelled by a last effort towards the kitchen door, a box and red geraniums on the window-sill passing him by like a splash of blood. One push, and he was standing inside, breathless, wiping his feet, claimed by the interior warmth. Grandma Merton looked up from her sock-darning. 'Hello, Brian, what brings you here?'

Sheets of newspaper protecting the recently scrubbed tiles were used as stepping-stones to the fire: 'Mam says she can't come to see you this week-end because Margaret's badly again.'

'Don't stand with your back to the fire, Brian, or you'll be sick, there's a good lad.' He moved, waiting for a proper response to his delivered message, hands in pockets and looking out at the last triangle of blue sky. 'I don't know,' she tut-tutted. 'What's up wi' 'er this time?'

'I think she's got measles, because she had spots on her face this mornin'.' She took knives and forks from the table drawer and laid them on the cloth for tea. 'You must be hungry after coming all that way' – looking out of the window as if to see in one glance the total distance of his journey. She went down the pantry steps and the rattle of the panchion lid filled his mouth with instant desire for the pasty she would bring. Will it be jam or mincemeat? he wondered.

It was mincemeat, and he sat on grandad's chair to eat it. A steel-blue flash across the window robbed one bite of its sweetness. 'It started thunderin' when I was comin' over the fields.' He noticed the tremor in her hands, filled with knives and forks. She's frightened as well, a fact that reduced his own fear.

Heavy boots sounded on gravel and cinders outside, and a tall man in a raincoat passed the rainspitted window. The door burst open and Merton pushed his bike into the parlour.

'You're back early, aren't you?' his wife said. He took off his coat. 'There's a storm comin' up, Mary' – dividing the embers and placing a log on the low fire. 'There's nowt to do at pit so they sent us 'ome.'

The storm roared as if threatening the house. Mary took steel knives and forks from the table to put them back in the drawer.

'What are you doin'?' Merton wanted to know, changing his boots by the fire. 'We ain't 'ad tea yet.'

She wavered, unable to stand up to him: 'You know I don't like to see steel on the table during a storm. It might get struck.'

He let out a terrific 'Ha!' like a bullet: 'You'd take 'em off the table just because it's lightning?' he shouted. Brian drew back: what's he getting on to me for as well? Merton jumped up, so that Brian almost lost his fear of the storm in wondering what he was up to. 'I'll show you there's no bloody need to be frightened at a bit o' lightning.' He scooped a bundle of knives and forks, flung open the window and held them outside, waiting for a flash of lightning while Brian and his grandmother froze by the table.

Had Merton been at work Mary would have taken an oil-lamp on the stairs, where lightning was invisible and thunder muffled. For whenever the faintest flicker of lightning carved up dark and distant clouds like a Sunday joint she would say to whoever was in the house: 'It's a bit black over Nottingham,' knowing that soon the storm would turn its deluge towards Wollaton. The children had been made to sit countless times on the stairs when they were young, and Vera never forgot the hours spent under the dim oil-lamp that created shadows of merged and huddled forms on the landing walls. Not until the last low rumble of thunder had died away would she tentatively open the stairfoot door and motion her children back into the kitchen.

A sudden fleet of hailstones bullied the geraniums, sang against Merton's cutlery and bounced into the house. 'Here it comes!' he cried, so that Brian, kept quiet by fear at the time, remembered the joy in his grandfather's voice. A sheet of blue light covered the window. I heard it, Brian said to himself. I heard it sizzle – shielding his face and looking through splayed fingers. He's dead. The dark kitchen was lit up, and immediately a thousand guns of thunder rolled over the house.

Merton slammed the window and turned round. 'You see? There's nowt to be frightened on.' Brian took his hands down: it hadn't touched him.

'God'll repay you for such things,' Mary said, 'and for frightening poor little Brian like that.'

'Go on,' he scoffed, slinging the cutlery back on the table as if contemptuous of its inability to kill him. 'Old Nimrod ain't frightened, are yer?'

Brian breathed hard; the circus act had seemed as much directed against him as his grandmother. 'No, grandad. Course I ain't.'

Grandad wasn't won over by this. He sat by the fire, an image of the inside storm, while hailstones and raintorrents outside fought hand over fist to get down eaving and drainpipe into the safety of water-butts placed around the house, a swishing and scrambling that discouraged Brian from talking for fear he wouldn't be heard. Hailstones smacked against the window-panes, zigzagged down the chimney and died in the fire, or ricocheted so quickly from the fire-back that they didn't melt until hitting the hearthrug.

Knives and forks stayed on the table, but Mary wouldn't touch them while lightning flashed. She lit the lamp and fetched tea food from the pantry, so superstitious that she did everything as if God were watching her: never threw bread on the fire (which was feeding the devil), never ill-treated a 'dumb' animal, never turned a beggar away from the door. Even forty years with Merton had kept these principles alive, and they were so strongly instilled into her eight children that their children would also live by them.

Brian left his chair and went to Merton. 'Grandad?'

'What's up, Nimrod?'

'What meks lightnin' an' thunder?'

'Nay, I don't know.' Merton was puzzled, forced to give something thought that he had taken for granted these last sixty years. Then his stern face changed to mischief and enlightenment. 'It's like this,' he said, leaning forward: 'as far as I can mek out, God asks Sent Paul to get 'im a load o' coal up from 't pit in 'ell, an' Paul gets wagons loaded up wi' some o' the best. Then 'e 'itches up ponies and trundles it up to 'eaven where God is. Well,' his eyes flashed with inspiration, 'when Paul unloads the coal it meks a noise, an' that's when it thunders.'

Brian's laugh was belief and doubt. 'It i'n't,' he said.

Merton grinned. 'Yo' ask yer gra'ma, an' see whether it's true or not. Hey, Mary, ain't that right?'

Salmon, pickled cucumber, bread already buttered, were spread on a white cloth, and they drew chairs in to eat. 'That's right,' she said, amused at such blasphemy since it put Merton in a good temper. Brian leaned across the table: 'Hey, grandad, well what about lightning?'

A forkful of cucumber was speared before the answer came: 'That's when they open the furnaces of 'ell, to see'f fires is still goin', an' if they need some more coal.' He grinned at his easy victory. 'Look, old Nimrod don't believe a thing I tell 'im. I don't know, I can see nobody'll ever be able to tell 'im owt wi'out he looks at 'em in that funny way, enough to call 'em a liar!'

Sun glistened on the wet slate wash-house roof across the yard. 'He only believes what his mother tells him, don't you, Brian?' Mary said. He shook his head, mouth full, at the sight of a hedge dripping with fresh rain. One line of hedge turned into another, bordering unused forgotten pathways, trodden deep between house-wall and pigeon coops where you stood and could see nothing, yet hear the throaty warbling like water going through a broken-down whistle from perches beyond hexagonal-holed wire. The front door of the house faced away from the lane, over a garden into which Brian went after exploring the suburbs of inhabited hedgerows. He saw the well, conventional and frightening, a fairy-book piece of architecture on a low hill. He wanted to touch the wooden triangular roof and turn the chain-laden roller of wood, to sit on the circular low brick wall and let down the bucket for filling. But he was afraid. When he said: 'I'm going out now, gra'ma,' she said, looking up from her pastry board: 'Don't go near the well then, will you?' He was eager to be off but asked: 'Why, gra'ma?' 'Because you'll get drowned,' she told him ominously. Sometimes he saw Uncle George coming from it with a yoke across his shoulders, walking down the slope with two lead-heavy buckets. 'When can I fetch water from the well, Uncle George?'

'Soon,' Uncle George told him, and went on to the house.

'Soon', he discovered over square-wheeled months, was a misfit, a no-good word, a trick to fob him off with because it wasn't a definite length of time like a minute, hour, week, or even year, but was whatever of those divisions he or she who said 'soon' wanted it to be. So from now on, he told himself, whenever anyone says I can do something 'soon' I'll say to them, yes, I know all about that you bleddy liar, but when, when, when? 'Hey, gra'ma, can I sleep here tonight?' he asked, bursting back into the house.

Merton spat on the hot bars. 'This'll soon be your second home, I reckon. Would you like to live here, you young bogger?'

'Can he sleep with you two?' Mary said to Lydia and Vi, looking up from her paper.

'He can for me,' Lydia replied. 'It'll be a bit crowded, but I don't mind.'

That was settled. 'Thanks, gra'ma. Can I play in the parlour?'

'Yes, but don't break the gramophone, will you?'

'No,' he said. 'Uncle George?'

George's forkful of egg was reprieved for another minute: 'What?' he asked, looking up.

'Can I build a Goose Fair with your dominoes?'

'Don't break 'em then, or I'll cut your nose off.'

'And you wain't look up to much wi' no nose,' Merton put in. 'Will he, Mary?'

The only time he'd seen anyone in the parlour was when his grandad went in there on Saturday night to change his boots before going out, and then to take them off for Sunday dinner after an hour on the razz-mataz in one of the beer-offs at Radford Woodhouse. Merton would lean back in a chair, and if Brian happened to be there, call for him, saying: 'Unlace my boots, you young bogger.' Then: 'Now pull for all yer worth.' Sometimes the boots would come off slowly and Brian would stagger back only one pace; often, pulling and lugging and all but twisting, they would loosen suddenly and send him crashing against the wallpaper, with Merton grinning from the chair when Brian on the rebound resentfully called out that he was fawce bogger, and boxed the curtain out of the way so that he could go into the kitchen.

Sometimes when Merton sat at ease in his high-backed chair at the fire he imperiously held out one of his long heavily knuckled fingers and called to Brian: 'Hey, Nimrod, pull this.'

Mary tut-tutted: 'Stop your tricks.' George and Lydia watched smirking – or perhaps would turn away and try not to watch. Brian suspected a trick but pulled hard and strong at the finger anyway, and Merton would let out a long unmistakable splintering fart as he did so, a performance that brought the house down, and caused Brian to remark: 'You dirty bogger' and walk off.

When Merton was at the pit, or otherwise occupied around

garden or toolshed, Brian was alone in the beamed parlour playing with Uncle George's dominoes on the polished mahogany table. The dresser was covered with interesting untouchables: curios from Skegness and Cleethorpes, a porcelain war-memorial, sea-shells, a ship in a bottle. On a stand blocking the front door was an enormous horn that played tunes when the gramophone handle was turned two dozen times. A cracked voice – impossible to say whether man's or woman's – sometimes sang:

'O my darling Nellie Gray
They have taken her away
And I will not see
My darling anymore . . .'

and when he asked his grandmother who Nellie Gray was she said she supposed it was some woman or other; and when he asked Uncle George he was told it was a horse, a grey horse; so he saw a woman in a grey dress with a horse's head whenever the maundering and cracked voice wove an arabesque through the cluttered room.

Above the mantelpiece hung a huge picture of a shy, narrow-faced, long-haired girl holding a posy that a waistcoated, muffle-necked youth by her side had given her. They were sweethearts, he said to himself, and when his grandmother dusted the parlour he pointed to the picture: 'Gra'ma, was that you and grandad?' 'No,' she answered. 'Who is it then?' 'I don't know.' But she must be having him on, for who else could it be but his gra'ma and grandad? Under the painting two lines were written, the last words of both sounding similar but for the first letter of them:

If you love me as I love you
Nothing will ever part us two –

which he chanted to the click of falling dominoes, or copied on the white paper bordering indecipherable newsprint, or sang to the tune of Nellie Gray when the whining voice of the man or woman got on his nerves, building his Goose Fairs until all light had been drained into the garden and killed by some monster there, when he ran into the oil-lamped kitchen because darkness made him afraid.

A double-barrelled shot-gun slung over his shoulder, Merton walked up the garden path and cut through a gap in the hedge, followed by Brian shouldering a stick, and Gyp the dog. Silently through a cornfield, they climbed a stile into a meadow, Gyp now picking a fight with stones that Brian ducked-and-draked for it over the grass. Brian stepped behind the tall upright figure of a grandad carrying a gun directly there was a feeling of birds in the blue sky, ink blots swooping to a rise in front.

Merton lifted the gun, and the persisting tune of Nellie Gray died on Brian's lips. There was a roar, a startling explosion that imperceptibly moved the right shoulder above and, looking from behind the legs, he saw birds falling towards grass on either side of a stream.

'Go on!' Merton shouted to Gyp. He smoked his pipe, waited for the dog to lay the limp and bleeding thrushes at his feet. 'Put 'em in the bag, Nimrod,' he said, 'then I'll let yer 'ev one for your supper.' Blood and feathers came off on to Brian's hands, and he was startled by another double-crash of the busy quick-firing gun.

Merton's hand made an eaving across his forehead. Brian saw a controlling skyscraper in half-way motion between a wave and a point, shouting: 'Goo after 'em, Gyp' – as if each word were shot out by the downward bash of a piston somewhere in his chest.

Brian ran, competing with Gyp at finding peppered half-stripped birds, licking blood from fingers as he peered under a bush for what the dog might have missed. Who was Nellie Gray, grandad? (His grandad was the one he hadn't asked, but he knew he wouldn't get a straight answer, so didn't bother.) 'Get down flat,' he was told, 'flat as a pancake, Nimrod.' And just as a nettle stung the end of his nose another shell exploded a hundred feet above, and before receiving the order to stand up three more thrushes slapped his neck and legs. He punched the dog and took them for his own pocket, making his way through the wheat to where his grandad was lighting another pipe.

Brian and Gyp followed the swinging bird-bag to the house.

'Thrush-pudding for supper,' Merton laughed, pipesmoke drifting over them, 'wi' custard.'

'Will they be sweet then, grandad?'

'Ay, like new-born cabbages.' Merton waited, pushed the dog in front with his boot, and Brian with his open hand.

'Them's not sweet,' he contested, looking round.

'Go on, you young bogger, you'll be tellin' me as rhubarb's not sour next.' He gave a satisfied grunt as he pushed open the door. Brian pummelled Gyp on the cinder path outside, getting his ears chewed in return for being a bully and not letting the dog enjoy its own world. It freed itself, but stood by him waiting to be attacked again, tongue falling so far down between two molars that he could have tugged it like a girl's plait at school.

'Gyp! Here, Gyp!' Merton called, appearing at the door with a bone. A fist crept to its face, then withdrew, and it waited for another knuckle-bound assault. ('Gyp! Gyp!') 'Go on,' Brian said, 'grandad's calling you.' The dog's eyes said: If I turn you'll jump on me. What do you think I am? When Merton called again it still didn't run for the bone, and the next thing Brian knew was Merton striding towards them with a stick. 'I'll teach the bloody dog to come when I tell it.'

Brian pushed it away. But his 'Go on' was too late, and the dog knew it, lost the look of playful complacency and shrunk its black and white patches to escape Merton's wrath. 'I'll teach you to come to me when I shout,' he said, holding his breath back at each blacksmith's swipe.

'Don't hit it, grandad,' Brian shouted, wondering why the dog didn't run. Head to one side, then under its front legs as if to bite its own tail, then up and sideways, until suddenly it winged across the yard, squealing on cinders because it couldn't get through a hole in the hedge fast enough. Merton threw his stick down and went into the house.

After dinner the dog wasn't back, making the difference between a full and an empty yard, for the others were shopping in Nottingham. He trod his way through the wheatfield, skirted the well, crossed into Cherry Orchard, and came up out of the lane to capture the gigantic tree whose bole was burnt out, making a room so big that he could walk inside and sit down.

When this novelty had worn he walked the five-mile half-mile over humps and hollows towards the Arlingtons' cottage by the wood, and met Alma when almost there.

'I've got a joke to tell you,' she said, wiping grass-juice on her white frock.

'All right then, tell it me,' he said impatiently.

She clarified her claim: 'It's ain't a joke; it's a piece of pointry,' then sat down.

He sat by her. 'I like pointry. Go on and tell it me.'

Her face saddened. 'I've forgot it.'

He was disappointed, liked to be told poetry and stories, except when he was made to learn them by heart at school. 'You're daft. You forget everything.'

'I'm not daft, Brian Seaton,' she pouted. 'If you say I'm daft I wain't tell you my pointry.'

'Did you make it up?'

Proudly, 'Yes.'

She's fibbin', he told himself, but didn't say anything because he wanted to hear it. 'Tell it me, then,' he said again. 'I didn't mean it when I said you was daft.'

She was happy at this. 'I've remembered it now' – and recited:

> 'I went to the pictures tomorrow
> I took a front seat at the back,
> A man gave me a plain cake with currants in
> So I ate it and give it him back.'

'That's a good 'un,' he said, laughing. She waited for him to stop: 'Now you tell me one.'

'I don't know any.'

'Mek one up then,' she ordered, 'like I did.'

'I can't,' he said defiantly.

She ran off across the field, slammed the rickety wooden gate and went into the cottage.

The fire-scooped hollow of the tree smelled of charcoal: who made such a big blaze to scorch out all this wood? Must have searched days for twigs and leaves to get it going. But what a fire, to burn yet carve a black hooded hollow big enough for a good many to hide in from rain or chasing gang, though it wouldn't make such a good hiding place because every kid in Radford knew about it. He went in, plucked a layer of charcoal and stamped it into the soft wet soil; picked off more to crush in his fingers and turn his flesh black. Must have smoked for days, everyone walking by and nobody thinking to piss on it even. Colliers riding past on their bikes, and laughing at it, letting it burn its heart into a hideout and shelter for when it rains, though it wouldn't be a good place if it thundered and lightninged because trees often get struck. Grandma ought to know because she's older than mam, and even she knows. But p'raps somebody had chucked a bucket of water at the tree to swill it down, watched it sizzling and steaming and gone off thinking it was finished, but as soon as it stopped steaming it started smoking again until it got red and went back to burning, which served the bloke right for trying to kill it out. He should have minded his own business and let it burn, because once fires start it ain't right to bother 'em, especially if they're in a field like this one was: you've got to let them get on with it and burn red hot, as any daft sod knows. Tons and tons of wood must a bin burnt in this tree and I'd like to a seen it. Mam says it's allus bin like this, that even she can't remember how it was before it was black and hollow.

By Sunday dinner Gyp hadn't come back. Merton was in an amiable mood, bland with a few pints of soothing brown ale inside him, and asked at the table if anybody'd seen Gyp. They hadn't. And no wonder, Violet said, after such a pasting as he'd given the poor bogger. For nothing, as well. Can you blame him for not coming back? Well, it should do as it's towd, Merton maintained, then it wouldn't get stick so often. I expect he's roaming the fields though. A forkful of mutton fat went into his hatch. He turned to Brian: 'Shall you come wi' me, Nimrod, and see'f we can find 'im after dinner?'

'Yes, grandad.'

They rounded to the houseback and set off up the sloping path, passing the sentinel well and making a bee-line for Serpent Wood. Was the stick he carried to help him on his walk, or to beat Gyp with for desertion? Yesterday he hated him for hitting the dog, but now, trailing behind in the heavy-clouded silence of green fields, he was unable to. Maybe they'd see Alma, he thought, hands deep in his pockets when his grandad had told him a thousand times to take them out, though he didn't suppose they would because she went to Sunday-school as a rule.

They turned south from the wood, towards the railway. Merton stopped now and again, calling: 'Gyp! Gyp!' each gruff cannon-ball shout met only by an echo, or by an uprising bird that didn't know how lucky it was Merton hadn't a gun with him. Two partridges took off from a bank, flap-winged over an elderberry bush, turned high in a steep curve and vanished beyond the railway.

Great clouds were piled high in the distance like a range of mountains suspended in space. Merton leaned on the iron railing as if wondering whether to cross the railway and search there. Bush leaves swayed with a noise like waves against sand when you put a sea-shell to your ear, and tree branches creaked. 'We'll climb the bank, Nimrod, and see'f we can see owt in Farmer 'Awkins' field. If we can't we'll goo back and see'f your gran'ma's mashed. It looks as if it'll piss down soon.'

Brian was already over and half-way up to the railway, then jumping from one steel rail to another, Merton close behind. He looked beyond, saw nothing but silence. Wheatfields swayed with the wind but made no noise, and smoke from a grey-roofed house went obliquely into the sky. It was funny, he thought, how soil smelled of rain when you'd think it'd be the air it came from. A steel-grey cloud-base stretched for miles, and there was no sign of the dog.

He shielded his eyes from an imaginary sun: 'Can't see 'im, grandad.'

'We'll go back 'ome then. 'E'll cum when 'e's 'ungry.'

Brian turned to re-cross the railway: the long stretch of track disappeared round a bend to the right, no trains flying. Then he turned his head leftwards and, about to face front and leap over the lines, saw something white tucked into one of the sleepers.

He knew what it was before beginning to run, stared at the

splashed blood on the ridge of each parallel track. It's been run over, he said to himself, it's been run over.

'Grandad,' his wavering voice called. He detached the blood-stained collar and folded it into his back pocket. They walked to the house without speaking.

Merton came later with a spade and buried Gyp in the field. While he was away Brian heard his Uncle George and Aunt Violet talking in the kitchen. 'He led the poor dog such a life,' she said, 'that it must have done itself in by laying on the lines till a train came.' Brian was sorry she said this because he'd been with his grandad when the dog was found and, walking back with him, noticed how he hadn't said a word all the way, which was, he knew, because he was sorry he'd hit the dog. George agreed with her: 'He's got too much of it.' Too much of what? Brian wondered. But they said nothing to Merton when he came in.

Brian went home that evening, for it was school in the morning. His small figure walked quickly along, waving a stick, his pockets jingling with pennies and ha'pennies that his grandad, uncles and aunts had given him.

5

Eight-wheeled lorries came by the motor-works and followed each other towards the high flat tongue of land that had been raised by months of tipping and was slowly covering a nondescript area of reedgrass and water. From nearly every precipice men walked to where they hoped the loads would be dumped. Empty sacks flapped over their shoulders, and they called to each other, waving sticks and rakes. Brian, having already used his judgement, was scraping into a heap of swarf and scrap steel picked clean days ago, but which still gave off a pleasant smell of aluminium shavings and carbolic, oil and the brass dust of big machines his father had sometimes worked. He kept one eye on the rapid movements of his flimsy rake, and the other on a small pile of wood covered with a sack near by. Bert had promised to be at the tips later, and Brian hoped he'd come soon to get something from the four lorries – and the convoy of high-sided horsecarts trailing at walking pace behind.

'Where's it comin' from, mate?' Brian asked. Steelpins were popped out and the back ascended slowly. Half a dozen men, waiting for the avalanche of promise, watched the heavy handle being worked by a driver who rarely spoke to the scrapers, as if he were ashamed of being set within the luxurious world of hard labour. Even uncommitting banter was rare, and the scrapers looked on, waiting, never offering to help so as to get the stuff rolling sooner to their feet. 'Prospect Street, young 'un,' the driver answered.

Them old houses. A few bug-eaten laths. Wallpaper, dust and bricks were already streaming down the bank, filling up oil-stained swamp-pools and crushing rusty tins at the bottom. A piece of wall made a splash like a bomb, and that was that. The back was wound up, and the lorry driven off. Brian rubbed pieces of cold water from his ear. Men were scraping systematically at the rammel, though expecting little from those poverty-stricken, condemned, fallen-down rabbit-holes on Prospect Street. Yet you never knew: such exercise in hope may gain a few brass curtain rings, a yard of decayed copper wire (from which the flex could be burned over the flames) or perhaps a piece of lead piping if it was a lucky day. A man whistled as he worked: speculation ran too high for speech.

Brian, having netted a few spars of wood, rubbed grit from his knees and stood up, gripped by a black, end-of-the-world hopelessness: Please, God, send a good tip, he said to himself. If you do I'll say Our Father. 'What's up, kid?' Agger called from the top of the bank.

'I'm fed up,' Brian said gloomily.

Men looked around, grinning or laughing. 'Are yer 'ungry?' Brian said no, scraped a few half-bricks to reveal a fair-sized noggin of wood. 'Sure? There's some bread and jam in my coat pocket if y'are,' Agger said.

'No thanks. I've got some snap as well.'

'What yer fed up for then?' He couldn't answer. Like the old man often said: Think yourself lucky you've got a crust o' bread in your fist. Then you can tek that sour look off your clock. But Brian couldn't. 'What does your dad do?' Agger wanted to know.

'He's out o' work' – already forgetting despair.

Agger laughed. 'He's got a lot o' cumpny.' Agger came on the tips every morning – in time for the first loads at nine – pushing an old carriage-pram, an antique enormous model that may once have housed some spoonfed Victorian baby and been pushed by a well-trimmed maid. There was no rubber on the wheels; all paint had long since blistered from its sides, and a makeshift piece of piping served for a handle. Another valued possession of Agger's was a real rake unearthed from a load of bricks and tile tippings, an ornate brass-handled tool of the scraper's trade with which he always expected to pull up some treasure, good reaching under the muck for good, but which he used with relish whether it made him rich or not. Other scrapers envied it: Brian once heard one say: 'Lend's your rake five minutes, Agger. I'll just get some wood for the fire.' The men around stopped talking, and Agger stayed mute: just looked at the man – a faint touch of contempt at such ignorance of the rules of life – though the blank look was forced on to his face mainly because the request was unexpected, and unanswerable if he was to maintain his sharp gipsy-like dignity. The man got up and walked away, beyond the fire's warmth. 'The daft fucker,' Agger said loudly. 'What does he tek me for? He wants chasing off the bleddy premises.'

Agger often referred to the tips as 'the premises' – a high-flown name as if 'premises' was the one word and only loot he had carried off under his coat from some short term of employment – at being ordered off them himself by a despairing gaffer. 'Premises' to Agger was synonymous with some remote platform of life where order might have been created from the confusion within himself, if only he could be respected as king for some qualities he hadn't got – but wanted because he knew them to exist.

Winter and summer he wore a black overcoat that reached to his ankles and flapped around his sapling body. On the morning when his weekly gatherings had been sold to the scrapshop for a few shillings, each deep pocket of his coat held a quart bottle of tea, panniers that steadied the folds of an otherwise voluminous garment. Each morning he coaxed a fire from the abundant surface of the tip, stoked it to a beacon with old oil cloth, tar-paper and arms of brackenish wood that had laid between the floors and walls of back-to-back houses during generations both of people and bugs.

On fine days, Brian noticed, some scrapers worked little, stood talking by the fire, and only ran madly with coats waving when a lorry came; others scraped industriously every minute of the day whether there was a fresh tip or not, working solidified rubble on the off-chance of finding something that might have been missed. Brian belonged to the latter sort, searching the most unpromising loads because hope was a low-burning intoxication that never left him.

While the damp-wind – seemingly foiled by jersey and coat –

concentrated on Brian's face, he forgot it was also reaching into his body. He whistled a tune through a mixture of brick, wood-chippings and scraps of slate, feeling snatched only when the division between an unreal cotton-wool dreamland and the scratches on his numbed fingers broke down and flooded him with a larger sensation: 'snatched' – eyes and face muscles showing what the innermost body felt even though he hadn't been aware of it, perished through and through, so that a blazing fire would only bring smarting eyes and a skin thicker though not warmer.

Agger worked near by, cleverly wrapped up and more impervious to cold because he had been on the tips longer than anyone else – straight from Flanders at twenty, he said. The useless slaughter of employable sinews had crushed his faith in guidance from men 'above' him, so that he preferred the tips even when there had been a choice. Sometimes he'd gaze into the quiet glass-like water of the near-by canal and sing to himself – a gay up-and-down tune without words – punctuating his neanderthal quatrains with a handful of stones by aiming one with some viciousness into the water, watching the rings of its impact collide and disappear at the bank before breaking out again into another verse that came from some unexplored part of him. Born of a breaking-point, his loneliness was a brain-flash at the boundary of his earthly stress. Still young-looking, though lacking the jauntiness of youth, perhaps out of weakness he had seen the end too near the beginning, had grafted his body and soul into a long life on the tips even before his youth was finished. The impasse he lived in had compensations however, was the sort that made friends easily and even gave him a certain power over them.

Brian broke wood into small pieces and filled his sack, stuffing each bundle far down. 'How are yer going to carry it?' Agger asked.

'On my back.'

'It'll be too 'eavy.'

'I'll drag it a bit then.' After a pause for scraping, Agger wondered: 'Do you sell it?'

'Sometimes.'

'How much do you want for that lot?' Brian reckoned up: we've got plenty at home. I wain't mek much if I traipse it from door to door. 'A tanner.'

'I'll buy it,' Agger said. 'I know somebody as wants a bit o' wood. I'll gi' yer the sack back tomorrow.' Brian took the sixpence just as 'Tip,' someone screamed towards a corporation sewer-tank veering for the far side of the plateau. Agger ran quickly and Brian followed, more for sport since his only sackbag rested by Agger's pram.

He scrambled down the precipice to watch the back open above the round oven door, a foul liquid stink pouring out. Then the body uptilted and a mass of black grate-and-sewer rubbish eased slowly towards the bank, coming out like an enormous sausage, quicker by the second, until it dropped all in a rush and splayed over the grass at the bottom. 'Watch your boots,' Agger shouted as he began scraping through it. 'This stuff'll burn 'em off.' He turned to Brian: 'Don't come near this 'ead, nipper. You'll get fever and die if you do.'

Brian stood back as half a lavatory bowl cartwheeled down from a lorry-load of house-rammel. 'Tek a piss in that, Agger,' the bowler shouted. It settled among petrol drums and Brian amused himself by throwing housebricks at it until both sides caved in. One of the men uncovered a length of army webbing: 'Here's some o' your equipment from France, Agger' – throwing it like a snake at his feet.

Agger held it on the end of an inferior rake. 'It ain't mine, mate. I chucked all my equipment in the water on my way back' – put his foot on it and continued scraping. The stench made Brian heave: he ran up the bank holding his nose, and stopped to breathe from fifty yards off.

At twelve they straggled to the fire for a warm. All swore it looked like rain, some loading their sacks to go home, though Agger and most of the others stayed through the afternoon. Brian took out his bread, and Agger passed him a swig of cold tea. Jack Bird lay back to read a piece of newspaper: 'Now's your chance, Agger,' he said, lighting a lunchtime Woodbine. 'What about joinin' up for this war in Abyssinia?'

Agger reclined on a heap of shavings. 'You on'y join up when they stop the dole and chuck us off these bleeding premises – when there's nowt left to do but clamb.'

'They'll never stop the dole,' Jack Bird said. 'It's more than they dare do.'

'It wouldn't bother me, mate,' Agger rejoined, 'because there'll allus be tips, just like there'll allus be an England. You can bet on that.'

Brian emptied pebbles from his left boot, shook the sock and put it on again. Holes were visible, and when he pulled to tuck them under at the toe the gaps ripped wider. He doubled the long tongue of superfluous wool underfoot to keep stones from his flesh, careful at the same time to leave enough sock above the boot-rims to stop them chafing his ankles. It was a successful reshuffle of wool and leather, he found on standing to walk a few yards, bumpy underfoot, but there wasn't far to go.

An empty tipscape stretched to the motor-works. Lorries wouldn't be back till two, and he swivelled his head to view the building at the opposite far end of the tip, where corporation carts unloaded dustbin stuff into furnaces. Its high chimney sent up smoke as thick as an old tree trunk, a forest giant whose foliage flattened and dispersed against low cloud. The red-bricked edifice was far enough off to be slightly sinister in appearance, an impression added to by its name, the Sanitation Department, or Sann-eye, as the scrapers called it. A miniature railway had been laid towards the tip, where men wearing thick gloves worked all day pushing wagons of still hot cinders along its embankment, emptying them into the marsh on either side and forming another tongue of land which would eventually join up with that made by the lorries.

'Then they'll make an aerodrome,' Brian speculated, 'to bomb old houses like ourn was on Albion Yard.'

'To flatten the Germans you mean,' a scraper put in.

'They'll build a factory,' Agger argued. 'Or a jail. I'm not sure which they'll need most by then.'

Along the high embankment by Sann-eye Brian saw his cousin Bert. Was it? He shaded his eyes and looked again. Yes it was – walking towards the tippers' camps – a long way off and coming slowly with hands in pockets, kicking the occasional half-burnt tin into the too-easy goal of waterpools below.

To meet him meant crossing the swamp by stepping-stones of grassy islands, and tin drums that had rolled from high levels. Brian's feet were pushed well forward as he went through spongy grass towards the opposite ash bank, surprised that such a varicoloured collection of mildewed junk could meet in one place: half-submerged bedticks and 'steads, spokeless bicycle wheels without tyres sticking like rising suns out of black oily water, old boxes rotting away, a dinted uninhabited birdcage in front like a buoy at sea. Farther in the canal direction lay a dog-carcass sprawled half out of the water, its scabby grey pelt smoothed down by wind and rain. I'll bet there's rats whizzing round here at night, he thought, big rats with red eyes, and maybe cats with green 'uns. The prevading stench was of rotting diesel oil, as if countless foul dish-rags were soaked in suffocation and held under the surface. Patches lay on the surface like maps of gently rounded coasts, making whorls of blue and purple and greyish inland, beautiful patterns that he now and again pelted with stones to see if they were real enough to stand explosions, but they merely let the stones through, and reformed to a slightly different design.

He walked on, excited at swamp-roving, zigzagging from what he sensed were deeper scoops and gullies. His no-man's-land was small, for he could hear the sharp-voiced scrapers on the tip behind, and at the same time see Bert almost above him on the grey wall in front, a ragged-arsed sparrow calling out:

'Don't come up: I'm coming down. I've got some chocolate 'ere' – patting his back pocket, walking to different parts of the slope before deciding which was freest of hot cinders. He waded through a pile of blue-shining burnt-out tins, stepped over ragged clinkers (like a cat on hot bricks, Brian thought), holding into the steep slope in case he should keel over and begin rolling. 'Who gen yer the chocolate?'

Without looking up Bert answered: 'Nobody. I got it from a shop.' He disturbed a mass of tins and ash: 'Never known anybody to gi' me owt, 'ave yer?' – and an avalanche rolled into water, drops splashing against Brian: 'Where did you get the dough from then?'

'Pinched it, if you want to know.' He walked to Brian and sat on a petrol drum: 'I pinched this as well, from Doddoe's pocket,' he added boastfully, drawing out a whole cigarette. 'He'll think our Dave done it, and paste 'im. And it'll serve 'im right, because our Dave batted my tab last night, for nowt.'

Sandy-haired and pint-sized, one of the many kids broadcast from Doddoe's loins, Bert's fever-eyes and white face marked him a born survivor. He wore long trousers, a baggy cut-down pair of Dave's. Like Brian he had first lived in the bitter snows of March, was suckled under the white roof of a pullulating kitchen, then set free from everyone's care because another kid was queueing up for air and milk behind. He pulled a match sharply against the drum and helped its flame to life in the cup of his dirt-worn adult hands. 'I like a smoke now and again. It meks me feel good. I had a whole packet once all to myself and I stayed in the woods smoking 'em.'

'I tried it, but it nearly made me 'eave.'

'Not me. I'm nearly ten, see?' He drew a half-pound bar of chocolate from his back pocket: 'Tek a bit. And break me a piece off as well.'

Brian ripped the blue paper away: 'How did you pinch it?'

'Easy. A shop door was open. I stood outside to mek sure it was empty, then jumped across the doormat-bell and slived my hand over the counter.' Brian passed him a double square: 'Anybody see yer?'

'No. I was dead quiet. Had my slippers on. Look' – he held up his foot to show the rubber and canvas rags of what had once been one-and-fourpenny plimsolls, now like the relics of some long and fabulous retreat: 'Quiet as a mouse. So don't say a word to a livin' soul. Not that I think you bleddy-well would,' he said, checking himself quickly. 'You're my best pal as well as my cousin, and I know I can trust yo' more than anybody else in the world.'

'Did yer nick owt else?' Brian asked. ('Yer want ter stay away from that Bert,' his father said when the Doddoes had left to live up Sodom. 'He's a bleddy thief, and if yo' get caught thievin' wi' 'im yer'll get sent on board ship. So watch it, my lad, and 've nowt to do wi' 'im.')

'I don't allus pinch stuff, yer know,' Bert said resentfully, as if he also had seen the pictures in Brian's mind. 'So don't think I do.' He skimmed a piece of slate across the water: it ducked-and-draked and took his annoyance with it under the surface. 'Want a puff? No? All the more for them as does then. I just saw this bar o' chocolate, see, and went in to get it. That ain't pinchin', so don't tell me it is. Break me a piece off then,' he asked, flipping his nub-end into a pool of water and laughing at the crackshot sizzle. 'We'll scoff it up and see'f we can find owt on the tips.'

He led the way: 'Watch that there; if you tread on it you'll goo under. A pal o' mine once got blood poisoning: cut his foot on an old tin and they kept 'im in 'ospital six weeks. Wish it'd a bin me. He got marvellous grub. Ever bin inside Sann-eye?' he called back.

'No,' Brian admitted. 'I ain't.' He turned for a snapshot look: the massive building still in the distance, a row of windows top and bottom, less smoke travelling from its chimney.

'We'll go in then later on, about five o'clock when the men's knocked off.' He pulled a bicycle wheel from the water and bowled it along with a piece of stick.

Brian asked questions: What about the nightwatchman? because he couldn't imagine Sann-eye without one. He visualized the burning fires, oven-doors like a row of monsters' mouths filled with flames instead of teeth, able to draw you in for devouring if you stood near too long. 'That's 'ospital,' said the voice of a girl who had taken him walks not long after he had learned to walk.

'Nobody's there. Fires is nearly cold by five. I went in last week with our Dave, up through the big winders. I'll show yer.' The wheel swerved off the path and disappeared under a nest of bubbles. Bert threw the stick after to keep it company. It floated. They were almost at the escarpment. 'I bet a good tip'll come this afternoon,' he prophesied.

'We could do wi' it,' Brian said. 'But there ain't much on tips today. I bin scraping since nine, and I on'y got a sack o' wood.'

Bert wanted to know where it was. 'I sode it to Agger for a tanner.' Both were on hands and knees, making slow progress up the bank. 'Yer got robbed,' Bert said. 'He should a gen yer a shillin'.'

Brian was being called a fool: 'It saved me carryin' it 'ome. We've got plenty o' wood anyway.' Bert relented, went on climbing: 'Well, as long as you get your sack back.'

'Course I will,' Brian said. 'What are you going to do for a rake though?'

'Mek one. Flatten a piece o' steel wi' a brick.'

'It'll break.'

'I s'll look for summat else then.'

'I'd like a good rake,' Brian said. 'I 'ave to mek a new 'un every day, as it is. After about six scrapes they break.'

'You need a steel 'un,' Bert told him.

'I know I do. I ain't got one though. The best rake I've seen is Agger's. It's got a proper 'andle. Most o' the time he don't use it an' all.'

Bert reached out for what he thought was a piece of iron: slung it away when he saw it wasn't. 'Why?'

'It's too good. He on'y uses it on loads where he might find good stuff. Most o' the time he keeps it in his pram.'

'A rake's no good if it ain't used,' Bert reflected, as they came up on to the solid tips. He found a sack without too many holes, in which he put scraps deemed useful enough for home: an old kettle worn thin underneath that Dave would mend with a washer, a cup with no handle, dummy bars of chocolate for the kids to play with, a coagulated mass of boiled sweets to wash under the tap and eat, and a few choice pieces of fresh-smelling wood for the washday copper.

The scrapers were leaving the tips under a misty silence: a scuffle of boots could be heard kicking the fire out, and the tin shed – put up when it had looked like rain – fell with a satisfying clatter against the stone. 'The rats don't come out till it's dark,' Bert said, which Brian was glad to hear. They walked without speaking, treading quietly through sedge, water seeping into all four shoes if they didn't go forward quickly enough. Topping the precipice of tins and clinkers, Sann-eye looked empty and locked up for the night, its chimney cold and unsmoking, frail almost against heavy clouds, as if it had to bear an unfair weight and couldn't for much longer.

Brian noticed Bert limping, remembered him walking with a strange motion ever since leaving the tips. Must have a stone in his shoe – yet it didn't quite look like that. He's acting daft I suppose. Still, he himself had often simulated a painful limp when on Goose Fair, asking people for pennies because he was hungry. It was an old and secret joke between them: 'I want some money, missis, because my crutches are in pawnshop and I can't afford to get 'em out. No, *I* didn't pawn 'em. Dad did. He was short for a packet o' Woodbines. I tried to stop 'im but he knocked me down, and I couldn't chase him because he'd snatched my crutches. Mam tried to get him as he was going through the yard, but he hit her with one of the crutches as well. So it's ever so painful to walk without 'em, missis, honest it is. They're in pawn for a bob, and I only want another twopence to mek it up. Thank you, missis, ever so much.'

And sometimes when that inner urge to beg was far away, they might limp because they felt like it. Brian often did so when alone, to look different from other people due to his uppity-down progress along the pavement, and also to make himself the object of sympathy to passers-by. After a while he'd realize he didn't know whether or not they felt sorrow because it was never shown, so he'd change his antics to a self-made interior tune whistled for his own benefit only. Like sometimes you thought people might at last feel sorry if you died, but you knew you'd never be able to see it, so it wasn't worth it anyway.

He was going to ask about the limp, when Bert said: 'This is where we goo up. I'll nip first and yo' can foller.' At the top he gave the sack to Brian, stared hard at the wall for a second. Then the patch of neat cemented bricks turned into an all-powerful magnet, for he shot across the few-foot gap at great speed, and was pressed like a flat frog against its vertical surface. His two hands clawed their way on to the window ledge, and with one heave he was up.

Brian saw a distinct hollow in the wall on which to grip, so that he too, after throwing up the sack, was all of a sudden flattened against the bricks, aware of his boots twenty feet free above the ground. Heavier rainspots tapped coldly against his hands. 'You'd better come up quick before you get drowned,' Bert advised.

His feet, like swinging pieces of iron – one of which felt dangerously heavier than the other – also found ledges. It was a fight to steady himself, and he stopped breathing to do so, pushing each finger as far as it would go into the ledge to strengthen his grip for the pull-up. He heaved, and began to lift slowly. At the same time his fingers dragged back, as if the rainspots that had fallen on to the ledge were grease instead of water. Before they could snap off and send him whistling like a bomb into the ground he lunged forward with his elbows, swung his body at the top shelf of stone, and landed in a sitting position. 'Yo' needed all day to do that bit of a job.'

'I didn't tek as long as yo' did,' Brian retorted. He looked back over swamp and tips, railway and distant factories, with not a living soul in sight, then turned to see a six-foot drop within the Sann-eye: mountains of dustbin rubbish ready for burning after the week-end, tins and boxes and cinders stretching in waves away from the wall to form an escarpment at the dozen doors of the cooling stoves. Dim light came in through high arched windows all around the great interior, and such vastness seen from the ledge he stood on made it seem like the inside of a church – except perhaps for the stuff of every dustbin piled below.

The oven-doors had been bolted and shutter-drawn; looked harmless, not like monsters' mouths any more but corpse-grey and a bit ghostly, sinister in their temporary inaction. The only remaining signs of heat were mixed with warm ash and a nose-cutting smell like that of old vegetables and fish. Something moved in the rubbish. 'A cat: they get the biggest feed of their lives here.' Bert's gruff voice echoed around the space still left between rubbish and ceiling.

'I'm off,' he said. He jumped a yard out from the window-sill and dropped into the rubbish, almost out of sight as his feet went in. 'It's like landin' on a feather-bed,' he yelled. Brian held his nose and took a clumsy flying leap.

The height, twice his own, looked immense, but was reduced to nothing by the crash that pulled at his legs like an electric shock and rolled him sideways a bit too soon after the leap. Shuddering, he tried to get up, but couldn't until Bert pushed a hand out and jerked him to where it was less spongy underfoot. 'It's like sinkin'-sands, if you ask me,' Bert said. A cold herring wriggled from his face. The green eyes of an angry cat speared him, outraged at the cheek of his intrusion. It's trespassing in here, he thought. We'll get sent off if a bloke comes in: there's nowt worth pinching anyway, so what's the bleeding odds? We should 'ave gone off and spent my tanner. He sat to look back at where he'd hit the rubbish, and peering through the grey of the foreclosing afternoon, used a few seconds to discover what it was piled in heaps and taking up nearly half of the whole Sann-eye. Herrings and mackerel and bloaters, he'd never seen so many, not even on the pictures when it showed you big steamboats bobbing around Newfoundland and pulling in nets-ful. Where did they all come from? 'I don't know,' Bert said. 'I expect it's all rotten though.'

'It don't smell rotten.'

'You can bet it is anyway.'

'What about taking some home?' Brian said. 'We can fry it for supper.'

'You can't; it stinks like boggery.' Bert seemed certain, so Brian was ready to take his older word for it, except for: 'It don't smell all that bad.'

'It wouldn't be 'ere if it worn't, would it?' Bert retorted. 'Use your loaf.'

'I'm using my bleddy loaf. Look, the cat's eating it.' He picked up a fish and smelt it, opened its mouth, turned its tail. 'It looks all right to me.' Bert was already in another corner, scraping through more varied heaps. 'Fish shops chucked it 'ere,' he called back.

'I've never seen this much fish in fifty fish shops.' He threw the herring back on the pile. 'I suppose lorries brought 'em?' Bert said they must have. A huge black cat ran from a window, took a fish in its mouth, climbed out. Other cats were round about, fixed in the windows like bats or owls, bloated with food, hoping for enough appetite to make another dive. Some moaned like babies in the dusk, unable to move, too loaded to live, dazed at the shock of an easy life, as if filled with a nagging fear that they would never recover from it.

'I suppose they threw it away at the shops 'cause they couldn't sell it? It's old stock; like them tuffeys you find on tips.'

'Why don't yer forget about that bleedin' fish?' Bert said. 'You're getting on my nerves. Come over 'ere to look for summat good.' There was boat-loads on it, enough to feed thousands: you could roast 'em over fires or fry 'em in pans, and fill your guts for a year of teas and suppers, as long as it didn't mek yer sick. 'Bollocks,' he shouted to Bert, making his way on all fours over tin cans and ashes towards him.

'They've nearly orluss got this much fish in.' Bert was too absorbed to slam back. 'It's bad though.' He tore into a wall of rubbish, and Brian had never seen him use a rake with such skill. Tin cans, bottles, cardboard boxes, orange peel and solidified masses of unnamable parts were burrowed into, while objects of doubt were hooked up to the failing light: either jettisoned or laid aside on the sackbag.

Brian looked closer to see how such quick raking came about. 'That's a strong rake you've got. Did you find it 'ere?'

'On tips. It was under a load of old swarf from the Raleigh.' With a boastful gesture and a satisfied grin he held it up, meaning him only to glimpse it before bending to work again.

'I'll believe you when I see it,' Brian said, already suspecting. The rake swung, so he grabbed out and pulled it close, which brought a laugh: 'What did you think I was limpin' all the way from the tips for? I couldn't let anybody see it, could I?'

'That's 'is best rake. He'll be lost wi'out it.' Brian cried indignantly: 'You rotten sod. Fancy doin' a thing like that.'

Bert tried denying it, in fun as much as hope of belief. 'It worn't Agger's. It was somebody else's. Honest. Cross my 'eart and cut my throat if I tell a lie.'

'I don't believe yer. I know Agger's rake when I see it. I'm not blind.' Bert gave up his act of innocence and turned on him: 'What if it is? Agger found it, didn't 'e? He didn't pay for it, did he? We needed one, didn't we?'

Brian admitted the truth of this barrage. 'You still didn't need to nick it.'

'I didn't. I found it in his sackbag. Anyway, our Brian, when I took it I seed 'e'd got about ten more. He finds plenty o' new 'uns every day. Or else p'raps he nicks 'em like I did.'

Maybe he does at that, Brian thought, and became absorbed in Bert who seemed to be carving a grotto from the bank of rubbish. He stayed back while the dexterous excavation went on, all kinds of domestic residue landing not far from his feet. He'll get through to the wall soon by the look on it. That's what came of nicking such a good rake: it worked like a machine, some sort of field thresher they often have near the Nook in summer.

A tunnel opened so that Bert was half hidden. What's he trying to find? I'll go in soon to see what it's like under all that rammel. Maybe he wain't let me. Course he will: he's my cousin. My pal as well. Our birthdays are nearly the same. A large tin from the top of the mountain rolled menacingly towards him, and the instinct to kick it out of the way was curbed by a thought that it wouldn't be safe to do so. Bert, adaptable and quick, capable of looking after himself, came from a long line of colliers, and cocked his ear as if he'd heard some mythical splitting of pit-props far down in his soul. Another tin rolled, followed by jars, bottles and wet paper, until Brian saw the whole mountain sway like an earthquake. A cat ran across the top to forage at the fish beyond, its green eyes looking momentarily to one side as if its light feet were causing the subsidence.

Bert jumped to safety while Brian was distracted by the cat. The collapse was almost soundless. Hundredweights of rubble settled back into place, and Bert was out of range, rolling down the bank, shouts and laughter chasing around the high ceiling. Brian leapt clear, disappointed that Bert's monument had been squashed out of existence. 'That was good sport, our Brian' – Bert brushed ash from his clothes. 'It didn't get me though.'

His hands were empty, black and scratched, an unbleeding cut between two fingers. 'Where is it?' he demanded of Brian in a warlike way.

'Where's what? What yer talking about?' Bert looked around, felt in pockets – but only knew the rake was lost when convulsed by a bout of swearing that shrunk his world to a black and thwarted brain. Brian looked at the flattened hill of refuse. It would take all night to delve: 'I'll help you.'

Bert could neither get over it nor act. 'A rake like that,' he kept saying. 'Would you believe it? A rake like that. Agger's best 'un.'

'It'll get shoved in the ovens with all that other stuff right enough.'

'I know it will.' There were tears between Bert's curses. 'I'm daft. I'm batchy. Nicked it and carried it right across the bleeding tips. For nowt. For bleeding nowt.'

Brian turned away, because four loud words hammered against the inside of his head – trying to get out. But he couldn't say it, except to himself, and even then he felt treacherous, as well as foolish. 'God paid him out,' they said. 'God paid him out for nicking Agger's best rake.' There ain't no God. God is a bastard, his father had often roared in response to his mother's taunt that God would pay him out as well. So maybe there is one. He scraped at the wall of refuse with a piece of stick while Bert sullenly loaded his sack.

And 'appen there ain't, because where will poor owd Agger be tomorrow when he finds his rake missing? He'll goo off 'is nut, 'aving to use old 'uns that break easy, and not getting such good stuff to sell. Maybe he'll think I nicked it. I'd better not go back for a while in case he does. What a bleeding look-out! Where'll I get wood for the fire? All through our Bert, the loony bastard. And then he went and lost it. I'm sorry for Agger though. I am. I'm sorry for 'im. Out o' wok and living off the tips. I don't know. Nowt but an overcoat and an old pram to his name; and not even his posh rake any more. I'm fed up, I am. God-all-bleedin'-mighty, I'm fed up.

They climbed through the window, too morose to think of safety during the high drop on to the path. 'I'm 'ungry,' Bert grumbled, trudging along. 'I ain't 'ad a bit t'eat since that chocolate.'

A straight road led from Sann-eye to the bright flares of

Wollaton Road. Lorries, cars, buses, were crotchets along bars of music, drumrolls as they roared by in the distance, loud and frequent because people were going home from work, 'I don't suppose there'll be any snap at our house,' Brian said, 'and that's a fact.'

'Nor at ourn either.'

There was a smell of spring, a lightness of moss and grass and fresh nettles that stung their legs when they went too far into the hedge. Westwards the sky had reddened, as if a nightwatchman behind the clouds had lit his fire for the night, sitting there to keep out intruders from what paradise lay beyond; and a glow from it was cast against the sheer grey-plated walls of looming gasometers, making them seem taller as they walked by. Brian felt in his pocket: 'I've still got that tanner Agger gen me for the wood, so we can get summat to eat. We'll buy some Nelson Squares and crisps, and stuff our guts on that.'

'Marvellous,' Bert said, putting his arm around Brian's shoulders, and they walked more quickly.

6

Brian watched two pigs near the coal heap, nibbling black bits from under the dust. 'Grandad, why are the pigs eating coal?'

Merton was mixing bran in a tub near the copperhouse door. 'Because they've got nowt better to do, Nimrod.'

Brian thought he wasn't getting the whole story. 'Is it because they're hungry?'

'Pigs is allus 'ungry.'

'But they eat bran, and taters wi'-their-jackets-on.' Merton stirred the soggy mess with a steel scoop. 'Ay, they'd eat owt. They'd eat yo', yer cheeky young bogger, if I served yer up in their trough!' He turned his back on questions and emptied a sack of potatoes into the tub. Brian saw Uncle George wheeling his bike up the path, a tall thin man wearing a cap, a wavy-haired god who worked at the Raleigh.

'Where yer bin, Uncle George?'

'To t' football match.'

'What for?' he asked, thinking: to play, or watch?

'Don't ask questions,' George told him, putting his bike in the shed, 'then you'll 'ave no lies towd yer!'

He followed him into the kitchen with a laugh, where his grandmother was mixing flour for cakes and bread. 'Did yer see owt on the placards?'

George bent to pull off his cycle clips, then looked up with them in his hand. 'They've captured Addis Ababa. It looks like the Abyssinians is finished.'

His mother tut-tutted in sympathy. 'Aren't them Italians rotters? Fancy gassin' poor black people as 'ave never done anybody any 'arm.'

'They reckon they were fightin' wi' umbrella sticks against machine-guns,' George said.

Them Italians'll suffer one day,' she prophesied, spreading jam over a flat sheet of paste. Brian listened with such interest that he unknowingly screwed a button off his shirt. 'Now look what yer've done!' she cried. 'Fancy piggling a button off like that.' He was given the jam-jar and spoon, and after scraping sucking licking came the prelude to further question:

'Gra'ma?'

'What?'

'Who won the war?'

'Which one?'

He was puzzled. 'The war.'

'The last war, do you mean?'

He stood, not knowing what to say, not wanting to be fobbed off with any war. 'Was the last war the one where uncle Oliver was killed?'

'Yes,' she answered.

'Well, who won that war then?'

'Nobody,' she said, taking the sticky jam-jar from him. 'Now go and wash your 'ands, there's a good lad.' He walked to the sink, puzzled. For how could nobody win a war? Nobody ever answered his questions, he brooded. Nobody. Nobody wasn't a word, it was a trick. There couldn't be a war without somebody winning it. Somebody won; somebody lost. That's how it was. And, washing hands and face from a bowl that his grandmother filled, he could hear them still talking about the war in Abyssinia.

Doddoe's spirit passed to his children. Merton saw them once, a straggle-lined caravan coming over Cherry Orchard, bearing misshapen apple-bosoms grown during a foray into someone's garden. They kept well clear of his waving stick, knowing who he was and fearing him for that reason. The close-browed demon of bull-Doddoe seemed more desperate in his offspring due to the fact that they often had to find their own food, which meant putting themselves in the way of fences to be climbed, palings and barbed-wire having good enough reason for being there: apples, potatoes, cabbages, or perhaps even more luxurious stores.

Sometimes a brace of them visited the Nook, hoping Merton was still at the pit. Mary would bring a jam pasty or piece of bread to the door, making them divide it fairly before they went away, which they did quickly, fearing the sudden expostulating wrath of Merton, regarded as more terrible than that of their father because they were less familiar with it.

While the Doddoes were discouraged from the Nook, Vera's children were welcomed. For some reason Harold Seaton's reputation had grown in Merton's eyes; he was now considered a quiet sort of man who thought a lot of his family and looked after them as best he could, worked hard when there was work to be had, and didn't throw his wages away on ale while his children marauded for what they could lay their thieving hands on – like the Doddoe Tribe for instance.

On the far side of Cherry Orchard, under the clouds of cloud and trees at the edge of Serpent Wood, were two farm-labourers' cottages, and Brian was acquainted with only a fraction of the children who spewed occasionally from the doors of both. On Saturday he walked over the open roughs, mesmerized by the long dark strip of forest crossing his horizon, drawn to it more than to the pair of cottages and often mapping it with an explorer's mind – though rarely going to open country beyond.

A gaggle of girls rose out of a hollow, wearing similar pink frocks and holding up hands made of daisies and buttercups. They came towards him, but stopped at an intervening patch of flowers to kneel and pick them. Brian went closer, paused. One of the girls looked up and said:

'Hello.'

He felt uneasy, thrust hands deep into pockets, dug holes in the turf with his shoecaps. 'Hello,' he responded.

'You live at the Mertons', don't you?' she said knowingly.

'How do you know?'

'We've seen you playing in the yard when we've walked past, haven't we, Fanny? Our Alma's towd us about you, as well.'

'I'll help you to pick some flowers,' he said.

She didn't like his manner, because he hadn't asked. 'If you like you 'elp our Fanny, 'cause I've got a lot already.'

Fanny turned shy but he ripped up handfuls from the moist grass, throwing them into a heap for her to sort out. 'Do you want any clover? I know where there's a lot.'

'No,' Brenda replied, 'I don't like clover. Fanny don't either.'

'Hey, our Brenda,' Fanny shouted from a hundred yards. She was all flowers now, yellow and white, a walking cornstack with arms and pockets full. 'Let's go and get some bluebells. I know where there's 'undreds in our wood.'

Brenda pointed to a distant hedge, and nodded. 'We'll shout Ken and John first.' Cupping hands over her mouth she screamed: 'Our Ken! We're goin' ter get sum bluebells. Cum on!'

The boys were running up and down over the hollows. 'What's your name then?' Brenda asked. He told her, grudgingly. 'Brian Merton?'

'No, Seaton. I don't live at the Mertons'. I on'y go up there when I'm not at school.'

He was astonished, almost angry, at how much Brenda knew of him: 'I *knew* you didn't live at the Mertons'. He's your grandad, ain't he? I know your grandad, *and* your gra'ma because sometimes they go out with our mam and dad and the Lakers into Wood'uss, boozing.' They walked towards Ken and John near the cottages. 'Your grandad sometimes goes shootin' and I saw him at the Farm Show last year. Once, when *you* wasn't there, I went an errand for him into Wood'uss, and Fanny went with me, didn't you, Fanny?'

The mute Fanny walking by their side managed a muted affirmative. 'He sent us to fetch some fags and a pint of ale.'

The boys came up. 'You don't go to our school, do you?' said Ken Arlington, a statement, not a question.

'I go to one in Nottingham,' Brian said.

'Ours is a rotten school,' Brenda complained. 'Miss Barber allus gives us the strap.'

Ken pushed her in the back. 'That's because you're cheeky.'

'I'm not cheeky,' she shouted.

'Yes you are. I heard you chelping her off when I walked by

your class window one day carrying a case of milk bottles. No wonder you get the strap every day.'

'You're a liar,' Brenda screamed. 'You tell big fibs.'

'I'll paste yo',' Ken said, 'if you call *me* a liar.'

'I'll tell your mam if you do' – which she knew would put a stop to his threats.

'Coward,' he grumbled. At the cottages Brian was fascinated by the waterpump in the Lakers' backyard. 'We don't have one of them,' he said to Brenda. 'We've got a well instead.'

'It's better having a pump,' she claimed.

'Can I have a go on it?'

'No,' she said in a righteous and holy voice, 'you mustn't. It'd be wastin' water.' They stood aside when Mr Laker came out of the door carrying a white enamel bowl. A few vigorous ups and downs sent water belching from the iron spout, flooding the bowl he held beneath. 'Gerroff an' play, kidders,' he said. His short hair stuck out like chaff, went suddenly limp under as sluice of water.

Brian set off across Cherry Orchard. A few hundred yards from the houses he sat down and took out a packet of cigarette-cards: flowers, sorting them into seasons.

Brenda appeared, and he gathered them back into his pocket. 'I've found some primroses,' she announced, falling beside him. 'In the wood.'

'I don't care.'

'You would if *you* found them,' she taunted.

'No I wouldn't.'

'Yes you would.'

'No I wouldn't' he repeated, 'because I don't like primroses. They mek me sick.'

'No they don't. Yes they do.'

'No I don't.'

'Yes you do,' she went on with stark uncompromising persistence, almost crying. He turned away. 'No, I don't like them.'

'I'll bash yer,' she cried, her face red with rage.

'I'll bash yer back,' he said.

She stood up. 'Well, if you don't like primroses you're daft, 'cause anybody who don't like primroses is daft.'

Deadlock. They looked at each other with blank faces.

Then she said: 'I love yo', Brian.'

He was baffled. Love? His mam and dad loved each other: black eyes, split heads, table tipped over, black looks and no fags for ever and ever. His teacher said that God loved everybody: Italians gassing blackies and mowing 'em down with machine-guns: dole, thunderstorms, school. That picture in his gra'ma's parlour was about love.

They looked at each other.

'What have we got to do?' he asked.

She glared at him, angry again. 'If you don't like primroses, you're daft' – and ran back towards the wood.

He gazed across Cherry Orchard, the Nook chimneys just visible over bushes and trees. Wind bent back the longer patches of grass, and thick clouds lay across the sky. Far away, along Colliers Pad, a man was riding on a bicycle, his figure flickering through gaps in the bushes.

He advanced, but behind outposts. Cherry Orchard was vast, remote, unfenced, a continental mile from house to house, treeless scrub and rise and dip breaking its green surface against the pillars and towers of Serpent Wood. It stained his unwary slippers or shoes with the juice of cowslip and celandine, hid him, exposed him, made him tired after a while, frightened him, but lured him on, into the wood where each leaf was alive and each stepped-on twig exploded through his vibrant nerves. By the stream bank he pulled smooth pebbles from the sand, loaded his pockets before passing between bushes and tall trunks, sometimes stopping to find a toadstool or an already rifled nest, or to skim his ammunition at a quick unhittable bird.

He crept under a fallen tree. In the wood's centre from where no fields could be seen and no sound heard except himself, he pulled his body into the lowest fork of a many-pronged tree, barkdust marking knees and hands, twigstumps scraping his groin as he went up. In a sitting position bushes were surveyed from above while many treetops were at eye-level: green humps and bracken dips of the jungle, his refuge from the punctuating black gulfs of school year and home-life that didn't bear thinking about at times like these. Sounds came to him, the stream running, a cuckoo's rhythmic and fluting whistle, a mooing cow from some bordering field. Primroses grew to each side of the track, and where the stream turned into a morass tree spaces were flecked with bluebells. It was a wet wood after a long winter, soil and fungus smells weighing heavily on the air, though sun in more open spaces had turned the soil a drier colour.

Brian put both hands to his mouth and made a Tarzan call, the mere shadow of an incompetent warbling scream flitting through the trees, to a swift end against the unbridgeable obstacle of distance. He listened to it dying, waited for silence, then shouted what many swear-words he knew, using all the air his lungs could muster to send them far away. He paused between each word until its echo was about to fade, then he let go with another explosive monosyllable, hands cupped in a message to which no answer was expected. When he grew tired of the game he leapt down and set out for midday dinner at the Nook.

In the quiet afternoon he leaned over the pigsty gate, tapping the pink-white pigs with a piece of stick as they gathered at the trough on feeling a human-being near. When they grew tired and wandered away he shook the gate-latch to see how quickly they would converge again on the trough, and was astonished at the squeals sent forth in protest at his taps. His grandmother called that he was to stop tormenting them, talked for ten minutes about cruelty to dumb animals, saying that God would put him in a big fire when he died, if he wasn't careful: and as he walked into the garden behind the house, ashamed at having been caught, he imagined a mighty hand catching him up, and flinging him into an enormous heap of burning embers. But then he doubled back from this scene of horror, and pictured a skilful escape before events led so far.

Cats made less noise. He sat on a bench under a wooden awning when one came stalking tail up between potatoes, grey-black and mustard and yellow, round face turning left and right to box a white butterfly, then coming for Brian's held-out hand. It had grown fat and trusting on a surfeit of cornfield and copperhouse rats, rubbed its flank against him and allowed itself to be lifted to his knees.

When it purred and rattled at its new-found nest Brian's knees opened and let it fall. Before it could amble away, he lay it again in the groove between his closed thighs. The cat liked it but, having lost self-confidence and being afraid to purr, preferred to leap down and find a warm patch of soil in the sun. Brian's hands caught it in mid-air and brought it back.

A few minutes' stroking of smooth fur raised the rattles of its purring again; then his knees moved a fraction, and the purring stopped abruptly. He knew when an escape was coming because the cat's back legs stiffened, whereat his arms grew ready to snap out and bring it back.

It took longer to soothe it this time, but Sunday afternoon was endless. His hands played slowly, rhythmically along the length of its soft flanks, backwards and forwards, from the top of its leonine head to the base of its tail, up and down, from the side of its mouth to behind its neck and above the hardly felt ridge of its comfortable backbone, until it purred as loud as if its throat were clogged with marbles.

He prodded it from behind. The indications of its pleasure ceased, but returned after a few seconds in which it sensed that the prod had been nothing more than an accident of nature which had gone away quickly and would probably not return. It did. Annoyed, it leapt from Brian's knees, but his hand shot out and set it firmly and with some roughness where it had been.

The tail, upright with righteous wrath, waved before his eyes. He took the end and held it still, feeling the force of it trying to free itself and continue its angry swaying. Letting it go, it swung completely to one side. When the back legs stiffened, his hands hovered above the cat's neck and, as it sprang, a hard grip descended.

It realized eventually that there was no real need to escape, that if it stayed still on the warm knees no harm would come. But the controlling demon of Brian – felt dimly by the cat between escapes – grew tired of waiting for a next attempt, and prodded with such force that it was almost clear before being snatched by hovering hands. Each time it thought to abandon its prison there was an unmistakable warning, but the interval between the jerk in its back legs and the sight of its body in mid-air grew shorter, until the warning jerk became so faint that Brian's heart almost stopped in an effort to stay aware of it.

Bored, he decided to let it free on the next sally, but the sight of the cat leaping to freedom was too much, and before it could scatter its four legs among holes and furrows, he had set it firmly down again on his knees.

He made a low fence around it with his arms, a tempting barrier that was hardly noticed; it stayed where it was, belly stiffened with rage, eyes staring, tail waving back and forth like the electrical-contact mast of a dodgem-car. Instead of bounding forward it swung away to the side, under his hand to the nearest bush. Brian threw himself down, held nothing but his tail end. The cat howled a slow threat, urged its strong body away from what millstone had caught it, from the vice closing tighter and tighter the more it heaved. Brian looked at the straining back, at fur-marks of black and grey and mustard yellow mixed in, at the ears trying to twitch, at the head bent forward like a bull's.

The long tail relaxed. A mass of sharp needles ran along the soft fleshy inside of his arm, leaving pale white indentations the size of small fishbones magically turning red.

But he didn't let go. He picked up the cat with both hands so that it was helpless, cuffed it twice about the head and threw it to the middle of the garden. With a scuffle of orientation it hit the soil, skidded towards the hedge and was free.

He dabbed at his bleeding arm with a black handkerchief, walking slowly to the house. His grandmother turned from the fire: 'What have you gone and done now, you silly lad?'

'I fell into a bush,' he told her.

She busied herself in a drawer for clean linen to bind it. 'I don't know, getting scratched like that. I'll bet you was after bird nests. You'll get sent on board ship if a policeman catches you at it, you will and all.'

* * *

Lydia promised him a trip to the Empire. She was a stout, good-looking thirty-five and still unmarried, and was making sure, so Brian had heard his mother say, of a good time before settling down. The man courting her though was grey-haired and thin-faced, and sent Brian running errands to a dozen different places every time he came to the Nook for an afternoon. He had consumption, Lydia said ('*She'll* never get it, and that's a fact,' Vera remarked, when discussing the case with Seaton.) 'What's consumption?' Brian asked, when Lydia was getting ready.

'Mek sure an' wash yer tabs out. It's a disease,' she informed him, taking the flannel and rubbing his ears violently, which he resented and struggled to evade. 'When yer badly an' wain't get better.'

'Do they tek everybody away then when they've got consumption?'

'Ay,' she said, 'they do. If you don't make haste, we'll be late and then Tom'll be mad.'

It was raining, and the muddy lane was darkened by wet hedges like rows of steaming camels on either bank. Lydia clutched his hand as they walked with heads bent: it was his first time to the Empire, and everyone spoke of it as a marvel, something more grandiose than the Great War, as legendary and surprising as the wooden horse of Troy. Well scrubbed, and dressed in a new coat, he was aware of being taken to somewhere posh and rare. 'What's going to be on?'

She pulled him along: 'Singing and dancing, and people who mek you laugh.'

'Cowboys and Indians?'

'No, not tonight.'

'Aren't there any lions and tigers and snakes?'

'Them's in a circus,' she said, 'Besides, you don't want to see such nasty things. They bite you.'

He had been so certain of seeing unique and astonishing scenes that he hadn't bothered before this to question it; and now his wide-open ever-deepening stage had shrunk to a few lights shining on a woman singing at one end and a man trying to make people laugh at the other. He bit his lip in anger: had he been forced to get washed for that?

When they got off the bus in Nottingham the rain had lifted and the world changed. Slab Square rose up and greeted him on the forehead when he tripped, leaving a mound soon forgotten in the well-lit confusion. The dull sky seemed to be held at bay by barking newspaper sellers who thrust folded *Posts* at Lydia as they went across the Square. Though big enough for his age she dragged him through crowds like a dog on a lead, mixing him with traffic while his eyes were elsewhere: in dazzling windows, on the highlighted cabs of advancing buses, on faces crowding their reflected images in the wet pools before his feet. A sonorous booming of the great council-house clock ruled over the tinselled darkness for eight long beats, drowning voices and motor-horns, leaving only a smouldering smell of petrol until the world opened again after the collapse of the final gong. 'Come on,' she tugged, 'what are you counting them for? It's eight o'clock and if we don't 'urry we'll keep Tom waiting.'

Tom already had the tickets, had got them half an hour ago, he said, and been for a drink to the Peach Tree rather than stand in the rain. Brian thought of him as old, dressed in a white muffler and good topcoat, hair well combed and brilliantined, tall and delicate and never saying boo to a goose – a phrase he'd heard his grandfather use about him. Merton found him easy to tolerate, even had a certain respect for his gentleness. He'd been a bit of a lad though once, Lydia said with some pride – though in lieu of this, consumption had given him dignity. Tom had worked twenty years in the tobacco factory, and it was assumed that dust had caused his consumption so that the Union made sure he had the wherewithal to maintain himself. Though in one way he appeared as strong as any other man, in another he seemed hardly to exist, walking on the world's rim as if ready to shake hands and say good-bye to it at a week's notice. He was in the rare position of a man regarded as dying on his feet, yet was looked upon by others with as much respect as if he had in some way proved himself a scholar, though as far as Brian knew he never read anything but newspapers.

Time went quickly. Brian kept his eyes on the stalls' clock, hardly laughed at what the funny men said though was amused when they fell about the stage. He liked the man with the seal best because it barked and flapped its feet when everybody clapped. The only thing he didn't like while fixed in his plush seat was the cigar smoke, and he felt sick until lost at what was happening on the stage. But the swirl of glaring colours clouted his brain and stupefied his ears with the music's tuneful and furious beating. His eyes stared when women danced across the stage in something that looked like a bathing costume, and pushed out even harder when someone came from the wings in what looked like nothing at all.

At the interval Tom and Lydia smoked cigarettes, something Lydia never dared do in the house. She opened the packet and folded back the silver paper with deliberate pleasure, handing the cigarette-card to Brian. When the ice-cream woman came down the gangway she said, feeling for her purse: 'Get three tupp'ny cups, Brian, there's a good lad.'

Tom pushed a shilling into his hand, and he struggled against solid tree-trunk legs along the row, elbowed his way up the blocked gangway. Many people stood talking, and he waited in an ice-cream queue for the freezing cardboard cups and wooden spoons, novelties he had never seen in such pristine condition, had seen them only crushed and mud-marked underfoot. He was reading the words on each when the lights dimmed for the second half.

Curtains opened, and a flourish of Oriental music was driven out from the orchestra as if at the crack of a whip. Brian guided himself down the gangway, looking along each darkening row for Lydia and Tom, and keeping an eye turned on the stage so as to miss nothing. A black-faced lady in flowing robes appeared from the proscenium, greeted by arabesques of eastern music. Brian stared at her elaborate robes and turbaned head-dress, at the silks and satins covering her figure with such neatness, was even more entranced at her sudden strange wailing. 'Hey,' he called, a few yards from his seat, 'Aunt Lydia, is she the Abyssinian Queen?'

'She must be,' came some answer.

'That's a good 'un.'

'She does look like it, and all.'

'I never thought of it myself.' Remarks flitted among the

laughter, and Lydia pulled him into his seat, convulsed herself. Brian peeled the top from his ice-cream, eyes still on the stage, half believing himself to be in Abyssinia except when he turned to see the red-framed figures change as the curtains swung to for a new act.

The bus made him feel sick on the way back so Lydia and Tom got out to walk. 'The trams never used to mek people badly,' she remarked. 'But these new trolleybuses is terrible.' They didn't mind the walk: it was fresh and without rain, and Brian saw a million stars when he looked up, like luminous breadcrumbs on some mighty tablecloth. Lydia and Tom stopped at a pub, left him outside while they had a couple at the saloon bar, and they came out after half an hour, Lydia bending with beer-smelling breath to give him a packet of crisps. They turned down the dark road, passed the fire of a night-watchman's hut where new drains were being laid.

'Uncle Tom,' he asked, 'is Abyssinia a long way away?'

'Yes,' he told him, laughing, 'ever such a long way.'

'How far?'

'Thousands o' miles.'

'I'd like to go there.'

'You will some day.'

'I want to go soon.'

'Them black people'll eat you if you do,' Lydia said.

'No they wain't. I'll 'ave a gun like they 'ave on't pictures. Anyway, Paul Robeson's Abyssinian and 'e don't eat people.'

'That's a good 'un!' Tom said.

Houses were left behind and they walked through the long tunnel of the railway bridge, where Lydia was always afraid with or without Tom's company. 'Come on,' she snapped to him, 'don't tread in them puddles o' water, you'll get your socks all wet.'

'I'd like to go to Abyssinia,' he said. 'I want to goo a long way.'

'I wish you'd stop talking about Abyssinia,' she complained. 'You're getting on my nerves.'

They walked for a time in silence. 'I'm going to draw a map when I get home, Aunt Lyddy.'

'You don't know how to draw maps,' she said, easier in her mind now that they were near the Nook.

'I do; it's easy.'

'That's the first thing I knew.'

'We do 'em at school,' he persisted. 'I like making maps up.'

Tom said he wouldn't go in with her, and they drew together by the hedge in what looked like a more desperate combat than that which was supposed to have taken place between St George and the Dragon. After a few minutes Tom went into the blackness of the lane, and Lydia opened the gate so that she and Brian could go into the lighted house.

7

Ada, by marrying Doddoe, had unwittingly outlawed her children from the Nook. Doddoe was a 'bad lot', Merton swore, a foul-mouthed drunken bully beyond the railings of reason or help or pity. His son-in-law would have laughed and agreed arrogantly with the truth of these random verdicts if Merton had said them to his face – which he hadn't bothered to do, though Merton's fiery stick-brandishing ostracism was nevertheless known.

Doddoe had an inside demon whose existence he was unable to acknowledge, a figure pictured by a friendly yet untrustworthy grin on Doddoe's actual face, that pulled the strings of his recklessness in the most haphazard see-saw fashion. Harold Seaton didn't like him, having frequently been put out when associated with Doddoe's misadventures, and nothing made Seaton more black-dog depressive than to be put out by something. There was the time when the pair of them collected all the spare underwear their wives possessed and pawned it for the pleasure of a pint and a seat at the pictures. In retaliation Ada had laid hands on Doddoe's Sunday boots and pawned them, for four shillings which she shared with Vera because neither had any food to put on the table. But these were minor tribulations of Ada's misery. Doddoe once blacked her eye before going to work, and returned after a prodigious stint of overtime in the evening to see not a limb of kid nor stick of furniture left in the house, whence it was his turn to roar all night like a stabbed bull in his misery. A month later they were back together again, and there seemed no denying on the night of the reunion that both kids and grown-ups liked it better that way.

Few people were fond of Doddoe, that tall sandy-haired muscular ex-bombardier sergeant of artillery who played a tempestuous forty-year centre-forward for whatever team could be persuaded to take him on. Navvy, collier, poacher by turn, he swung from job to job, content that his wages should leave him a bob for booze, allow him to sit taciturn in the pub and drink a few pints that came as his due either by treat or credit after his meagre shilling was exhausted. Doddoe placed himself too often at the mercy of bum-bailiffs, coppers, publicans, gamekeepers and bookies, mostly to the damage of himself and always to the detriment of Ada and their underfed children. Yet butties and chargehands were glad to call on him when work was going, because Doddoe, once set on, had a knack of harnessing his energies into careful prodigies of labour that outshone all other workers and often encouraged them. He toiled within a slow-moving pantomimic world of his own, behind a barred mind that had to be told the time before he would bring himself to cease work in the evening. For him, overtime was like free money: unfortunately it came too rarely, and when it did his children clamoured in such a mighty voice that he could not but give them a good share of what he had earned.

One Friday when Doddoe was ably labouring at a semi-detached row near Wollaton, Bert was told by Ada to take him a parcel of shirt, suit and bowler hat. The message was clear though Brian was also forced to memorize it: Doddoe was to change on the job, after finishing work, and come into town without stopping at any pub to meet her for the first house at the Empire. 'Mam thinks I'm daft and can't remember owt,' Bert grumbled, carrying the enormous parcel, arms holding it in front so that Brian had to lead him by the hands to stop him burying both face and parcel in some thorn hedge. 'I'll tell people I'm blind and maybe somebody'll gi' me a penny,' Bert said. 'Hey, missis,' he bawled to a woman, 'I'm blind,' but she walked on without looking, so he passed the load to Brian.

Wet trees overarched the road, and they kept well in so that cars and buses wouldn't splash their legs with mud and water. Fields stretched away on one side, and high moss-covered park walls on the other. Brian suggested he'd carried the parcel far enough, complained it made his arms ache, so Bert walked bent double with it on his back for a hundred yards. Brian found it harder work to help him stop it falling than to carry it himself, so he shouldered it for good. The too-long pressure on his arms made him relax unwittingly, and Doddoe's bowler rolled into a hedgerow.

'Christ,' he exclaimed, 'we'll cop it now. Doddoe wain't be able to put it on.' But undismayed Bert lifted it from the mud with a piece of stick, scrubbed it clean with sleeve and spit and carefully refolded the parcel.

Doddoe was up a ladder with a hod of bricks, and they hung around till knocking-off time, kicking their feet in fresh-pared shavings and inhaling the omniscient tar-smell that came from them. 'If we wait a bit Doddoe might give us a penny out of 'is wage-packet,' Bert said. 'Besides, we've got to tek 'is wokkin' clo'es back 'ome.'

Doddoe slung his jacket on a heap of ochred bricks, bent to swill his face at a tap. 'Got them bleeding clo'es?' he called, wiping himself on a piece of old rag.

Bert handed them over. 'Mam says you've got to go straight there.'

'I bleddy-well know that. She's towd me fifty times already,' he said, and went behind a lorry to change.

'And not go in no pubs,' Bert added, ready to duck and run. But Doddoe was singing, 'Daddy Wouldn't Buy Me A Bow-wow'; jacket, cap and shirt thrown on to an empty cement bag, boots and socks and trousers following, until he stood in clean shirt and bowler hat, about to don his handsome well-pressed blue-jacket trousers. 'How's yer mother?' he called out, laying bricks on the cement bag to stop it taking off in the wind. 'Is she still grumblin' at me?'

'She was getting ready when I left,' Bert told him.

'What was she wearin'?' Doddoe asked.

Bert came nearer. 'A red coat and 'at, I think.'

'She would,' was the deprecating comment. 'You'd think she'd got nowt else to wear. Whose lookin' after t' young 'uns?'

Bert ticked the kid-register off in his mind. 'Beryl.'

Doddoe grunted. One leg was over one foot, and his shirt-flap waved in a sudden breeze, showing a bare arse. 'It's bound to bleeding-well rain,' he swore. Brian noticed someone in the lorry-cab, and the roar of an engine sent heavily rubbered wheels spinning in ruts of sand and shavings.

'Bleedin'-ell!' Doddoe shouted, his screen moving away. It churned up a circular cement-making bed and turned by a brick stack from where the driver could see what he'd uncovered. 'What the bleedin' 'ell der yer think yer doin'?' Doddoe bawled.

The engine roared loud, then decreased in sound for the Irish accent: 'You should 'ave changed in one of the houses, then you wouldn't be showin' us everything you've got.'

Doddoe belched obscenities so quickly that the man hadn't time to drown them with his motor. He then shuffled into the rest of his trousers, pulling his shirtflap violently in as if blaming it for all the trouble. 'You leary bleeder,' he threw at the driver, massaging his sandy scalp before a pocket mirror. It was dusk before he gave Bert the parcel of old clothes, and tuppence between them for their trouble. 'Now get off 'ome, you little boggers. Keep out o' them allotment gardens and gas-meters or you'll get a clink across the ear'ole wi' my fist.'

They went off into the dusk. 'Yet know what I'm goin' ter do when I grow up?'

'What?' Brian asked.

'I'm goin' ter find a big wood and right in the middle o' this wood I'm goin' ter build an 'ut. An I'm goin' ter grow all my own grub in a garden, and shoot rabbits and birds so's I'll live like a lord wi' lots to eat.'

'Smashin',' Brian agreed. 'Can I live there as well?'

'You can if you want.' Brian pondered on the geography of it, brewing pertinent questions: 'Where will yer put this 'ut?'

'I ain't thought about it yet – somewhere in Sherwood Forest, I suppose, near where Robin 'Ood lived. Then when I pinch stuff from shops in villages, or poach rabbits like our dad does sometimes, I can do a bunk back to my 'ut in this wood, and the coppers wain't be able to find me. They wain't if it's far enough in, anyway. And if I pinch stuff I'll hide it away, and live off it in winter when grub don't grow and it'll be hard to shoot it.'

'What about fags, and bullets for your gun?'

'Easy. I'll just'ave ter pinch enough to last me all I want. And maybe I'll pinch ale as well so's I can get drunk now and again like dad does. But I'll eat rabbit stew, and tomatoes and bacon if I can, and bread with best butter and strawberry jam on it, and I'll sit in my hut in winter when it's snowin' outside, and I'll have a big fire in the grate and put the kettle on, and I'll just sit there day in and day out mashin' tea and readin' comics. That's what I want to do when I grow up: live in an 'ut all on my own, wi'out a thousand kids swarming all over everywhere. It'll be smashin', our Brian, I'm tellin' yer. When I'm in this 'ut I shan't care if it rains every day, as long as I'm inside with the winders and doors closed. Nobody to bother me, that's what I want when I grow up. That's why I want to find an 'ut like I'm tellin' yer and fix it up just for me. Then p'raps yo' can get an 'ut like it not far off, and you can come and stay with me now and again, or nip in fer a jam-jar o' tea when you're passin' with your gun to shoot rabbits or summat, and I'll see yo' in your 'ut sometimes. It'd be smashin' if that's how we could both live when we grow up.'

'Wouldn't yer want to go t' pictures?' Brian asked. 'Or go down town for a walk?'

'Not me. If I'd got this 'ut I wouldn't want to do owt like that. I'd 'ave too much work to do. I'd be out wi' my 'atchet every day choppin' wood for the fire, or plantin' lettuces, or settin' nets and traps for rabbits. If you lived in an 'ut on your own you'd 'ave plenty to do and wouldn't bother wi' goin' to the pictures. That I do know, our Brian.'

A dominating question had to be asked. 'What would you do if it thundered?'

'Nowt,' came the ready answer. 'I'm not frightened o' thunder like yo'. It wouldn't bother me a bit. In fact the more it thundered the more I'd like it. I shouldn't bother if it thundered and rained and snowed for months, as long as I'd got plenty o' grub and wood inside the 'ut. That's what I'd like more than owt' else to 'appen: to be stuck in my 'ut for months and months wi' plenty o' grub so's I'd never 'ave to worry about nobody or nowt: just listen to it pissin' down and thunder goin' like guns, while I drank tea and puffed at a Woodbine.'

'Smashin',' Brian said. 'That's what I'd like to do. And I'll do it, as well, when I grow up. I shan't go to wok when I'm fourteen like mam says I will. I'll run away from 'ome and go to Sherwood Forest and live there. I don't want to wok in a factory, do you, Bert?'

'Not me. If I 'ave to wok I'll wok on a farm or summat like that. Out in the open air. That's what Doddoe says: it's best to be a navvy or wok on a farm, then you wain't get consumption. That's the on'y wok I'd bother to do – diggin'. I like wokking wi' a spade, diggin' taters up, or shiftin' sand, or shovellin' coal into t' cellar grate, or chuckin' rubbish about. A spade is what I like because it's easy an' yer've got to be in the open air wi' a spade. And blokes as wok wi' spades aren't on dole as much as other blokes are.'

'My dad's allus on dole,' Brian informed him, 'and 'e's got a spade. It don't mek no difference, 'cause when there ain't no wok there ain't no wok. Doddoe's often on dole as well, an' yer can't say 'e ain't. Nearly all the kids at school 'ave got dads on dole.'

'Well, if they can't get wok,' Bert said, 'then they've got to go on t' dole, ain't they? It's better than nowt, though it ain't enough to manage on, is it? That's why I want to get an 'ut when I grow up, because then you can get your own snap and you don't need to go to a factory or some new 'ouses to get a job because you can grow all your own grub. And then if you do that you never 'ave owt to do wi' gettin' the dole. That's why I'd like an 'ut. It's the best way to live, if yer ask me.'

'It is an' all,' Brian agreed. Lights gleamed along Wollaton Road, a double line of mist dispersers with traffic roaring between them into town. 'It's cowd,' Brian felt, so Bert set the parcel down and took out Doddoe's working jacket, passing it to Brian who put it on and folded it around him like a topcoat. Bert wrapped his father's trousers around his arms and shoulders, topped his head with the too-big cap, rolled the newspaper into a ball and kicked it before them to the goal of home, passing with quick footwork to Brian and screaming 'GOAL!' every time he shot it along the pavement. 'Doddoe says he's going to mek me a jockey when I grow up because I'm little, but I'd rather be an outside left for Notts Forest. I'm getting quick as lightning with a ball. A crack shot when I get near a goal. I'll never be as good as Doddoe, though.'

'You might,' Brian put in, booting the ball of paper back.

Bert pulled him to a stop, gave the ball a final slam away. 'There's a lemonade lorry outside Deakins' shop – look.'

A weak roof of light came from a gas-lamp further down. 'It's loaded,' Brian said, 'with bottles. Do you think they're all full?'

'Some on 'em,' Bert said, 'so let's walk by quiet, on the outside, and grab a bottle as we go. Then we can drink it in our house.' They sauntered along the middle of the road and closed in towards the lorry. The street was empty, not a footfall or murmur anywhere. A door banged far away and did not matter. Brian looked into the lorry cab, but no one was there so he stepped back a few paces and closed his hand around the neck of a bottle and drew it from the wooden crate.

'Round the back,' Bert said when they reached the house. Once inside and safe Bert put two bottles on the table, Brian one. All dandelion and burdock. Bert cursed: 'I wanted lemonade.'

'This is better than nowt.' Brian screwed the stone top off, lifted the bottle to his lips. Three younger children clamoured for a drink and Bert gave them an opened bottle which they took into a corner to fight over and spill. 'It's a good job Colin and Dave ain't in,' Bert said, 'or we wun't a seen much o' this lemonade.'

'They wun't get my bottle,' Brian affirmed, who had no elder brothers to lord it over him.

'Let's drink up and go out to the Nag's 'Ead,' Bert said. 'I went there las' Sat'day an' 'elped to collect glasses and the bloke gen me a bar o' choc'late and tuppence.' They buried the empty bottles in the garden with one of Doddoe's spades. 'We'll tek 'em back to the shop in a week or two,' Bert said, 'and get a penny each.'

Still sharing Doddoe's cap and coat they clambered over five-foot boards on to the railway, crossing it as a mighty train took the bend out of Radford Station. They kept together in the pitch-black fields, calling out when marsh became blood-sucker pool and flooded their shoes. A railway signal-box stood like a lighted watchtower, a man walking to and fro between banks of levers as they drew near the drier path and went through allotment gardens, a route high-bordered by privet and thorn. 'Me and Dave came up here last week and scrumped a load o' taters and lettuces,' Bert told him. 'We was 'ere till twelve at night, Dave diggin' 'em up and me loadin' 'em in a sack. Nobody seed us, but we nearly got run over by a train when we was crossin' the lines.'

'I went scrumpin' once,' Brian said, 'up Woodthorpe Grange, for apples, but on the way back we found they was all sour, so we pelted the high school kids wi' 'em on Forest Road. Jim Skelton was wi' me, 'e can tell yer. 'E's in my class at school.'

'Well,' Bert said, 'a mate o' mine got sent to 'prove school for breakin' into gas meters. That was two years ago, an' 'e ain't cum back yet. 'Is mam says he'll be back this summer, though.'

'I'd rather not pinch than get sent to Borstal,' Brian said. 'Anyway, Dad'ud kill me if I got sent away. He says so. So if I pinch owt I'll mek sure I wain't get found out, that's all.'

'Sometimes yer can't 'elp gettin' found out,' Bert informed him. 'Our Johnny pinched a bike lamp last year, an' a bloke seed 'im an' towd a copper. So 'e got put on probation for a couple o' years, and 'e's still on it, though it don't mek any difference, 'cause 'e still can't keep 'is 'ands to hissen.'

'A lot o' my pals is on probation,' Brian said. 'All they do is go down town every Thursday, and they get their bus-fare paid, as well. Our dad goes down town every Thursday to get his dole, but he don't get his bus-fare paid.'

The path widened to Bobbers Mill Bridge. Across the tarmac fork shone the Nag's Head, where people crowded at tables set out between parked cars and a children's playground. Bert and Brian decided on a visit to the fish-and-chip café near by. Hunger gnawed as it always did, even after a Sunday dinner, or during a week of inexplicable surfeit. They gazed inside from the half-open door, at tables reaching far back into the large saloon. Few people were eating, but at some tables were plates not yet gathered by the waitress.

They advanced into the hall, went from table to table, scooping each plate clean, gathering up cold chips, tasty cod-shells of yellow batter, or crusts of bread and butter. Neither spoke, and the whole operation went on in silence. A man digging into a pile of steaming fish and chips stared at Bert, who was composed enough to take up the vinegar bottle and sprinkle it over what was in his hand, giving the impression either that he worked in the place collecting scraps like this, or that this was a form of super-cheap meal served by the café to unobtrusive waifs and tramps. Bert cleared another table, glancing now and again at the chatting waitresses near by. A blonde-dyed, heavily painted woman passed Brian half a cup of still hot tea, which he drank too slowly for the job he was out with Bert to do. He set the cup down, and a man who had seen him drink the tea covered his meal protectively. Brian had never done this before, might normally have been afraid to come into a café and play locust to its cast-off food, but he was too surprised at finding such edible nutriment set out plainly for the getting to worry about who was looking on.

They sat under a wall, their findings spread on a newspaper that Bert had collected with the same insouciance as the food. Both ate hungrily, sorting minuscular chips that had been fried as hard as fishbones and using them to stab big soft ones, but liking the batter best – which meant a scrupulous sharing out. Some had fried fish left in the folds by fastidious eaters, and these prizes were scooped with thumb into ever-ready maw.

Brian dragged Doddoe's coat sleeve across his mouth and stood up. 'Why do people leave such smashing grub on their plates? That batter was marv'lous. I never knew you could get snap for nowt like that.'

'Well, I've got lots o' things to show yer yet,' Bert boasted. 'Colin an' Dave tell me 'ow ter goo on. Yer should see the things they get up to. Last week they pinched a box o' reject fags from Player's and when they got 'ome Doddoe batted their heads and said they shun't pinch things like that. Then 'e sat down to smoke 'em 'issen. I bet 'e sowd a lot of 'em later as well, because 'e got drunk that night and 'ad a big row with mam, and they was swearin' and bawling till two in the morning. The next day mam 'ad a black eye and Doddoe 'ad a big bump on 'is 'ead. It's allus like that in our 'ouse.'

'Our old man's a rotten sod as well,' Brian contributed. 'I wish we was rich, don't you?'

'I do an' all. If I was I'd buy a bike and ride off on it wi' my pockets full o' pound notes. I'd go to Skeggy an' never come back.'

'I'd get on a ship and go to Abyssinia,' Brian said.

'What do you want to go there for?' Bert wanted to know. 'There's a war on.'

'I'd go to India then, and ride about on elephants, and shoot at tigers.' Bert pulled the over-large cap down to his eyes. 'Let's go to the Nag's 'Ead and 'elp 'em to get empty glasses in. People often drop dough when they're drunk, so don't forget to look under the tables, will yer?'

'I'm not lucky at findin' things like yo' are,' Brian answered. 'I don't think I've ever found owt like that in my life.'

'Keep on lookin', though,' Bert said, 'because you never know what you'll find. If you see any big nubs pick 'em up and put 'em in your pocket so's I can smoke 'em later, see?'

People sang beneath dim lights, and Brian's ear caught the hypnotic clash of money as some table paid for its beer. 'I'll never waste my dough on booze when I grow up,' he said. 'I'll save all I get and buy a bike.' Bert's eyes were elsewhere. White-coated waiters were unable to cope with the flood of work, so he hooked up half a dozen glass-handled jars and carried them to the counter.

The rhythmical often-beating pub piano thumped and jangled as Brian went from table to table with thread-looping fingers, making his route back to the counter when a maximum load of wet and slippery handles was reached. In darker corners men and women kissed, arms folded into well-coated bodies – for the night was fresh – doubleheads flush against the wall, undisturbed at the rattle of glasses as phantom Brian stole up to collect – wondering what they found in it all. A man sitting alone was seen to have a tiny pus-filled wound above the bridge of his nose at which he occasionally picked and dabbed with a handkerchief. Brian stared at it every time, and Bert said the man came there often, knew Doddoe in fact, who'd said that the hole had been shot there by the Jerries and wouldn't heal. Bert pushed a chocolate biscuit into his hand: 'The waiter gave me a couple.' Near ten, few glasses were left to look for, and both stood by the see-saw, hawk-eyed for put-down empties and ready to leap at any snatchable tankard. Brian was tired, wanting to go home. 'So'm I,' Bert said, 'but let's wait a minute. They might gi' us a tanner for what we've done.'

A cold wind blew, as if each gust were fitted with grappling hooks to scale walls and search out those without vests and jerseys. 'I hate wind,' Brian said. 'And rain and snow. I like it most when the sun shines.'

Bert pointed to a table. 'Summer'll be 'ere soon, then we wain't need coats. Get them glasses in, and I'll do the next lot.'

Fair was fair. They were at the far end of the yard, two halves left on an empty table, hooked with an easy experienced swing while pushing the rest of the biscuit into his mouth. The pub was about to close – towels overspread the three-handled beer pumps inside – and he walked quickly through the last-stand inebriated bawlers. A chair was pushed into his track by someone too drunk to get up slowly, and Brian skidded on a banana skin he had seen from a distance and meant to avoid.

The glasses went out at arm's length, hooked too firmly to be thrown off in time. No one looked up at the musical crash, too busy swigging final drops, reaching for handbags, fur coats, walking-sticks, and Brian lay with orange sparks flicking and jumping before his eyes. Then in one sick flood he knew himself to be the cause of two priceless glasses having been destroyed, that could never be paid for because he had no money. Prison, Borstal, his father's big fist flashed before him in a bloody picture, and impelled him in a mad bullet-like charge towards the gate and clear of the pub.

A car came one way, a bus advanced with calm assurance from another, but he ran between them to the dark side of the road, back among the safe high hedges of allotment gardens, then into a ghost-ridden funereal zone of pathways that he wouldn't otherwise have taken. Mud splashed him, thorn bushes scraped his face and pointed a way to drier land by the railway.

A goods train went slowly by and he watched the blaze from its engine-cab, feeling more comfort with the dynamic unknowable monster than with the ordinary overalled men wielding shovels within. It went under the bridge to the colliery, leaving him wishing for a ride even though it was heading back for the pub. He kept its sound in his ears as long as possible, until it slid into a murmur, swallowed and killed by the bigger and all-embracing fog-dragon of night.

A voice replaced it, coming from paths he had traversed, rose gruffly and stayed high for a second, then tapered off. Blackness won a further round, voice dead as well as train gone. A hand tingled as if biting-ants were running over and, holding it up, he saw two jar handles firmly fixed into his middle fingers. With the other hand he forced them open, pulled off the glass and threw it as far as the blackness would allow.

The voice lifted again, nearer this time: 'Brie-ie-e-errrn!' He sucked blood from his cuts and stayed quiet, listening for footsteps to back up the voice but hearing only frogs leaping in a near-by stream. 'Brian, where are yer?' the gruff voice called from near by. They weren't chasing him, because it was only Bert. Why weren't they? He'd smashed two glasses, hadn't he?

He answered: 'I'm over here,' gripped a blackened handkerchief in his teeth, held the other corner with his good hand and bound it around the cuts.

'Are yer orright?' Bert asked, by his side. ''Ere y'are, I'll tie it up' – snapping it so tight that no blood could leak. 'Why did you run away?'

Brian was surprised at the question. 'I broke two glasses. Didn't yer see me?'

'It didn't matter,' Bert said. 'Nobody said owt.'

'I thought they would. And I couldn't pay for 'em.'

'Glasses often get broke.' By the railway embankment he gave Brian three pennies. 'Your wages. The publican handed me a tanner for what we'd done.' In the streets of Sodom it was late, most doors closed and few people about, the dandelion-and-burdock lorry gone. Brian wanted to get home quickly. 'I'll see yer tomorrow night,' he said, outside Bert's front door. 'Is the "Count o' Monte Cristo" on your wireless?'

'No, it's nex' Tuesday, I think. We'll listen to it then, because mam likes it as well. Let's go on t'tips tomorrer, eh?'

'OK. So long.'

'Abyssinia.'

8

Mr Jones was a gett, a four-eyed twopenn'orth o' coppers, a sludge-bumping bastard who thumped Brian six times across the shoulder with a hard knotty fist because he didn't open a book quickly enough. 'The Merch-chant of Venniss,' he screamed, each syllable a synchronized crash of pain on Brian's bones. 'Got it?' he demanded. 'Got it, you oaf? When I order you to open your book don't spend five minutes over it.'

A parting bat on the tab for good measure left him more or less in peace, staring at a coloured picture on which his searching had stopped. A man called Shylock it was, tall and with a beard, a knife in one hand holding them at bay and a pair of taunting scales in the other, grey eyes set hard on a pack of getts like Mr Jones, the same puffed-up bastards after a poor old man that were after Brian – and all because he wanted some money back he'd lent them. Old Jones was against Shylock – you could tell from the way he read the story – and Shylock was good then because of it, a poor old – Jew was it? – holding the world's scorn from him, standing there with his knife and scales – as though he'd just stepped out of the Bible like that other bloke going to carve up his son because God told him to – while some posh whore in the court talked about rain and mercy. (Jones liked her; you could tell from the way he read that too.) Shylock was clever and brave, an old man who in the end lost money, pound of flesh, daughter, while Jones and his side got everything and went on thumping and being sarcastic and batting tabs with nobody to say a word to 'em. Only Shylock had defied these cock-sucking persecutors, these getts and clap-rags. When Jones made them sing hymns about all things being bright and beautiful/I vow to thee my country/green hill far away, Brian and Jim Skelton turned every word to a curse. Brian knew that if he had to choose between Jones and his copper's narks who had recently sent Bert's elder brother to approved school after knocking the living daylights out of him so's he'd tell them where he'd hid the gas-meter money, and poor done-down sods like Shylock, then he knew whose side he was on and who would be on his side if he could suddenly come to life and step out of the printed book before him.

Mr Jones was enemy number one, a white-haired tod who stalked the corridors during school hours, peeped his white moustache and purple face over the glass partition that he could reach only by standing on tiptoe. His steel-grey eyes looked in at the class, moving left and right to make sure the teacher had the boys well controlled. Signs of slack discipline would bring him bursting in, arms flying at unlucky heads as he marched between rows of desks, a navy-blue pinstriped suit sagging as he got thinner and thinner through summer and winter so that soon, everybody hoped, he would kick the bucket in some horrible way. If Brian were lucky enough not to feel the stab of his random fist he could tell by his jumping nerves when Jones was coming close, and when he had passed Brian glimpsed his white collar and putty-coloured spats over his shoes: 'If I had old Shylock's knife,' he thought, 'I'd bury it in his bony back.' He laughed to himself: 'I'd get my pound o' flesh, half a stone in fact, and no posh whore would stop me.'

Headmaster Jones was never without a ball of plasticine, an all-year everyday possession rolled between thumb and finger, furiously moving yet keeping shape as he bashed the drum of somebody's back with his free hand. Once, the plasticine rolled under a desk to unhoped-for liberty, so he stopped hitting the boy and walked up and down to make sure the rest were still 'paying attention' to the teacher's droning lesson but actually fixing his eagle eyes on the floor, hoping to see his precious ball of plasticine that was, as it turned out, squashed and held under the boot of a raging boy he had recently thumped.

His tigerish walks were a nerve-racking gamble for the class. Brian had a game. Listening to the soft padding of his footsteps approaching behind, he said to himself: Will he stop and hit me?

I'll bet he does. I bet a bloody quid he does. There, what did I tell you? The bastard. That's a quid somebody owes me.

Even the teachers disliked him, Brian saw, always on the watch for him peering into the room, and when he did come in they immediately relinquished all power over the class and handed it to him – seemingly in the hope that something would go wrong. But nothing ever did that could not be solved by an erratic scattering of fists among the gangways.

Mr Jones's mouth turned down at the edges, and it was agreed in the class that he could not have been a very pretty baby, some sixty-odd years ago. Brian tried to imagine him as a boy even younger than himself so that he could look back on the age and see him more clearly – to fix an image of a youngster in his mind, visualize him walking over a field with hands in pockets, whistling, and heaving a stone now and again at birds. Impossible. Even as a boy Brian saw him a blank-faced nonentity, face gradually becoming more shrivelled until a moustache appeared and the mouth below bent at the side, and the short trousers turned into those of a blue pinstriped suit, and the head of fair hair burst through starkly into white, and the meadow across which he had been walking lost its greenness and became the polished wax-smelling floor of a classroom, and then there was the actual awful figure beside you and you knew that whatever Jones had been like as a little boy it didn't matter a bogger because Jones was what Jones was now and all you had to do was keep your eyes skinned for him and learn to bend your head right forward on feeling the first smack of his folded hand on your backbone.

Whenever Mr Jones opened a book, either to ask questions or read a story, it seemed to Brian an unnatural combination. Books and Mr Jones did not go together. The comfortable rustle of pages and the crack of his stick or fist did not belong in the same room, were disparate qualities that confused and annoyed him, and weren't calculated to bring out the best side of his uneven intelligence.

At home there were no books, but he found a store at the Nook, ancient dust-covered Sunday-school prizes with the names of his uncles and aunts inscribed in impeccable writing within the front covers. He took them from the shelf ('Don't destroy them, Brian, will you?' his grandmother said) and read their titles: *John Halifax – Gentleman*, *The Lamplighter*, *What Katy Did Next*, *The Gipsy*, opened them and smelt the mustiness from years of damp storage. A book was too strange an object to read, so he built them into a tower, watched it wobble, gave a push if his construction showed no sign of falling. He placed them in two piles, side by side so that they didn't fall, took one from the top and opened it. 'Once upon a time there was a gipsy named Meg Merrilees . . . Nowadays the gipsies . . .'

Merton could not read, but liked someone to reel off the front page of the newspaper to him. 'Come on then,' he said sharply to Brian, 'read me what it says.'

'I don't know the first word.'

'Course yer do,' he said gruffly, thinking him obstinate. 'Read the first bit on it.' Brian looked hard: 'Art,' he said slowly. Merton waited for him to go on, demanded when he didn't: 'Is that all? Art? That ain't a word.'

'No, there's a lot more yet. It's a big word I don't know.'

'Gerron wi' it then.'

'Tek yer sweat, I'm going as quick as I can. I'm building it up: '"Art-ill".'

'You're a bloody slow-coach,' Merton scoffed. '"Artill!" I never heard such a word.' He turned to everyone in the room: 'What's "artill"? I don't know. I'm boggered if I do, do any of you lot?'

'It ain't finished yet,' Brian protested, lifting the paper again.

'Well finish it then, Nimrod. Come on, I want some news. What's "artill"? Is that the beginning o' t' word, or all on it?'

Brian was indignant: 'I'll finish it if yer'll shurrup an' let me. Artill-er.'

'That ain't it, either.' Merton prodded him and winked at the others, who looked on. 'I thought yer was a better scholar than this,' he said with disappointment. 'There must be summat else besides artill-er.'

'There is,' Brian retorted, now seeing the joke Merton was having. 'On'y a bit, though. Listen. I've got all on it now: art-ill-er-y.' Then slowly: 'Artillery, that's what it is.'

'It's as bad as ever,' Merton pronounced, puzzled. He turned to Lydia: 'What's . . . what was it, Nimrod?'

'Artillery.'

'Artillery,' Merton repeated.

'Nay,' Lydia said, 'I don't know.'

'It's guns, ain't it, George?' Merton asked, half sure of himself.

'Yes,' he was answered.

'Go on then, Nimrod.'

Slowly he read: 'Artillery preparations for the bombardment of Madrid . . .'

He'd heard of scholarship papers that you took at eleven, but someone said that you had to know Latin to pass. One weekend he sat in the Nook kitchen: 'What people speak Latin, gra'ma?'

'I don't know, Brian.' So he turned to Merton: 'Grandad?'

'What, Nimrod?'

'Who speaks Latin?' He was still plagued by the possibility that Merton, being a grandad, must know everything. 'Nay,' came the answer, 'I've no idea.'

'Do you know, Uncle George?'

'No, lad.' He went back to his book puzzled. Who spoke Latin? He'd asked Ted Hewton, and Ted Hewton didn't know. To ask Jones was inviting a crack on the tab for being so stupid as not to know a simple thing like that, even when no one else in the class knew, and it was better to stay ignorant than get a pasting, he felt. It was obvious that Spaniards spoke Spanish, French people French, and Germans German, but who spoke Latin, that puzzling language on the back of pennies? He copied it out: GEORGIVS V DEI GRA: BRITT: OMN: REX FID: DEF IND: IMP – worse than Abyssinian it seemed. Mr James told him, a quieter teacher who didn't hand out pastings when asked questions: 'But it's dead now,' he added. 'Nobody speaks it any more.' And that was that, all that fuss for nothing.

He stopped the playground flight of a paper aeroplane that, it turned out, was made from a French Grammar. He unfolded the would-be bomber and tried to read its message: articles and nouns on one side, a picture-map of Paris on the other. He gave a dozen marbles for what was left of the book, then searched out Ted Hewton to show off his bargain.

Black-haired pallid Ted already knew how to count in French. 'Our kid on the dole gets books from the library, and learns French because 'e ain't got nowt to do. So 'e learnt me to say some.' They sat in a corner reciting: OON DER TWAR KAT SANK SEECE SET WEET NERF DEECE.

'What's eleven?' Brian asked.

'I forget,' Ted said. 'I'll ask our kid and tell yer tomorrer.' The first ten were memorized in a few minutes, would stay in a pocket of the brain all his life, but eleven and up was another thing, like a row of strong bolts opening on to the unknown.

He turned the page of his grammar. 'What's an article?'

'A thing,' Ted explained, 'anybody knows that.'

'I know they do, but this article ain't a thing, it's a word, like "the", for instance.'

'Don't be daft,' Ted scoffed. 'How can "the" be an article? An article's a thing. I'm tellin' yer.' Brian pushed the book under his nose: 'Look. *Le* is an article, it says, and it means "the". So how can it be a bleddy thing?'

'It don't mek sense,' Ted remarked. 'Maybe the book's out o' date.'

'It'd better not be,' Brian said savagely, 'or I'll get my marbles back.' He flipped over more pages. 'It's still a good book, because it's got lots o' words in it. Maison, chemin, chapeau, main, doigt,' he said slowly, following the mock-pronunciation beneath each. Ted grabbed the book for a second look, as if he did not believe all those words were in it. 'Ay,' he said approvingly, 'it's not a bad book at that.' He flipped through its wad of leaves to the back cover: ''Undred an' ninety it goes up to. It's long.'

'I gen twelve marbles for it,' Brian reminded him, snatching it back as the whistle blew for end-of-playtime.

Geography, history and English: in each there was a possibility of learning about other countries and people. In *Lands and Life* were coloured pictures of camels by big ships on the Suez Canal, and snow-covered mountain tops on the Equator; and in *Foundations of History* he read how Greeks captured

Troy by hiding in the belly of a wooden horse and being dragged inside by Trojans who thought the gods had sent it from heaven as a present (daft people who didn't know any better); and often for English Mr James read *Coral Island* or *Ungava*. But geography won, meant notebooks with blank pages on which the teacher pressed a roller that left an outline map when he lifted it off, and set strange names on the blackboard that you copied against the map. Brian scoured the food cupboard for labels from foreign places, found pictures of other continents in magazines to stick on the blank pages in his geography notebook until it grew fat with insertions and notes.

Six columns formed up to be marched in by the prefects. The asphalt yard sloped down to lavatories, and along the wall of the infants' and junior girls' departments was written in large white letters: CLEANLINESS IS NEXT TO GODLINESS – by order of Mr Jones, who called in a man to repaint the letters so that on the first few days of each term they shone and glittered with reproach at the yardful of ragged-arsed down-at-heel and often unwashed kids.

Black clouds gathered across shining roof slates, and cold rain blew as they marched inside. Any inside was good in weather like this, and Brian felt happy that an English lesson was on the timetable. His belly was full from a meal at the dinner-centre, and he anticipated a ha'penny from his father when he got home, it being Thursday dole-day.

Mixed telegraph messages of clacking desk-lids and stamping feet filled the teacherless room. Rain streamed down the window-panes and, as no one had been told to switch on the lights, the gloom that lay about needed much noise to dispel it. Brian made for the steampipes with Ted and Jim Skelton, and they watched two bodies rolling and pitching in a gangway fight. A smell of damp coats and trousers mingled with breath and polish smells, and a further violent surcharge of rain against the outside glass increased the recklessness within.

A sly face rose slowly above the door panel, stayed still for a few moments. 'Get back to your desks,' Brian hissed. A phenomenon detached from the turmoil, the livid vivid face of Mr Jones turned this way and that to take in everything before entering the room. Seconds went by like minutes, and Brian looked away from the face at the window to meet the equally distrusted visage of the Laughing Cavalier on the opposite wall, then turned with a half-laugh to the front and stared at nothing.

After the crash of the door and the sight of eyes hollow with rage, the only sound left came from tangible rain outside. Mr Jones grabbed four boys who had been fighting and hauled them one by one to the front, a few well-placed punches getting them into line.

'What were you fighting about?' he roared, shaking the nearest boy. The noise of rain flowered like a burst dam, for everyone in the room except the frantic expostulating Jones seemed to have stopped breathing. The life had gone out of them, but for hatred and fear. The boy could not answer, and the sound of flesh meeting flesh at great speed jerked silence out of the room. 'What were you fighting for, you lout?' Mr Jones shouted again, into the ear he had just hit.

'Nothing,' the boy blubbered.

'Nothing?' he bawled. 'Nothing what, you jackanapes?'

'Nothing, sir,' came between the sobs. With a faintly sarcastic smile he lifted the desk-lid and took out a stick. His body doubled with spite as he leapt at the culprits: 'You don't fight for nothing, you idiot,' he yelled, hitting the nearest boy furiously across the back and shoulders. 'You don't fight for nothing, do you? Do you? Eh? If you want to fight,' whack, whack, whack, 'then fight me. Come on, fight me,' whack, whack, 'fight me, you nincompoop.'

He's barmy, Brian thought. He'll go into a fit one of these days and wain't be able to come out of it. I'm sure he will, as sure as I sit here. Either that, or somebody's dad'll come up and knock him for six.

'Get back to your seats,' he gasped, straightening his royal-blue tie. 'And come out the monitors.' Four boys, a piece of yellow ribbon pinned to each lapel, walked to the front. 'In that cupboard you'll find two stacks of books called *Treasure Island*. Give one to each boy.'

They went to their tasks with avidity. 'I'm taking you for English literature during the next few weeks,' Jones went on, 'and I'm going to start reading *Treasure Island* to you, by Robert Louis Stevenson.' A hum of excitement was permitted. *Treasure Island*. Brian had heard of it: pirates and ships and other-world adventure, a cinematic hit-and-run battle among blue waves and palm trees taking place a million miles away yet just above his head, as if he could reach up and touch cutlass and cannon and tree branch to heave himself into hiding.

'And' – the plangent voice of Mr Jones made an unwelcome return – 'every other Thursday I'm going to ask you questions on what I've been reading' – his grey eyes glared, eyes empty if you dared but look at them, which wasn't so dangerous as it seemed because they stared back at nothing when he wasn't inclined to bully – 'and woe betide anyone who hasn't been paying attention,' he concluded ominously, opening the teacher's clean copy the monitor laid before him.

He had a good voice for reading, rolled off the first paragraph in a booming tone that lit each boy's imagination like a powder trail. They saw the captain as Jim Hawkins first saw him: a proud suspicious renegade stomping along the clifftop followed by a wheelbarrow bearing his far-travelled sea-chest, heard him demand a noggin o' rum, and tell Jim to keep a sharp weather-eye out for a one-legged villain called Pew. He ran fluently on through several chapters, before the class was sent flying home through a real world in which the rain had stopped and a mellow sun shone on rainbows of petrol and water in the middle of clean streets. Brian was glad to be free, and could not think of the good story he had heard without imagining a wholesale tab-batting when Mr Jones questioned them on what he had so far read.

It rained the next day and was cold, so that no one knew whether the year was coming or going. A mere drizzle fell by playtime, and Brian pledged his last four marbles against a boy from top class. He knelt, and aimed one at the blue-and-white of the bigger boy some yards away. It seemed a great distance, since he was not sure of his aim and his fingers were cold. He shivered in his jersey: I might hit it – hoping he'd hit something soon with only four left, because there'd been nineteen in his pockets that morning. The bigger boy was impatient, so that

Brian needed an even longer time setting his sights. 'Look sharp,' his adversary said. 'I want to play Smithy next, after I've skint yo'!'

The playground noise swayed about him: two hundred surging boys watched by a teacher walking up and down under the shed. He'd got his aim, couldn't miss, drew back an arm to release the marble from between his fingers. A boy from his class walked over the target marble, and when he lifted his foot it was no longer there.

Brian looked around and up in the air, even felt in his pockets and opened his other hand. Where the marble had rested, the asphalt paying was blank. He could only stare at the boy who had walked over the marble, now at the other end of the playground, and saw that he was limping. He'd walked evenly before, but Brian guessed that the boy's boots were so full of holes that it had caught in one of them. He watched him lift his foot to see what caused the limp, extract the marble and glance back to where Brian was standing.

The bigger boy swung round, demanding: 'Ain't yo' shot yet?'

'No,' Brian answered.

'Well, gerron wi' it then.' He was tall and truculent, a dash of hair falling into his eyes, and even more holes around his clothes than Brian had in his.

'The marble's gone,' Brian informed him. You big-headed bleeder, he swore under his breath. Big-head glared at the blank paving, spun with an accusing war-like snarl: 'Yer've pinched it.'

'I ain't,' Brian denied. 'I ain't a thief, if yo' are!'

'Gi' me that marble.'

'I ain't got it, I tell yer.' Big-head edged closer: 'I'll bash yer up if yer don't gi' it me. I know yer've pinched it. Yer can't gerraway wi' that.'

Brian was about to tell him what happened, but held back. 'I ain't got the marble. It must 'ave rolled somewhere.' But threatened with a nose-bleeder he was forced to hand over a marble to Big-head; then went with his last three to play somewhere else.

* * *

In summer and winter, snow and rain and frost, and now again sunshine, Brian set out up the early-morning street with his brothers and sister, telling them to hurry otherwise they'd be late at the dinner-centre. With plimsoll shoes and peacock jerseys he led them to the long hut beyond the recreation ground where at morning and midday meals were served to those whose fathers were on the dole. They were caught up from warm troughs of sleep by Seaton's rough voice at seven o'clock: 'Come on, Brian. Dinner-centre.'

'Come on, Arthur and Margaret, Fred,' he said to the bundles beside him in the bed, 'dinner-centre.' the bottom room of the house was merely part of the route, though on his way through, Brian wished they could eat breakfast there, but saw nothing on the table except a mug of tea to be drunk by his father.

Caution was needed to get his charges over the dangerous boulevard, for often out of the morning mist buses or lorries came rushing by like cliffs, and he had to arrange them level at the lights, wait for red to show and walk them quickly across in line. Often they were first there and stood near the green-painted iron gates waiting for Miss Braddely. Other children appeared from the mist, shivering and silent, redfaced and still sleepy, and Brian would help carry the crate of cold milk bottles up to the kitchen door when Miss Braddely herself came short-stepping it from a different world from theirs. Brian went in the kitchen and watched her put cocoa on the stove to boil, then saw her work the bread-cutting machine and spread thick butter over each slice. He took Fred and Margaret and Arthur to their places in the hall, sat them quiet while they waited for breakfast to be pushed through the hatch, immersed in the low quiet talking from two dozen other children at the tables. The breakfast, when it did come, was magnificent: three thick half-slices of bread and butter each, and a mug of milky cocoa. There was no breakfast to beat it, as far as Brian knew, except tomatoes and bacon, but that was a dinner.

At half-past eight they walked back through the rec to school, now very much alive, noticed little bead-like mounds of soil made by worms among the flowerbeds, discovered the ground to be less white, though their breaths still turned to vapour, so that Margaret put a piece of stick between her lips and shouted: 'Look, our Arthur, I'm smoking! Don't tell mam I'm smokin', will yer?'

Brian met them at half-past twelve and played shepherd again over the much busier boulevard for dinner. As many as two hundred children (who had not bothered to go for breakfast in the morning) milled and played around the dinner-centre door waiting to be let in by fat Miss Harvey. The door opened inwards, and the crush was often so great that even the bulk of Miss Harvey couldn't stop a dozen children falling into the hall, so that she beat them about the shoulders with a wooden spoon for not showing more restraint. Brian disliked the dinner – cabbage, potatoes, liver, and pudding – and often slid it quietly to his cousin Bert when Miss Harvey wasn't looking. The meal lacked the clean simplicity of breakfast. Its smells were too diverse and often unidentifiable, and you had to eat whatever of the food you might like in too great a hurry. Often Miss Harvey made them sit quiet and say 'grace' before dinners were handed out, a practice that the gentler Miss Braddely forwent in the too-early morning. Afterwards they splayed like confetti out on to the greensward of the rec, and on sunny days Brian fought for the swings or a place on the see-saw, slide, table-top or monkey climber, pulling Arthur and Margaret and Fred on after him, and forgetting the world till schooltime at two.

The second session with Mr Jones came round, and everything was quiet when he entered the room. 'For this lesson I want you to draw a pen-picture of the Old Sea Dog, when he comes to the Admiral Benbow Inn.'

There was a rustling from every desk, as though a gala of paper-chains had fallen down at Christmas. It's funny, Brian thought, there ain't any drawing paper in our books. Anyway, I'd rather do it in pencil because it seems daft to draw a picture with a pen. I suppose that's what he means, so I'd better get on with it or I wain't be finished in time. I don't want his fist flying around me today. A pen-picture's a picture you draw with a pen, he reasoned, still unsure of what exactly Mr Jones wanted. What else can it be? Stands to reason. The whole class was engrossed in the exercise, and Brian sketched in the roof of the Admiral Benbow Inn.

Mr Jones walked up and down the gangways, watching for signs of progress. The first thing Brian heard was someone being furiously thumped a few desks away. He trembled inwardly. 'Idiot! Nincompoop! Fool!' Mr Jones bellowed with each resounding bat of his hand. 'Begin all over again.'

This made everyone wonder whether they were doing the right thing, and after several similar demonstrations Brian felt Mr Jones peering over his shoulder. Blows exploded against his back and fell about his ears.

'This is the limit! Oh my goodness!' Mr Jones wailed in mock-despair. 'Oh dear! Would you believe it? This clown has actually *drawn* a picture! Actually drawn one!'

With hands bent over his head he wondered: Why is he hitting me like this? It's bad enough hitting me, but why is he telling the class I've made such a daft mistake? It was hard not to weep at such thoughts, and he was saved from tears only by a surge of hate; he let forth in his mind a stream of awful words he had heard his father use under his breath to his mother. Mr Jones still hovered, ready to crack him again, while vivid barbed-wire images flashed through Brian's mind. Why don't he die? still building a dyke against the tears.

'You're supposed to *write* a description of what the captain looked like. To use words,' Mr Jones bellowed. 'Do you hear?' Brian said in a low voice that he did hear, and after a parting hit, Mr Jones went on his way.

More drawings were discovered, and those who did them paid for their mistake in the same way. Mr Jones reached his desk clenching and unclenching his burning fists in an effort to cool them, the silent hatred of the class turned against him for the rest of the lesson. 'I didn't know we had so many artists,' he said, grey eyes twinkling in a dangerous good humour. The few clever ones who never made mistakes laughed at his joke, having correctly sensed that they were supposed to.

'If I had made such a blunder in my class when I was a boy,' Mr Jones went on, 'I'd have been thrashed with the leg of an easel. *My* schoolmaster used the leg of an old blackboard easel to knock sense into us.' Another joke, though fewer boys laughed than before. Brian's shoulders still ached. 'Daft bastards,' he said under his breath. 'It's nowt to laugh at. I wish old Jones would die though, that's all I know. Why don't he die? Why don't the old swine die? He must be sixty if he's a day. But he'll never retire because he likes hitting kids too much.'

9

One Thursday afternoon Vera said: 'Go up Ilkeston Road, Brian, and meet your dad. He'll be on his way back now from the dole-office. Tell 'im to get five Woodbines and bring 'alf a pound o' fish for our suppers. Go on, run, he'll gi' you ha'penny if you see him.' Brian gathered what brother was available, and did as he was told.

Vera had been glad to see the back of Seaton that morning. Hunched by the fireplace, sulking because he had no cigarettes and was out of work at thirty-five, he suddenly stood up and took his dole-cards from the cupboard. 'I'll have a walk,' was his was of putting it, 'and call in at the dole-office on my way back.'

So she was shot of him for an hour or two, free from black looks, and filthy talk if she dared give him a black look back. Day in and day out, from dole-day to dole-day, he sat by the empty firegrate, fagless and witless, a rotter to everybody that got near him. It worn't his fault, that much she knew, but he could be better-tempered than he was. Sometimes he would get up from his black despair and send Brian to a woodyard for a sack of waste, spend a day chopping sticks so that Brian and Fred could hawk them a penny a bucket from door to door. Or he would buy a few pairs of shoes from Sneinton Market and set about mending them. Sitting on a box in the backyard, his mouth full of tacks, he hammered new-cut leather on to the last-held shoe. A semicircle of kids stood watching, and Vera swore to God he didn't know they were there, held fast as he was in his work. The shoes were then sold cheap around the neighbourhood. He paperhanged and whitewashed, dug gardens or pushed loaded barrows, went coal-scraping with Abb Fowler, though such windfalls of work fell rarely in his way. But when the hands were happy and one side of the heart at ease, the other was wary and sly, adept at evading that ubiquitous bogey of the means-test man who docked your dole and sent you on 'relief' if caught doing work not registered for. Brian and Arthur would meet their father at a whitewashing job, to come home with them, boy-scouting a hundred yards ahead while their father walked behind with the ladders. If Brian saw anyone who might look like the means-test man he was to nip back and give warning, and when once he did Seaton dodged into a yard while the means-test man went unsuspecting by. But the dole couldn't go on for ever, Vera thought, and hoped it wouldn't, for a fifth child was about to join them.

Seaton enjoyed his two-mile walk to the dole-office – except when it rained. Tar-smells of clear-skied summer or the lung-stinging frost of winter were all the same, pleasant to get out of the house into, from the walls of the house to farther apart walls of roads and streets which had no roof and let the good sky in on you. It was warm summer, and he stood in the long queue for his dole. Old friends were occasionally missing from the line – having stepped into the aristocrat class because they had got jobs, but Abb Fowler was always there, still the same wide-nosed sandy-haired moonlight-flitter, wearing his cap at a cocky angle, dismayed but unbeaten at being out of work. He carried a ragged copy of the *Daily Worker* and talked about the war in Abyssinia not long finished, and the war in Spain not long begun. Every Thursday for months he'd thought of volunteering to fight in Spain, but never did. 'I'm a communist, 'Arold,' he would say, 'and I don't mind gettin' shot at, if you want to know, but not in Spain. It's the bleeders in this country *I* want to stand up against a wall.'

Seaton came home with his thirty-eight shillings and handed them to Vera. He thought of the money she had given him not long ago: ten bob for scrubbing out an office every morning for a week. Farther back than that, she had gone with Ada, collecting for an old woman who had died on Ada's street. At nearly every house they were given a penny or a ha'penny, and at the end of the street they went on into the next, even though the old woman wasn't so well known there. Nevertheless few people would refuse a ha'penny towards a wreath. So off to another street, and then another, the old woman's name bringing less response on being mentioned after doors had opened to their knock. Ada had the cheek to collect in a pub as well, escaping by the saloon bar door when the publican strode over to throw her out. Fifteen shillings made a magnificent wreath for the dead woman, bigger than she could ever have expected on her meagre pension; and the few shillings made by Vera and Ada spread the tables of each house with a good meal that night. He had to laugh at the thought of it: what a couple o' boggers they are! and black-haired sway-walking Harold broke into a shilling for a packet of Woodbines and enjoyed his first smoke since yesterday.

Vera took ten of the thirty-eight shillings to the corner shop, to pay for what food they had fetched on strap during the week. Then she went with Brian up Hyson Green, to cheap shops where she could stock up on tins of milk and packets of margarine, sugar and tea and bread, vegetables and sixpenny-worth of meat for a stew that night.

Job or no job, there was usually a wireless set in the house. Seaton, after drawing his dole the following week, came in smiling broadly: 'I've got a surprise on its way, my owd duck!'

'What? Have you won a thousand?'

'No, nowt like that.'

'What then?'

'A man'll be 'ere in a bit wi' summat yo'll like!'

'And what's that?'

'A brand-new wireless!'

By way of confession he told how, gazing in a shop window on his way back from town, he had spotted a good set that would blow the house apart if turned full on, and that without thinking he had gone in and settled the deposit.

'You know we can't afford to pay for a wireless every week,' Vera shouted, but soon smiled and left off taunting his extravagance, knowing they both had to do such things now and again, otherwise put their heads in a gas-oven, or cut their throats with a sardine tin like poor Mr Kenny up the street.

They managed the payments for a time, but after a few months of free music and news it was disconnected and carted back. Then Seaton bought a wireless for six bob that didn't go, though with a few hours of clever intuitive tinkering a powerful pan-mouth Gracie Fields blared-out over the house and yard. Seaton knew nothing of such machines, yet took it to pieces, tightened a nut here and a valve there, until the electrical maze of wire miraculously 'went', stayed on the dresser as a monument to luck and ingenuity.

On Sunday afternoon, after a pause of nothing from the wireless, a voice would announce: 'Foundations of Music' – a title that intrigued Brian because one of his favourite books at school was *Foundations of History* and somehow he imagined the two same words would generate a similar itensity of interest, but nothing more survived that the title, for his mother would immediately say: 'Take *that* off, Harold, for God's sake!' and the knob would be swivelled on to the sugary music of Debroy Somers, or the rackety drive of Henry Hall.

Time and again Vera told herself that she shouldn't be riled by Seaton's moods of animal temper, for it only made things twice as bad. But after the dole money had been spent to the last farthing he would sit by the firegrate in the small room, head bent low, nothing to say. She would know all he was thinking, that he was cursing his existence, her and the kids, the government, his brothers, her mother and father, anyone and anything that flitted into his mind, and she hated him for letting the lack of a few fags upset them. He looked around the room, from wife to children, and children to mother, until all but Vera went out. Then she would say: 'You're lookin' black again, aren't yer? What's up, ain't yer got no fags?'

He glared savagely. 'No, and no snap either.' Each tormented mind fed the other in diabolic fashion: 'Well,' she said belligerently, 'I can't help *that*, can I?'

'Send Brian to borrow a couple o' bob from your mother,' he suggested, a last desperate remedy he knew she wouldn't take up. 'I can't' – her voice loud and distressed. 'We owe her something from last week.'

'Them skinny boggers wun't lend owt.'

'We wouldn't need to ask 'em if you went out and earned some money,' she said, near to tears at his and her unjust words. He was dimly aware of many answers to this, but could squeeze only a few words of protest from his locked-in despair: 'I'd get wok if I could. I've wokked 'arder in my life than anybody's ever wokked.' He remembered his fruitless expedition of yesterday, returning to a scene that had happened time and time again.

'Did you get it?'

'There was too many.'

'It's a bogger, i'n't it?'

He was bitter: 'Don't bother. They'll want me soon. I know they will.'

'You all ought to get together,' she said, 'and give 'em what for. Mob the bleeders.'

'You can't fight wi' no snap in you. Look at what 'appened to them poor boggers from Wales: got the bleddy hosepipes turned on 'em.'

'They'll suffer for it one day,' she said. 'They'll have their lot to come, yo' see.'

'Besides, I give you thirty-eight bob, don't I?' he said now.

'And how far do you think that goes?' was all she could say.

'I don't know what you do wi' it,' was all he could think of.

'Do you think I throw it down the drain?' she screamed, going to the door.

'It wouldn't surprise me.'

'Nowt surprises yo', numskull.'

She waited for him to spring up and strike, or throw something from where he was. But he sat there.

It went on, stupid, futile, hopeless. Brian listened outside the window, each word worse than a dozen blows from Mr Jones's fist. 'They're rowing,' he said to himself, a knotted heart ready to burst in his mouth. Margaret stood by him: 'What are they rowing about?' 'Money,' he said.

'Tell me when they stop, wain't yer, our Brian?'

'Wait with me here,' he said, looking through the window, seeing his father still sitting by the grate, shoulders hunched and face white. His mother was at the table reading a newspaper.

'They ain't stopped yet,' he told her. They stayed out till dark, then went in hoping that somehow their father would be in a better mood, that their mother had miraculously been and cadged or borrowed, begged or stolen or conjured up out of thin air some cigarettes for him.

One day when a quarrel was imminent Seaton put on his coat and rode down the street on his bike. He returned an hour later on foot, a cigarette between his lips and a carrier-bag of food in each hand. Brian followed him in, saw him put the bags on the table and give Vera a cigarette.

'Where's your bike?'

'*I've* got you some food,' he said, proud and fussy.

She smoked the cigarette and laughed: 'I'll bet you've sold your bike.'

'I 'ave my owd duck.'

'Yo' are a bogger,' she said with a smile.

'I'd do owt for yo' though!'

'I know you would. But I don't like it when you're rotten to me.'

He put his arm round her: 'I'm never rotten to you, duck. And if I am, I can't 'elp it.'

'You're a piss-ant,' she smiled: 'that's what you are.'

'Never mind, Vera,' he said. 'My owd duck.'

'How much did you get?'

'Fifteen bob. I sowd it at Jacky Blower's on Alfreton Road.' He'd had it over a year, always working on it, reconditioning a lamp, new brake-blocks he'd been given, a bell he'd found, hours spent cleaning and polishing. She'd never imagined him selling it.

'I went to one shop and they offered me six bob. Six bob! I said: "Listen, mate, it ain't pinched," and walked out after tellin' 'em where they could put their money. I did an' all.'

'I should think you did.' He took off his coat and cap, pulled a chair to the table. Seeing Brian he stood up again, saying: 'Hey up, my owd Brian! How are yer, my lad?' – caught him in his broad muscled arms and threw him to the ceiling.

'Put me down, our dad,' Brian screamed, frightened and laughing at the same time. Seaton lowered him, rubbed his bristled face against his smooth cheek, then let him go. 'Come on, Vera, mash the tea. There's sugar and milk and some steak in that bag. If you send Brian out for some bread we can all have summat to eat.' The kettle boiled and Seaton stirred his tea. When Brian wasn't looking he put the hot spoon on his wrist, made him yell from the shock and run out of range. Brian was glad when no one quarrelled, when they were happy, and he could love his father, forget about what he had thought to do when he grew up to be big and tall.

Vera often saw in her children similar rages and moods that she detested in Seaton, diversions of petty misery created between the big one of no fags. When Brian came in from the street she asked him to go out again for a loaf. He slumped in a chair to read a comic. 'Wait till I've finished this, our mam.'

'No, go now,' she said, pounding the dolly-ponch into the zinc sud-tub of soaking clothes. 'Come on, your dad'll be 'ome soon.'

He didn't answer, glared at the comic but saw nothing more of Chang the Hatchet Man. Vera emptied fresh water into the tub. '*Are* you going,' she demanded, 'or aren't yer?'

'Let Margaret go. Or Fred.'

'They aren't 'ere. You go.' He could hold on for a while yet. 'Just let me finish reading this comic.'

'If you don't go,' she said, wiping the wet table dry before setting the cloth, 'I'll tell your dad when he comes in.'

'Tell 'im, I don't care.' Having said it, he was afraid, but a knot of stubbornness riveted him, and he was determined not to shift.

When Seaton came in and sat down to a plate of stew he asked for bread. Brian wished he'd gone to the shop, but still didn't move. It's too late now, he told himself, yet knowing there was time to ask his mother casually for fourpence and go out for the loaf so that his father wouldn't know he'd been cheeky. He stayed where he was.

'There ain't any,' she said. 'I asked Brian to go for some ten minutes ago but he's too interested in his barmy comic to do owt I tell 'im. He's a terror to me sometimes and wain't do a thing.'

Seaton looked up. 'Fetch some bread.'

He held his comic, as if courage could be drawn from it. 'Wait till I've finished reading, our dad.'

'Get that bread,' Seaton said, 'I'm waiting for it.'

'The devil will come for you one of these days, my lad, if you don't do as you're towd,' Vera put in. He dreaded the good hiding he knew he'd get if he didn't move that second, but picked nervously at a cushion.

'Don't let me have to tell you again,' Seaton said.

When Brian didn't move Seaton slid his chair out from the table, strode over to him quickly and hit him twice across the head. 'Tek that, yer little bleeder.'

'Don't hurt his head,' Vera cried. 'Leave him now.' He got another for luck. Seaton took a shilling from the shelf, thrust it into his hand, threw him to the door and bundled him into the street. '*Now*, let's see how quick you can be.'

Brian sobbed on the step for half a minute and, still crying, slouched along the wall towards the corner shop, making fervid plans to kill his father with an axe, if he could get an axe, and as soon as he was strong enough.

To reach the bednight attic Brian led the three others up through mam-and-dad's room, then climbed a broad ladder to a kind of loft, a procession of shirts and knickers going up there out of sight. Arthur at three was ready to do battle with the rest, and the flying mêlée of fists and feet that broke out as soon as the makeshift latch had been dropped caused Seaton to open the far-below stairfoot door and bawl: D'ye 'ear? Let's 'ave less noise or I'll come up and bat yer tabs.' He stood for a few seconds in the electric silence to make sure it continued, then went back to his supper. It was all Arthur's fault, Brian whispered. He'd put his foot into the communal last-Christmas trainset as soon as he got into the room. So let's jump into bed, or dad'll come up and posh us.

He spread the sandwich packet and placed the bottle of water on the table, threatening wiry Arthur with his fist as he grabbed at the paper. Margaret held him back saying: 'We'll share it, now,' while Fred looked on from a secure position on the bed. Night was a picnic time, when Vera filled a bottle with water and Seaton sliced bread and dripping, saying: 'All right then, I've cut yer a few slices. Yer must 'ave summat t'eat after you've climbed that wooden 'ill. Come on, Brian-Margaret-Fred-Arthur, it's time you was up that wooden 'ill!'

With each divided portion scoffed they blew out the candle. 'Go to sleep now,' Brian bossed them.

'Tell us a story,' Margaret said.

He'd known they wouldn't sleep unless he did: 'What shall I tell you about?'

'Tell about war,' Fred said, his lips breathing from the darkness of bedclothes.

Arthur's sharp feet seemed to attack every leg and backbone at the same time. 'Stop it,' Brian called, 'or I'll thump you.'

'Thump you back,' Arthur threatened, but kept his feet still. 'I'll tell you what,' Brian said, 'I'll tell you all a serial story.'

They approved and curled up to listen. Arthur's feet-stabbing subsided, and Brian narrated how three men with machine-guns sat in a cellar that they used as a den, drinking whisky, planning how they would rob a bank. In the middle of the night they came out of their den and drove up the dark street in their big black car, and when they came to the bank they put ten sticks of dynamite under the big doors and stood on the other side of the street while it blew up with a great big bang. And when the smoke had cleared and they could see again they all rushed in through the high doors shooting off their machine-guns. When they got to the strong safes there was a night-watchman who said: 'Get back or I'll shoot you with this gun under my coat.' But the robbers took no notice of him and shot him stone dead and put more dynamite under the safes. And when this blew up they went inside and took all the money, millions of pounds. And when they'd put it all into sackbags they had with them they ran out of the bank. A man tried to stop 'em getting into their car, and one of the bandits said: 'That's the means-test man; let's blow him up.' So they shot him dead. And then another man jumped on 'em, and the boss said: 'I know him. It's the school-board man. Let him have it.' And they killed him dead as well. So they got into their big car and drove off over Trent Bridge and out of the town into the country at ninety miles an hour. But later they stopped at a caff to have a drink of whisky and something to eat and a detective called Tom Briggs was in the same caff having something to eat with his girl. And as soon as Tom Briggs saw these three men coming into the caff he knew they was robbers and that they'd just robbed a bank because he saw money-bags that they had under their arms. 'Stop, yo' lot,' he said, and pulled a gun out that he allus carried, but they had their machine-guns ready and tied him and his girl up, and when they had them tight tied up to chairs, the boss of the robbers said: 'We're goin' ter kill 'em now.' And he put some more bullets into his machine-gun and held it to their heads and said: 'Is everything ready, boys?' And the other two said: 'Yes, let's kill 'em. It's all ready.' So the boss of the robbers said: 'All right, I'll shoot 'em now,' and he started to pull the trigger of the machine-gun, and in two seconds they'd be dead. He killed 'em anyway, and then one of the bandits said to the boss: 'Look out o' that window and you'll see we're surrounded with fifty coppers. It looks as if we're done for.'

'And that's how part one ends,' Brian said. A car crashed through the silence below. Arthur breathed softly. 'It's smashin'.'

'What happens next?' Margaret demanded.

'I can't tell you,' Brian said, not yet knowing. 'Part two don't come till tomorrer night.'

'How many parts has it got?' she asked.

'Four, I think.'

'Serials at pictures have twelve,' she said. 'Sometimes they've got fifteen.'

'Do the coppers get 'em?' Fred demanded from down the bed.

'I'll tell you tomorrow.'

Arthur put his spoke in: 'Now.'

'You're ever such a good story-teller,' Margaret said. So he told them more, and went on till no one was left awake.

On his way to sleep Brian heard the whistle from a train rumbling out of Radford Station: like a squeal of surrender in the lead-heavy night, a downward note hurled from a black cavern by some unknown terror. He shuddered, rolled in a half-sleep, suffocated among bundles of bodies. The fearful low piping followed him into overarching slumber, the train gone and the whistle alone was an almost visible monster crying in the mouth of the night. 'Dad!' he wanted to shout. 'Dad!' being afraid, and when he looked from wide-open eyes, he saw the Devil on the end of the bed.

The sad long wail sounded again, muted and resigned and more discouraging than before, coming from what was beyond his experience because it was nearer than he to the pits and brink of dying. His fear was of the coal swamps, a million years back and a million years on, the dead already calling from the future behind the black flames of life, as if dying and living were no more than a vast circle broken at one tiny place – where he was. The whistle persisted its soul-in-agony hooting, imprisoned in the dark spaces of his brain, even while his eyes were staring at the Devil on the end of the bed.

The Devil wore a crimson triangular hat, had a grey round face, a snubbed nose and big loose grey lips. Brian was aware of him grinning, and when the whistle blew again it was part and parcel of him, and the jaggle of trucks on the railway line was chains rattling when his arms lifted (though his body did not move); and they were the chains with which he was to take him away.

The small dark room ignored the sliver of moon outside, and shrunk in size until the Devil seemed closer. The squat figure grinned and beckoned, and his chains rattled again, impatient to take him to the owl-whistles and mastodon coal swamps. The grey face leered, and Brian stared at the crimson triangular hat that, even in the darkness, he saw was the colour of dried blood. The Devil had come to take him away, and he didn't want to go. Brain and heart and fibre were against it, and he opened his mouth to cry out. Nothing. Dad! Dad! Dad! No sound came. He couldn't breathe, as if a giant hook were fixed into the mechanism of his lungs, though in a way it seemed more tolerable to cry out than breathe, except that his cries made no sound, and the figure of the squat Devil sat waiting, patient and assured, wearing an oxblood, triangular hat and rattling grey chains in grey invisible hands. The whistle stopped, as if the train had fallen sheer over the missing span of a bridge joining two banks of night; and Brian without knowing it dropped into sleep.

He told his father he had seen the Devil. It was only a nightmare, Seaton said. You often have nightmares from eating too late at night. Brian didn't believe it. It was the Devil, who had come to take him away. Yes, his mother said, it was the Devil right enough, and if he didn't behave himself and do all her errands from now on, then the next time the Devil came he *would* wrap them chains around him and take him away, for good. Then he'd never see anybody again, not even his grandad Merton.

10

After a hefty downward press of his boot Merton swung back the fork and lifted an abundant root of potatoes, shook them vigorously to the soil, then cast the useless tops aside for Brian to load on the small red barrow.

Brian didn't yet know how hard he worked, was enjoying himself, having been in the garden since breakfast, unplugging weeds and nettles and gathering broad beans for one o'clock dinner. He pronged up potato-tops in Merton's wake with his own quick-working fork, piled them high on the barrow, then fixed himself into the shafts – like a pit pony, as Merton said. He ran a sleeve across his forehead, brought it down mucky with sweat and a couple of squashed thunderflies. The hot days lasted a long time, making his face red, then brown below his close-cropped threp'nny haircut whose front scrag-ends dipped over, turning his normally high Seaton brow into a lower Merton one and falling almost to his angled blue eyes.

With dug-in heels the barrow was heaved from a self-made rut, drawn between flowers and marrow patch towards a dumping ground by Welltop Hill. A series of lorry-like manoeuvres sent the wheels climbing a mound of weeds and heads already brown from the sun. Every week-end Merton started a fire under them with a sheet of newspaper, and Brian stood back with him while flame and grey smoke rose, then returned to see the circle of black ash at dusk. He charged like Ben-Hur back to the garden, taking corners at full speed and axle-catching the gatepost as he went by, to see that his grandfather had scattered more tops and carried several buckets of potatoes into the arbour-shed.

Merton leaned on his fork to watch Brian fix another load on to the barrow. He liked to have Vera's lad with him, working strenuously yet not breathing hard, thrusting the fork under a load of refuse and testing its weight to make sure it wasn't too heavy before swinging it on to the barrow. Each sure movement was recognized as an unconscious work-rhythm that he with his oft-lotioned back was beginning to lose.

He smiled widely at Brian, who did not know he was observed, admiring him for a good worker, a quality that made him fond of anyone. Yet he recollected him in the kitchen at evenings, head down over a book or pencilling an imaginary map, pastimes he couldn't reconcile with the innate good sense of toil exhibited by the Brian now before him. It was an amusing combination that did no harm, and he didn't suppose it could, as his grandson in yellow shirt, short trousers, and burst plimsolls loaded more weeds and potato-tops.

'Come on, Nimrod,' he called, standing erect and shouldering the fork, 'stop doin' that for a bit, and we'll go and cut some rhubarb. 'Appen yer gra'ma'll mek you some custard wi'it for your tea.'

After dinner he was equipped with brush and scraper to clean out the pigeon hut, a job he didn't like but accepted because – apart from it pleasing his grandfather – he'd been promised a penny at the end of the day. A scraper-blade in his teeth, he crawled through the low opening and out of sunlight. Letting the scraper fall, he used his mouth for breath after the first force of the smell brought water from his eyes. Gradually he was able to see and move about, pushed his scraper along half-rotten boards, heaping excrement and feathers towards the far wall. He gave up trying not to dirty his clothes, and sat down whenever he felt tired. Working open-mouthed from corner to corner, he isolated the large central patch; then he cut lanes through it and gradually enlarged the island of clean-scraped board in the middle, until only a broken perimeter of filth remained. When this vanished he pushed the scrapings from the door with a dustpan dragged in from outside by his muscular sleeve-rolled arm.

On Sunday afternoon the Arlingtons and Lakers trooped out of their woodside cottages and came over the Cherry Orchard, passing the Nook on their way to Sunday-school. Brian leaned over the fence, sleepy from an excess of dinner, waving and calling out. When they returned at five o'clock he would join them as far as the end of the Cherry Orchard, hearing talk about what the teacher had read from the Bible. He couldn't understand why they went to school on Sunday, when five days a week was more than plenty for him. Besides, there seemed something shameful about going to church or Sunday-school, a place you went to only if you were a sissie, or if you were posh. His grandmother said he should go. 'Why do people go to Sunday-school?' he demanded in a tone of contempt.

'To worship God,' she told him. 'Besides, if you're a good lad and go every week the teacher'll gi' you a book.' Even this didn't shake his obstinacy. It was a rainy afternoon and he sat in the kitchen, competing for some hearthrug with the cat. Merton had shed his best boots and gone up to bed, leaving his wife to make bread and cake at the table. A saturating drizzle sent water down drainpipes and splashing into water-butts, and the obliterated landscape edged the whole house slowly to sleep. Even the pigs left off grunting; the dog dozed in its kennel, and the silent cocks were petrified on their perches. Only the rain had energy, suddenly pitting at the windows. 'Why do we have to worship God!' he asked in the same tone.

'So that He'll love you.'

'What does it matter if God loves us?'

'Because if He does,' she catechized, 'you'll grow up strong and wain't ever come to harm.'

'I don't want God to love me,' he said.

'Ay,' she ended it slowly, 'you don't now, but you might some day.' He stood up and walked into the parlour.

The first light after the ending rain would be seen from there, and while waiting for it he put 'I'm Forever Blowing Bubbles' softly on the gramophone. He looked at the picture above the mantelshelf. 'If you love me as I love you, nothing will ever part us two.' He used to think the boy and girl were his grandparents when they were young, but now it looked as if the girl with the auburn hair could be Brenda Arlington in a few years' time, and as if he might grow into the youth who was trying to give her a bunch of flowers. But not likely. They didn't live in his world, had no connexion with his brain just vacated by 'I'm Forever Blowing Bubbles', were people who lived beyond his boundaries of school and tips and house and Nook and the swivel-eyed dole-packet that kept him alive and kicking. And while he gave his brain over again to the green-hearted spinning rhythmical record, the sky grew lighter, and beyond the window huge clouds were marshalled away like obsolete continents by the wind, and the sun like a drowned rat asserted itself over green and dripping fields.

Like the sun, the dog dragged its chain and came out of the kennel, and cockerels were letting it rip from behind their high wire. Mary took bread and cakes from the oven, and went out with a shovel for coal before the fire went too low. Merton pulled on his shoes and fed the grunting pigs. Brian sat down with them to salmon and cucumber and lettuce, rhubarb and custard, and jam pasty.

Merton said one morning: 'They're comin' to mow the field nex' week.' Blue flowers lay around the hedges, and corn was ready for cutting. The weather was dry and hot, and Brian had stayed at the Nook the whole five-week holiday.

'Are you gooin' to 'elp like yer did last year?' he asked, having seen him, tall, strong, wielding a long scythe, the high corn falling heap on heap in front. Merton's white-spotted handkerchief wiped tea from his mouth. 'Nay, Nimrod, I shan't. Not this year. They'll cut it wi' a machine and when it's finished all they 'ave to do is pick up the stooks an' stack 'em, then wait for 'osses to cum an' tek it away.'

'Can I watch?' Brian asked, mopping bacon-fat from his plate with a piece of bread.

'As long as you don't get in anybody's way,' Merton said. 'Your grandmother'll be busy. Farmer 'Awkins is goin' ter send flour and bacon so's she can mek the farm 'ands' dinner. They'll 'ev it in the yard 'ere.'

Bay rose and poppies were pictures of midsummer fires that surprised him at the turn of each hedge corner when crossing to spread the harvest news among Lakers and Arlingtons. He walked between white mats of daisies, rugs of buttercup, patches of yellow dead-eyed ragwort peeping from hedge bottoms, and entered the territory of a herd of cows. A breeze came between sparse prickly bushes and he whistled away the too-hard stares of the big dumb animals that slowly surrounded him. He could easily imagine becoming afraid, but walked whistling on, till the brace that stood in his path moved to one side and changed the circle into a horseshoe, leaving him free to walk out to the Arlingtons' cottage.

'Is Ken in?' he asked.

No, he wasn't, but his mother stood in the doorway, holding a colander of shelled peas, a small woman harassed from too much work, whose sharp quick eyes reminded him of little Miss Braddely at the dinner centre. 'He's gone to get some blackberries.'

Brian made for the dark glades of the wood, treading an undergrowth way from point to point of a map pockmarked on his mind, until the protesting scream of Brenda leapt to him through a belt of bushes. Ken and Harry were monkey-swinging on a branch that barely held them, while Alma and Brenda filled their frocks with blackberries below. Brian broke himself a stick, ripped away twigs and leaves. Harry Lake came down to earth, doubled from the impact and sprang straight like a Japanese doll. 'They're playing,' Brenda protested, again 'while we work; it ain't fair.'

She was on tiptoe, stretching her fingers for the richest clump. 'I'll get them,' Brian said, plucking two at a time. He hadn't given Brenda time to reply, and she spurned his offer, retorting: 'No, don't bother, I can get them,' but she slipped and clawed her arm so that blood and blackberry juice mixed on it.

'Wipe it with my hanky,' he said.

Crimson with shame and anger, she sucked away the blood as if it were milk. 'I don't want your hanky.'

'All right then,' he said, 'don't have it.' Ken had a claspknife that cut through wood like chocolate, so they made bows, and launched into a game of Robin Hood. With aprons of black-berries Brenda and Alma sat on a tree-trunk by the stream, and when the game of Robin Hood had worn itself out Ken shouted: 'Let's see'f they've got many berries yet. That's not many,' he said, breaking through the bushes. 'I'll bet you've been eating some.'

'No we ain't,' Brenda denied. 'They got spilled.'

'She did eat 'em,' Alma accused, 'our Ken.'

Brenda turned: 'Clatfart! She's had a lot as well: look at her mouth.' Alma wiped away tell-tale stains that weren't there, but Ken settled the argument: 'All right yo' two's had a lot, so we'll finish 'em off. Come on, Brian. Come on, Harry' – thrusting his hand into the apron. 'You big 'ogs!' Brenda shouted. 'Gerroff!'

Ken smacked his lips, remembered the promise to take some home, so all began another collection. 'They're mowing corn in the field near our house next week,' Brian said, putting a blackberry into his mouth.

Brenda was distant: 'Are they?' He was about to eat another, but dropped it into her apron. 'You're a greedy 'og,' she said. 'You're eating more than you put in my pina.'

'No I'm not.'

'Yes you are, because I'm counting 'em.'

'There's plenty more,' he said, reaching to the bush top. 'Is your grandad going to cut the corn?' She looked at him with brown inquisitive eyes.

'No, Farmer Hawkins' men are doing it.'

They walked down a path almost closed in by bushes. 'I might come then,' she conceded.

At the stream's narrowest point Alma was nervous and wouldn't cross. Ken found a large stone and plunged it into the middle with such force that everyone leapt to the bushes for fear of being splashed. 'You needn't a thrown it in like that,' Brenda cried. 'It's a steppin'-stone for our Alma.' She put her foot on it, swung to another stone, became rigid at seeing the distance left to cross.

'Go on,' Ken called. 'You'll be all right.'

A wave of panic masked her face, and with a sudden shrill cry she collapsed into the water, a dozen blackberries bobbing in the disturbance. Ken hauled her out, bedraggled and shivering.

'Oo you won't 'alf cop it, our Ken,' Brenda sang with a dead-set serious face. 'Oo you'll cop it. Not 'alf!'

'I didn't push her in,' he shouted, 'it's your fault. You knew she was going to fall, so you should have grabbed her.' They walked out of the wood, arguing bitterly, Alma a silent round-face heroine shivering between them.

Still in bed Brian heard work going on in the field: horses neighing and the jingle of harness, men shouting to one another, and harvest machines splutter-chugging up and down the lane. He ran to the window in his shirt: it was true right enough, they'd started; pulled on his trousers and walked downstairs holding shoes and socks. His grandmother laid some breakfast. 'The tea's nearly cold, lazybones, but I din't bother to wake you because I knew the noise'd do it sooner or later.' She poured a mug of tea: 'Anyway, it's on'y eight o'clock so you've plenty of time.'

He washed, and bolted through the hedge. Merton was talking to Farmer Hawkins, so he stayed back. Drays and wagons stood in spaces already cut, and Brian felt a lingering fear of the huge juggernaut wheels of the wagons because three years ago near haymaking time he had asked his grandfather: 'What do they carry the corn off in?' 'Drays and wagons, Nimrod.' 'But wagons eat you,' he exclaimed. Merton cried in surprise: 'Eat you? Wagons?' 'I read about it at school,' Brian said. 'Well if you did, all I can say is they teach you some funny things,' Merton laughed. Brian was disconcerted: 'Well wagons do eat you, because Saint George killed one.' 'He must 'ave 'ad a bit o' bother then stabbin' the wheels,' Merton said mischievously. 'I suppose it was loaded wi' bottles of ale, and that's why he wanted to kill it!' Lydia broke in: 'Sent George didn't kill a wagon, Brian. It was a *dragon* he killed.' 'Ah!' Merton exclaimed. 'I thought there was a catch in it somewhere.'

Even now Brian half expected a snorting scaly monster to come charging at him and felt disappointed on seeing a clumsy inoffensive thing on four wheels unable to move without the help of horses. At dinner-time he went down the lane to fetch Merton a quart of ale and with the change from a shilling bought himself an ice-cream cornet. A wind had risen, and though a hot sun shone, someone expected there'd be rain tomorrow, so they had to finish the field today. Brian sat on the gate and watched the wheat swaying in a charmed dance under the wind that fell on it from the long embankment of the railway. It turned and lifted like a gentle sea of yellow and gold. The field had shrunk since morning, was half the size of yesterday, would soon be a mere wasteground of short stems that stuck into slippers that walked over them. All heads were lifted and lowered, then went in a beautiful movement all at once from side to side as if making the most of a narrowing existence and knowing that by evening it would be flat and finished.

Something was wrong. Everyone stood around a horse that, still in the wagon-shafts, lay on its side, half strangled and tilting the cart that was in danger of falling. 'What's up?' Brian asked his grandfather.

'That 'oss's gone mad.'

'What are they going to do with it?'

'Shoot it, if they can't get it up.' The huge grey horse lay neighing and snorting, its unmoving eyes on the men around, sensing itself in an unusual position yet unable to break through the dim mists covering its brain and gather strength to get up. Foam was like snow on its mouth and no one would go close and try heaving it on its feet. On its forehead was a red sore the size of a florin, a dozen flies buzzing over it. 'Does it was some water, grandad?'

'It's 'ad a drink,' Merton answered brusquely.

'But it's sweating' – he pointed to glistening enormous flanks: the body twitched, and grey eyes rolled emptily. Farmer Hawkins, a heavily built man wearing a panama hat, pushed his way through the onlookers demanding: 'Ain't you got the bloody thing up yet?'

Nobody spoke, seemed afraid of him. Merton smoked a pipe some distance off, and Brian stood by his side. Farmer Hawkins cracked a whip over the horse's head, hoping it would leap up and pull the wagon away. No good: it lay like dead. He tugged at the harness, but was forced back to his whip, which made red streaks down its flanks. It tried to rise at each crash but its head fell in a dull half-paralysed heap. The farmer saw it was useless, threw his whip aside and sent the labourers back to their work.

'Got a gun handy, Jack?' he called to Merton. Brian edged closer: its body shimmered with sweat and fatigue, eyes showing grey, tail swishing feebly against attacking flies. Then all movement subsided, and he turned at hearing Ken Arlington shout from the hedge. Brenda's wild face roamed over the field and stopped at the prostrate horse. 'It's gone mad,' Brian told them. 'Grandad's gone to get a gun.'

'They don't ev ter shoot it just 'cause it's gone mad,' Brenda said, 'do they?'

'Course they do.' Farmer Hawkins cleared them off when Merton came back and they walked to the embankment hoping for trains, Brenda between them. 'What's up?' Brian asked at her silence.

'Nowt,' she answered. Remembering the horse's face he wanted to get far away before it was killed. 'Why can't they make horses better when they're badly, like people?' she cried. 'Can't they get a doctor to it?'

'Don't be daft,' Ken threw in sharply. 'That hoss is too old. It'd be too much bother to try and get it better.' He plucked at blackberries. 'Come and eat some o' these, they're ever so juicy.' Brian collected a handful and gave some to Brenda. Still eating, they sat on the railway fence. Brenda's hair blew about: 'I hope they don't kill that 'oss,' she lamented.

They heard a train. Brian leapt from his perch and ran up the green slope, lying flat in deep grass near the top, already feeling a vibration from the approaching train. The others crashed on either side. 'I hope it's an express,' Ken whispered, his voice low as though the driver might hear him. Brian remembered how Bert near New Bridge laid flat on the tracks while a goods train rumbled over him – a dare-devil who dared the others to do it as well, though nobody would take his 'dare'. He bet Brian a pound, but Brian said: 'Where will you get the pound if I do?' 'Rob a meter,' Bert said, but Brian hadn't done it anyway.

Before its thunder grew too loud to hear anything else, a series of sharp echoes fled from the cornfield. Brian felt a pain in his chest, as if the bullet struck there. He tugged a handful of grass by the roots and chewed it, and when the train screamed by opened his green mouth to cheer, an arm waving above his head. Engine, wheels and carriages came to within a few yards, ripping the view into tatters of blue sky and field, each in a decimated second dancing between the carriage-gaps. A column of smoke curled like a black long stocking into the sky, its head quickly dispersing at the shock of finding nothing to keep it in shape.

He followed them down the slope and over the fence. 'I want to go away on a train like that sone day,' he said, slashing at nettles with a stick.

'Where do you want to go then?' Brenda asked as he drew level. He hadn't thought about it. 'Anywhere. I don't know.'

'I'd be frightened to go a long way,' she confided. 'And trains might crash.'

'Well,' he said, a note of anger in his voice, '*I* wouldn't be frightened.'

11

Seaton was a secretive man, and his dark complexion may have been more than skin deep because of his inability either to read or write. This bred in him – when surrounded as he imagined himself to be by a fair world of literacy – a defensive wish to create his own peculiar brand of pencilled autobiography. He acquired notebooks and filled them with dates and columns of figures, copied monthly calendars on to sheets of cut-out cardboard, on which he starred each dole and signing-on day. In the books he kept accounts of what wages he came by on his short-lived expeditions into the world of employment. A spacious old toffee-tin held bills, lapsed insurance policies, pink forms of one sort or another, fading official letters he had some time received, birth certificates and two photographs of his dead mother. All these items, as well as each added-up column of wages, were signed by his name in broad rugged handwriting, the only thing that, apart from figures (at which he was remarkably clever and quick), he knew how to write.

This private office, which gave him a sense of still being part of the world when it no longer needed his labour (yet of being master to a tiny and exclusive life of his own), was kept under lock and key with a tool chest he had made himself. Brian watched him saw the remaining hard gut out of half-rotten planks, plane and bevel, sandpaper and mortise-tenon the lid and sides. Within, on hooks or in equal compartments, lay screwdrivers and hammers, gimlets and bradawls, saws and chisels, hinges and brackets and bolts, and bits of shoe-leather (for he was a miser and threw nothing away except cigarette-ends), all of them begged or borrowed or stolen, found perhaps but seldom bought. Brian was sometimes around when it was opened, and out came a smell of upholstery and bicycle inner-tubes, tobacco and sweat and leather, and the beginnings of rust from straightened nails.

Seaton delighted in using his tools, worked with an animal absorption within self-found carefully-defined limits of intelligent usefulness. His creative world was the result of necessity finding its own level in a man who might otherwise have made his family suffer too much, and infect them completely with his own melancholia, spite, and despair.

Brian saw him unlock the cupboard on certain evenings, spread papers and notebooks over the table, watched him set out a clear life in dates and figures and signatures with no explanatory prose, in the only way he knew how to record it. These were the times of his greatest contentment, and an aura of calm descended over the house.

Brian copied him, bought a penny notebook and in awkward, uneven writing put down the names of schools he had been to and the dates at which he had left them, the streets he had lived on for as far back as he could remember. He saw other boys standing at street corners with pencil and paper collecting car numbers, but his own game was part of walking up Denman Street on Sunday morning to buy a sixpenny roast from a cheap butcher's (pushing up to the counter and always hoping the roast would be bigger than last week's), stopping on his way back near a corner plastered from top to bottom with cinema billboards: big letters in yellow and black, red and purple and gold, forming titles of adventure and destiny, and names from the brightest of heavens such as Robert Donat and Jack Hulbert, Jean Harlow and Clark Gable. Shopping-bag by the wall, he took out his book and selfconsciously gathered on to paper the shining words of poetry around him, imagining the thoughts of passers-by: What's he doin', writing in a book like that? – for he would stay a long time laboriously copying and turning pages, while his mother waited at home to get the meat in the oven.

The game came to an end one evening when he opened his grandmother's *Evening Post* and discovered two long columns on the inside page already filled with words he had so arduously hunted for and copied down. In one way it was like finding a goldmine, corn in Egypt that dazzled his eyes as he strove to take in such a fabulous concentration of titles. Though they lacked the colour and layout that went right into him at the hoardings, his game was finished.

At the beginning of September time threw in its reserves of frost and fog to break down the year's resistance, and he wore a coat, began in the chill and darkness of evening to anticipate Goose Fair and Bonfire Night and Christmas parties at school. Rain came, cold and persistent, drainpipes and gutters working overtime to wash away the dead from a battlefield of leaves and matchsticks. Houses grew farther apart in the misty odours of each earlier dusk, became more compatible for Knock-a-door and Spirit-tap and Dustbin-lidder in the form of Brian, Ted Hewton, and Jim Skelton, moving like wraiths from lit-up lamp to lamp in laughing agony at the distraught tormented who opened his or her door after mysterious noises, to see – their eyes still blind from an electric-lit room – nothing.

Brian with hand-bat played rounders, sent a tennis-ball smacking from wall to wall and corner to corner in half-darkness, sometimes cracking a window and bringing an irate man in shirtsleeves shaking a fist into an empty street threatening to have the shadows 'sommonsed'. Those for the leap in Leapfrog sang as they went for the leap:

'Rum-stick-a-bum
Here I come
With my finger up my bum!'

A game of snobs went on across the pavement, or marbles in the gutter, and in the middle of the street a solid bundle of bellicose kids split into a dozen fragments when a car came by, or slowly dispersed when haggard mothers from doorsteps called them in one by one for tea or bed.

On Saturday morning a scraping of pennies and ha'pennies sometimes succeeded in mounting to threepence, the price of a matinée seat at the pictures. Brian collected rags and iron from the tips, cadged a rabbit skin from his grandmother, a stray beer-bottle from Merton, and traipsed them in a sack to junk-yards on Alfreton Road. When Seaton did a paper-hanging job he was able to take Fred and Margaret to the flickerdrome as well. They stood hand in hand, an hour before time, in a long queue of shouting and restless children. Ice-cream barrows attracted knots of them by the kerb, and Fred absentmindedly kicked the wheelspokes of one before he thought to slide his ha'penny on to the cool-looking lead-covered tub, then came back crying because his ice-cream had thrown itself from the cornet-mouth and was melting on the pavement as if it couldn't disappear fast enough. Brian tried to pacify him, but a hard fist screwed towards weeping eyes, and the mouth beneath wailed: 'I want another cornet!' at which Brian tried threats: 'If you don't be quiet I wain't tek yer into the pictures at all.'

'I want another cornet,' Fred wept, and Brian had no staying power before tears. Weeping seemed the greatest disaster that could ever happen, much greater than what had caused it, which should already have been forgotten. Tears, more than faith, should move mountains – but what a pity they were shed so easily – as Fred went on roaring and everyone turned to look.

Margaret tut-tutted, as she had heard her mother do many times: 'I'n't 'e a mardy-arse?'

Brian relented. Had it been anyone else crying he would have felt anger against them, but for his own brother he mellowed, became soft and almost afraid for them both. 'I'll buy you a cornet,' he said, and pushed a ha'penny into his hand so that Fred stopped the tap as if by magic. 'Don't let it fall out this time,' Margaret shouted at the stolid back of his head by the ice-cream barrow.

Cars and buses catapulted down the cobbled road, dodged by Brian to reach the paper shop and buy a *Joker* comic. He stood on the pavement reading the latest machinations of Chang the Hatchet Man, immediately drawn into a strange landscape, himself an unseen spectator standing by a broad riverbank, watching a junk loaded with dynamite carried by the current towards a dam, by which it would explode and bury both valley and distant plain in water. He was filled with admiration for such grandiose ideas of destruction, looking upon Chang with some sympathy, almost as if he was some long-lost great-uncle a few times removed, roaming the wastes of China. He knew Chang was a villain, and that three English youths standing hopelessly by the riverbank would have saved the dam if they could, but Chang was greater than these, the brigand who had set the junk in motion from farther upstream and was the real hero of the piece. The junk exploded, a thousand fragments suspended in mid-air till next week – and even this didn't make him aware of Chang's creator, of the fact that Chang was no more than a few pen marks on paper, lit into something bigger than real by the escape lanes of imagination.

He moved up to see the queue moving, and asked for three thre'pennies at the cash desk. The musty, scent-smelling cinema was already half full, and he led them to the front row; Margaret wanted to sit farther back, but stayed with them because her mother had drummed it into her that she mustn't leave Brian at any time: 'You might get run over or talked to by a dirty old man if you don't come home with the others.' Brian found it easy to imagine a bull double-decker grinding on its brakes, its meat-chopping radiator smeared with blood and bone and gristle as the bus capsized by the barber's to a grinding of tin, a tinkle of glass, and a thump of fifty people and shopping baskets hitting the kerb. But a dirty old man – what did he want with little girls? Anyway, if I caught a dirty old man doing owt to Margaret I'd rush him and kill him.

Red lights dimmed from the fourpenny backs, bringing a tide of darkness and increased cheering towards the screen, a blackout of noise that went on and on. A length of boarding ran under the screen and the manager beat an iron bat against it, creating gunshots of rapid fire. Brian folded his ears in, one flap over the other and his flat hand over that, while more shots ricochetted as far as the balcony even when the cheering and booing had stopped.

'All right,' shouted the demoniac manager, a little man become giant-sized in the silence. 'It won't start until I can hear a pin drop.' Even those in for the first time knew better than to create more noise by laughing at his joke, one that Brian disliked and distrusted because at school old gett-faced Jones used the same catch to get you quiet before hymn-singing and prayers, different in that the stick he held was always still swinging from action before he got to the 'pin-dropping' smirk.

At the consenting flash of the manager's torch the Three Stooges came like jumping-jacks on to the screen, and pure untrammelled laughter grew like fireworks. At the end of the serial, when Jungle Jim was one side-stroke away from the scissor-jaws of a faster crocodile, all exits burst open and Brian kept Margaret and Fred before him, arms held out to stop them being wedged too tight in the flood. Fred shot out first, his mouth fixed in a Tarzan scream, until Margaret told him to stop it or she would thump him.

Brian led them running home because of a thin drizzle falling. The electric light was already on, and Vera was cutting doorsteps of bread, pasting it with margarine and plum jam. Seaton sat by the fire smoking a cigarette, cup of tea on the hob. 'It was ever so good at the pictures, our dad,' Margaret said, and he pulled her to him with a laugh, covering her rain-cold cheek with loud kisses: 'I love my little gel, I do an' all!' He listened absorbed to her re-hashed tale of Buck Jones and Jungle Jim. Brian bit his way through a doorstep. 'The Three Stooges was best because there was women in the other pictures. I've never seen a big picture wi'out a woman in it.'

'And you wain't, neether,' said Vera, setting up a line of cups and mugs for tea; 'the men like to see 'em too much.'

'Yo'll see enough o' women some day, Brian,' Seaton said with a laugh.

As Vera drew curtains across the window the urgent voice of a vendor shouting 'Special' electrified the room. They could hear people buying papers, and the clink of money given in change when the newsman stopped under the window. Brian was afraid, feeling the blowing up of bombs and black death and screams of gun-and-bayonet war, whenever he heard anyone shouting 'special', because his mother once told him that Specials meant war. Vera broke the silence: 'Shall I go and get one?'

'I shouldn't bother,' Seaton answered. 'I expect it's on'y summat about Spain, and we'll get it on the wireless soon.' When the man's voice had gone Brian said: 'A man came round to gran'ma's sellin' *Old Moore's Almanacks* for tuppence, and when she bought one off 'im I read in it that there'd be a big war soon.'

'There wain't,' his mother scoffed, spreading more bread, 'don't yo' bother. An' if there is, yo' wain't be called up.'

'I 'ope not: I'm frightened o' wars.'

Seaton grunted: it was a difficult sound to tolerate – an employment of bitter sarcasm while everyone knew him to be feeling fine. 'It's no worse in a war than it is now. You get boggered from pillar to post and get nowt to eat, just the same.' He pulled Margaret on to his knee with a laugh, a revolution in mood: 'Come on, my curly-headed baby, tell me some more about what was on the pictures, then I'll let you sup some o' my tea.'

They looked into the deep black canyon between the canal locks, a far-down shine of water fitfully seen by cloud-belaboured moonlight, like a coal-hole dug so deep that water had filled it, glinting like boot-polish. A few yards away, up and over the bridge parapet, cars and buses roared into the city from a wilderness of fields and woods, and headlit javelins of opposite desires left the huge illuminated rag-patch of town for Brian knew not where.

They were alone, sidetracked beyond lights and out of notice. Bert kicked the pram: 'I'd like to chuck that in as well, but I'd get a pasting if I went 'ome without it. Our Midge is on'y four and mam pushes her up to t' clinic every week to get her leg seen to.' He flashed his torch, a flat model for one-and-four-pence bought from money cajoled with the Guy in town. His fingers gripped it, pressed – and light came again from the one eye of Polyphemus bulging white out of the top.

Brian drew back from a twelve-foot fall into bottomless water, not only cold but wet as well, heavy on your clothes, and nothing to grip down there but smooth walls when and if you surfaced. 'Come on then, let's get the Guy Fawkes. Yo' tek one arm; I'll tek the other; and we'll let go.' He looked over again: 'It wain't 'alf splash.'

'It's a crying shame' – Bert shook his head. 'It'd burn well if we took it 'ome and saved it for the bonfire.' Brian hated a change of mind. It made him uneasy – because his own unsure mind was inclined to follow every switch. A simple decision often meant hard work, and to break it an extravagant waste of spirit. The decision to buy torches with the Guy Fawkes money had been easy to make, but both were now guilty at not splitting the three bob between their families for food, and needed to get rid of the Guy to prove, when recriminations flew at their faces, that it had been stolen from them by bigger boys before they could earn a penny. 'It might not sink for all we know,' Brian said. 'And when a copper comes along in the morning it'll look like a man who's chucked 'issen in. Then the copper'll sling his hat and coat off and goo in as well.'

That decided it. 'P'raps he'll drown if he does,' Bert said. 'Yer never know. Not all coppers can swim.'

'Coppers don't drown though,' Brian said with conviction, fastening the Guy's coat as if it were a paralysed and much-loved brother in danger of catching pneumonia. 'If a copper dived in he'd get out. We wouldn't, but he would.'

'He might not' – Bert held the agreeable vision for as long as he could make it last – 'he might get cramp. It's cold enough for cramp, if you ask me. Once you get cramp you're a gonner. A lad at Poor Boys' Camp got it in his leg last year, and he went under twice before anybody could get to him. He didn't die though.'

Brian caught on to his vision. 'Well, if a copper got cramp and I was near, I wouldn't help him to get out.' The Guy lay between them, flat like some derelict drunk, a sackbag arm across button eyes, as if not wanting to see what the world had in store for him next. One leg was akimbo and Bert kicked it straight. 'Even if I'd got a lifebelt I'd chuck 'im a brick. Coppers is bastards. I was down town last week and opened a car door for a bloke. A copper cum up and batted my tab. He said I'd get sent to Borstal if I didn't clear off. I worn't bothering nobody.'

Brian flashed his torch, revelled in the magic of it. 'Rotten bogger.'

'All coppers are like that.'

'I don't know why they have coppers,' Brian said. 'They're worse than schoolteachers.'

'No difference,' Bert said, lighting his nub-end in the darkness. 'It's all part of the gov'ment. They're all Conservatives, as well. I know that for a fact, because dad towd me. Conservative' – he was proud of such a posh formidable word – 'if ever yer vote Conservative, dad said, I'll smash yer brains out. And 'e showed me 'is big screwed-up fist to prove it. Then on Saturday night I seed him thumping a bloke outside a pub, and I suppose it was because dad 'ad got to know he'd voted Conservative. He bashes mam sometimes though, but I don't know what for, because she don't vote Conservative.'

'Millionaires vote Conservative. John Player and the bloke who owns Raleigh.'

'Well I wouldn't. Even if I'd got ten million pound notes I'd still vote red for Labour.'

'Me as well,' Brian said. 'Shall we chuck the Guy in the locks then, like 'e was a copper?' And an idea came quickly. 'Let's get a couple o' bricks and fasten 'em inside, so's he'll sink right to the bottom.'

'Nobody'll think it's somebody drowned,' Bert objected. 'It wain't be seen.'

Brian's face exploded into a laugh, the force of a decision that took no deciding, happiness giving character to his face unseen in the darkness. 'It'll mek a big splash though,' he managed to say at last, and Bert, relaxed and disarmed, knew that it would.

Labour, Brian repeated, bending to pull up his share of a huge stone. Labour – the word had a stern ring about it, like the hard labour they gave you in court. Perhaps this was soft labour since everybody voted for it. Or like Manual Labour, the Spaniard fighting in Madrid: cloth-cap, rifle and a thin cigar. His father was Labour, red Labour, and so was everybody else he knew (except old Jones the headmaster at school: you could tell a mile off that he wasn't), though that didn't make the word and meaning of it more acceptable. The stones were tied and centred into place, and he hooked his fingers around an arm and a leg. 'We'll count three,' Bert said, 'Soft though.'

'Back then,' Brian responded, feeling the straw-like texture of the Guy. Conservative – it was an official word to be distrusted, hated in fact. If a van stopped near you in the street at election time and some fist shot out and thrust into your hand a bunch of blue streamers, you didn't stop to wonder why you'd been daft enough to accept them but threw them down immediately and kicked them to bits with your shoes – or else. Even being Labour like your father and street and suburb, you risked being battered to the pavement following the eruption of a gang of red-streamers like a steam-engine out of the nearest corner. You might hold your breath long enough though, hang on to the blue streamers and pin them to the door of someone you did not like, someone who had once sent too readily for the police when you played loudly on the near-by cobbles.

The final drawback, then a masterly satisfying swing of the stone-bellied straw corpse into the air and over the welcoming water. Labour was the best thing – and if Brian ever felt distrust for that sympathetic organization it was only because all big names seemed like devil's threats to hold his soul in thrall – and he wasn't sure enough of his soul yet to trust it with such things.

It was late enough for a traffic lull along the near-by big road; a rough silence reigned between the corridor of its lights, and among the distant railway yards. The Guy, leaving their lunging arms, spent a glorious moment of freedom suspended in black harmless air, then, a straw-emasculated monster, it descended while Bert and Brian held their breath with anticipated delight.

It hit the water with a justified explosion, a reverberating thump creating havocs of sound in the canyon of the deep lock, while Bert and Brian embraced with roars of delight – and then set to pushing the now empty pram back along the towpath, their newly bought flash-lamps making spaces of clear light before them.

On rainy days clothes steamed in the classroom, emitting invisible yet olfactory vapours from waterlogged shoes and soaked jackets. Hot pipes were a December godsend, to be sat on before lessons began, stayed close to during them so that the hand could stretch slyly out and touch their luxurious warmth. At home when he and Arthur and Fred ran in crying from the bitter cold of hot-aches, Seaton would pull them to the hearth one by one and press his fire-warmed hands over them: 'Have a bit o' fire. There's plenty more where that came from' – making Brian's bones ache from the pressure of strong maulers.

In winter he saw the Nook as a snowbound igloo set in the desolation of stark countryside, Merton and the rest plodding in or out for wood and beer and groceries. If not snow, then the fields were dull and wet under a grey sky, and there was no comfort in crossing fields and mud like a fugitive walking beyond the world of sound. Silence and rain surrounded it – not even a horse or lightning. Streets were better.

To subscribe penny by penny at the corner shop for some toy or Selection Box of chocolates ravaged his deepseated natural inclinations. But it had to be done if Christmas was to mean anything at all, it being better to spend two shillings straight off than twenty-four pennies bit by bit. A concentration of resources left a more solid memory of having been rich for a day instead of stingily solvent for many.

'Who'll join the Christmas Club?'

'I wouldn't join two pieces o' string,' Seaton said, 'except to 'ang myself, 'appen.' But he laughed as he said it.

Trimmings and Christmas trees and toys were in every shop window, aquariums of light and colour, impossible to buy but good to look at. Seaton was still on the dole, with money harder to come by than it had ever been, though food and presents usually landed from somewhere at Christmas. Vera's mother sent a Christmas pudding boiled in the outhouse copper of the Nook six weeks before; Ernest sent a parcel of discarded toys from last year; a sister sent clothes and gave Seaton a few shillings when he walked to Carlton for them.

A Christmas tree came into the house. Seaton trimmed the ragged rim of a two-pound tomato tin, filled it with soil, laminated it with blue crêpe paper. It stood like a god with multiple green arms on the dresser. Out came the box of decorations, saved like gold from previous years in beds of tissue paper. A delicate yellow pear was held aloft: 'Where shall I put this one?'

Arthur stood at tiptoe on a chair to point out a branch half-way up the stem, shaking the sideboard in his eagerness. Margaret bawled at him not to knock owt over. 'Just there,' he said firmly.

Vera put down her cup of tea. 'Come off that chair, then, our Arthur; you'll fall.'

'And where'll I put *this* one?' Seaton asked, holding up a coloured model of Santa Claus. Brian had seen enough Christmases to lead the chorus of: 'Right on top! He's the chief! Up top, our dad.'

'Ah,' Seaton responded, high on the chair, 'you'll be 'earing 'im on Christmas Eve if you listen 'ard enough. You'll 'ear 'is reindeers trotting across the chimney pots, wain't they, Vera?'

'Santa Claus i'n't real,' Margaret scoffed.

'That's what yo' think,' Brian countered.

'He i'n't,' Arthur said, and his baited breath settled it.

'Our dad hides our toys in the pantry, don't yer dad?' Fred said.

He looked at Vera. 'Ain't he a sharp little bogger? You can't tell these kids owt, can yer?'

'Yer can't,' Vera said, pulling Arthur's shoes and socks off. 'Not like when we was kids. Believed owt, we did. When I was ten, only a little gel, our Oliver towd me to go up Canning Circus to gerrim some orange peel. When I asked him what he wanted it for he said he'd bat my tab if I didn't goo. He said he wanted it because he'd got an 'eadache though. So I went. Silly bogger *I* was. It was miles away, and I was terrified coming back in the dark, under them bridges. I though an owd man was going to run me. And when I got back wi' me pina full of orange peel our Oliver just laughed. All on 'em did. I said: "Yer rotten bogger" – and chucked it in 'is face. Then me dad gen me a penny, and said it served 'im right. He was a bogger though, our Oliver was. But he was good as well though, a proper card. Everybody liked 'im. My dad cried like a baby when he got killed in the war.'

Brian had heard it before, yet always found it hard to believe in grandad Merton crying. He pictured someone bringing a telegram to the Nook: YOUR SON KILLED FOR HIS KING AND

COUNTRY it would have said. Kicked to death by a drunken mule; Oliver's pals had given it rum to drink before he led it across a moor – being a blacksmith like his dad and on his way to shoe it. Maybe they did it for a joke on him because he was having 'em on like he had his mam on. But everybody says he was a good bloke though, so he was sorry he'd got killed because that was one uncle less. A sprig of mistletoe was tied under the light. 'Come on, Vera, let's 'ave the first kiss of Christmas,' Seaton said.

'Stop it, 'Arold' – struggling, aware of four kids looking on. 'Don't be so bleddy daft.' But she was kissed.

The week-end before Christmas, Brian went to the Nook, stayed overnight and the next day felt sick as he was about to start back. He stood by the door with a stick in his hand, ready to walk out and home under the black sky that looked like sending fists of rain at the hedges before he got far. He couldn't move, and Lydia turned from her making-up at the mirror. 'Look at 'im,' she said to her mother, 'he's badly, the poor little bogger. Come on to the fire, Brian. He's as white as a sheet.' He leaned his stick in the corner and walked back. She undressed him and walked him up the stairs in his shirt, the smell of her newly applied powder and rouge bringing the sickness into his mouth so that she just got him to the pot in time. 'How is he then?' Mary asked when she came down.

Lydia took two lemons and filled a jug with warm water. 'He was as sick as a dog. I'm teking him some o' this up.'

'He'd better stay 'ere over Christmas if you ask me. Shall we get a doctor?'

'No. It's only a bilious bout.'

Brian curled into a ball, half-slept in a colourful incomprehensible world under the blankets. His tightly closed eyelids held in flickering lights of orange and red, and while he wanted to open his eyes in the hope of driving them away – they attacked him like bluebottles that stung – he did not want to lose the sense of repose that closed eyes gave. He fought this problem for a while, until he was forced to push his head above blankets and look at the flowered wallpaper beyond the bed because open eyes steadied the equilibrium of his stomach and saved him from being sick at that moment. The dance of the flowers slowed down; the swaying ceased and eventually he eased his eyelids together and fell back into less dangerous rest.

On Christmas morning there was a train-set on his bed, and its silver lines were held like a horseshoe as Merton's heavy tread sounded on the stairs.

'Hello, Nimrod, is that bilious bout about gone?'

'I feel all right now.' He was in the middle of the wide bed, looking beyond brass posts at wiry tree arms outside that the teeth of winter had picked clean. Merton pulled the window open. 'I think we'll get yer up later.'

The railway line circled an uneven terrain of blanket. 'Gran'ma said I couldn't yet.' A wind blew sunlight into the room, the damp breeze sharp as smelling-salts after the sick odours of three days' breath. 'Ay, 'appen she did, but yer'll never get better stayin' in bed. Yer want a bit o' fresh air round yer now.' He closed the window, stood at the end of the bed. 'What yer got there, you young bogger? I suppose Santa Claus brought it for yer?'

'No, yo' did, and gran'ma and the others. You all put to and brought it me from Nottingham.'

Merton laughed. 'There's a little sharpshit for yer. Don't believe in Santa Claus any more. I don't know. But yer believe in Sent George and the Wagon though, don't yer?'

Brian laughed, stood the trainlines up like a child's drawing of the Big Wheel at Goose Fair. He let it fall. 'No I don't.'

Merton took the lines: 'Let's see'f we can't get this contraption going.' He set them on the floor and turned the engine key until it came against the stop. Brian leaned over the edge of the bed: Merton lined the carriages behind the engine, stopped whistling when the caravan set off. 'There,' he said, 'nowt to it.' After a dozen times round he set an empty cup on the track, and they stared down on the whirring colourful train going by the counterpane that hung to the floor, then circling to Merton, then towards the washstand legs, finally turning with a clack into the cup, knocking it aside and going round and wearing itself to a standstill.

'Put a shoe on now, gran'dad.'

'Why, you destructive little bogger,' he said, feeling under the bed for one. It jerked the train sideways, sent it trundling at an angle: Brian heard a hollow thump as its snout smacked at the skirting board. 'That did it,' Merton said, satisfied at Brian's laughter. 'Now yer know how to break it, I'll leave yer. Though I expect yer'd a found out soon enough on yer own.'

He went down for Christmas dinner, and later found himself alone in the kitchen, the others either out or in bed. He was sitting on the rug, dressed, torn between a book on shipwrecks and the mountainous red shapes licking above the fire-bars. The book didn't hold, except that it was new, another present. He tried a page: everyone stood on the deck and sang God Save the King, while the boat descended into a sea of sharks. Why didn't they shoot the sharks, make boats, drink ale perhaps? It was nothing to sing about. When he was totally interested in a song, book, a picture, his face went dead, his pale snubbed features carved in wood, life only coming into his face when he didn't understand something and was trying to. Like now with the men singing God Save the King and sharks waiting to snap them up.

A grey and mustard cat purred in a hump by his knees. Merton would have booted it out of the way for being too near the fire. Brian prodded it, but went back to his book to read the end of the story over again. The cat's paws flattened along the rug, its green full-empty eyes staring. Men were struggling in the sea: no more singing. The women were far away in rowing boats, wailing at the terrible grey sea that melted like mountains and then shot up again. The cat looked at him and he offered it a piece of mincepie from his plate. The next story was about a steamship with funnels – with ten times the number of people on board. The cat came eagerly forward to take the pie: put its claws on his bare knee, sniffed the pastry and put out its pink tongue. Everybody said the ship couldn't sink. Well, let's see how it does. The cat went back to its half-sleep, unable to understand why Brian was eating with such enjoyment something it found uneatable, suspecting that what Brian ate changed from meat to dull flour by the time the cat got to it. An iceberg ripped the bottom out. There was a complete silence both in and outside the cottage. Even the dogs slept, gorged for once on scraps and bones.

Brian returned to school and snow, which fell so deep that gangs made barricades across the pavements and fought like revolutionaries in *Les Misérables.* White cannonballs spun through the air, soft and harmless as they collided with coat or neck, carrying cold instead of fire. After an hour contestants would melt away to nurse hotaches, tired and jangled after charge and countercharge. The enemies of winter were snow and flu, and Brian was a reluctant casualty of the latter. He was in bed for a week, fed on rice-pudding, toast and margarine, and hot drinks of Oxo. Elbows on the window-ledge, fingers pressing against his cheekbones, he watched it snowing protected from the outside world of cold and wet by the glass pane that nevertheless smelled of the wintry desolation when his nose went to within an inch of it. A jersey over his shirt, socks on for warmth, he singled out a particular snowflake, determined to keep it in view among the hundreds around, slowly bringing his eyes lower, as if it were a white butterfly pinned within his control by hypnosis and taken as a special privilege out of its secret den in the sky for safe conduct to earth and a better life.

Flat, triangular, an ordinary shape (yet different because it was the one he'd fixed on) – changing to oblong – others had decided to come with it, not wanting to be left back there alone. They were all pals, except that there were too many of them and they got in each other's way. So he lost it, but looked on down into snow just the same, where it would by now have fallen. It was near evening. Snow along the street had been trammelled into ruts by passing traffic, but the pavement was still thick and inviolate, a long smooth bed of untroubled snow. Until a man-shadow rounded the corner, and went off towards home, hooked out of sight by another corner, only footsteps left behind, plain and deep.

The opposite rooftops were covered by snowblankets made to measure. He thought of the Nook: saw larger snowflakes through the immediate curtain of his eyes burying doors and pigsties and even the house chimneys; then saw the chimneys without smoke and the dogs gone, the doors firm but guarding emptiness. Street lamps one at a time came on.

Undaunted at losing the first, he lifted his eyes to single out another snowflake. The storm thickened in silence. Crowds and crowds of soundless snowflakes elbowed and bullied each other out of the way in their hurry to escape from something in the sky that was terrifying them. He looked up, but couldn't see what it was, again losing the chosen snowflake.

He went back to bed, still seeing a sky full of white butterflies when he closed his eyes.

12

Singing in the rain and walking up Alfreton Road one Saturday morning, Brian and his cousin Dave whistled the actual song that came from a wide-open radio shop as they stopped at a big window to wonder what they could buy. Dave carried the money because he was seventeen, and, so he claimed, could therefore look after it better than Brian, and this was all right by Brian because if it hadn't been for clever Dave he wouldn't be staring in a pawnshop window with a half-share in eighteen-pence, a fortune earned by searching for takebackable beer bottles on the tips and collecting a penny on each after washing them well in the tadpoled cut.

Dave was Doddoe's eldest, tall and curly-headed, with sunken cheeks and dark prominent eyes. His sharp face missed nothing as he scanned each window and (like a high enough camera) took in the pavement from doorways to gutter, bending to pick up a threepenny-bit that Brian would never have seen but which brought their moneybags to one-and-nine. Jobless Dave wore long trousers ragged behind, a brown-holed jersey and a pair of shoes that let wet in. Brian's clothes were ragged also, but his boots at the moment kept his feet away from the rain. They passed a second-hand furniture and junk shop, and Brian read whitewashed letters painted across the window: GET YOUR GUNS FOR SPAIN HERE. 'Are they still fightin' in Spain?'

Dave nodded, trying to disentangle two pieces of steel as he walked along, a Penny Puzzle bought farther down the road. 'How long will they go on fighting then?' Brian wanted to know.

'Till they all drop dead,' he was told. The road was wide and cobbled, bordered by scrapyards, toyshops, pubs, pawnbrokers, cheap grocery stores, the live-wire artery for back-to-backs and factories hanging like clags on either side. People carried bundles to the pawnshop or sackbags to the scrapyard, or came up from town with untouched dole or wages in their pockets so that trading went on every day of the week.

Dave was fixed by the window of a radio shop. A wireless on show was dissected, and he explained how to make it work: a valve here, a condenser there, an impedance at such a place, fasten an aerial at that point, but Brian was bored because he couldn't understand it. 'If I bought that owd wireless for five bob I could fix it up,' Dave claimed, 'and I bet I could sell it for thirty bob then.'

It stopped raining, and meagre sun shone on wet pools in the road. Buses came slowly for fear of skidding, and a man whose bike brakes didn't work dragged his boots along the ground when he appeared from a sidestreet. Dave demanded: 'Who's the two best singers in the world?'

'I don't know,' Brian answered. 'I can on'y think o' one and that's Gracie Fields.' Dave walked on and said: 'Paul Robeson's the best, and the next is Al Jolson. So don't forget.'

They looked at the glass-framed stills outside a cinema. 'Would yer like ter goo ter't pictures s'afternoon? You ain't seen *G Men* 'ave yer?' He said no, he hadn't. 'It's a good picture. James Cagney's in it. About gangsters. It starts where he throws a pen at a fly and pins it to the door. Then a man's fixin' 'is tie in a mirror and the mirror gets shot to bits.'

'What time does it start?' Brian said, excited at these details.

Dave took the money from his pocket and began counting. 'They wain't let us in for another 'alf an hour, so we'll 'ave summat t'eat fost.' He pointed out several shops across the road. 'Go into that baker's and get two tuppenny meat pies, then go into the paper shop and ask for a buckanachure. The buckanachure will cost sixpence.'

Brian drew in his breath at the long word: 'What's a buckanachure?'

'Nowt for yo',' Dave said brusquely. 'Yo' can't understand yet what a buckanachure is. But just go in that shop, give the man sixpence, and tell 'im yer want a buckanachure. Understand?

Brian muttered it aloud as he crossed the road: buckanachure, buckanachure, and said it to himself in the pastry shop: buckanachure, buckanachure, so that he wouldn't forget such a strange big word and wouldn't let Dave down by going back without whatever a buckanachure was.

The word seemed ridiculous when he stood in the silent shop. Newspapers hung all around, rows of murder books lined the wall at the back, and in the window he could see magazines with bare women on the cover, and bare men as well, like Tarzans on the pictures. When a man in shirt-sleeves asked what he wanted he slid the sixpence across. 'A buckanachure.'

'A buckanachure.' He would have stood there repeating it till he dropped dead, for the word was engraved on his lips for ever. The man looked hard, then rummaged beneath the counter. 'Who do you want it for?'

'My cousin,' Brian told him. Nosey bleeder.

'I hope *you* aren't going to read it.' He passed a green-covered paperback across the counter, let the sixpenny bit fall into the till. Brian picked the book up as though he were a thief, walked out and paused at the kerb to look at it: 'Book of Nature' – he said it to himself, then aloud: 'Book of Nature, Book o' Nature – Buckanachure – so it's a book about nature. He'd heard of the Book of Daniel and the Book of Job, but he didn't know there was a Book of Nature. He opened it and saw drawings he couldn't understand, but it seemed to be about science, and he thought Dave must be clever to want a book like this.

Dave snatched it from him, munched his meat pie rapidly and skipped through the book with avid interest. When the first unnatural edge had been taken from his curiosity he slipped the book into his pocket and set to finishing his meal. 'Do you ever read books?'

'At school,' Brian told him.

'Have you read *Dracula*?'

'No. Is it good?'

'Yes,' Dave laughed, 'it frightens yer ter death.'

Brian laughed also. 'I'm goin' ter buy a book though. It's called *The Count of Monte-Cristo*.'

'I 'erd that on the wireless,' Dave said. 'A serial as went on for months, so the book'll cost a lot o' money.'

'I know, but I've bin savin' up for a long time. Whenever I get a tanner I tek it to Larker's downtown, and the manager's savin' it till I get half a crown. Then I can 'ave the book.'

Dave was impressed by the purposeful method: 'Ow much 'ave you got so far?'

'Two bob. I can fetch it nex' week if I get sixpence more.' Dave fleeced his pockets of every coin, looked them over shrewdly: ''Ere's threepence, Brian. I'll gi' yer the rest on Monday. I've got a lot o' rags ter tek an' sell, so I'll cum ter your 'ouse and give it yer.'

Brian could hardly believe it: weeks might have passed before the final elusive sixpence had come his way by pennies and ha'pennies. 'Thanks, our Dave. I'll let yer read the book when I've got it.'

'No,' Dave said, 'I can't read long books. Yo' keep it; if I take it to our 'ouse they'll use it for lavatory paper, or Doddoe'll write bets out on it. Anyway I've seen the picture, so I expect it's the same as the book.'

He screwed up the meat-pie paper and threw it into the road. They talked about films and filmstars, until a man began opening doors on either side, and a smell of cloth upholstery that had been locked up in the depths of the small picture house all night wafted out into the street. Then the doors slammed and a woman went into the paybox. 'Come on, Brian, we can goo in now and find a good seat.'

They emerged three hours later. Saucers of sunlight danced before Brian's eyes, and they ached from the shock of such bright day, when in the cinema he had expected it to be equally dark without. A trolley-bus at Canning Circus swept them down one hill and up another, past Radford Station to Lennington Road, on which the Doddoes lived.

The long straight pot-holed street of newly built houses ended at a railway embankment. 'They're all bleedin'-well Jerry-built though,' Dave pointed out, his finger towards the doors from which paint was already peeling. 'You have to prune twigs off your doors and windows every so often.' Three children flashed by on a home-made scooter, pram-wheels and a piece of board: 'They'd better watch out,' Dave laughed, 'or the means-test man'll tek it away' – as he batted the tab of the rear rider.

A tune from 'Top Hat' was bursting from the radiogram as they went into the house, and Dave turned it down, so that Brian heard a pan sizzling from the kitchen stove. 'Where you bin, our Dave?' Ada called accusingly. 'It's about time yo' brought some money into this bleedin' 'ouse.'

'I would if I could get some,' he said. 'I'll tek them rags in on Monday and you can 'ev a few bob.' Ada was a good-looking blonde of forty, with six kids and one expected, boss of a family reduced by approved school and Borstal – Bert having been taken to the former for lifting bicycle lamps, and Colin to the latter for impersonating a gas-meter man. The table over-flowed with pots and half-eaten leftovers, and Dave nearly choked on a line of clothes strung across the room. 'Look where yer goin', daft bleeder,' Doddoe said from the hearth, speaking for the first time

Brian found a chair, sat and watched fourteen-year-old Johnny mending one of his father's poaching nets on the other side of the room. Johnny was gaffer of the kids while Colin was in Borstal, a self-appointed sergeant-major with meaty fists, and a sense of righteousness because he brought money into the house without stealing. He had done time at an approved school, and had learned to recognize authority and know what it meant to knuckle under to it. If you did as you were told at approved school the masters put you in positions of power over the other boys; and though Johnny could hold dominion by toughness alone, it was double-sweet and sure to have your power sanctioned by those above you. He was generous and good-hearted, though firm and inclined to bullying when his righteous will was disobeyed. He was Doddoe's favourite, though it wasn't acknowledged, and they rarely spoke to each other. But Brian felt an alliance of likenesses, so obvious in fact that it was recognized and commented on by others of the family, though beyond words to Doddoe and Johnny.

The unifying quality was one of fearlessness. Unable to get work and with a family to feed, Doddoe was absolutely convinced that it was right to go poaching in order to get food. It was more a question of good and evil, for while food in the form of rabbits was running on four legs around estates of the rich, who anyway had all the grub – and more – they needed for themselves, then Doddoe was right and fearless in his pursuit of it. He went on his bike most nights into the country, dressed in an army overcoat and wearing a cap, a knapsack slung over his shoulder to carry nets and whatever fur-covered victims ran into them – of which he would have plenty by dawn. A cosh sticking from the pocket of his topcoat was useful for knocking rabbits on the head if they struggled too long in the net, or for swinging at the gamekeeper should it come to a fight.

Johnny was equally strong, though in lesser ways because still young. Brian remembered a time when a pair of shoes dropped off Johnny's feet and he lacked an overcoat in snow-covered months. Johnny had made the best of things: knocked the high heels from a pair of his mother's, put on one of her fur-collared coats she had cut down for him, and walked off well-protected to school. No boys had laughed, but his teacher made a reference to his woman's attire and Johnny, the words cutting into him like knives, couldn't hide his bitterness from Ada that night. Nevertheless he went to school clad the same next day and half-way through the class was astounded to see his mother walk into the room. 'Your name Martin?' she demanded, standing by the teacher's desk. He was even more stunned than Johnny at the buxom fierceness of blonde Ada. 'Yes,' he said, 'what do you want?' Ada's fist landed hard across the side of his face. 'That'll teach you to tell our Johnny off because he's got no clothes' – and walked out of the room. That same day the teacher took him to the nearest shop and rigged him up with a new pair of boots. 'It just shows what a lot o' good you can do when you stick up for your kids,' Ada remarked before breaking into a laugh when Johnny clomped into the house that night.

Doddoe sat by the table, bare feet stuck on the range for warmth, a basin of tea in his hand. He turned and greeted Brian: 'Hello, yer young bleeder, what are yo' doin' 'ere?' He was out of work and his hard grizzle-haired head wasn't in the best of tempers. Brian was on the point of answering when Dave said, just back from a scrounge in the kitchen: 'I brought 'im 'ome, dad. He wants summat to eat.'

'He'll get nowt at this bleedin' 'ouse,' Doddoe said. 'We ain't got enough to feed our bleedin' sens.' And he turned back to staring in the fire. Ada came in with a plate of bacon and tomatoes, and Dave sat down to eat. 'How are you, Brian, my owd duck? Is Vera all right?'

'Yes.'

'Has rotten Harold bin on to 'er lately?'

'No.'

'I'll bet you're 'ungry,' she said. 'Are you?' His answers were short, discouraged by Doddoe. 'Well, just wait five minutes and I'll get yer summat.' Dusk filled the room with gloom and shadows, and Dave, chewing a piece of bread from his hand, stood up to switch on the light. 'Yer'd better put that bleeder off,' Doddoe said without turning round. 'We'll have the man 'ere soon to collect some money for the radiogram and we've got nowt to give 'im.'

But Ada said it should stay on: 'When he comes for money Dave can go to the door and tell 'im we're not in. I'm not goin' ter sit 'ere wi'out any light.' Brian ate bacon and tomatoes, dipped his bread in juice and fat, uneasy at eating with Doddoe in the room, though so hungry he couldn't but enjoy the meal.

Johnny finished the net, rolled it up for his father. 'Thanks, Johnny. You're a good lad. I'll gi' yer tuppence in the mornin' when I've sold the rabbits.' Doddoe swung his bare feet from the range, dragged boots from beneath the table and pulled them on without socks, tugging each lace tight through faded eye-holes. He went into the kitchen, and they heard him slinging cold water around his face. As he was donning his topcoat a sharp knock sounded at the door and everyone stopped talking, eating, dressing, playing. 'That'll be the radiogram man,' Ada hissed. 'Go and see 'im. You know what to tell 'im.'

Dave stood up: 'I should. I've 'ad enough practice' – strode to the hallway. Doddoe was both into and out of his topcoat, like a half-draped statue, and Ada held the teapot, about to pour a last cup of tea before he left for the night's poaching. Brian's mouth was full, stayed that way until the crisis was over. The two children stopped playing on the rug, as if they had been trained like seals to be silent at such times. Only the fire flickered in the grate, and that was all right because it made no noise.

Dave opened the door – was greeted by a polite brisk voice saying: 'Good evening.'

'Evenin',' Dave slurred, towering over him.

'I'm from Norris's,' the man explained. 'Is your mother in?'

'She's gone out.'

'Do you know when she'll be back?' He stood in the rain, trying not to get his boots wet. 'She wain't be in tonight,' Dave said, into his stride. 'She's gone to her sister's at Leicester.'

'Will she be back in the morning?' he probed. 'I can call around then.' The briskness was leaving his voice, as though he knew it was a hopeless task.

'She might be away a week. Her sister's badly in hospital and mam might 'ave ter wait till she dies.'

'Oh dear,' the man said consolingly, 'that is bad.' He had a certain technique as well, but it could never succeed. 'You can't get blood out of a bleeding stone,' Doddoe had often said.

'It is, an' all,' Dave agreed.

'Did she leave any money for Norris's man?'

'No.'

'Are you sure? It might be behind the clock.'

'I've looked everywhere for money,' Dave shook his head, 'but there ain't a tanner in the 'ouse.'

The man was on his track: 'Surely she wouldn't go to Leicester for a week and not leave any money to feed the family?'

'Well, she don't know 'ow long she'll be away,' Dave went on, 'an' she said if she's away a long while she'll borrow summat in Leicester and send us a little postal order.'

'I see,' the man said, 'but what about your father? Is *he* in?'

Dave shook his head sadly. 'I don't know where *'e* is. We ain't seen 'im for three days. I 'ope nowt's 'appened to 'im.' Had it not been raining the man might have stood long enough to be fobbed off with a shilling. 'All right,' he said, putting the books into his mac pocket, 'I'll call in three days, on Tuesday say, to see if your mother's in. Tell her if she doesn't pay something soon our men will come to fetch the radiogram back.'

'I'll tell 'er.' Dave shut the door in his face, for he always knew when victory was at hand. The tableau inside dissolved at hearing the man walk up the street. 'Poor bogger,' Ada said with genuine sympathy, 'he's come all that way for nowt.'

'If 'e'd stayed much longer arguin',' Doddoe said, swinging into the other half of his topcoat, 'I'd knocked 'im across the 'ead wi' this cosh.' Brian went on eating, and Ada finished pouring tea for Doddoe. Having milked and sugared it she turned the radiogram on softly, saying: 'I expect we shan't 'ave it much longer.'

'Not if I know it,' Doddoe said, between gulps of tea. 'It'll be in the pawnshop soon.'

'Yo'll get six months for that,' Ada said.

'I'll get no ale if it ain't,' he laughed. 'The dirty rotten bastards wouldn't let a bloke live these days. I allus work when there's work to be had, yo' know that. I'm not going to see my kids fucking-well starve.'

'Yo'll get drowned tonight,' Ada moaned, 'goin' poachin' in this rain.'

'Well,' Doddoe said with finality, crashing the cup down on its saucer, 'we've got ter live, and that's a fact, so there's nowt else for it. I'd rather sit in the Crown all night wi' a jar of ale, but yer'd soon start bleedin'-well moaning if there was nowt on t'table tomorrer.' They listened to the rain a few seconds: 'Anyway, it keeps the gamekeepers quiet.' He took a lamp from the dresser, walked to the back door. 'See yer tomorrer' – and they heard him drag his bike from the shed, then the rickety clack to of the gate before he rode off in pouring rain.

The only verdict was Ada's: 'Poor bleeder.'

'P'raps it'll stop,' said Dave.

Brian stayed to hear a thriller on the wireless, against the background of Johnny in the kitchen sawing wood to make a stool. Dave was right: the world never stayed black and wet for ever; it dried now and again to let Doddoe do his poaching and

Brian make his way home to bed. Stars ran between clouds, and children played within circles of beneficent gaslight as he looked back from the railway fence. One heave took him over, and he went up the embankment with bent back in case he should be silhouetted and attract attention from cops or shunters. A light twinkled far off across the field, then went out as if someone had lit a cigarette. Signals clanked up on another branch of the line and, wanting to beat the train, he leapt wildly from one steel band to another. Stones skidded underfoot and he slipped, scabbing his kneecap when his hand went forward and didn't hold. This unexpected letdown of his limbs filled him with panic, increased by the sound of a locomotive gathering strength from the station, and a low far-off whistle from another train on this jungle network. Gasping and crying out he reached the end rail, and saw the dim expanse of safe and marshy fields in front.

He sat in the nearest grass to get his breath back, as the train charged innocuously by along the embankment above. A horse moved and neighed by a bush. Two people approached, merging like shadows, and talking softly: a courting couple. He counted the concrete steps mounting to the bridge: thirty-two. Lights shone from the colliery below, but it was so dark walking down the lane that he imagined daylight would never come, and fear didn't leave him until he entered the kitchen at home and sat before the fire with a cup of tea and a slice of bread and cheese.

True to his promise, Dave donated the final threepence. Saturday afternoon was warm and dusty, and he walked to Canning Circus, past old houses being knocked down, lorries lining-up to transport rammel to the Sann-eye tips. Crossing the complicated junction he descended via Derby Road, looking into each shop, wondering as he skirted Slab Square what his mother and father would say when they saw him come into the house holding a thick and fabulous book.

A large atlas was opened at a map of the world, surrounded by dictionaries and foreign language books – the only section of the shop that interested him. He went in, and told a brown-dressed girl by the cash-desk that he wanted to buy *The Count of Monte-Cristo*, started to explain the simple financial system into which he had entered.

She left him standing with four pink receipts and the final sixpence, and came back with the manager. 'I know him,' he said. 'He's a customer of ours.' He turned to Brian, took the receipts and the money and spread them on the cash-desk. *The Count of Monte-Cristo* wasn't it? Go and get it for him, will you?'

The book came, and he had only time to glimpse the picture-cover of a man holding a sword before it was taken away and wrapped up.

He opened the packet outside, flipped the hundreds of pages through his fingers, from cover to cover and back again. A posh woman's voice said from behind: 'You're going to be busy, aren't you?' He turned and said yes, ran his eyes up and down the formidable list of chapter titles.

No one was at home, and he sat by the fire to read. The room had been scrubbed and the table cleared, and in the congenial emptiness he sped on through the easy prose of the story, had reached Edmond Dantès' betrothal ceremony before his parents came in. They took off their coats. 'That looks a nice book,' his mother said. 'Where did you get it from?'

'I bought it from downtown.'

'Who gen you all *that* money?' his father put in.

'It must 'ave cost a pretty penny,' his mother said, spreading the cloth for tea.

'Nobody gen me the money,' Brian told them, closing the book carefully. 'I saved it up.'

Irritation came into his mother's voice: 'How much was it?'

'Half a crown.'

'Yer've wasted 'alf a crown on a book?' his father exclaimed. He'd imagined they'd be pleased at his cleverness in bringing such a thing into the house, but it was the opposite. It was as though he'd been split in half and was bleeding to death. All for a book. 'It was *my* money,' he cried, anguished and bitter, because instead of buying the book he should have given the money to them.

'You're bloody-well silly about books,' his father said, a

definite threat in his voice. 'You read till you're bloody-well daft.' His mother came back from the kitchen: 'You stand need to spend half a crown on books when you ain't got a bit o' shoe to your feet. And you're a sly little swine to 'ave money in the 'ouse all that time when I've often bin wi'out a shillin' ter buy some snap.'

'I didn't have the money here,' he explained. 'I took it bit by bit to the bookshop, like a Christmas club.' This was even worse, because he'd made sure that, starving or not, they hadn't been able to get their hands on it.

'You'd 'ave 'ad more sense to a got yoursen a pair o' shoes,' Seaton cried. 'I've a good mind to throw it on the bleddy fire.'

''E's got no more sense than 'e was born with,' his mother said. Brian was horrified at his father's threat, saw flames already at their work. 'It's *my* book,' he shouted.

'Don't cheek me,' Seaton said, 'or you'll be for it, my lad.' His tears were open, and they saw it. 'I hope there's a war on soon so's we're all killed,' he raved.

'What a thing to say,' his mother said. 'I don't know where he gets it from.'

A smack across the head from his father. 'Say one more word, and I'll show yer what I'll do wi' yer.'

'Wait till I grow up,' Brian cried.

But Seaton only said: 'He'll be a lunatic one day wi' reading so many books.'

He sat by the fire while they drank tea, trying to force back the sobs, difficult because he saw too easily how he had done wrong. But hatred and pity for himself surmounted this, and so he couldn't stop. Vera passed him some tea: 'Come on, it ain't the end o' the world.' His eyes were drawn to the book cover, where a brave man held a rapier as if he didn't care for anyone in the world, as though nothing could ever trouble him. And if it did, the face and sword said, it would be an easy matter to fight a duel and dispose of whatever it was.

He ate bread and jam, and went on reading. The story grafted itself to him, slowly becoming him and he becoming it, and he left behind with each second the light and noise in the house and went on wondering footsteps down into the dungeons of the Château d'If with Edmond Dantès, following the guards and slipping invisibly into the cell, and all night long he listened to the tappings and whispers that came from the granite floor, heard the patient scraping and scratching of freedom, was shown that even dungeons and giant prisons were unable to keep men in for ever, though fourteen years was longer by four than he had so far lived: he listened to the chipping of home-made tools, and voices whispering as if from the dead, that talked of knowledge and freedom and hidden treasure on the Island of Monte-Cristo.

13

Mr Bates was powerless to stem the tide of commotion in the classroom. With good reason the boys were excited, everyone talking to everyone else. The regular timetable dissolved as if by magic, and the map of South America – in white chalk for the coastline and brown for the long curving rib of the Andes – was being rubbed out by the prefect, who even forgot himself and shook the chalk rag in the classroom, so that brown and white dustclouds penetrated layers of light slanting in through the windows.

Assembly and prayers had gone by and, to the intense joy of the class, Mr Bates stayed writing at his desk. Brian was close enough to hear the reedy turmoil of his pen and the rustle of overturned paper. What was he writing on a day like this? For whom could he be using these unique minutes? Maybe it was the best he could do while waiting to see what happened, because had he ordered the class into the hall and set them to singing hymns, they would possibly have mutinied, or acquiesced so truculently that hall-discipline would have been impossible.

'Bosworth!' Mr Bates cried, glancing icily at the prefect when dust settled on his coatsleeve and notepaper. 'How many more times do I have to tell you to shake that thing outside?'

But Bosworth recognized his words as a protest, not a threat. 'Sorry, sir,' he said, hung the duster over the easel-lath and went back to his seat after seeing his apology met only by a bent preoccupied head and the sound of a pen scratching across foolscap like the exploring claws of a badger.

Anybody'd think he was writing a book. The noise rose to a climax, a sea beating against the sound-barrier of Mr Bates's pen, until suddenly the stream of his thought was taken in the flank: 'Quiet!' he shouted. The sea didn't fall back, for only those closest, always careful not to make much noise anyway, heard him. 'WILL YOU BE QUIET!' he bawled.

The sea-roar stopped, the waves receded, but the unbearable throb of excited unanimous conversation was replaced by a silence that paralysed Mr Bates's pen. He assumed a stern expression and looked at the forty faces before him, adjusted the spectacles chafing the back of his ear: an unnecessary movement, but he could not at that particular moment keep his hands unoccupied. Every face, from four rows of ancient name-scratched desks with two boys frozen at each, converged on the focal point of his own. He knew quite definitely that each one was waiting, with their silent collective gaze, for him to tell them something – and the passing seconds assumed a pandemonic quality because he did not know what to say. He who held his class always within the bounds of discipline – though never tyrannically so – wavered because for once he could not give them their rightful due of words on a subject spreading like a thornbush through every brain.

'I suppose you all know,' he broke out firmly at last, 'that gas-masks are to be given out today?'

A question to which no answer was needed. Everyone was relieved that he had addressed them with such satisfactory wisdom. Tension drew from each face, and he was aware of a smile growing like an apple rolling as if before wind among them.

'Also,' he went on, easy now that a beginning had been made, 'there won't be any geography or arithmetic lesson.' The smiles became definite, and Mr Bates thought of his half-completed letter. 'Go on talking, but keep your voices down. Mr Jones may be in soon.'

Once more his pen scratched, disguising paper with a camouflage of ink, and slowly – like a great hoarse dynamo that has difficulty in starting – the noice of speculation grew until reaching a level that stopped Mr Bates being aware of it.

'I'm glad there's a war,' Brian said to Jim Skelton. 'Dad says he'll be able to get a job if there is. Then he'll give me a penny every Friday. As long as we aren't gassed, though.'

'I'm not frightened,' Jim replied, 'but what about mam and dad and Maureen and Frank and the others? There's seven of us and we can only just fit into our cellar if bombs start dropping.'

Brian absentmindedly tipped the viscid contents of one inkwell into another, making a black pool on the wood and almost blotting out the first carved letter of his initials. 'But perhaps everybody'll have guns,' he ventured, dabbing at the ink, and wiping it on his jersey.

'We won't get guns,' Jim said. 'Everybody'll have to stop in their cellars. I can't think what we'll do.'

'Your dad'll have to build bunks,' Brian advised. 'He's a joiner, so it'll be easy for him. But our house don't have a cellar to it.'

'You'll go in air-raid shelters, then.' No one had attended to the flowers in the window jars, and their yellow heads drooped for want of water; neither had those detailed entered the temperature or barometer readings on the graphs that stretched in coloured undulations along one wall like a mountain panorama in the geography books; it was inkwell morning and no one had filled them; and no books had been given out. Lack of timetable discipline convinced them that there was no need to be silent, to read, write, or sing, because it was marvellous, miraculous confusion, with all hoping beyond hope that disorganization had come to stay, thinking that if war was this then it wasn't so bad after all.

Brian's idea of war was Napoleonic, at any rate in tactics, with barricades in every street while a gas-masked Waterloo exploded from Clifton Grove to Gotham Village. Moulded by an addiction to *Les Misérables* he saw wagons of paving-stones and sandbag-parapets blocking Denman Street and all approaches to it, while a higher blockage sealed each main road off from the country to stop tanks. His picture showed a tin-hatted soldier with rifle and bayonet running along the cobblestones of Radford streets, while Mr and Mrs Skelton and all the little Skeltons gazed anxiously up from the grill of their cellar grate. Then a bomb would fall and blow up a house, grey bricks shooting into the air, now coloured grey though they had been red before the explosion. Perhaps he, too, like Marius Pontmercy would go off with a rifle to the barricades and fight the Germans (a rifle picked up from a body in the street) and kill many men, saving the Skeltons who, in the proscenium of his mind, still looked anxiously from their cellar grate at the soldier running up the street with bayonet fixed.

Then a container would fall – silently almost – and lay in the gutter, and after a few seconds a slit would open in its side and a yellow vapour spill out and ascend a few feet, then thickly spread. And Brian would put on his gas-mask (which miraculously appeared, for he did not have it a few seconds before) and clamp it over his face. If he saw someone without a gas-mask he would give it to them: for himself, he knew exactly what to do, which was to soak his white handkerchief in water that somehow appeared in the gutter, and lay it over his face. That would stop the mustard gas – or so uncle Doddoe had told him.

And hadn't his mother said there were to be trenches on the Forest, as in the last war? He saw people wearing gas-masks filing into them as twin-plane aircraft came over to drop bombs – like he had seen them blasting the slum-dump ruins of Albion Yard. Then a change of scene as enemy – German of course – soldiers came over the green-painted railing far away and advanced through mist towards the trenches, so that conveniently and from nowhere English soldiers streamed out to repel them, and Brian somehow mixed himself up with them and killed so many Germans with the rifle he carried that he was asked to organize a schoolboy battalion, of which he would be commander-in-chief.

'You won't get a gas-mask.'

Gruff and indignant: 'What do you mean? Why?'

'Because you've already got one, ugly mug.'

Through the glass partition of the next classroom chairs and tables moved, feet shuffled, and orders were carried out. A report was passed from a daring observer: big boxes were being heaved in from outside and laid on tables. There was a smell of rubber. 'Frenchies,' someone called, 'that's what they are' – as the words Large Medium Small were shouted time after time.

Brian caught the note of jubilation that swamped the class: it was after ten, and would soon be playtime so that a rush for straws and milk could commence.

A second later he filled his underbreath mind with swearing, telling himself that he above all should have known that such freedom was too good to last: Mr Jones walked in. Mr Bates did not push the letter out of sight as he usually did, but left it lying on his desk and turned his chair to look at the small tight dynamite headmaster as he entered the room. There was no need to tell the boys to stop talking, for even the sea would fall silent at Mr Jones's shadow. He stood compact within a vacuum of silence, and Brian felt an itching behind his neck, but held his arm fast from scratching for fear of drawing notice to himself. Jim Skelton's eye went into a winking match but Brian did not take him up on it, seeing his lips curl up at one corner as if to smile. He'd better not make me laugh, the rotter. A lorry roared along the street and pulled up at the school door. The milk's come, he guessed, but when he didn't hear the clash of filled cases coming through the hall he assumed it was another load of gas-masks.

'They weren't very quiet,' Mr Jones said. Brian watched his plasticine pellet: if it rolled quick, he wouldn't hit anyone; if it rolled slow, he was bound to.

'It's hard to keep them quiet on a day like this,' Mr Bates said as he casually slid the letter in his desk. Mr Jones became sarcastic: 'I feel sure you could have done better than that.'

'They're excited.'

Picture-clouds of war plagued every brain, and the outposts of fear that preceded Mr Jones as he walked among masters and boys had been neutralized by the overwhelming bomb of a question that smoked to varying shades in the hearts of boys and masters alike. 'I still say there's nothing to be excited about,' he snapped.

When is the old bastard going? Brian wondered. Why can't he leave us to talk, or let Mr Bates read summat good to us? If there's a war I hope that old bastard's the first to cop it, with a great big bomb (the biggest bomb in the world if it can be managed) right on to his spiteful white loaf. Or maybe a Jerry will get him with a rifle when they start sniping from chimney-pots. You never know, these days.

'They wouldn't be excited if they knew what war meant.'

'Boys never know what war means,' Mr Bates said.

'It's a pity they can't be told then, and have some of this excitement drained from them.'

Mr Bates's eyes gleamed, as if about to water; he smiled to stop them doing so. 'There'd be no cannon-fodder for the war after the one that's about to start if that happened.'

Mr Jones looked hard at him, then at the class. 'Are they all here?'

'Ten are absent.'

'Too excited to come to school, even?' A few bold spirits began to whisper, and hisses passed from across the room like jets of escaping steam. 'Silence!' he roared, his anaemic face flushing.

There was silence.

'What do you intend doing?' he asked Mr Bates. 'They can't go on like this, war or no war.'

'I'll probably read to them.'

Mr Jones snorted. 'Let me use your desk.' He moved aside and sat in a chair, a stack of 'Foundations of History' rearing at the back of his head.

'I suppose you all know that they're giving gas-masks out today?' Mr Jones addressed them.

He knows bleddy-well we do.

'Any of you know what a gas-mask is like?'

Not yet, but we will.

'I'll describe one to you. A word-picture of one.' Brian remembered: the first Jerry shooting from a chimney-stack ought to put one right into his four-eyed clock. 'There's a rubber facepiece, with a celluloid frame you can see through, and to this are attached straps that you pull back over your head to hold it on. Very neat and well thought out. Now, under the chin is what's known as a filter. This is what you breathe through. This is what makes the poison gas harmless before it gets to your mouth and nose. Simple, isn't it? Any questions?'

No questions.

'I didn't think so. You've all got heads made of putty. You wouldn't think a putty-head would need a gas-mask, but it does.' A few crawlers laughed. Mr Jones grinned at his own joke. 'All right, putty-heads, I've told you what a gas-mask's made of. Now I'll tell you what it's *for*. It's to be used in case (or should I say when?) German aeroplanes drop poison-gas bombs on Nottingham.' He paused, possibly for questions, perhaps for some reaction, but they hadn't heard enough.

'Anyone know what a black-out means?' No answer. 'Well, putty-heads, it means that no lights of a city can be put on, that everything's kept in complete and total darkness so that German planes flying above won't know where they are. And at such times you'll all have to go to bed early because there'll be no sense playing in the streets when it's pitch dark. And you'll carry your gas-masks to bed with you, careful not to drop or damage them. If you do, then you'll be in a fine fix when the bombs fall, won't you? So you'll take the gas-mask out of its cardboard box and place it by your bed for when the air-raid warning sounds.'

He settled himself comfortably at the desk. All day, Brian moaned. 'Of course, when they do go and you hear bombers coming over, there'll be no need to put your gas-mask on. Only when a man comes around the streets with a klaxon do you do that, and when gas *is* dropped you all act very quickly – except the putty-heads, of course – and pull the masks over your faces. Naturally, if any of you have smaller brothers and sisters you'll help them with theirs before putting on your own.'

His bloodless head turned from one side of the class to the other, and as his face passed the front both eyes were blotted out by circles of light as big as his glasses. 'Something else,' came from his mouth: 'Do any of you know when poison gas was first used in a big battle?'

One hand did: 'In the Great War.'

'Ah. So you're not all putty-heads. Yes, quite right. Fifty thousand Frenchmen (and many British) were gassed by an afternoon breeze at Ypres. All the troops saw was a greenish yellow fog coming towards them at dusk and soon scores of hundreds of men were choking from it. Those who got away from the trenches were blinded or injured for life, and lines stretched for miles as each man followed the one in front to the hospitals behind the lines. Yes, war is a lamentable business, and isn't worth getting excited about, is it? IS IT THEN, YOU PUTTY-HEADS?' he roared, his gunburst lifting even the sleepiest from their daydreams.

A few voices sent out a mixture of yes and no.

'It's hard to tell you what war is, but I can promise one thing: there'll be plenty of pain flying about. I suppose the easiest pain I can think of in war is when you have to queue all day in the snow for food or coke, and when you have to eat horse flesh at the end of it, and when you have to listen to the noise of sirens. Not much pain there, is there? However it's possible that the war will still be on when you're men, and one of the hardest pains perhaps is when one is left wounded after a battle without water or food. War is taking place in China and Spain at this moment, and happened in Abyssinia not so long ago, so what I'm telling you shouldn't seem so impossible, though judging by your faces you aren't bright enough to take in much of what I'm saying.'

He knows we're all waiting to get to the playground for our milk, Brian said to himself, but he's keeping us in out of spite, the sly bastard. 'Do any of you really know what pain is? I suppose you think it's pain when my fist clouts your putty heads to make you pay attention? Well, let me tell you, it's not. It's nothing to what pain is in war. Ah, yes, I know, you're all excited about the gas-masks and the war that's coming. Well, you should be praying to God that by a miracle it doesn't begin. For war means nothing but pain. Some people escape it, but don't let that be a comfort to you, because during a war the earth will convulse with pain, and it will get you and me and possibly everyone else. So let's have no excitement over the thought of war.'

He broke off and strode out of the room, and they heard the next class fall quiet as he went among them.

It's all lies, Brian thought. Even if it's the truth, it's a lie. But he also scoffed at his own fiction of the barricades and pyramids of dead on paving-stones, convinced of nothing except the bursting top of his milk bottle at playtime and the pushing in of a straw before sucking cool liquid into the dry chalk of his mouth, a liquid that nevertheless still tasted like the dull and sluggish iodine-pain that old Jones had blabbed about.

At four in the afternoon he ran home clutching a cardboard box, and burst into the house as his father was having tea. There'd been a rumour in class while waiting to be served the respirators, that everyone had to pay for them, so much a week, and Brian had been pleasantly surprised to note when it was actually put into his hand that payment hadn't been mentioned at all, at which he assumed that he had been given an expensive piece of equipment absolutely free. 'Look what I've got,' he called out, swinging his treasure-box on its string. They were uninterested. Then he saw three others on the floor in a corner, their boxes already bent and battered, a strap hanging from one, Arthur doing his best to break up another. His mother was reading the *Post*: 'There'll be no peace in *our* time,' she said scornfully, laying it aside to pour Brian a cup of tea.

'No,' Seaton answered, in splendid gruff prophecy, 'nor in any other bloody time, either.'

14

Mr Jones walked in with no preliminary spying. Dapper, smart, his jaw like that on a ventriloquist's dummy, he held up a slip of paper and called, not overloud, 'Robertson, come out.'

Brian heard a movement behind, and a gangly eleven-year-old walked to the front. Mr Jones stood by the blackboard, hid Ceylon with a head as fiercely threatening as the cobra that represented the island. 'So you're Robertson?'

He admitted it, though reluctantly; not knowing where to put his hands, he tried to get them into his trouser pockets but was baffled when their entrances seemed to have closed up against him. 'Keep your hands by your side when you speak to me,' Mr Jones roared, smacking him across the ear. He held the menacing piece of paper up to his nose, chafing it like a fly so that Robertson got a smack on the other ear for trying to brush it off. 'I've had a complaint about you from a lady who lives near by. She says you broke her window with a football and used foul language when she came out to you.'

Robertson looked to one side, and said nothing.

'Well?' – in a roar that told the whole school he was on the warpath again. Parts of his face were streaked with tiny purple veins, like rivers on a finely drawn map, though his lips were bloodless. 'Have you nothing to say, blockhead?'

Out of a sound of slow choking came: 'I didn't cheek her off, sir.'

Clap! 'That's for being a liar as well. I'll teach you to use foul language, and lie to me.' He turned to the motionless teacher sitting at the high stool by his desk: 'Give me your stick, Mr Bates.'

The boy did not move when ordered to hold out his hand.

'Are you deaf?' Mr Jones screamed. He's looney, Brian said to himself. If we all rushed him though, we'd pulverize 'im. Robertson made as if to turn to the rest of the class, but no one could help him, being arranged at their desks in a helpless dead silence. 'If you don't hold out your hand, I'll make you hold it out.' He brought the stick back and slashed at the boy's shoulder with all his strength, but Robertson dodged it and ran, opened the door with unrehearsed dexterity and slammed it behind him. He was heard clattering to safety along the street, running to the protection of his unemployed father. Mr Jones threw the stick down and strode out.

Brian missed both verse and chapter from the Bible-reading that followed. On the streets, in your own land when playing at night, you still weren't safe from the long arm of Mr Jones. Even miles away in quiet and hedge-bound fields his rage seemed out to get you: next morning in school he might confront you with stick and piece of paper with your name on both demanding to know why you were in a certain field last night when a notice on the gate said quite plainly that trespassers would be prosecuted. Trespassers will be persecuted, more like it, persecuted by bastards like old dead Jones.

The only place he felt safe was at the Nook. Beyond the valley of the Lean and across the new boulevard he made his way every week-end of the autumn. After the harvest a pig was killed and the pork salted for Christmas. Mary made a list in the back of an old laundry book of those who wanted to buy a piece, and Brian would carry a loaded basket under the railway bridge and deliver to different houses in Radford Woodhouse.

Merton had set the date for the slaughter. 'Percy'll be 'ere at three, so I'll not go upstairs to bed.'

Brian was at the table shelling a bowl of peas: 'What pig are yer goin' ter kill, grandad?'

'Come wi' me, and I'll show yer.' He took his stick, and as he walked out and along the yard Brian noticed for the first time his slightly bent shoulders. Maybe he is very old, he thought, remembering his father's reference to him of 'that owd bogger'.

Merton pointed into the pig-sty. 'That one, Nimrod. See it?'

Black and pink, they huddled together near the trough, squealing at the expectation of an unlatched gate with buckets of food to follow. 'See it? That fat bogger as can 'ardly move.' He turned away to roll a cigarette.

'Will it hurt it when you kill it, grandad?'

'Nay,' Merton said, his face lost in smoke. 'A man comes up special to kill it. I can't do it myself 'cause I ain't got a licence.' He turned and smacked one of the pigs across its rump for pushing a nose too insistently at the door of the sty, then took a steel scoop from the wash-house wall and stirred the large barrel of crusts and old potatoes, meal and bran. Brian unhooked the latch, and the pigs, smelling food, squealed and crowded at the empty trough so that Merton couldn't get to it. He put the buckets down: 'Pass my stick, Nimrod: I'll get the boggers out o' the way.'

Buckets of meal splashed into the trough, the pigs congealed into a solid row, gurgling and gobbling, Brian fascinated at the swill-level going down before his eyes.

The pig to be killed was driven from the food by Merton's stick, kept wild-eyed and squealing in a corner until the rest had finished and were looking round for more. It was as if the sky had altered colour for it. While the rest seemed happy at not having been singled out for this limbo before death, the victim walked round the sty with nose to the ground, sniffing with nervous quickness. Its steel grey eyes, deeply sunk into an obese face, gazed at the sty fence that Merton and Brian leaned against; then it walked back to the trough, still unable to believe it had been left out, and expecting to find food there, hoping that its last sensation of having been set apart from some incomprehensible purpose had been only a dream. But it kept walking around the sty, repeating these expeditions to the trough, in between time squealing loudly with fear at the incontrovertible difference thrust upon it.

The pig-killer arrived, a small man of forty with a brown wrinkled face and a grey moustache. He wore a flat greasy cap and lit a cigarette as he stopped near the kitchen door. Over the cross-bar of his bike hung a small sack, in which he carried knives and an apron. 'We ain't hard up for time,' Merton said.

'So we'll 'ave a cup o' tea first.' Brian followed them into the kitchen: 'Can I watch the pig being killed, grandad?'

'Yer can for me. It wain't hurt yer to see a drop o' blood.' His grandmother overheard. 'Don't let 'im. It ain't nice. You'll see enough blood when you're a big lad.'

'He'll be all right,' Merton said.

But Mary didn't want Brian to see it. He'd have bad dreams, she maintained, and Merton agreed: ay, maybe he would. Mary in fact wished the pigs could have gone to the slaughterhouse, for such piteous dying squeals chilled her; so she stayed in the parlour, turned chalk-white when the death blow was struck. It was impossible not to tremble for them: 'Poor thing!' she muttered. 'Poor thing!'

A large tin bath was placed on the table outside. Percy sorted his knives, got Brian to tie the strings of his apron: 'Mek a tight bow, there's a good lad.' A continual grunting and squealing came from the sty, as if the pigs were somehow able to smell the last bloodstains already washed from the slaughterer's knife. Buckets of boiling water were carried from the wash-house copper until the bath was two-thirds full. 'I might 'ave another done next month,' Merton said, 'if I get enough orders for this one.' More people were wanting meat than last year, for work was coming back on the market. 'You know where to find me,' Percy said.

The final column of hot steam was poured into the bath. 'I'll mek it right,' Merton promised. 'There'll be a good piece for yo'.' The poultry hatches were abnormally quiet: even the dogs and cats had fled from the vicinity of the house, though would be back for scraps when the carve-up began.

Brian felt afraid at this silent inexorable display of purpose. Each twig of the near-by tree was significant and isolated as before a thunderstorm. His grandmother had forgotten he was outside, and had gone into the parlour until it was all over. Part of the yard where he stood was empty, for Percy and his grandfather had gone to get the pig from the sty. A wall of cloud darkened the yard and, strangely enough, even the pigs weren't whining any more. He knew this to be a good time to escape without being thought foolish by his grandfather, yet he was unable to go indoors, was held by a gap in the hedge that showed him the dead fixity of a stubbled cornfield.

Squeals came round the corner, with scuffling and the smack of Merton's stick across a pig's back. Then the vacuum of silence was overfilled by every pig screaming at once.

They dragged the half-crazed animal along the ground, its eyes staring like ball-bearings to where it was being taken, but seeing nothing because the squeals were in its eyes and blinding it. Legs kicked from its podged body. Merton cursed, hit it with the stick he still managed to hold, but the blows only confirmed the animal's instinct that it was going towards some terrible fate, and so caused it to squeal louder.

Those left in the sty were infected with its fear, joined the lament in the hope that they would not be next. With one heave the pig was on the table. Merton held its hind legs and Percy the front. It stared at a patch of blue sky through the branches of the alder tree. Then its head went to one side, and in the distance Brian heard a train passing, as if the pig had turned to watch it at that moment. Percy reached for a wooden-handled knife, held it above the pig's throat. The blade curved, almost sickle-shaped: like that picture of Shylock, occurred to Brian. His arm came down strongly, pierced the throat and ripped it sideways. A metallic, almost human cry covered the house, and died quickly, like a train whistle.

Blood was aimed into a bucket and nearly filled it. They lifted the pig (heavy like iron now) into the bath, and the steaming water changed magically to pink. 'Well,' Merton said, 'that's that.' Percy wiped his knife on a cloth.

That's what pigs is for, Brian said to himself. Its trough-searching snout was dead meat, ready to be cooked and eaten. On the point of tears he remembered its struggle: that's what it's for though, and now he had seen it. He went into the house.

'Is it dead then?' Mary asked.

Merton was angry that she looked so pale. ''Course it is, why?'

'Nothing.' She filled the kettle to make tea.

'There yer goo agen,' he exclaimed, 'worryin' yersen to death over the bleddy pig. Anybody would think I was a bleddy murderer. The soddin' ta-tas we 'ave over this. Don't ye know you've got to kill a pig to get summat t'eat?' Brian had heard his mother say that these words passed every time between them. 'I know. But they squeal so.'

Merton took a packet of Robin from the shelf and offered Percy one. 'Well, that's their fault. We kill 'em as neat as we can. I hope I die as quick, that's all I can say.'

After tea, the oil-lamp lit, Mary stood in the pantry salting the pork. There was a great block of salt on the kitchen table, and Merton knocked off lumps, crushing them to powder with a rolling pin, filling basins for Brian to carry down the pantry steps. Slabs of pork hung from the ceiling, so clean that it seemed life was still in it. Bowls were filled with blood and lengths of intestine ready for blackpuddings next day. All Brian's sympathy for the pig had gone – except that on his way to bed faint squeals from its dying returned, and during the night mixed with train whistles that made excursions into his dreams.

Pink houses of new estates were spilling into the countryside. Men with black and white poles and notebooks came across the new boulevards into lanes and fields; they set theodolites and dumpy levels pointing in sly angles at distant woods, into and over the Cherry Orchard where the Arlingtons and Lakers lived, invading Brian's hideouts, obliterating his short-cuts and concealed tracks towards the Nook.

After the surveyors came the clearance men, groups of pioneer navvies breaking down hedges and making trenches in a straight line out from the boulevard. It was no longer a lonely walk from Radford: trees were ripped out of the soil, ditches dug, and the first markings of a road skirted the Nook by a few hundred yards. Brian walked out with his grandfather one day. 'What are they doing all this for?' It was like pictures he had seen of the Great War: an open landscape scored with trenches, stretching over to the black wall of Serpent Wood. 'Going to build 'ouses and shops,' Merton told him, sounding as though he didn't like the idea of it. 'What do they want to build 'em just 'ere for, though?'

'Because they've got nowhere else to build, I suppose.' He

slashed at the remaining twig-sprouts of a bush, as if angry that it had let itself be pulled to ruin so easily. Brian liked the idea of buildings going up: he would see men coming along with machines, trains of lorries bringing bricks and mortar. Instead of woods and fields, houses would appear along new roads, would transform the map in his mind. The idea of it caught at him like fire: 'When will they start building then?'

'Not for a long time, Nimrod. They've got to finish clearing yet. Then there's the drains to be put down. It might be a couple o' years before they get the first one up.' But Merton was wrong. Allotment gardens, football pitch and wheatfields were soon under the hammers of annihilation. Brian looked one Saturday from the bedroom window to see enormous lorries unloading drainage pipes not far from the Nook. The bricked-out foundations of houses were already visible near the boulevard.

Seaton was able to get a job on a factory site downtown. There was even an urgency for overtime, and he would be out of the house for twelve hours in fine weather. On the first day Brian took him a can of tea, saw him among a gang of other men shovelling sand from a lorry. He waved and came over to the fence, his black hair hidden by a new cap, and wearing a workjacket too big for him. Having subbed a pound from the gaffer, he was able to push money into Brian's hand: 'Here y'are, my owd flower. Tell yer mam there'll be a lot more on Friday as well.' He turned back to his work. Brian shouted out a good-bye and walked off, unwilling to look at his father who, he thought, might for some reason be angry if he did so while he was working. To Brian he was captured, taken from being king of the house and set among strangers where he seemed insignificant.

Yet it was worth it, everyone agreed, for there was more food in the house. There was also more money, and though it had been supposed up to then that the lack of it had been the cause of all their quarrels, it was soon clear that they went on anyway from force of habit. Seaton was born with his black temper and would die of it, and Vera had never been able to express and defend herself, first against her father, then against her husband.

The only thing she could do with any thoroughness was worry, which probably sprang from thinking she hadn't had the best out of life and never would. If there was nothing tangible to worry about she was bored, so there was always something to be harassed into a problem. The house was too small to keep her busy all the time, and rather than make or repair clothes she found it easier to buy cheap new ones. Her hands were clumsy and without confidence: patches and rips to be sewn were swiftly bodged, and in spite of washday and family meals there was still time to worry, often over lesser things of the house that didn't really matter. Now and again the whole family became embroiled in explosive quarrels about nothing: pots flew and fists struck out, and everyone from mother and father down were isolated by bitterness and misery, until the violence of it, after several hours, thinned itself out into their bloodstreams and brought them happily together again.

By another long bout of saving, this time more open, Brian bought his second book: *Les Misérables*. He'd heard it as a serial on the wireless, had been enthralled by the grandiose surprises of its plot. 'Nineteen years for a loaf of bread!' was a cry rising like a monolith of burning truth from the placid waters and unruffled jungle that hid the murderous go-getters of Treasure Island, and stifled the inane parrot-cry of 'Pieces of eight! Pieces of eight!' Hounded by the police, impervious to bullets at the barricades, carrying a wounded man on his shoulders through the serpentine arteries of the Parisian sewers, Jean Valjean's lifelong fight and death seemed an epic of reality. It was a battle between a common man, and the police who would not let him be free because he had once stolen a loaf of bread for the children of his starving sister. And after such terrifying adventures of this man who did not want to be an outlaw, death was the only freedom he was allowed to find by the author of this bitter and sombre book. Good and bad were easily separated. On one side were Thenardier and Inspector Javert – both against a society of equals because Thenardier needed the rich to thieve from, and Javert the poor to persecute. On the other side were Fantine, Gavroche, Jean Valjean, Marius Pontmercy, Cosette – the weak, the young, the revolutionaries – those who could not live with the former in their midst. The barricades were stormed, the insurgents killed, but the novel was read and re-read, and read again.

There was no fight when he brought the book into the house: 'Why!' Seaton said with a laugh, 'the little bogger's gone and bought another book. I don't know. I wish I was as clever as he is. He beats me at being a scholar.' He gave him fourpence to see the film of the book, and made him tell all about it when he came home. The last creditor of the week-end had been fobbed off with a shilling, and Seaton sat by the fire, with a basin of warm tea beside him on the hob. Vera switched off the noisy row of a football match and went back to darning a pair of socks. The light was on, and Arthur could be heard up in the garret-bedroom playing with a hammer.

'And when Jean Valjean came back to the bridge to keep his promise,' Brian was saying to his father, 'Javert worn't there any longer. And when he looked over the bridge into the water he saw that Javert (Charles Laughton played 'im) had chucked hissen in and was drowned. That's where the picture ended, but the book goes on for a long time after that. Shall I tell you 'ow the book ends?'

''E don't want to 'ear it,' Vera said, a tone that made Brian uneasy because he couldn't see whether or not it was meant as a joke: 'Do you, dad?'

''Course I do, my lad.' He finished his story, pronouncing the French names in the imitated accents of the radio serial. Margaret stood before him, her long straight hair framing a mischievous laugh. It wasn't long before her gaze penetrated: 'I could die at our Brian saying them funny words.'

'If yer do,' Brian said, 'I'll bash yer.'

'I'll bash yer back as well, wi' our dad's bike pump.' She edged towards the window, to observe in safety his increase of rage. 'He thinks 'e can talk French; I can talk it better than 'im.' She gabbled quickly, imitating a foreign language.

'I'm tellin' yer,' Brian threatened.

'Pack it up,' the old man said.

Margaret stopped a moment, but the more afraid she grew the more something inside her said he knew she was becoming afraid, and that she should continue taunting to prove him wrong. 'Booky!' she cried. 'Allus reading books.'

'Leave 'im be,' Vera said to her, 'or I'll start.' Brian felt the flesh at his mouth jumping, such a high twitch he imagined all could see it. Maybe there *was* something shameful in reading books, in imitating French, in writing, in drawing maps, that he was putting himself beyond their reach. He couldn't quite grasp or understand the sense of betrayal, though its connexion with books had been clearly seen and picked out by the others as his most exposed nerve. He knew he should show indifference to their taunts, but they touched something too deep for that. He stood by the table, a few feet from his tormentor. 'Look,' Margaret sang out, ''e's goin' ter cry!'

'I'll mek yo' cry if yer don't shurrup,' he exclaimed. Seaton came out of his huddle by the fire: 'Now stop arguin' or you'll get sent ter bed out o' the way. You're allus on, the pair o' yer.'

'She started it,' Brian said bitterly. 'She's allus causin' trubble.'

'No I didn't, our dad,' Margaret threw back. 'It's 'im: 'e reads all them books till 'e's daft.' She had heard her parents say this, and it cut into him like a knife.

Brian ran, sent a couple of quick thumps to her shoulder, and made for the door before his father could get at him. He was in the street, and heard Margaret crying as he went by the window, and his father saying: 'Wait till the little sod comes back, then 'e'll get it.'

But he didn't return for two hours, by which time everybody had forgotten his attack, except Margaret herself. The parents were out, and she clenched her fist on the other side of the table, showing it to him menacingly while he cut himself some bread. Soon they were playing Ludo.

Some mornings Seaton turned a deaf ear to the knocking-up man, and even to Vera when she railed by his side: 'Come on, Harold, if you don't get up you'll be late. The knocking-up man's bin a long time ago.'

At the third nudge he mumbled from the sheets that he wasn't going. 'Don't be idle,' she said. He went back to sleep with: 'I'm not effing-well going in' – meaning that if he was to lose a day's pay he was certainly intending to get the bliss of a lie-in.

Later, downstairs and eating, he would say: 'They did without me for six years, they can do without me today. I'm at no effer's beck and call.'

'You'll get the sack,' she said, taking the pots away.

'Not any more. There's a war coming. And bring that cup back: I want some more tea.' These days and mornings off weren't so frequent as to cause alarm. Vera knew he wasn't idle, and Seaton knew it too. Work had always been blood in his veins, but since his life-sentence to dole and means test he didn't find it so easy to climb down from the scrapheap. On those days when he hadn't been to work Brian would come home from school and find him in a blacker fouler and more vicious mood than he'd ever got into even on the most desperate of penniless dole days.

One Monday morning Mr Jones didn't turn up at school and word was tom-tommed around that he was ill, had caught a cold going home in the rain on Friday. The lessons went on as before, only more relaxed. Why can't 'e allus stay away? Brian wondered. There don't need to be a headteacher. He liked learning, but now and again during the free week he somehow expected Mr Jones, by a supreme effort of spite, to come, still sick like a phantom from his bed, and scare the happy class merely by showing his gargoyle face above the partition. In any case, after a week-end gang fight Brian was apprehensive lest some parent, whose boy had been cut above the eye by a flying stone, should have reported the skirmish, and that Mr Jones would break in during the scripture lesson and read out names from a list he waved in his hand – Brian Seaton being at the head of it.

He didn't return the following week either. There was a lack of desperate noisiness in the yard at playtime, which meant more laughter and less nose-bleeders. Brian went early to school one day because it was his turn to enter the temperature and barometric readings on the wall-graph. Several boys were already in the classroom talking softly, and something was obviously up, for two looked as if about to weep, and one actually was making silent and helpless tears as if somebody had blown cigarette-smoke into his eyes. This was the prefect, and the others were favourites of Mr Jones who had never been under his wrath. They tolerated Brian's company however because his examination results were often as high as theirs.

'What's up, Johnnoe?' he asked, entering the readings.

'Mr Jones's dead,' Johnson told him.

The thought gave him pleasure, extended the vista of easy lessons. 'Don't kid me.'

'He's dead. I'm not fibbin'.'

'It's true,' somebody else said. 'It was last night: from pneumonia.' The graph finished, Brian dashed from the room and met Jim Skelton coming into the playground. He hugged him, pulled him into an embrace and tried to dance.

'What's up?' Jim asked. 'What's up, Brian?'

'Jones 'as snuffed it,' he said. 'He's stone dead and kicked the bucket. Honest-to-God and cut my throat if I tell a lie.'

Jim's ginger hair blew in the wind: 'You bleeding liar. Stop 'aving me on.'

Brian laughed: 'That's what *I* said to 'em, but it's true. He got pneumonia and kicked it. Johnson just towd me. If yer don't believe it go into the classroom and see 'im and 'is pals blubbering.'

It sank in; they seemed ready to cry at the good news, just as the others were crying at the bad. 'Well, owd Brian, it's about time, ain't it?' He brought out a packet of marbles. 'I'll share 'em wi' yer, then we can play.'

Prayers were said, and collections made for a fitting wreath: Brian dropped a ha'penny into the box. Any boy wishing to attend Mr Jones's funeral, it was said, would be given half a day off. Brian measured the pleasure of a break from lessons, and decided it wasn't worth it. Three teachers went to the funeral, and under the lax discipline there was a subdued air of rejoicing.

15

Water, gravel, cement and sand were shovelled and poured into the circling cannon-like mouth of the concrete mixer. With these ingredients well shaken to a grey pulp the mouth lifted upwards, still turning, stayed there for a time as if wondering whether to let itself go and spit its cement up at the cloudless sky. Then, as if remembering its humble fixed purpose in life, it gave a shudder of regret, and turned its mouth over to the side opposite Brian to pour its cement-guts dutifully into a huge vat.

He walked on, weighed down by four blue mash-cans of scorching tea. Fresh-planed woodplanks slanted from doorways and windows, clean smelling of resin and tar, giving off newness even more acceptable to the blood than buds in spring. A man, hosing down a stack of bricks, called: 'Yo' got my tea, young 'un?'

Brian stopped: 'What's yer name then, mate?'

'Mathews. That's it, that one there.' Brian had found it hard at first to remember who owned what mash-can. Four or five faces were fixed in his mind when he collected them, but when he got back he stood desperately trying to distinguish between them while at the same time looking as if he'd merely stopped for a moment to watch the progress of work – until a man would call out for his can. Brian would give it to him, and no mistakes were made, though by the time he caught on to the ease of this system he knew most of the faces anyway. Mathews slid the can from his wrist: 'I'll pay yer grandma Friday, tell 'er.'

'All right, but if she says no, I'll cum back an' c'lect it.'

He looked around. 'Will yer now? You're a bleddy sharp 'un, an' no mistake.'

'I've got to be, ain't I?'

'Wi' some, I dare say you 'ave. 'Ow much do yo' get for this, anyway?'

'Grandma gi's me a bob on Sat'day.'

'Not bad for a young 'un.' Brian's summer holidays passed in fetching and taking their cans, running to Woodhouse for more tea and sugar, and gathering the money on Friday. The boundaries of fields had been trodden in by lorry ruts and brick stacks, and houses had made a rush forward during the spring as if they'd grown with the leaves. Some by the boulevard were almost finished, their tops still grinning like the pink tents of an army or circus – urged on, it seemed, by the totem poles of factory chimneys in the smoking city behind. The sputtering sound of concrete mixers blended in the hot summer air with the klaxon-throated cockerels from the Nook, and privet hedges by the gate were dusty from powdered concrete.

The Nook was lighted by electricity, was magically blessed with water-taps so that the bucket-yoke hung as useless as a souvenir on the wash-house wall. The surface of the land was changing, becoming covered like memory, though Brian realized as he walked for the first time along new-laid pavements that the familiar soil underneath would never be difficult to reach. There was even soil under Slab Square in the middle of Nottingham, he realized, but that was harder to believe in.

With the money he earned he bought novels, dictionaries and maps, browsed through the threepenny boxes in the basement of a secondhand bookshop downtown. His father hammered a shelf together in the bedroom so that they wouldn't litter the kitchen. Books fitted into a separate part of his life, divided from reality by the narrow pen-knife cut of a canyon that he could cross and re-cross with ease. The book world was easily defendable because he was alone in it and without competitors – though it was occasionally threatened by his father's resentful glare if he had them strewn over the table when supper-time was near and tea called for.

From where they were working on the foundations, past the singing of trowels as bricks were tapped into position by plumbline and spirit-level, to where whole walls were complete and surrounded by scaffolding, Brian walked with his final can of tea. He watched a man ascend a swaying ladder with a hod of bricks: he was tall, thin and agile, blessed with a good sense of balance and seemingly without fear. Someone from the top platform shouted out that he be careful, but he responded by a wave of the arm and by tackling the next few steps without holding on, ending his antic by sending a few swear-words like handclaps into the air. Brian wondered where he'd heard the voice, seen the lanky figure before: stood watching him unload his bricks and talk – friendly despite his swearing – with the bricklayers up top. He took off his cap to scratch his head, then came down the ladder swinging the emptied hod round and round like a mace. One man called to another: 'Owd Agger's a real glutton for wok. I ain't seen nobody as can goo up ladders like he can, ev yo'?'

'He wants to be careful though. I 'eard as a bloke on them new houses near Bilborough broke both his legs last week. He'll get a lot o' compo though.'

Agger went to a stack of steaming bricks, and Brian decided to go close and greet him: 'Ey up, Agger.'

'Hey up, kid' – only a glance. He was the same, a combination of the words 'jaunty' and 'gaunt', and his lined face had the regular features of a hard exterior life without realizing it too much within. He seemed easier though, relaxed compared to a year ago on the harder more uncertain battlefield of the Sann-eye tips. His eyes had lost some of their haunted ironic glare, were as agile and good-humoured in fact as his limbs at the climbing of ladders.

'Don't yer goo on tips any more?' Brian hoped he wouldn't crack him one at thinking he and not Bert had stolen his prize rake on that far-off day.

'Not since I got a job. I di'n't want to stop all my life on t' tips, kid. Anyway, my missis passed on.' He spoke as if to an adult, and Brian wondered what his wife dying had to do with getting work. He counted twelve bricks being placed on the hod. 'So I couldn't mess about much longer. I knock up above fifty bob a week now, you know.' He felt Agger's pride: his father was in work, hadn't been able to get it up to then simply because it wasn't on the market. Why didn't Agger say this? 'It's an 'ard life on the tips, kid. This is better graft for us' – was as far as he would go.

'You said it,' Brian agreed, realizing that he had been taken as a full-time worker and feeling pleased about it. Agger smiled: 'They've set you on as a mash-lad, 'ave they?' Brian told him the tariff drawn up by his grandmother, and Agger said he'd like a can as well, every morning at ten if he could manage it. 'I'll gi' yer a tanner on Friday.' He hoisted the bricks on his shoulder, and was half-way up the ladder before Brian turned to deliver his last can of tea.

Merton didn't like the idea of leaving the Nook, and said as much to Tom who came for his fortnight's rent. Mary laid the open book on the table, four half-crowns and sixpence down the dividing line of the middle. 'I thought they were going to leave it a year or two,' she said, 'what wi' tekin' so much trouble putting in water and electricity.'

Tom scooped up the money and wrote it in: 'It's the land they want you see. As far as the railway and over to the woods.'

'Aye,' Merton grunted, 'they're bleddy gluttons for it.' He stood near the window, a tall thin figure wearing black trousers from an old suit, a brown cardigan and well-polished laced-up boots. He'd finished his momentous fifty-odd years of work as a blacksmith, and now gave his strength to the garden, to chopping wood and seeing to his pigs and poultry – taking it soft, as he termed it. There was no work for Brian to do; Merton shouldered it himself as if, despite his fifty years' hard labour, he hadn't yet worked the violence out of himself, as if he had been put on the earth to attack life rather than live it, to subdue it with hammer and pickaxe, tunnelling his way through until he dropped within sight of the lighter daylight of death. He had a long way to go yet: stood erect, white hair cropped short, his blue eyes steadily taking in the view, an ironic fierce gaze set upon the tatterdemalion camp of wood and bricks and cement bags near by. He turned back to the cups of tea Mary had poured: 'Not that I 'adn't bin expectin' it.'

'It ain't that black,' Tom said, not sitting down to drink.

'They've got another house for yer: in the Woodhouse, on Vane Street.'

'That's summat to be thankful for,' Mary said.

'Besides, it's only two doors up from the beer-off.' Tom had a gnome face topped by a nicky hat, the sort of face that seemed to have dried-up riverbeds running down it to meet at his pointed chin, a worried expression that tried to do nothing but please because the vanity behind it wanted everyone to think him a good bloke and not insult him. He buttoned his mac. 'Thanks for the tea, Mrs Merton. You've got a month or two to think about moving.'

Merton thought about it: and since he had been expecting the upheaval he wasn't so disturbed as he led everyone to believe. It would be a change to live among shops and pubs and be nearer to bus stops for the city. Lydia thought so as well: that there'd be no walking down the muddy lane and under the lonely bridge on dark nights. Mary said the house was like being in the middle of a graveyard all through winter, and now they'd have neighbours and company for a change. Merton was galled most of all at the smaller garden. 'I've seen 'em down there,' he said, 'and they aren't big enough to tek a piss in.'

The new house was in the middle of a long row inhabited mainly by miners working at Wollaton Pit. Merton sold up and moved in, George and Lydia glad because apart from being comfortingly nearer the town there was less work for him to set them to. Brian walked there along the main road and down by the canal side, went for the first time one afternoon and found no one in but his grandmother who dozed by the fire. He sat on the sofa waiting for her to wake up. The kitchen was arranged exactly as at the Nook, with the same mixed pervading aroma of tea and spices, kindling wood and tobacco, baked bread and stew. Brass candlesticks towered on the shelf, with two black and white statue dogs that reminded him of Gyp about to leap for birds before Merton had killed him, and white pot ornaments were placed between seaside souvenirs of Cromer and Skegness, Cleethorpes and Lowestoft. A magnifying glass hung from a nail, waiting for Merton to come back from his walk and look closely at the photographs in tonight's *Evening*

Post: Brian always hoped to borrow it, to set fire to a piece of paper in the garden by holding it under the sun. On the other side of the room was a glass-faced cupboard of tea-services, and rows of Merton's prize horseshoes. His grandmother sneezed and woke up. 'Hello, Brian, I di'n't 'ear you come in.'

'Well, I knocked first, grandma.'

She looked at the clock: 'I'd better get some tea ready for when the others come. I'll get the sack if I don't.' She went into the scullery to put the kettle on the gas. Brian wondered where his grandfather was, pushed the cat away from the fire with his foot: 'Shall I get some coal up from the cellar, grandma?'

'Yes, you *can* do that. Fill me two buckets, there's a good lad. It'll save your grandad doing it later.' He clattered down the steps whistling. Sunlight came through the grating, showing many small pieces of coal at the foot of the neatly stacked heap. But he pulled down an unwieldy lump and smashed the half-hundredweight of it to pieces with the hammer. Then he filled the buckets and trundled them back up. 'Wash your 'ands and I'll gi' you a piece o' jam pasty,' his grandma said.

Black liquid streamed down the sides of the white sink, and his hands smelt pleasantly of carbolic. The table was laid, and a half pasty and a cup of tea waited for him. 'Pull up a chair and get that down you,' Mary said. The *Evening Post* had just clattered through the letter box, and she went to get it. He interrupted her reading. 'I'm going up to the Nook tomorrow to see what's 'appened. Then I'll go over the Cherry Orchard to see Ken and Alma Arlington.'

The paper rustled to her knees: 'You'll find it altered. The Nook's down already, and I did hear that the Arlingtons was going to have to leave as well.'

He slept at home that night, and woke up the next morning with Fred on one side and Arthur on the other. Pushing Arthur's knee from his back he remembered he was to explore the Cherry Orchard, and an hour later he set off down the street, turning over the Lean towards New Bridge. From its summit he saw that apart from the immediate fields below, the countryside had gone. Nothing was the same, and beyond the broad new boulevard were houses, in which direction there seemed no set point worth searching for any more. He could go on walking on and on and not meet anyone he knew, could lose himself in the mountains of Derbyshire and reach the Atlantic at Wales without being able to stop a friendly face and say Hello how are you and Which is the way back to Nottingham.

He leapt streams and climbed over stiles in the pocket still left. Flowers hid among hollows and hedgerows, or stood in the wind of hillocks. His hair blew about, and most of the sky was blue. A horse nibbled at clover, and Brian thought it was the same horse that had nibbled there during the last four years he had passed through the field on his way to the Nook.

Across the boulevard he entered streets of new houses, and at the corner where he should turn and see the Nook, neither smoke nor roof was visible. The hedge had been trampled down, and the gate torn from its hinges, and instead of ochred walls he looked through into space towards the dark shade of the yet untouched wood. Nettles and thorns caught his ankles, and only the foundations of the house remained, and he stood in them, walking from section to section, kitchen to parlour and down into the pantry – filled with bricks, filth and glass fragments that had once been part of windows showing him marvellous fields and gardens. It hadn't taken them long to flatten it, he thought, and imagined it being done, beginning with roof and chimney-pots cascading into the yard, then the slow ripping down of walls, and lorries carting everything away.

The garden was a jungle, and he walked through it to the well. The fairytale headstock was no longer there, and he dropped stones down the depths still left: the noise of stone sailing down to stone hypnotized him as he lay over the parapet of rubble, a great peace sounding between the stone leaving his hand and striking the depths below.

The Cherry Orchard was untouched, still in the country. Noises of machinery fell away, giving place to the whistling of birds, and bushes bending in the wind. The silence made him afraid. In the distance he could see the two cottages of the Lakers and Arlingtons, but as he got near there was no sound of water being drawn from the squeaking pump.

Their gate was also smashed. The cottage doors were boarded

up and chimney-pots hung slantwise, as if youths had taken shots at them with bricks. He stood still, unable to speak his thoughts that were too deep to be fished up by the bent pin of sentiment. But the disappearance of his friends disturbed him, and trying to put his thoughts into speech was like an iceberg that grows hands in the middle of the ocean attempting to lift itself out of the water. The wood at the end of the garden sent out birdsounds: but no twigs cracked unexpectedly under other children's feet.

He went into the wood. Where had the Arlingtons and Lakers gone? He knew the land of Nottingham and a few miles beyond, but all was unexplored after that, and his consciousness of it slid over the rim of the world like the sailors in olden days who had no maps. But there were farms, he supposed, other towns and woods and fields, mountains and oceans that went on for ever and ever, until you came back to where you were standing now.

Clear water ran along the stream, and he leapt over. Where had they gone to live though? He had been to Skegness on a train when he was three, and vaguely remembered the rhythm of the wheels, a green blur of fields as he fell into sleep on his mother's knee. Then the grey boiling sea burst on to the sand. He brushed fingers over yellow nipples of bittersweet, unknowingly trampled the curved vetch. They've gone to another farm I expect. I wish I could go somewhere, a long way off, to jungles and mountains and islands. I'll draw a map when I get home. He ripped leaves from an elderberry bush and rubbed the stain over his hands.

He lay down for a long drink, legs outspread and knees bare against humps of dried earth. Stones on the bottom were of different sizes and shades, with sand and green weed between, like a landscape, a miniature world under glass, uninhabited by minnows or water-boats: an ideal country of No-One-Else, ripe for filling and exploration. His eyes bulged as he swallowed and caterpillars of stone-cold water jerked into his stomach.

Reaching the footpath he kicked loose stones about, running them gloriously into imaginary unguarded goal-posts. Whistling out of the wood he charged over the new road and across the field, sat on the embankment fence to watch an express train go fleeing by. Must be going to Skeggy, he thought, forgetting to count the carriages. I wish I was on it.

The ground plan of the Nook was on view to the sky for a long time, because men and materials couldn't be spared for building houses, due to a war that had started. Its clear markings stayed until the war ended, and Brian didn't notice that it had been covered with prefabs until he came back from Malaya, by which time its obliteration was looked on as a good thing.

PART THREE
The Ropewalk

16

Malaya soaked under rain. Brian swore he had never known anything like it: a mountainous backbone labouring against such a punishment of water. It seemed strange that the near-by sea could take so much and, walking to the door, he almost expected to see that the waves – after each flat-handed bash at the sand – had leapt over the beach and were worrying the billet supports like ferocious green dogs. Sand was hurled like pepper through the open door. 'For Christ's sake put wood in th'ole,' shouted a telephone operator. 'That stuff'll blind me; I wain't be able to see my dirty pictures then.'

'Belt up,' Brian called back, enoying the grey fury of the storm. 'I want to see how much longer we've got before tekin' to the boats.'

'I'd feel safer if I was in one now.' Bush-hats, wellington boots and capes: a hundred yards from breakfast at the mess had forced him to change every stitch. Dampness gave the illusion of cold, and those not on watch sat around in jerseys, a thing unknown since landing from England five months ago. He remembered a conversation with a melancholic Welsh regular at the transit camp: 'The grub's rotten out there, man. You sleep in tents, what's more.' His long Bible-backed face wagged over the pint Brian had treated him to: 'I wouldn't go to Malaya if they paid me danger money. Terrible. Insects drive you insane. Not to mention snakes getting in your bed. No pictures, not even on the walls. And boy, you should see it in the monsoon: so much rain you drown if you slip. I'm telling you – you couldn't go to a worse place.' The memory of the sing-song voice whose owner didn't take himself seriously made

Brian laugh: he closed the door and went back to finish his letter.

'Dear Mam' – he looked at the envelope already addressed, ON ACTIVE SERVICE scrawled across the top, which made him laugh because the War had been over a good two years. I can't act, and I'm nobody's bleeding servant. I'm just on a free trip. A poor man's Cook's Tour to the Far East. He threw the envelope away and addressed another, writing the initials OAS in the bottom left corner where he hoped no one would see it.

'Dear Mam, thanks for the *Daily Mirrors*. I had a good read when I was on watch in my hut in the paddy field, where I sit sending out Morse Code every day. I went to Pulau Timur the other day and got drunk. I go once a month when I get paid. I go with a gang of pals, and we take a boat two miles over the water.

'I hope everything's OK in Nottingham. Does Pauline come to see you? If not, why don't you visit her? She don't have much time with the kid, and neither of us are having much married life, me being out here. Give my love to dad. I wish he could write to me sometime, because I'd like to hear from him.' A washbowl near his foot was set to catch water from the leaking roof, and he pushed it dead under the main fall when it missed a few drops. 'It's raining at the moment,' he wrote, and rounded the letter off: 'Your loving son, Brian.'

Half an hour remained before going on watch, so he lay back for a drag, staring up through his mosquito-net at the rafters and palm-leaf roof. They'd dished out the new identity cards that day, and the photo turned it into a convict passport, with details splayed to the left of it: Aircraftman Second Class Brian Seaton, nineteen, five feet nine, medium build and blue eyes. No distinguishing marks. That's not much of a description, but I suppose it's the best they can do because if I was a hump-backed cripple I wouldn't be here, would I? He took the card from his shirt pocket. What a mug! I've gone thinner since I came, so I'd better be careful or else I'll sweat mysen to death. I've got the same mad starers as the old man, except that mine are blue and I look a bit cross-eyed on this. A good tan and hair like pig bristles. Christ, I'd better put it away.

Maybe they got a file on all of us at Base, like coppers: 'I sentence you to two years' hard service in Malaya, which is the maximum sentence the law allows. That will perhaps teach you to be eighteen and think you can get away with it. Next case.' He imagined the extended dossier:

Politics: socialist; used to read Soviet Weekly.

Sex-life: plenty until he fell foul of the authorities and received his two years. Five-fingered widow now.

Complexes: Mother, father and inferiority.

Patriotism: nil. Wants watching.

Favourite film star: Jeanne Crain.

Anything worthwhile: Good at wireless operating and earns his six bob a day. Works sixty hours a week – so we won't let him go yet.

Discipline: none. Even wears civvies on duty.

An argument brewed up between Hansford and Kirkby. Hansford was a brawny dark-haired southerner, a nineteen-year-old know-all half-way between callow youth and a dead-set staidness. He had an upper lip permanently curled, a disfigurement of spirit rather than physical defect, for it accentuated all his moods. When happy and good natured in the canteen others drew around him for the hilarious fun that was bound to break; but when broody and irascible he infected the whole billet, with the risk that the others might turn on him. This vacillation in his hare-lipped nature – hardly any fault of his – tended to make him unpopular more than anything. He was naked now but for a small towel lapped around, stood truculently holding soap and flannel. He'd have been out the door in five seconds, except that, nosy and intelligent, he happened to hear Pete Kirkby tell someone that he hadn't been called up but had volunteered. Hansford fastened the towel tighter around his waist, a set disbelieving expression that was in itself an insult to the person doubted. 'You didn't volunteer,' he said with a hard drawl, implying that no one could be that barmy. 'Come off it. Tell us another one.'

'I did,' Kirkby answered calmly. Brian reached for a tobacco tin to make a cigarette. His tastes in smoking varied according to mood and, often, affluence. He tried a pipe, black Chinese stoogies, ready rolled or tailor-mades – each label signifying calm or agitation, contempt or well-being. Hansford lifted his lip of incredulity still farther: 'Come off it, you bloody liar.'

'Belt up,' Brian called out. 'It ain't got owt to do with yo' whether he volunteered or not.' Kirkby was an old pal, a Radford lad from a long time back, when they'd known each other at the cardboard-factory where both had worked at fifteen. Kirkby was short and well-built, as strong as a donkey, taciturn yet now and again struck with the bright light of humour which had flared particularly when Brian in the factory tried to indoctrinate him with his own politics. As labourers they had worked like a team, lumping sacks of flour and alum from outside lorries to inside pastebins, or hanging up trolley after trolley of wet fresh-made cardboard in the stifling heat of the drying-rooms. 'I volunteered because I was fed up,' Kirkby had the patience to explain. But Brian knew it wasn't the right way to tackle Hansford, who responded: 'Christ, I'd never get that fed up.'

'Don't worry,' Kirkby said, 'I'll be out the same time as yo', 'cause I only cut my throat for the Duration of the Present Emergency. I'd 'ave bin called up anyway.'

Brian blew clouds of tobacco smoke over his row of shining boots, hearing the dull woollen punch of breakers on the near-by sand and shattering bouts of rain flailing the roof – punctuating deadly boredom between watches. Che-Din, the Malay youth, worked well to keep the shine on their boots. You'd think they were his pride: two lines of glistening toe-caps along each side of the billet – though Brian imagined he hated their guts even more than he did himself, which was saying a lot. Che-Din was small, compact and delicate, sometimes came to work in a sari and trilby hat. He once pointed out a tree at which Malays and Chinese had been shot by the Japanese, and Brian asked him whether he preferred the Japs to rule in Malaya, or the British. Che-Din shrugged and said: 'What does it matter? They both make us work for nearly nothing' – a response which infuriated the unpredictable Hansford, who threw a boot that clouted his shoulder, bringing tears of shame to Che-Din's eyes and driving him from the billet for three days. 'I didn't mean to hit him,'

Hansford said by way of apology to the others who cursed him as much for the bad luck of his accurate aim as for the impulse that led him to pick up the boot.

'I suppose you got more than you bargained for when they sent you out to this bloody pig-sty.' He sat on his bed, as if to set his argument in for the evening, when Kirkby only wanted to get back to his western. Yet Kirkby was sometimes flattered when people quarrelled with him: 'I enjoy it out here. I'd never 'ave seen this country if I hadn't joined up, would I?'

Hansford wiped his crutch. 'I can think of better ways to see the world than being shipped out like cattle on a troopship.'

'So can I, mate. I'd never earn the dough to do it though.'

'You should sign on,' Hansford said, a dry cocksure assumption that he'd got the upper hand. 'Twenty-one years would do you just right.'

Kirkby grinned. 'You think I'm loony?' trying to hide irritation behind his grin, but not succeeding. 'Three years never hurt anybody.' Hansford descended to the centre lane-way: 'The best three years of your life, don't forget.'

'Come off it,' Brian chipped in. 'Every year's the best year of your life.'

'Not if you're in uniform.' He turned from Brian's effort to bring the argument against him, and looked hard at Kirkby as if he'd like to hit him but wasn't sure of the reception he'd get. Brian could have told him. He was madder than Kirkby now, and Kirkby's grin became genuine because he'd noticed it as well. 'The three are going OK for me,' he laughed.

'You must have a warped mind,' Hansford threw back. Others were listening, looking up from books, cigarettes, thoughts or emptiness. 'Not so much of the warped, Hansford,' Thompson shouted threateningly, who was in for seven-and-five. 'As long as my mind's warped the way I want it to be,' Kirkby said, 'I don't give a fuck. I'll be going back on the same banana boat as you, but I'm not griping all the same. I like the sun and I like swimming. I even get paid for being here. Not bad for a year or two.' Hansford could not penetrate such satisfaction: 'You ought to get a job writing recruiting posters,' he said, and padded down the steps to take his shower. Brian stamped on his fag-butt with bare feet, then pulled on his wellington boots.

Quarter to six: he slung a cape over his shoulders, took up his haversack with, 'See yo' lot in the morning,' and walked into a wall of rain. He couldn't hear himself think above the noise it made, spat out a gust that raced across his mouth. The covered lorry stood fifty yards away, and he climbed in the back. Singing came from a near-by billet, an antidote because so much rain was frightening, gave the impression it would never stop until the universe filled up and the world sank. Coconuts now and again fell like Big Bertha shrapnel: a quick swish as they came through branches and thumped themselves on to wet soil.

He banged against the cab and sheets of water took to the air as it made for the road. Malayan police at the gate stood under palm-leaf shelters, capes outspread under their glum heads. The lorry roared up the coast road, and all he could see were grey waves, grey clouds, and roaring mist a thousand yards out. He was glad to be leaving the camp and the apprehension that had descended with the first rain. Everything became subdued under it, all inmates on edge waiting for it to end not long enough after it had begun. Out of the crowd he felt better, freer, happy enough to whistle the latest song hit from Radio Seac. Fires tended by women for the evening rice, burned by the native huts-on-stilts.

From the back he only saw what the lorry left behind, not what its blunt-nosed radiator was heading for – suddenly turning to pass the ramshackle control tower and race up the wet shine of the airstrip that seemed as if it were being laid like a carpet as he looked at it. He was going to the outlying DF hut set in the middle of a vast square paddy field and connected to the runway by a thin path of mud now hazed under needling rain. When the lorry stopped he leapt out, drew the cape about him, and made for the distant hut.

At the same time the operator he was to relieve began walking towards him. The water was continually pierced with weighted rain, was churned to a murky and cancerous colour, and the earthen lifeline between runway and hut had in places been well eaten into by the force of it. Brian trod slowly to avoid slipping into the three-foot depth on either side, whistling a monotonous tune as if it would help him keep balance. Tall, fair-headed Baker came level, his myopic eyes looking superciliously through the rain, thin lips firmly closed, giving the impression that they were about to break out into a smile, though the opposite was true, for Brian knew he was browned off and dead to the wide after his afternoon grind. 'Anything going on?'

'Not much.' Baker spoke tersely, his hat brim uptilted by a gust of wind. 'You might as well close down at seven. A Dak coming up from Singapore should be landing in half an hour.'

'He'll 'ave a job to land in this stuff.'

'Got to land somewhere, the poor mutt.'

'As long as he don't flatten his snout on that runway,' Brian said. 'I wun't like to try it.' They were already fed up with each other: Brian eager to get into his isolation, Baker to escape from it, so there was no sympathy between them. They passed. On the far shore invisible hands of wind were trying to duck the heads of palm trees into the water, bending their supple trunks that sprang back time and again in defiant protest. White flashes of lightning skidded across the water, to meet thunder out on the runway.

The hut stood on a square of ground, surrounded by four aerial poles whose wires joined above the middle of the patched and often-mended roof and went down through it into the direction-finding receiver. The smell of water and dampness was so strong that it threatened to block the nostrils, made it difficult to breathe, as if the earth were soil to its core and soaked through and through. Baker had plugged in the speaker, and atmospherics scuffled with the noise of rain by the hut door.

He went in, shedding cape, hat and haversack, cursing Baker for an idle bastard because he had let rain drip on the accumulators. I suppose he was reading his motor-bike catalogues again; the no-good worker should have been a mechanic, not a wireless operator. He struggled with the long heavy boxes on to a form, which he pulled to a dry corner, then signed on in logbook and diary, and called up Singapore to ask the strength of his signals.

The first flexible key-tapping of his nightwatch went out clear and neat, the long and short of each letter piercing his ears with birdlike music, balm to his brain, intoxicating yet sobering, like the first drink of a dipso. He wore his earphones half on and half off, so that while hearing the solid low-pitched thumps of the superheterodyne dots-and-dashes he got the clicking of the key at the same time, as a reassuring echo fed back from desk to ears. He was on his own, and in control of a radio-set, had only to press a key for other lonely operators hundreds of miles away to push a hand forward and tap out a reply. Tonight their replies were all but inaudible, just as his own calls to them, he realized, were pounced on over the jungled mountaintops by saw-toothed atmospherics and torn into unrecognition. His beloved fourteen-hour stretch of isolation had begun, and despite rain battering against all sides of the small and flimsy hut, he felt good being at work, and paused from filling in the log to open a tin of cigarettes and have a smoke.

The leeward side of the hut lay open to the grey rainfilled daylight of water and low cloud. The aerial wires generated a ghostly morse of their own, soon dominated by a message from the approaching aircraft asking for a weather report. He spun the phone handle to get the met office – once, twice, three times – but the wire was dead. Must have been chewed through by water. 'None available,' he told the plane, but the operator came back fast saying they had to have one.

He stood in the doorway to observe the weather: cloud base two thousand feet, visibility a mile, wind westerly at forty knots, raining; went back and tapped it out. Not very accurate but the operator in the plane seemed happy. He then wanted a bearing to bring him in, but the aerials must have shorted because they wouldn't give a reliable reading. Third class, Brian sent back, so don't rely on it. 'I won't,' said the ironic operator.

Christ, what rain. It came with frightening elemental force, as if it had an animal mentality and imagined it would win its battle against the land after one final effort. The paddy field was a lake as far as the trees, and ripples appeared, as if the DF hut were a boat on the open sea but approaching the coast. Water dripped through the roof, some splashing on to the Sten gun and annunition. Maybe it don't work any more: he took it outside, stood with legs apart and fired off a magazine, aiming level across the paddy field. The sharp fireworks-sound of bullets was muffled by the storm and taken harmlessly into its belly.

Soaked, he went back in the hut, stripped to the waist and sat at the set. What a life! He'd a date with Mimi tonight, hadn't expected to do a watch, but the corporal who was to have taken a turn had reported sick, and looked like being in dock for a couple of weeks. He called up the French operator at Saigon, using a mixture of Q signals and pidgin French: 'Any planes flying around your way tonight?' Maybe he was reading a book and didn't want to be disturbed, but he sent fast and nervous through the interference: 'What do you want?'

'Nothing,' he tapped, and waited a few minutes.

Saigon came back: 'My name is Henri. What's yours?'

'Jean Valjean.'

Brian felt his mystification, repeated the name.

'How old are you?' Henri tapped out, making several mistakes. 'Thirty-five,' Brian lied, enoying his game. 'And you?'

'Twenty-seven.' Brian asked if he liked Saigon, and back came the wireless operator's laugh: dah-dah-di-di-di-di-dah-dah. 'Where were you born?'

Brian told him: 'Nottingham.'

'Give me the address of a hot girl then.'

It was forbidden to send plain language, but Brian had never known any conscript operator that didn't. What can you do, O what can you do, But ride to your death on a kangaroo? was a rhyme he had made up, and it came into his head now. He sent out a fictitious name and address to Saigon, and they gave the wireless operator's handshake by simultaneously pressing down on their keys.

He watched the Dakota landing: it hovered low over the palm trees, came bouncing on to the tarmac and hurled itself like a cannonball in the direction of the control tower. He sent out his closing-down message – good night, good night, good night – and switched off the set, leaving the ether free for the confused legions of atmospherics. Darkness closed over the water, and he fastened the doors to stop insects getting at the lights and feeding on his cold sweat. The primus flared when he tried to light it for tea, so he kicked it away and drank water with his bread and cheese.

The thought of eleven hours still to go was appalling. Lightning winked at him under the slit of door, as if mocking him because he could have been in bed with Mimi. I'm not lucky enough for this world, though it's better to laugh than curse your luck. The wind brawled with the hut like a hooligan. God knows how I got here, I don't. I don't mind being cut off, but this is like clink: not even a bleddy telephone to call the control tower.

'Look,' the old man said that night when I told him I'd be eighteen in the morning, 'if I catch you joining up I'll punch your bleddy 'ead in. Mark my word.' I'd come back late after a session with Pauline on the sofa, and felt marvellous. 'You don't join up,' I told him. 'In case you don't know, they've been calling people up for six years.'

'Don't be so bleddy cheeky,' he said, scowling as black as thunder, as if he'd bosh the teapot over my head, though instead he poured me a cup. 'I don't care whether or not they call you up: they didn't get me, did they?'

'Well,' I said, 'thanks for the tea, but that was because you di'n't pass your medical though, worn't it?'

''Appen so. But I swung the lead a bit as well. After all them years on the dole I swore I'd never fayt for 'em, the bleddy bastards. Not after all me and yer mam and yo' lot 'ad ter put up wi'.' He cut me a slice of meat, all fussy in a rare bout of letting himself go in talk.

'But don't you see, dad, they'll call me up, because I'm fit. I wain't be able to get out of it.'

'Dave and Colin got out on it all through the War. *They* beat the bleddy redcaps.' He looked vacantly towards the curtained window. 'They was boggers, our Dave and Colin was.'

'They got 'em though, di'n't they?' I said, remembering the time with regret.

'Ah,' Seaton said, laughing, 'but the War was over by then.' He took a fat swig at his tea. 'So stay out on it.'

But he hadn't wanted to keep out on it, because that would mean staying in Nottingham when he wasn't sure he wanted to any more. Not that he was afraid to desert either, but felt he would be more of a deserter in letting himself be called up than roaming like an outlaw around the night streets, and in fact might miss something if he didn't let himself go for once where the wind took him. The old man went on and on:

'Our Eddie deserted in 1917, got on a bike and rode to his sister's at Coventry. The crafty bogger didn't go by the road for fear the coppers 'ud stop 'im; he went along the canal bank and didn't meet a soul. It was twice as far, but it paid him in the end. She hid him for six weeks, but the loony sod missed Nottingham and came back one day, so mother and dad had to look after him. A pal saw the coppers coming to the house and towd us, so he skipped off and stayed out in Wollaton Roughs. The poor bogger nearly froze to death. I used to ride out on my bike every day with snap my mother had packed up for 'im. But one day I worn't clever enough: the bleddy coppers follered me, right to where Eddie was hiding – and got 'im. Three months later he was in France, and a week after that he was a prisoner with the Jerries till the end of the War. We had to laugh: our Eddie was fawce bogger.' Another round of hot tea was poured in the lighted kitchen.

After a drink of water Brian groped a way to the charpoy bed and spread sheets across it. Baker had let the accumulators run too low before phoning the transmitter compound for renewals, and there wasn't enough light left to see a shadow by. He lay on the bed, listened to rain hitting the hut like thousands of grains of rice, the water harvest of South-East Asia. What would Colin and Dave have done in my place? Packed up and gone. But they wouldn't have got this far, and I've seen things they'll never see: 'Did I tell you about that time I saw a python, our Dave, when I was in Malaya? In a paddy field it wor. Must a bin twenty feet long, as thick as my thin raps and splashing about like boggery. Di'n't waste my time watching it though.' 'Better yo' than me,' Dave would say. 'I'd rather see Tarzan at the pictures.'

Large rats were scurrying on endless journeys up and down the hut, having a pow-wow on the roof about the rotten weather, and how it had flooded them out of their nests. He couldn't relish such company, spun the telephone handle in the hope that somehow the cable had miraculously mended itself out in the swamps. But it was dead, useless as a picked lock, and after another drink of water he lay down in a cold sweat of sleep.

Livid wounds lit up the hut and penetrated his eyelids, forcing them wide open, so that, staring at wind and thunder that sounded as if some lunatic had been set loose with matches among touch paper, the noise seemed louder than when his head was down. The sheets were quickly wet, and he wondered if water had been dropping down without him knowing it, was comforted to realize it was only his sweat. The thought of moving the bed out of raindrips seemed to demand a too impossible effort through his fatigue.

Lightning flashed continually, as if the sky had turned itself into an enormous signalling lamp and he was lying right by it: at one time he woke and tried to read its signals but they didn't make sense, unintelligible morse quickly erased by a follow-up of thunder.

He noticed a dull grey light in the hut, felt it before opening his eyes, as if it were a tangible thing, a ghost that rain had pushed like a letter under the door while his face was turned. He had mixed feelings about waking up, and such noise greeted him this morning that he would rather have stayed asleep. The storm had rampaged all night, still went like a full-grown battle that, though covering the whole country, seemed to centre on the paddy field and the DF hut in particular. Something else infected him with worry as he lay on his back. He shivered from the clinging touch of the cold sheet and the intense smell of mould, grew colder from a fit of coughing, so pulled his shirt on and sat up. A foot of water came nearly to bed level, covering his wellington boots and a tattered Penguin book. The flood: I'll thumb a lift from Noah as he goes by. Roll on the boat. What can you do, Oh what can you do? Can it, and belt up. What a bastard though. I'd better move. I can't hear myself think with this thunder: I want earplugs – and an eyeshade for the lightning. Water curved from his wellingtons, which he emptied and put on, paddled to the receiver and pulled down switches. He pressed the key to bring himself on frequency, which elicited a Good Morning from Mingaladon in Burma. 'What's good about it?' he tapped back. That stopped his gallop. It was seven o'clock.

He looked out from the leeward door of the hut. All but the far-off trees were covered, and the path across the paddy field – now a lake – leading to the higher ground of the runway was nowhere to be seen. Rain still pitched itself into agitated water, as if it would go on falling until the hut collapsed and floated away. He saw it clearly, and his first thought was to desert the hut, to wade through the paddy field and reach the runway, for in this mess the aerials were useless for bearings.

He paddled to the desk, and by some miracle got through to the control tower by field telephone, began spinning a sorry though vivid tale to the officer on duty. His description was cut short: 'Close the hut then, and get back here. A lorry'll take you to camp.' But what about a boat to get me to the runway? he thought as he slammed the receiver down so hard it almost cracked. The loony bastard.

Whistling a tune he stuffed logbooks and ammunition into his pack, disconnected the accumulators and lifted them to the highest point. A bloated leech, as big as a small snake, wriggled between his boots and made its way into the hut through a gap. 'You wain't find owt in there: I just got out in time,' he called after it. The hut sides were a crawling mass of spiders and other insects that had taken refuge from the rising flood, and rats squeaked in fear from the roof, running down to look at the water now and again, then hurrying back to tell the others it hadn't gone down, might in fact come up to get them yet.

His boots found the path, two feet under the surface. A lit cigarette was soaked and blown across his face, and he spent most of the journey spitting tobacco-bits back at the wind. With the Sten gun looped over his shoulder he waded slowly, for in some places the path had been washed away, and he floundered almost up to his armpits trying to find it again. He was sweating under the rain, afraid of meeting snakes, remembering the many he had seen and particularly the python splashing not long ago near the hut. Maybe they all swam off to the trees, was a happy though not convincing thought. He swore aloud and talked to himself. It's an adventure right enough, and I'm so far away as I ever wanted to be, about three times farther than Abyssinia, which is sayin' summat, but Christ, I'll be glad to reach that runway where I can't get bitten, and get back to camp where I can swill some tea. He pulled the cape around him to keep out the driving rain. If only the old man could see me now: 'What did I tell you?' he'd say. 'You daft sod, up to your neck in that rheumatic water. If you like water that much you'd a done better going for a swim in the Trent. I towd yer not to join up. They never did owt for us, so why should yo' do owt for them? Eh?'

A mile trek along the runway was made against a spearhead of wind, and he felt his face being blown out of shape, cape flying back like Bela Lugosi the vampire-bat man, hat twisted like an old gold-digger. Soap bubbles came from the toes of his wellingtons. He was even too fed up to worry about a plane pouring down the runway behind and flattening him. All I want now is a warm billet and a long novel, and a shovelful of grub every four hours to keep me fed. It's an easy life, though, except when a wet sky falls on top of you.

The control tower wasn't much better off than the DF hut. Water poured through the roof, and maps covering the walls were discoloured beyond recognition: Burma was running hell for leather into the Bay of Bengal, and French Indo-China was making a sly move against Singapore. Sumatra was going red, which gave him a laugh, though he thought it was a shame and a waste about the good maps. A large shed opposite the tower, which catapulted a firetender whenever a plane was expected to land, had been blown flat to the ground. That'll cost 'em a bob or two to put right, he smiled. The flying control officer gave him a few dirty looks because he was dressed in a civvy shirt instead of a uniform, but Brian smoked obliviously in the doorway, feeling the dampness getting into his marrow.

The relief lorry arrived through the mud, Baker landing in a pool of water he couldn't have seen as it pulled up. 'Is the camp still there?' Brian asked when he'd finished cursing. 'Or has it bin swept away?'

Baker refused a cigarette: 'We've got to go back to the hut and bring the accumulators out.'

'You can't get back yet. The paddy field's flooded.'

'The signals officer says we must.'

Brian felt as though he'd been thumped at the back of the head, red stars winking in front of his eyes. 'The jumped-up bastard, what does he know about it? He wants to come out and get 'em himself instead of knocking back whisky and cornflakes in his jumped-up mess.'

Baker had been to public school, was hidebound and full of games, mutinous only within the limits of King's Regulations. 'We have to do it anyway.'

Brian came down the steps. 'Back through the slosh for a couple of mouldy accumulators.' The lorry took little over a minute to do the runway mile, and Baker was daunted to see the water so high. 'Come on then,' Brian called out, already waist into it, 'frightened o' getting wet? Don't mind the odd snake: they run away from yo' first.'

'Balls,' Baker shouted, in with a splash. Brian waded quickly, only stopping to point out a gap in the path, feeling more courageous now that someone was with him, and he was in the lead. Still, if you had somebody shooting at you from them trees you wouldn't even think about snakes. 'The boys in the hut have been feeling sorry for you, out all night in the floods,' Baker called. The rain no longer drove like needles but splashed against the dull putty of Brian's skin, was unfelt through his fatigue. A snake rippled on the right. 'Thanks,' he shouted to Baker.

'We're going to operate the DF frequency from the signals section while the rain lasts. Is there a gap here?'

'No, come on a bit. There, it's not deep though. They should a bleddy well thought o' that yesterday.' Still, it was good: the signal section was only fifty yards from the billet: he'd be able to nip down the road and see Mimi more often. He unlocked the door of the hut, and the bloated leech swam out again. 'The gale blew a tree down on to one of the bashas last night,' Baker told him. 'No one was hurt though.' They lifted the accumulators to a chair. Brian sensed he was seeing the last of the place, that no one would operate from there again. Baker thought they should bring in the auxiliary aerial and went outside to get it, but he let go as if it were electrified: spiders, leeches, centipedes and scorpions scrabbled for the protection it offered against the flood.

'God,' he exclaimed. 'Let it stay.'

I'll be out here another year, and on the boat by next autumn. The thought gave him patience. There's something good about being here though, and interesting, because in a way I wouldn't have missed it, in spite of what the old man said. After all, there worn't any scorpions in Radford, and I've allus wanted to travel. But what a way to do it! Shouted at like a rag-bag all the time for not wearing a uniform. I wouldn't be seen dead in it, though I have to put it on to get my pay.

He covered the accumulators with his cape (soaked to the skin, he didn't need it any more) and they carried them slowly to the lorry. 'Better not slip,' he said, 'or you'll get an acid-bath. Imagine gettin' a pension for rheumatics and a scorched arse.' One foot slowly before the other, it took all his willpower not to speed up against the driving rain. 'You wouldn't be able to settle down, would you?' Baker said, happy because they were half-way across.

It seemed as if the rain would never end. A glittering sea of blue, equal sky above green hills and the pastel colours of Muong across the straits, with red and black ships in the harbour and yellow strips of beach north of the town, seemed like a dream already, even vaguer than memories of Nottingham. On fine days it was a treat out at the hut sitting in the basket chair stark bollock naked to get brown, while some poor aeroplane belted his morse lungs out for a bearing or met report. He'd make a fire and have sardines on toast, wearing down another tin from the endless supplies in the grub chest. Once he'd given a few tins to the Chinese rice sower who drove his ox and plough by the hut, and the man had made him feel foolish by bowing his thanks about half a dozen times. That's the worst of doing a good turn to an ignorant bastard; he ain't got the brains to know that everybody's equal. Still, bowing to them's like shaking hands with us, according to Mimi. The continuous rattle of rain was the only real thing at the moment, a cocoon of water that enveloped his brain and the whole world.

From the back of the lorry he saw the DF hut, a small dark block in the middle of a vast square lake of grey. Then it was out of sight and they were roaring as fast down the runway as an aeroplane trying to take off. Wet and hungry, he would get cleaned up and go to the canteen, drink as many bottles of Tiger Beer as he could take. In a day or two he would see Mimi. Baker prodded him: 'You were going to sleep,' he said.

17

Left from the main road (ignoring a notice saying: BEYOND THIS POINT OUT OF BOUNDS TO ALLIED FORCES) meant cutting himself off from the forceful grip of lights and traffic, and entering dark groves of palm trees. The narrow lane was indented with cart-ruts, and trees rising on either side overlapped it with shadows. He felt a criminal every time he parted from the traffic, committed to some irrevocable step though in fact he was only going to see Mimi. Walking, he pictured her framed beyond the darkness, behind the fireflies that now and again glittered in pairs and seemed to put out their lamps when he went too close.

Black night was a good camouflage until danger had passed and you could light up again, proving that fireflies knew a thing or two. He pictured her, the collar of a blue kimono dominating the bones of her round face, sitting maybe at her rattan table to make up before he came. Or perhaps, wearing her pyjama dress, she stared vacantly into the mirror, a mirage of green or yellow, at a small face and slow-moving finely made hands. He couldn't see her features clearly when she was out of his sight: the image shifted or became blurred, taunted him with having no memory. It was the same with most things. After getting back from watch and as the camp came in sight – a score of long huts clear and sharp among slim-poled palm trees – the airstrip and DF hut he had only half an hour left were already vague and beyond description, shimmering in the open heat and the dreaminess of wide spaces. Absence makes the heart grow fonder only because memory plays you false. The strange, beyond reach whether in the past or future, was always more tasteful than what stood before your eyes, made itself even more illusive if you tried forcing your eyes like antennae into the dim corners of it. He couldn't for instance recall certain parts of Nottingham, or old faces, no matter how much he screwed up his will to do so; yet they would come vividly when he was least trying or expecting them, so sharply that he once stopped tapping morse in the middle of an urgent message, and, with an aircraft waiting at the end of his signals, was transfixed until the picture departed. Such visions made the power of his memory seem unreliable and weak.

He stopped to light a cigarette, and in the accentuated darkness left when the match went out, saw the glow from lights in the village. But the dark trees in front gave greater promise, and he walked on. He hadn't seen Mimi for a week, which was bad enough, but worse when measured by the appetite each visit left him with. An application to the signals officer for a temporary all-night pass had been turned down because the reason for asking it had been guessed. Three dollars a day wouldn't cover much more than a weekly visit to the Boston Lights taxi-dance hall where Mimi worked, and in any case there was a one o'clock limit to these expeditions. He was lassoed from left and right by legislation devised by some genius for persecution: permission for this, permission for that – still, what did I expect when I let them call me up? I should have told them I had an old blind mother to support and that I believed in God and Jesus Christ and all that pack of rotters. Then maybe they'd 'ave let me off. And everybody at home used to think I was clever because I read books! Christ, I knew a hundred words of French before I was able to tell my left hand from my right, and I knew the capital of Bulgaria at the same time as I learned to read the clock. Bucharest, wasn't it?

The vision that had stopped his morse dead in its tracks was when he went to get a job at fourteen. I had to have a medical and the eye doctor said to me: 'Now look at the circles on that card, son. You'll see that the circles are broken on the left or right side. Starting from the big circle at the top I want you to tell me what side the gap is on every circle, left or right.' What a laugh. I never felt so ignorant in all my life, though it didn't stop me getting the job.

The track was dry, a shallow bed of powder, for the monsoon

had been over some weeks and the one-season year was three-quarters on to Christmas. A hand in pocket, he recognized by the motion of his legs the peculiar swaying walk of his father, though it was hardly noticeable to someone looking at him, and most of it had been eradicated by parade-ground drill in England. But it was there and gave him comfort as he walked in the darkness, accentuating his own self and setting him apart from the camp and all it stood for. A Malay in white shorts and pith-helmet came by like a phantom, and Brian said good night in the man's own language, a reassurance to both that they were passing human beings and not ghosts. There was no reply to his greeting, and he wondered whether his Malay had been understood. He knew the days of the week and how to count, a few common words of food and drink, a verb or two, but no more. There were classes in Malay at the camp but he couldn't bring himself to go, was unable to take the learning of it seriously, half thinking that Malay didn't matter as French and Spanish might, and half not being bothered to master it. He had seen it was easy enough to learn: you could put words together in a string without bothering about such complications as grammar, of which he knew nothing.

The Patani swamps weren't far off, and vegetable decay, rank and bittersweet at the same time, mingled with the smell of fish and rice being cooked on glowing charcoal fires from huts among the trees. The bungalow was across a clearing, half a dozen rooms on stilts with rotten floors, and a palm-leaf roof that leaked in rainy weather. But the feeling of it, when in Mimi's room drinking tea, or lying with his head across her and his thoughts in comforting oblivion, with the smell of joss impregnated in the wood of the widow's room and drifting through to them, was of a last refuge, an outpost of his forward-pushing consciousness that in some strange way was similar to certain patches of his life now left so far behind that he couldn't draw them to him, let alone fit them with words.

He saw a light from the corner window: Mimi's room. The Chinese widow who let it was on her weekly visit to Muong, and wouldn't be back until the last ferry – which docked when Brian was to be in camp. He didn't go up the front steps, but using his guile in case the widow hadn't yet left, made for the back, kicking his way through the tangled garden and thinking in one panic-stricken moment that he had trodden on a snake. Maybe it's dead, he told himself, walking along the veranda. He hoped Mimi hadn't heard him, looked in through the unshuttered window and saw her lying on the bed wearing only the bottom half of her pyjamas, the nipples of her small pointed breasts ready to embrace the roof. She seemed to be staring blankly at nothing, but her eyes moved, and following them he saw a lizard on the ceiling hunting insects. 'Why don't you climb in?' she said, not looking at him.

He hesitated. 'You can see the lizard better from inside,' in a small persistent voice hard to disobey. He leaned his elbows on the sill and smiled: 'I'm watching it from here. I'll disturb it if I come in.' She looked a treat, with her short black hair, a round face with sallowy yet youthful skin, and heavy unmoving eyelids. Like a doll, he'd said at first, but that was for the story books, the lucky dips of ancient Christmases, a twisted picture of geography given out at his no-good school. He remembered the first night's dancing at the Boston Lights, talking to her and buying round after round of drinks and wanting to sleep with her, seeing her mouth well shaped by lipstick and strangely angled eyes that looked so profoundly blank in the few seconds when nothing was being said that he felt momentarily panic-stricken on realizing the distance between them both. But that was a few months back, and he knew now that there was no bigger gap between them than had separated him from Pauline at the start of their long bout of passionate courting in Nottingham over four years ago. Even here I can't get her from my mind, though I'm married, so who can wonder at it? It plagued him like a magic lantern out of control, switching from one thing to another, Mimi to Pauline, then back to the here and now of Mimi, because it was like having the blade-point of an axe paining your lungs to dwell too much on Pauline, and the way he'd betrayed her as soon as she was out of sight.

Returning from the dance hall on that first night, having lost Mimi to her other customers, he separated from the gang he was with on the ferry and walked down to the third-class deck. A small Chinese girl in black sat with legs curled up on a form, twisting her fingers together and holding the entangled result to the light to see what she made of them. Then she got tired of this and began to cry: Brian dropped a handful of coins into her lap and she stopped, her mother wondering what it was that woke her now there was silence.

The boat was in mid-channel: Muong like a row of dying embers, while northward the smooth sea was empty for a thousand miles as far as Rangoon and the Irrawaddy. The black lifeline of the opposite shore had long since faded, but for the encrusted lights around Kota Libis pier waiting for the ferry's touchdown. Back on the first-class deck, stepping over outstretched legs, he saw Mimi gazing at Muong from the rail. The night air was warm and she stood in her yellow dress, clutching a black handbag. 'A penny for your thoughts,' he said.

She turned quickly: 'Oh, it's you. I'm sleepy' – and looked back at the water, as if only the ploughed-up phosphorescence of it could give rest from the vivid colours her eyes had been seeing the last five hours.

'Do you work as hard as this every night then?' He noticed her ear-rings, small yellow lanterns whose shadows were thrown on the flesh beneath her ears by lights from above. 'You get tired whether you work or not,' she informed him. He kissed her, felt the touch of cool ear-rings as he drew back. 'Stop it,' she said, turning away. 'I have to be wide awake with you boys.'

'Not with me,' he said; 'I only want to know where you live.' It was beyond him that she hadn't simulated anger at his kiss – though he expected the going to get harder. But she smiled: 'What you want to know for?'

'To come and see you.'

Instead of resistance, she teased him: 'What for?'

He sensed that this sort of humour would never leave her, even when she was tired. It was a mask. Because of it he didn't know whether to think she was younger, or older, wondered how an invisible listener would have seen it – then spat into the water. 'Because I like talking to you, instead of always to the others in camp.' Slyness seemed as good a way to break through as any. Mimi was a giggling child one minute, much younger than him; then was in touch with a life into which he could never reach either because of age, or because she had access to depths that went off at a tangent to his own. Himself, he felt young and old in stages, knew nothing but the fact of being on the boat with her, future and past and everything else obliterated except the lights and water and wooden decks of the ferryboat around them fastened by booze and sentiment within the prison of himself at nineteen, which didn't help towards an easy flow of conversation.

'Tomorrow's Sunday,' he said, taking out a packet of cigarettes. 'So I don't suppose you work.'

No longer smiling, she wouldn't have a cigarette, so he lit one for himself. 'I don't,' she said.

Not caring about being persistent he asked: 'Can I see you then?'

'If you like.' She was listless, and he hardly noticed her joyless agreement in the surprise he felt at it. The fact that he was taking advantage of her came to him dimly and didn't bother him anyway. When he didn't look like speaking, she smiled: 'Don't you want to come?'

'Yes, course I do.' The lights of Kota Libis were large, and they saw people moving about and waiting as the boat did a half-turn ready for the approach. His spent fag dropped into the water. 'Where shall I meet you?' sliding an arm around her.

'At seven, outside the photo shop. In the village.'

The lizard hadn't moved for ten seconds. What sort of a view did it have of her, upside down on the ceiling? 'This is a long game,' he said; 'it can go on all night.'

'The children play it,' she said.

'Like my mother: she says she used to sit in the kitchen when she was a little girl and watch the clock hands move. It was a game that lasted hours.'

'That would bore me.'

'I like lizards as well,' he said. 'Out at my DF hut I've got a pet chameleon, green on top and duck-egg blue underneath. It waddles over the floor every morning and I feed it a saucer of bread and milk. We're pals now, in fact. He went off for a couple of days not long since, and I thought he'd got eaten by a snake, but then he came back with a female, so he must have been courting. Now I've got two of 'em supping at the saucer. I reckon they know when they're on to a good skive.'

She was laughing, a sort of distrustful giggle, flattening her breasts and sitting up on the bed: 'Why do you tell me such stories?' He leapt over the window-sill and sat next to her. 'Because it's good to tell stories. Anyway, that's the on'y time you like me, i'n't it?'

He drew her close. 'You're so funny,' she whispered. Many of her remarks seemed like meaningless counters, long since detached from inside her, with no real connexion to her own self. These he imagined her having used freely to other lovers she must have had; he recognized and resented them, jealous because they stopped him getting close to her. 'That's better than having a long face all the time,' he said, 'like some people I know.'

'But funny people are sadder than anybody.' It was strange to him: her old man had become a shopkeeper, she said, bone-poor, though, at first, from Canton, and he imagined him with a stick over his shoulder, like Dick Whittington, only Chinese, coming south-west in a junk chewing a plug of opium to help him on his way. He saw him as young and steel-faced, hat on his head shaped like a handle-less dustbin lid, living off a handful of rice a day and shaking hands with endurance, handsome perhaps, but making a hard go of it in Singapore. The thought was terror to Brian: in Nottingham yes, but he would have died over a life like that, scraping cent by cent from kerb-stall to backstreet shop that even now, Mimi said, wasn't all that easy. But Mimi had been to High School, and this difference, with female and Chinese thrown in, not to mention a couple of years in age, had for some time mixed up his attitude towards her, though things between them seemed to be improving at last.

The High School hadn't lasted long and he was touched by the sad way she had left. A boy-friend who worked for some political party (he was in no doubt as to the sort of party, using his instinct accurately nowadays as to left and right and knowing enough about Mimi) had got her pregnant at sixteen, then disappeared because the British police were after him. The Japs came soon after, and no one had seen him since. They didn't see the British police for four years either, except in chain gangs.

She sat with legs under her, away from him. He wanted to lean forward and embrace her, but the wish deadened because of the look in her eyes. 'You're the sad one,' he said. 'I suppose you get so fed up with having to laugh every night of the week that you can't even act yourself when you're with me.' He walked away, sat on the one chair in the room. 'So I tell you funny stories to make you laugh. That's the best way, i'n't it?'

'Sometimes' – like a child who cannot understand what is being said to it. He said: 'I knew a lump o' wood once that joined the air force and got sent to Malaya. It was a smart and chipper piece, not a big lump of wood, about half a pit-prop if you want to know, that parted its hair on the wrong side of its head, but still it met a lady pit-prop that spoke Chinese when she was asleep, but when she was awake she spoke slow English and said she loved him. How's that for a good beginning?' In the teeth of everything there was a spun-out ebullient story he couldn't stop himself telling and acting out, as if several whiskies had already taken effect and sparked it off – except that he'd touched none. The story became another limb, crazy and uncontrollable, used without thought, a joyful rigmarole spinning words out of the night of himself. It was a bout of inspired clowning, like a flash of sheet lightning that opens – and glows metallic and incandescent against the horizon of the mind until the story or clowning has gone.

She was laughing by the end, brought over to him by a short-circuit that avoided the separate complex depths in each of them. It was silence or laughter, and though he could find out little or nothing in face of either, he preferred to see her laughing, which meant at least a warmer welcome. She lay out flat and shook off her pyjamas, naked but for a bangle on her wrist, an oriental maja. Her fleshy nakedness was matched to the damp perspiring night, was connected in some way, he thought, looking up, with the dance of death around the moth lamp of electricity: what the dark bellies of the geckos missed, the sun captured and sizzled to death. He thought back through her nakedness to his sweetheart girl-friends of Nottingham, of how true it was that no matter how many times they had made love together he had never seen any of them completely bare of clothes (except Pauline, his wife, but she did not count), not slept the night and seen them as he saw Mimi now, talking as if her birthday suit were the latest fashion advertised in the *Straits Times* – something to be shown off and proud of, acquired at enough expense to justify revealing it in the flattering half-light to Brian for whom she had a sort of love that neither could explain nor yet feel compromised by. There was uncertainty as to which was more real: to go slowly through layer after layer of tormenting yet hypnotic cloth and cotton and discover the smooth whiteness with exploring fingers, or take one nakedness straight to the other or your own. It was a matter of climate and locality, a difference as much evident in his own body and brain as between two far parts of the earth: jungle with field, swamp and wooded hillocks, a sea of sharks and stingrays, to the slow meadow-winding of Midland rivers whose banks were sometimes as heavily clothed as the girl he lay with while watching their heavy cumbersome unwilling serpentining through the winter.

'I'll make some tea soon,' she said, returning his kisses, 'and then we'll be cooler.'

'It'd need eight pints of beer to stop my thirst, but then I'd be good for nothing!' Tea was a natural division of their meeting time, after which they made love, a ritual evolved through many visits. 'When I get back to Nottingham I wain't be able to drink the steaming mash my mother makes, with sugar and milk. I like it cold and weak now, served up in bowls.'

Her thin arms slid away from his neck: 'You'll soon get back to the English way.' He was used to the rhythm of her voice, so that while complete sentences registered more quickly he lost the facility for reading hidden meanings in them, accents and stresses being removed as the need for repetition waned. His dexterity at reading Morse rhythms had proved a loss in that it enabled him to master Mimi's too soon, and because her own language was Chinese, she was able to hide so much in her flat deliverance of English. 'I'm not going back to England,' he said.

She seemed surprised. 'Why? It's a very nice country. That's what it says in the *Straits Times*!'

'It might be, but I don't like it.'

'Well, you've got to go back,' she smiled. 'You promised to send me those books and things.'

He'd forgotten about that: books of sexual technique and contraception. 'You know enough of that without me sending you books on it.'

'I like to read about it though,' she said petulantly; he seemed to be going back on his word.

'All right,' he said; 'but I've still got a year to do out here. I might even stay on longer.'

Insects were worrying her: she disentangled a sheet and drew it up. 'You haven't got a job in Malaya, so you've got to go back.'

'I could get work as a rubber planter. It wouldn't take me long to learn Malay, if I really tried.'

'What's England like?' she asked. 'Tell me about England.'

'I don't know anything about England. But I'll tell you about Nottingham if you tell me about the jungle. If the insects are bothering you, pull your net down.'

'They're not: they never do. If you became a rubber planter you'd be in big danger.' Neither spoke. They heard the croak of bullfrogs and crickets working their looms of noise in the deep grass outside. Dogs barked from the huts, and the surviving wail of a steamer siren from Muong harbour came debilitated after its fight with tree shadows and avoidance of village lights. He laughed: 'You sound like a gipsy giving me a warning. There's no danger in being in Malaya.'

The bed creaked as she faced him more fully, her coal-like eyes shining with concern: 'You think you're living in a peaceful country then?'

He smiled – for the benefit of himself. It seemed peaceful enough: tigers, snakes and a no-good climate, but what did that matter? 'It's OK,' he said. 'Just take things in your stride, then you'll be all right. I ain't been in the jungle yet, but I might even do that soon. Some of us on the camp are thinking of climbing up to Gunong Barat to see what mountain-jungle is really like. Uphill all the way, I suppose.' He remembered seeing Pulau Timur for the first time, an island viewed from twenty miles and six thousand feet away as the Avro 19 roared high along the coastal swamps up from Singapore. Pulau Timur was an inanimate crumple of green hills lying in bright blue sea just off the mainland, looking from so high like the plasticine relief models he used to make at school, glittering under the light-bulb of the midday sun.

The Avro closed in low over its port of Muong, climbed the wooden hills behind and threw a shadow on empty sea to the west. Brian's stomach didn't turn willingly with the plane, whose belly seemed to scrape a hilltop when it turned back over the island and descended for a run-in across the two-mile straits. Down over blue water, the runway was like a glistening slice of canal, widening between trees in front. He saw sand under the water, a couple of sampans hastening out of the way, fishing traps sticking from the surface like knives ready for the plane's belly, then a long sandy beach passed in a yellow line on either side and the engines dipped ominously. This was the moment of fear, when science seemed to desert them and silence take over. Brian looked to the left and saw a huge mountain far off to the north, its grandiose peak pointing skywards, indicating a direction that he'd never before taken note of. The isolation of it reached to something in himself, the solid independent greyness beyond heat and cold, half-way into another world that attracted him, in a few seconds, more than anything else ever had. The far side of the moon seemed as familiar as his own cousin compared to this new dimension of life glimpsed far off beyond the water and coastal swamps. Then the vision went as engines roared and the plane passed over a tarmac road along the shore where cars, lorries and bullock carts waited for its descent, rolled by a few wooden buildings, palms, ramshackle control tower, until a bump and jerk brought it on to the runway and gave him a feeling of relief to have landed. A few evenings later he stood on the beach watching the sky above Palau Timur, orange, yellow, green and bloody colours streaked like a horizontal waterfall over the hills, stretching south to north and boiling away towards Siam and Burma. Palm trees bent over the water, and night-fires burned in fishing villages, pointing to the mountain he had seen from the plane. He had discovered its name: Gunong Barat – the mountain of the west – and seen its height marked on a map as four thousand feet. It stood separate from the main range of Malaya, a series of peaks and humpbacks divided by forest, filled gullies and watercourses, culminating in one pinnacle that dominated the landscape for miles. On nights of full moon its sharp ridges stood out as if it were an island, rearing up from mangrove swamps, king of the small towns and paddy fields of the coastal plain, far more complex in structure, he saw than had appeared in one simple glimpse from the plane window. He hoped to be able to climb it, but didn't suppose the opportunity would ever arrive. It was twenty-four miles north of the camp, covered in thick jungle, trackless and, he thought, probably wouldn't be worth climbing anyway. 'I don't know what you want to go up there for,' Mimi said. 'Nobody lives there.'

'How do you know? I've heard that right on top is a caff where they sell cream buns and coffee, run by a bloke from Yorkshire. He's been there thirty years and don't get much trade because everybody thinks nobody lives up there.'

'You're pulling my leg,' she laughed. 'But you don't know what I mean. There's going to be a lot of fighting in Malaya because people don't like the British being here. There'll be a war.' He knew there might, having read in newspapers of murders on rubber estates, of people being shot for mysterious reasons that the newspapers couldn't fathom. Not long after coming up from Singapore he asked a telephone corporal why it was still necessary to put ON ACTIVE SERVICE across all letters, and he replied that the Malayan People's Anti-Japanese Army, supplied with arms during the War by the British, had now turned awkward and didn't want to give them back, were in fact becoming an anti-British army because they wanted independence. 'And it'll get worse,' the corporal said, a prophet who knew everything. 'There'll be such a bloody bust-up one day. I only hope I'm not here to see it, though I suppose it's my luck I will be.'

'Well,' Brian said lightly, 'maybe I'll just go back to England as soon as I can and take a nice safe job in some factory or other. Then I'll be able to send you them books on sex I promised you.' He pulled the sheet gently down and caressed her. 'I don't want to go back though. I want to stay here for keeps.'

'This isn't any good for you. What will happen when the fighting starts? Everybody thinks that a communist army is going to come out of the jungle and kill the British. Nobody can stop them, they think. And maybe a lot of Chinese and Malays will get killed as well.'

'I don't know. Anyway' – half facetious and serious – 'I'm a communist, so maybe I'll be all right.'

'You shouldn't joke.'

'I'm not joking. You ask me to tell you something about England, don't you?' He lit cigarettes. 'The smoke'll scare the insects away. I come from a scruffy old house in Nottingham, and before the War I remember seeing my old man crying – in tears – because he was out o' wok and unemployed. He hadn't worked for years, and there was never any dough and hardly enough grub in the house. The kids were better off, mind you, because they had free milk and a hot dinner every day – they had to mek sure we'd be fit for the War and to fight communists, the sly bastards. It's a bit better now, but why should I be against the communists?'

'I don't know,' she said; 'but you are, aren't you?'

'That's what you think.'

'All the rest of the British are.'

'Don't be so sure. I'm not. I can tell you that. I've got a mind of my own.' His serious mood was shattered by Mimi's serious face, by some air bubble that broke in the bloodstream of his imagination. 'So if you know any true-red communist wants to buy a Sten gun and fifty rounds of ammunition, tell 'im I've got one. If he can't afford to buy it all at once he can pay me ten dollars a week. Or a crate of Tiger Beer now and again.'

'You're crazy,' she laughed. 'I've never met anyone so crazy.'

'I'm a no-good loon, and that's why you love me, i'n't it?' he said, kissing her mouth, neck and breasts, pressing her scarcely perceptible nipples in a black rage of passion, a bolt of lightning forcing his hand around the back of her. She broke away and reached for a dressing-gown: 'Get undressed. I'll fetch some tea, and we can drink it in the dark.'

Silence was the melting away of a stockade that released his thoughts. They came like pictures from the past, less clear than reality, though more definite than dreams, but at the same time more tribal than thoughts, let in by a disabled present. The darker more tangible tide of Nottingham streets and people sent tentacles to the jungled hills of Malaya, assailing him at their own select times, sometimes infecting him with the poison needle of nostalgia, though often with a whirlpool of dislike and determination never to go back there if he could help it, to let its huge sprawling mark shrink and rot in some far-off lumbered-up corner of his memory. Reactions were strong because at nineteen the future did not exist: present passions were based on what had gone before, and Nottingham found it easy to jostle Malaya from his brain.

He unbuttoned his shirt, sat listlessly on the bed waiting for her to come back. Unlike in the wireless hut, he hated to be alone here – as if dangerous ghosts were waiting to spring from each corner. It was a strange room, too much filled with the personality of someone and something else, a staging post through which many people had gone before. He smiled: well, you couldn't blame anybody for that. It smelt of perfume and perspiration, talcum powder and musk from the outside trees, blended with a subdued odour of Patani mud and joss. His hand touched the bed where Mimi's warm body had lain, and he lay back deeper in a foreign land than he'd ever imagined, and smiled to think he hadn't been far wrong when he swore to grandad Merton as a kid that he'd go one day to Abyssinia. I expect he'd a bin satisfied wi' this, right enough. 'The dirty young bogger,' he'd have said. 'Trust 'im to get 'old of a woman as soon as 'e gets there! He's a chip off my block all right.'

The tray made a faint rattling along the veranda, night music muted by the soft tread of her returning bare feet – careful for splinters in the worn boards. He listened in a daze, as if sounds concerned only some far-off neighbour of himself, was abstracted and motionless almost until she reached the door; then, still without waking, merely as if his state of abstraction had quickened, he slipped off his shorts and pulled the sheet over him, reaching for a cigarette to which the match flared as Mimi's hand put out the light. The last sight as he lay back at ease was of the gecko shooting forward and devouring a mosquito that had been whining up to then around the room for blood. The skin behind his shoulder itched slightly, so he was sure the mosquito had had plenty, and he grinned at the thought of part of himself being twice removed in the depths of another gut, like that far-fetched tale about Jonah fast in the raps of a whale.

She set the tray on the floor, and he felt her breathing as she bent over to give him tea. 'Marvellous,' he said as they drank. 'I'm croaking to death.' She crouched by the bed, laying the tea aside after one sip, and putting her arm on him. 'Brian, Brian,' she whispered. There was no tone in the words, and he didn't understand them. 'What's up?' he said loudly. 'You think the bullfrogs'll get yer?' His tea had gone in one gulp. 'I can't tell what I think,' she said. 'Neither can I,' he answered, disturbed because he knew he should be able to. Maybe he could, yet wouldn't. Thinking was like swimming under water: you have to develop a knack of doing so while holding your nose so that you don't drown. If you couldn't think sometimes, you floated, but that was no good, for all the colours and delights of the world were often under the surface: rocks and seaweeds, water-snakes and fantastic fishes – dreams and cartwheels of the imagination. But he couldn't swim under the water at will: mostly when he tried his lungs and ears seemed ready to explode, and he surfaced quickly to get out of danger. Sometimes, though, he stayed under long enough to enoy sights and sensations, and he felt that if he concentrated on breaking over the effort and fear he would eventually be able to master it. Thought was like this, almost as impossible to master as the water, yet always drawing him as if holding out the promise that one day he would be able to descend safely into his own mind, much farther down than he was able to now.

His hand roved up and down her, along the smooth skin of a backbone that seemed well marked because he couldn't see it. She laughed: 'I've got you in a hurry at last.'

'I was thinking,' he said, half teasing her but keeping his hand around. 'I'm always in a hurry, you know that. We've been 'ere hours already, and I've got to get back soon.'

'It's silly,' she said, 'and sad for me.' He didn't know whether she meant it or not, but couldn't care now because she stood up and put off her dressing-gown, and he knew them both to be enflamed and ready, feeling her hand at his groin as she lay beside him. The sensation turned him into a lion of kisses, and his past and present merged and were conquered so that there weren't two places on the earth for him but one, united by the flames and aches that both of them were scorched with, streets and green jungle joined into one moment of now.

'You're my love,' he said, 'and this is the only way I can really understand you.' Maybe time and places were joined for her too. 'I love you, I said.' Silence between them – Mimi never spoke when they made love: words stood no chance against the orgiastic working of her limbs and body.

Both were still, as if drawing breath before the fire. Life in the trees outside was a roar over their peace, filling the room with sounds, bullfrogs mating, crickets by the thousand spinning miniature klaxons as if at some voiceless football match, and the dull and distant noise of breakers burying grey heads in the sand at all they had seen below them on their journey across the shameless sea – the common speech of the night air in Malaya.

He lifted his body and thrust forward.

18

I've only to say I hate Nottingham, he thought with a silent ironic laugh, for all the years it's put on me to come into my mind as clear as framed photos outside a picture house. He was in Radford at fifteen, going to work on Easter Sunday to clean the boilers and chimney flues while the fires were out, a volunteer because double-time was paid and he was saving up for a bike. One and five an hour instead of eightpence ha'penny was corn in Egypt – or would be if you got it all the time. He left the house while the night was black, making his way along the silent streets at half-past five, avoiding dead-headed lamp-posts for fear of knocking himself flat. A fine rain fell and he pulled up his coat collar, shivering at the sudden impact of water, yet happy because he hadn't far to walk. Seaton had told him not to go in: 'You don't need the money all that much, my lad; and you'll work harder enough when you're older.' He recognized the onus of unnecessary overtime that Brian was going into blithely, and took on his own shoulders and into his own heart the distaste his lad should have felt but couldn't. To Brian it seemed a step forward, to work when hardly anybody else was and win the self-esteem of double time.

A group of over-sixteens had already done a ten-till-six night shift. Light stemmed from the door at the end of the corridor, and stars shone above the sheer windowless walls of it – one wall taller than another so that the sky looked like the jewel-studded underside of an enormous cutting blade. At his feet was a manhole with the lid off, and half the gangway was choked by piles of soot and clinker excavated from the factory bowels. So this is what we have to shift, the sight of it already making his throat dry and wanting cups of tea. He looked down into the boiler room, at a host of pipes and dials upside down over a cavernous circular door out of which, arse backwards and legs kicking, came Jack Parker. His face, hands and boiler suit were blacker than the back of dominoes, and he stood up cursing because of it. 'I'm glad I don't have to clean that lot out in there. There's mountains of soot and it's 'ot yet at back.'

'I suppose the young 'uns 'ull 'ev ter do it then,' Ted Bosely the mechanic said. Brian had been told by Samson the manager not to clock in for this extra work: 'It's against the Factory Act, seeing as you aren't sixteen yet,' Bosely said, 'so keep it quiet.' He walked through the shadowless cellars, between huge rolls of paper stacked almost to the sprinkler valves. What a fire there'd be if this lot went up, he thought, warmed by the image of it. There'd be no black-out then. 'Appen the Jerries'll get it one night, though I suppose the raids wain't start any more. A nub-end might do it, and if it did I'll bet it'd tek more than the sprinklers to put it out. Parker was taking off his beret as he went into the stoke-hole, revealing a springy mop of flaming auburn hair. 'Your turn now,' he said, seeing Brian.

'It ain't six yet,' Brian answered, watching his rights. Nevertheless he took the spade. On either side of the furnace mouth were two flue holes about a foot square, the left one going parallel with the furnace, then rounding the back and emerging to the right of it. 'I've shovelled a good bit from the front,' Parker said, taking out a pocket mirror: 'Christ, I look like a bleeding collier.'

'Aye,' Bosely said, also ready to go off, 'they'll 'ev yer in the pit yet.'

Just after six Brian looked into the stoke-hole flue but could see nothing, then got on his knees and pushed himself in to the waist to find it black and suffocatingly warm. With one heave he was right in and flat on his stomach, taking care to drag the shovel and keep it by for when he needed to begin excavations. He wriggled forward over brick flooring, intrigued at the lugubrious new world he had pitched into. It was black and tight around him, all sounds blocked from the outside. He lay still, astonished, pleased in a way that he'd been allowed to stumble into this fabulous mechanism of the industrial world, unwilling to start work before revelling a moment in it. It was warm, and frightening if he thought too much, but he went on a few feet until reaching drifts of hot dust piled almost to the top bricks. It was impossible to stay there, and he went on for as far as he could go, his body and face almost immersed in the powder, nose eyes ears filled with it. He tried to turn round, and the discovery that he couldn't in the confined space sent a spear of panic through him. Dust kicked up by movement stopped his breath and he lay as if dead in his endless coffin, yet breathing quickly so as to make the least ferment. He had been out of school more than a year and this was his second job, so he regarded himself as an experienced member of the labour market, a man of the factory world already smoking and passing himself off for eighteen in pubs where the waiters turned a blind eye; also he was courting what girl he could get hold of, and had been in a fight last Saturday so wasn't going to be beaten by a bit of tubercular soot.

Lying still, his apprehension went. I'll just drop out for a breather, then get stuck in proper. He had to move because the bricks were too warm for much hugging. It's hot and I'm smothercating, though I suppose there's worse things at sea. The impression was of a coffin with lid on tight but minus head and foot, and having to work in the dark set him thinking of coalmines and pit ponies, and the fact that he would go crackers if he didn't get out and prove he wasn't buried a thousand feet underground. Jean Valjean traipsing through the sewers was better off than this, though I expect Edmond Dantès in *his* tunnels didn't feel too good either. He gripped a handful of soot, hoping it would solidify, but it fell like the fine sand of an egg-timer through his opened fingers. If I had to do this to escape from prison I wouldn't give a bogger, would get crackin' and work my balls off, be out in no time, but as for the slave-driving penny-pinching poxetten getts of this flyblown factory – I'll do as I like; and if they don't like it they can whistle, because they wain't be able to see me for a start. Knees and hands were burning, so he pushed backwards until his feet hung in mid-air and light over his shoulder told him he was in the clear breath of the open cellar.

The bulbs dazzled him. 'That was a quick look round,' Mr Wheatcroft said. 'You was only in two minutes.'

'It felt like a bleeding year.' Brian rubbed hands and knees, batted soot from his clothes, wanted to look at his face but couldn't see a mirror anywhere. 'I'll get back now though and dig a bit out.'

'That's a good lad,' Wheatcroft said. 'Don't stay in too long at a time or you might conk-out on us. I'll set Bill Eddison starting from the other side. You'll soon 'ave it done between yer.'

Per'aps, Brian said to himself, back into the black soot of the tunnel. 'Don't volunteer for owt,' the old man had told him time and time again, but he'd never taken notice of him, though his common sense should have said that anything needing to be volunteered for was sure to land you smack into the clutches of hardship. 'Don't join owt, not even a Christmas club, not two pieces of effing string.' And Brian realized, from the deep passion of experience ringing in the old man's words, that he couldn't but be right. The trouble was though that you joined or volunteered even before you knew you were going to do so. A trait you knew nothing about and certainly could never trust lurked within, waiting for a weak moment when somebody asked you to volunteer or join, and then before you knew where you were you were fighting for breath like now in the Black Hole of Calcutta, shovelling soot for all you were worth at seventeen pence an hour. Sweat flowed out of him. This is how you get TB he thought, by breathing black dust like this for hour after hour. I'm croaking already.

He devised a system: dragged a load of soot, shovel by shovel from in front, then (having found a doubling-up technique after many try-outs) turned himself to face the isolated mound and push it bit by bit to the opening. Then back to the soot-face to part off another load. I'll get an X-ray next week, he thought. He'd been asked by Jim Skelton to go with him for one weeks ago, but hadn't been able to make up his mind. He knew he was afraid, and wasn't shy of admitting it, but now thought he ought to go because of the double doses of fine dust already causing him to cough for half a minute at a time. If I've got it I've got it, and if I ain't I ain't. You've only got to die once. It was a disease he'd been afraid of all his life because everybody seemed to die of it, even more than war. Aunt Lydia's bloke Tom had kicked the bucket, eaten to a shadow by it. Less to feed maybe, but it was a bleddy shame. Mrs Coutts died of it as well, and so had a good many more whose names he'd forgotten. It was a disease he was yellow of, just as he'd been frightened of being blown up when bombs were falling a year or so back. So I'll keep the X-ray date with Jim Skelton and see where I stand.

He worked his way up the tunnel. Soot was lukewarm on top but scorched his hands and knees when he scooped down to the bricks. He'd retreat a few feet until his hands cooled, then go forward to make a few more rapid sweeps with his shovel. Why am I going like a bleddy mad-head? he asked himself. To get it finished, he answered, pushing another load out of the opening. He'd been eight months at Robinson's cardboard-factory: a tall building blackened with age and the odours of sweated labour in the middle of a long street of two-up and two-down houses. At first he was an odd-job lad, lifting, carrying, running errands and sweeping up. He clocked in at eight every morning, and for a few weeks was set helping the charwoman to clean the offices during the first hour. This was a light and leisurely job, something that helped the morning go quicker in that he didn't begin real work in the factory till nine. Tea-break at ten, and before he knew where he was he was clocking out at one and running home for dinner. Each director of the firm had his office, and in Mr Rawson's was a huge war-map of Europe, well coloured and of sufficient scale to show the names even of small towns recaptured by the Russians – each one announced by Moscow to the accompaniment of ten salvos from three hundred and twenty-odd guns, and repeated on the nine o'clock evening news by the BBC. Solnetchnogorsk, Volokolamsk, Kalach, Ordzhonekidzegrad, Debaltzevo, Barvenkovo, Taganrog – names of steel and defence in depth, signifying disaster for the Germans on a scale that even they couldn't comprehend, brute force triumphing this time on the right side and smashing inch by inch towards the belly-button of Berlin. In full black flower the Germans had gone goose-stepping into the land where all factories and property were owned by the people, and had made it grim and awful with starvation and suffering, a country which would one day become the promised land of the earth where bread would be free and men would work only four hours a day

The very name Russia Russia Russia touched Brian like a root-word (even before he knew it meant much more than a country) and gave him an understanding of its invincibility, so that when he first heard that Germany had gone into Russia he was glad because the war had started to end. Meanwhile the German image was rampaging: a giant figure with buckshot teeth and a crossbow face, piked hands and hatchet feet, gun-metal eyes and barbed-wire hair, a sandbag forehead and armoured body – yet reeling now, bleeding from Stalingrad and Moscow, smashed everywhere by the Red Army, the returning hordes of the working man washing in like broad rivers of retribution making for the bigshot nazi rats of Germany. He laughed, buried in the black hole of Robinson's factory, pushing soot under his belly and back towards his feet like the dead dust of burned-up Germans.

At home he had his own maps of the Russian front, not so grand and durable as Mr Rawson's, yet sufficient for him to mark by pencil the sinuous band of scorched earth and death. It was a game, listening for the latest towns to fall and changing the front accordingly. If the Soviet line of advance bulged too far west between Bryansk and Kharkov he knew that the Germans along the Donets farther south would be cut off unless they skedaddled quick. There were few newspapers at home, and at the beginning of the invasion he had difficulty in equating the place-names given on the wireless with their written forms on the map. He'd searched hours before finding one particular locality, had pored over the map with his cousin Bert – who was also taken with the War game set loose by Hitler. The difficult name ended the uphill climb of comprehension, for after this had been marked and mastered, every other town came easy. The six syllables at normal announcer's speed went too swiftly into Brian's ear, sounded like a saw going into wood: BYELAY-ATSERKOV. Battles raged around it for days, until the noise of it sunk in: BYELAYATSERKOV. Bert helped him look for it, a word joining their thoughts and difficult to forget after so much repetition, a holy grail searched for within a vast circle of Kiev. Bert spotted it first.

Mr Rawson's map held a series of red-headed pins marking the Russian front, and Brian, on the first morning of his office-cleaning, saw they were too far east, hadn't been moved for a week or two. Maybe Rawson had lost interest; it certainly wasn't because he was too hardworking to shift them, for he was one of the younger and less hard-driving directors, a man about thirty-five with a squat face and ginger hair matted back, a good-natured man, it was assumed, since if he passed when you weren't working he didn't tell you off about it. He wore a big pair of spectacles over his heavy moustache, was a safely married man in no danger of being called up for the forces because his work at Robinson's was said to be of national importance. Some held this freedom from the army against him, saying he should be fighting even though he was a relation of big boss Robinson himself, but one or two of the old sweats said he was doing well to keep out of it, and good luck to him.

Brian swept his office, emptied the wastepaper basket, dusted the Remington (after typing out his name and putting a few paper-clips in his pocket), then studied Rawson's map of Russia, offended that the pins had been neglected for so long. The front still led from Leningrad through Moscow to Stalingrad and into the Caucasus, whereas vast areas had passed again within bounds of the Red Army. A crippling thought came to him: maybe Rawson had only been interested in the farthest limit of the German advance, and couldn't bring himself to rejoice over land recaptured by the Soviet forces. He laughed and, in a frenzy – it was five minutes to nine – began moving pins to their rightful places, and before he took his brushes and rags and tins of polish back to the cleaning woman the Russian front was fixed in accurate positions once more.

He felt better, from then on made a more thorough job of cleaning the office, and of moving the pins each morning to their rightful places as fresh towns were captured. One day he didn't resist the temptation to write in pencil SECOND FRONT NOW on the bottom margin of the map. A lark, he told himself.

I'll see'f he notices it, find out whether he's altogether fed up with his toy pins or not. Maybe I'd better rub it off though: some blokes don't like the Russians; either that or they're fussy about people writing on their posh maps. Yet he left it on, for somehow he'd hoped for recognition, a sign perhaps, a few words at least, from Mr Rawson saying that he was knowledgeable and clever at being able to find the complicated names of Russian towns and in plotting the front line with such vivid accuracy. Who else out of the two hundred working at the factory could have done it? No one as far as he knew, and that was a fact. You'd have thought old Rawson would have come along and said: 'You're a bit of a hand at the maps, Seaton. We's'll have to see if we can't find you a job in the office one of these days.' But they don't do things like that. And what can you do if they don't? You can't go up to him and say: 'Eh, Mr Rawson, have yo' seen what I've done to your map? I thought it was a shame it being such a good 'un and the pins in all the wrong places.' In one way he might think it a bit of a cheek, me taking his game over without saying a dicky-bird, though on the other hand he can't be offended if he don't even see what I've done, and neither in that case can he offer me a job in the offices. Not that I want one anyway, because you'd have to wear a suit and a clean shirt every day, and where would I get the dough to find owt like that? Mam wouldn't be able to do it. I'd rather stick in the factory and rough it with the rest of the lads.

By dinner-time he'd cleared soot from the first half of the left-hand flue. The length behind was now too long to push the soot out with his shovel so he went in with a couple of deep pans, and when both were filled he dragged them to the opening. Near the far turning behind the stoke-hole, soot drifts went up as far as the ceiling, and the heat was fierce under him. Sweat became mud on his face, ran to his mouth to be blown away when it chafed, or wiped if he had a free hand. He rested after every six pans, curled up on his side like an experienced collier, craved a cigarette or a mug of tea. Accustomed to the work and heat, confined space and lack of air, he grew to like his temporary double-pay job. There was a feeling of toughness, even danger to it, and if his mother or Aunt Ada or grandad Merton could have seen him now they would have said: 'It can't be good for him, in that hot tunnel. Still, he's a hard worker so it wain't do him much harm.' Also it was good to be on his own where no gaffer could see how much shovelling he did – though for one thing he was doing a good share of work, and for another, he grinned, burying his spade again in the soot, they wouldn't dream of coming up here to see how I was getting on.

Most of the foremen and chargehands had been at Robinson's anything from twenty to forty years, for the firm had a fixed reputation in the neighbourhood: if you get a job there, even though the pay would shame any union into calling out a strike, you could be sure of being kept on for as long as you worked like a slave and touched your cap to the gaffer every time you passed. It was one of those firms that had a tradition of benevolence behind it, meaning hard work and little pay to the right sort of people – those who would serve the firm through their thick and your thin. And before the War, when men were scrabbling for work, those at Robinson's were careful not to give offence to the gaffers and get pitched on to the dole, even though it would have meant a mere few bob a week less, with no work or arse-kissing or danger of getting sacked into the bargain. Wage rates at Robinson's had been carefully regulated – set at a fraction above the dole money, enough to give the incentive of a regular job, but hardly enough to keep its employees far from a harrowing exercise in near starvation. Brian laughed to think of it. Thank God there was a war on: I can allus go somewhere else if they try to come the hard gaffer with me, though I'm not much of a lad at swapping jobs and would rather stay at one place a couple of years to get my hand in and make a few pals. I can't understand people being here forty years – worse than a life sentence – especially when they can get better money at other places. And what do they end up wi' if they plod on here for that long? A cup o' cocoa, a copy of the Bible and a five-bob pocket-watch to time out the days of idleness left to them. Not even that though: I'm making it up. They're lucky to get a thank you, and become hot and bothered with gratitude if they do, or only spit the smell of thank you out when it's too late to do much else about it, such as drop a nub-end on a heap of paraffin rags, to trip one of the gaffers into a manhole. It's too late then, no matter how they feel. Earlier on they thought they'd got a trade and wouldn't turn to labouring – put up with blood-tubs telling 'em what to do as if they was skivvies. But forty years is a lifetime, a waste of breathing in which you could have lived in every country in the world, seen everything, done everything, instead of staying a cap-touching loon in Robinson's rat-warren.

Talking to Bob Thorpe the other day I said that old Robinson was a Bible-backed slave-driver, a two-faced twisting dead-head who'd sell his grandmother wholesale if they came more than two at a time. Old Thorpe said I shouldn't talk like that, and had better not let Robinson or any of the other gaffers hear it. 'What would happen if they did?' I asked, laughing to myself. 'Why,' he said, an almost terrified look on his long face, 'you'd get the sack.' He's a pasty little bloke of sixty. 'That'd be terrible,' I said. 'I'd have to get another job, wouldn't I?' Then he brightened up and said: 'You won't be so cocky after the War, when jobs is hard to get again.' 'Don't bother,' I said, quick off the mark, 'Old Fatguts with the big cigar will be out when the War's over, on his neck with the rest of his government. It wain't be the same again. Them days is over.' At least they'd better be. Yet nobody could be sure, and neither was Brian, despite the look of dead certainty on his face; for he dreaded the return of his father's means-test fate on himself. I'll shoot myself first, he thought. No, better shoot the other bastards, then maybe it'll alter before I do it to myself.

After three months' general work at Robinson's the foreman set him on as a pasteboy, mixing water and flour into brown paste at the bins, a sprinkling of alum added as the whole mass came to the boil. He carried hundredweight sacks of flour from a near-by stack and poured it in from the encrusted wooden rim of the bin. There was only one thing to compare the stench to: and his spit at the end of a day's work was coloured orange. A plug under the bin could be released by a lever from the rolling room in the cellar where the cardboard was made. When both vats were full he would stand in the spare minutes at the top of the steps and watch the three or four sheets of paper being drawn into the set of old-fashioned trundling rollers. Bob Thorpe was in charge of the whole operation, a master card-board-maker who had been thirty years with these same machines, an old bald bachelor, gentle and quiet-spoken, said to read books, only ferocious when enough paste from the bins in heaven above wasn't available to feed his beloved and all-powerful rollers. Then a cornered gleam would come in his eyes and fear of the sack would make him shout to Brian all the filthy words under the sun. Brian cursed back, though set to making more paste. The rollers ran only two days a week, and it was pandemonium in the cellars and around the pastebins, the antiquated machinery jangling and shaking the cellar roof, and even the ceiling of the department above that. Brian became strong in carrying sacks and mixing paste, felt his body and muscles hardening so that what had been almost intolerable burdens were now easily tackled. The heavier the work the more he revelled, drew both physical and spiritual elation from it, going home in the evening tired and dead to the wide on the surface, yet feeling alive and glowing with a sort of interior energy that kept him vivid and active for his long walks with Pauline in the fields and woods.

For the rest of the week he transported trolleys of wet cardboard up on the hoist to the steamheated drying-rooms at the top of the factory; hanging the sheets to dry with a row of other boys, then wheeling them back to the presses, and from there to the cutting-room; finally to the women packers and stacking the bales for railway vans to take away. There was often a time lag when the last wet sheets were finally clipped up and weren't yet dry, a recognized perk that allowed the boys on the job to lounge around until the boards were crisp and so razor-sharp at the ragged edges that they had to be careful not to slice their fingers in taking them down. It was a pleasant relaxed greenhouse atmosphere that reigned, the half-dozen of them sprawled on the warm and dusty floorboards talking or reading comics, far above the drone of traffic and engines working below, left in the heaven of the factory that Brian –

from the black flues of the boiler-room – realized was the opposite of constriction and soot.

Now and again in his underground burrow he put down his spade for no reason and stared open-eyed, unseeing at the darkness, too aware of the roof an inch or so above his head, and the wall on either side nudging at his elbows. The sensation that it was getting smaller struck him like a knife across the eyes: he lay flat on his belly and drew his arms in, stiff and silent to create the illusion of more space around, slowing his blood by an act of will, whistling a made-up tune in the hope that the theme music from a recent film he'd been trying to remember all day would come back to him. When bored with being calm he resumed work. Sometimes the attack was too quick, and he was in a panic before any control was possible, so he wriggled back to the opening with the speed of a snake, fell out on to the stoke-room floor, and stood five minutes for a breather and smoke, laughing at the shock he had given the others. He spent much spare time in the drying-rooms teaching Bill Eddison map reading. Sixteen-year-old Bill was a corporal in the Army Cadets who had been promised a third stripe when he passed his Cert A examination. He was a strong, forceful bull-like youth, quick on the draw with wit when talking about jazz and women, but dense on such mathematical subjects as cartography. He played knick-knacks to accompany his dirty songs, jumping up and down to the ballad of 'Eskimo Nell' or swinging away to a neatly worded march of Sousa.

When not courting with Pauline, Brian would go on the pick-up with Bill, starting off of a Sunday night in the fourpenny gods of the fleapit Grand, watching a show of some trash film until bored even with the ironic loud laughter at the old-fashioned style of it; then they'd sneak farther up and find a couple of girls to slide their arms around. Sometimes the girls were out for a thrill as well and they'd soon be locked in mouth-to-mouth combat from which no quarter was given. It was the kind of sport Brian liked, and he often tried to go the whole way while still on the back row so that even Bill Eddison was shocked. One night Brian had a girl's blouse undone and her breasts exposed to his roaming hands, and was bending her so far over the seat that a little girl to the left became more fascinated than at movements on the screen and asked, in a bright inquiring voice, 'Mam, what's that man doing to that woman?' Bill prodded him, piqued at not getting half so far with his girl. 'Let's get cracking before you get thrown out.' At which the four of them clattered off for fish and chips before the usherette came back with the manager.

Mostly though, Brian spent his evenings with Pauline. They liked going out with each other, and she had come to him the first time out of the dark back seats of the Savoy picture house: when the cheap war film was winding to a shindig finish and all interest had gone (why didn't the hero, who you knew would live, get killed? And why didn't those who had death in their sad eyes live?), he turned and saw her, isolated among seats, face set on the screen, quietly looking at it though without the intent fastening he often felt in his own gaze. He moved over, a lone wolf tonight, sat by her side and talked. 'I can't stick pictures like these: they give me a gut-ache.' After a pause she said: 'Why do you come then?' ''Cause I thought it'd be good.' 'Well, now you know, don't you?' At least she was talking: a good start. 'I do an' all. I wain't come again though, unless yo' do. There's a better film on next week: a musical. Kay Kaiser and his band.' 'I like Harry James best.' 'I do sometimes. That big trumpet makes me feel as if I've got frogs in my tab-'ole though.' 'Wash 'em out, and then it wouldn't, would it?' His arm was around the shoulder of her seat. 'I'll walk home with you, if you like,' he said. 'I've got somebody,' she told him. While God Save the King played they made for the exit, and a youth came down the aisle and took Pauline's arm. 'Lay off, mate,' Brian said. 'I'm seeing her home.' 'That's what yo' think,' the youth said. 'That's what I know,' Brian told him. There was some disappointment in him at the girl not coming over to his side, though he grinned at the fact that they didn't even know each other's names. So why should she? He had one arm, and the other was taken by the tall youth, who looked brawnier than the picture he carried of himself in the wallet of his heart, though that might have been because of his heavy dark overcoat and the white muffler around his neck. Brian thought he knew him from some factory or other.

The black-out blinded him. She didn't try to shake the youth off, nor get rid of Brian, but walked calmly between them both, as if knowing that it would resolve itself somehow and that when she ended up with only one of them, she'd then decide whether or not she wanted him. I suppose I should scram, Brian thought. If they are courting I ought to leave them alone. They might even be engaged for all I know. His instinct was to undertake himself into the darkest part of the black-out. Maybe they're childhood sweethearts and I'm breaking it all up. But he kept a grip on her arm (later they were able to laugh over it), his mind blank with stubbornness, walking with her and the youth across the dark main road and into a quiet street.

The youth pulled them to a violent stop, and Brian was treated to a blood-red oilgusher spouting before his eyes, a multicolour flash that made him let go of Pauline and stagger backwards to a chapel wall, roaring at the shock. The blow carried the seed of retaliation, he swung his fist against the youth's head, clenched fingers ringing with pain as if he had struck concrete or iron. Pauline stood in the middle of the road like a shadow, waiting for one or the other, and Brian decided it would be him, his mind changing to not-so-sure as he wheeled again into the wall from a strong thump in his chest. He gasped, realized that it was no play-acting, that this was a total fight from which there was no running away. He lost his nerve and drove wild, made to the left of the youth as if to give the impression of cunning, feeling for some weak spot in his perimeter before returning a blow. With head down he charged, under the fists and coming up too close to be struck, gripping him around the waist and pulling tight, knowing his strength would be able to bend him down double and drop him to the kerb. Both hands locked, he squeezed inwards, the youth's arms fastened safe, Brian's chin grinding his chest bones, working the strongest pitch of a sack-carrying strength into his adversary – until the youth gave way and dropped. Brian let go, unable to control the deadweight of him, but the youth was up before he could sink his boots for the grapefruit crush. Brian kept close, and after a quiet grunting scuffle he found a head under his arm. In a split second he saw what had come about, tightened the vice of his arm muscles, held the head and beat his other folded hand unmercifully into it, thankful for such good luck – as the pain from the youth's first blows began burning his own face.

The youth kicked and struggled. Brian was gone, sent beyond the world and into a dream of primeval vicious light. 'Stop it,' Pauline cried. 'Stop it.' The words came to him, and his fist, liquid running over the stone of it, held still. 'Yo' 'ed enough?' he demanded, releasing the head. The youth groaned and fell.

'Come on,' he said, 'let's beat it.' She took his arm and they walked off. 'You needn't a done that,' she said angrily. 'He'd a gone in two minutes, I'm sure.' She slung his arm from her.

'You weren't courting?' he said.

'Course we worn't. He'd only been sitting with me a minute before you came. He asked me if he could tek me home, and I never answered him.' Brian kept quiet, and she said no more for a while, for which he was glad because he felt tears on his cheeks. He wanted to walk away and never see her again, to bury the shame he felt. A dark wave swamped him, but he needed even more to stay near her, to feel her close because the pain in his heart would then be less. It would tear him apart if he went on his own into the darkness. He kept telling himself to go back and see if the youth was OK, yet at every genuine agonizing demand he was getting farther away. 'I suppose he's all right.'

'I expect so,' she said, taking his arm again. Blood flowed through his pains, an evening on spec at the pictures had ended like this, and he was glad to have fought for this girl, whom he hadn't yet seen in full daylight, and won. 'What's your name, duck?' he asked, pulling her to him in a kiss. A car droned by, lights dim towards town. 'Pauline,' she said. When he got home and dipped his hands into a bowl of water, the water turned pink. Next morning his face was no sight for sore eyes.

In the drying-rooms Brian would pick up a reject piece of cardboard and test Bill on conventional signs, grid references, scales and representative fractions and on how to allow for magnetic variation in true and compass north. The board would become a mass of complex symbols, Chinese to anyone who didn't know what they meant, and Brian also taught him how to make a profile plan from a line across contours, explaining glibly the difference between vertical interval and horizontal equivalents. His knowledge had come from a manual of map-reading discovered one Saturday afternoon in the bookshop downtown. He had studied the book passionately for a few weeks, but had forgotten it when his involvement with Pauline began, until Bill had blurted out one morning that he was having a hell of a bloddy time studying for Cert A because he couldn't make head nor tail of maps.

Bill also had volunteered for the double-time of flue-cleaning, but Brian, now working late into the afternoon and having cleared almost one whole side of the stoke-hole (fed up and dead to the wide, choked with soot and sweating like a pig), suspected he'd been set on an easier job, such as standing in the fresh air of the yard and hauling soot-buckets up on the rope, ready for the lorry. Or maybe not. He'd heard the gaffer say he was to help on the right-hand flue later because they hoped to finish it that day so's the stoker could light up straight away. If Bill's shirked though, he'll get no more map-reading out o' me, the jump-up card. What a pal, though he's a bleddy sight better for a bloke than the no-good gaffers. All they want is higher production and more money in their pockets. They can afford to be patriotic; so would I be. Rawson's supposed to be the best of 'em, but even he's a bastard: Brian had lost his soft first hour of a morning because Rawson had seen and presumably disliked the words SECOND FRONT NOW along the bottom of his office map, Brian being told by the cleaning woman that another boy had been sent in from the factory to take his place. Which is all the thanks and appreciation I get for moving his pins to the proper places.

He swallowed a mouthful of dust and kept going, almost at the turning where he hoped to meet Bill Eddison coming up the other side. He was bitterly tired, as if someone or something were pressing cotton wool on to his eyelids, and the temptation to put down his shovel and go to sleep was hard to resist: it was the sort of acrid tiredness that afflicted him most afternoons with a softening of the limbs, a combat to keep his half-closed eyes from completely shutting off the active world. Usually it carried itself on with too much colour in the revealing glare of light or sun for him finally to ignore it, but now pitch darkness was allied to warmth and the soft breath-catching atmosphere of dust that he automatically shovelled into the shallow pan between his legs, and the natural urge was to curl up to the odorous bank of soft soot and say good-bye to the conscious world of his thoughts. But though the undermining desire was there, the words were not, and his fight against the desire gave the words no chance to break through. His simplified existence was kept in balance by the renewed swinging of his spade, its dig soundless when soot lay high, softer than butter to go through, like skimming the top of velvet. The noise was satisfying when bricks were reached, a muffled scooping of the steel blade along them. In some places near the back the soot had solidified into small porous balls, and here it was hottest, an intolerable climax of his flue-cleaning day.

He did a belly-crawl away from the front line every few minutes and lay on his back until hands and knees had cooled, then he rolled over and went forward again. I'll bet there aren't things much worse at sea. You might die quick there in a storm by drowning, but here you could easily snuff it by inches, of consumption – though God knows I can't say which is worse: a life on the treadmill or to be hung, drawn and quartered. Thank God I don't have to take my pick. A shovel's all I need, so's I can dig myself out of a grave as well as into it like I've done today, or look like doing if I'm lucky and get cracking faster than I'm doing now. It's no good staying here too long, buried like a corpse in the dusty guts of Robinson's old factory, shovelling the gold of my heart out for all I know, hour after bleeding hour where I can't see a thing – though I expect I'd make a good collier. Even though I'm not small I'm getting practice sticking a thing like this, so if I'm lucky I'll get to be a Bevin Boy instead of being sent to fight the Germans, though I'd rather do neither but go my own way to Kingdom Come.

He was working faster than he'd done all day, driven by some inner motor to a higher speed instead of slackening off, slicing the spade into the last few feet of soot to be cleared, scooping it into the pans and using the flat of his hand as a sweeping brush to gather into a heap what the spade was too clumsy to reach.

The day had gone: he hadn't seen it get light and wouldn't see it get dark. I'd go off my loaf if it was like this every day. It occurred to him that he was working too fast, heart racing and throat bone dry, arms aching too much to control. Why? he wondered. What for? he asked himself. Come on, can you tell me that? Why are you going so mad-headed? Why don't you take your sweat, you barmy bleeder? He had already stopped, pushed back the pans and lay full length, a blissful stillness going like a pint of thick mild into his limbs. What's the point of going so hard? If you don't finish today you'll finish tomorrow.

But he wanted to get out of the earth, to see daylight and smell fresh air, to walk in the wind-thumped streets even if only to see the odd star above dark rooftops, to be out, away, a thousand miles off. He opened his eyes: 'I'll leave this putrid firm. I'll get my release and go somewhere else, even if I have to bike five miles there and back every day. I've had enough of this, one way or another.' The thought made him happy and his spade scooped at the wall of soot. Between lying half-asleep and a refreshed burst of action, his mind had been blank; he wasn't aware of thinking about getting back to work or making a decision – but a spark of life had exploded in his limbs and he was going forward even faster, ripping away the obstacle to he didn't know where.

A spade that didn't belong to him flew past his face and chipped a piece out of the brickwork, and suddenly Bill Eddison's voice bellowed a foot away from the blackness in front: 'Well if it ain't owd Brian! We've finished the bleeding thing at last.' They threw their arms around each other, and went on laughing in their victory.

19

Alone in the Camp Library, a mug of tea at his elbow just left by the char-wallah, he unrolled an outline survey map of Pulau Timur. A fresh batch of radio operators had been flown up from Singapore, and fourteen days' leave at Muka holiday camp had at last been handed out to him. He felt fresh after a shower, not yet sweat-soaked from the uprisen sun, dressed in immaculate white shirt and shorts brought back by the Chinese dhobi woman an hour since: his finger traced the coast up from Muong and stopped at Muka – a palm-lined bay facing Gunong Barat across the few miles of flat, variously marked blues of the water. Between swigs of tea his eyes roamed the map: printed in 1940, he noticed, a time for history books – over the hill and far away, an iceberg melted by the ever-turning suns of time, a year he remembered vividly as the date when his cousins Colin and Dave one by one went into the army and one by one, after a few weeks, came out again. He watched them return when everybody else seemed to be going, a strange thing, though underneath his quiet curiosity at their khaki uniforms draped over a chairback like the skin-trophy of some animal was a profound and unquestionable certainty that they were doing something right and good. Ada helped them, and so did the rest, for both climate and tradition were right for it. Out of a dozen able-bodied men in all remotely connected branches of the family, only two went into the army and stayed, and one was killed in Tunisia. 'I told you so,' was the verdict of the rest, who either deserted or found their way into some sort of reserved occupation. It must be a record, Brian thought, for one family. Nobody can say we didn't do our bit for freedom; though what I'm doing here I don't know – except that there isn't a war on.

His world and everybody else's had changed since then, and it had been about time, though his life at the moment seemed like an island set aside from the main coastline of his well-trod continent. Malaya was an interlude, he felt, and he was set out in the blue, like the song that had been sweeping and saturating the country for the past six months: 'Beyond the Blue Horizon', records of it being played in the cafés, whistled, sung, let forth like opium from wireless sets. On Radio Malaya's request programme it was called for by dozens of people, Malays, Chinese, British, week by week, an inundation of names so that eventually the announcer didn't bother to read the list but just let the sugary music fill out over the country. For weeks also Brian hadn't been able to cut it from his mind. One minute he liked the tune, then hated it, but whistled it unknowingly as he crossed the airstrip every morning, walking from the control tower with waterbottle and haversack swinging against his thighs, crossing the burning runway into the scrub-waste of the other side – out, it seemed, into the middle of nowhere with the blue horizon burning all round.

But in the emptiness a square patch of ground had been cleared and set-off for a new DF hut, and it was his work to help two mechanics unpack a straddle of enormous crates and fit hut-sides, roof and aerials into position. The three of them laboured all day in the sun, stripped to the waist and burned brown. The new hut would be a luxury box compared to the old one, set on dry ground and fed by electricity by a half-buried cable alongside a new track that would take lorries right up to the door. The station when finished and fully rigged would be operated day and night, a twenty-four-hour watch whether planes were up or not – though Brian knew that no one would give a sod about a nod or two of sleep at the deepest pitch of the morning. For weeks there had been talk of building a new DF hut, and now, out of the weak-willed climate, one had arrived and was being knit together by plan and numbers as if it were a Meccano set. A new PBX had been set up as well, and several radar devices installed in the runway. There was even talk of replacing the antique control tower by an indestructible skyscraper. The airstrip was being tarted up for a night out

– as if for a war or something, Brian thought, a cramp in his guts at the idea of it. Everyone was busier on the camp also, giving it an alien breath of being there for some purpose, which it hadn't possessed when he first arrived. He noticed it caught in the increased rush at mealtimes, in the latrines when in a hurry for a shower before dashing off to see Mimi, in the signals section when more channels were being worked than ever before, or in the new smartness of those who worked in the long headquarters hut. Sometimes you'd think a bloody war was already on, except that he felt the main combat as yet to be between himself and the threat of discipline emanating from HQ. The shift workers of the signals section were the last to be touched by it: they were excused all parades and guard duties, allowed in late for meals on production of a chit, which any enterprising wireless operator could take from the signals officer's drawer and sign himself. If the orderly officer came through the billet late in the morning and wanted to know why he was dead to the world and tight-rolled in his sheet he grunted from under his net that he'd been on watch the night before – so that the OO walked on, a bit quieter if anything. The seven months' hard studying for a sparks badge certainly paid off.

It was a simple map, and easy to memorize. He sat back in a wooden arm-chair to drink his tea, and wait in peace until the lorry drew up at eleven to take a gang of them across to the island. A fortnight's leave had been something to anticipate and when that was over he could look forward to operating the new DF hut, and then something else would turn up, and finally he would find himself on the boat chopping the blue waves back to England. Time went faster when there were agreeable events to hope for – when they arrived you noticed that the intervening weeks or months had been killed mercilessly stone-dead, hadn't even the value in memory of the sloughed-off dried skin of a snake.

Already 'Roll on the Boat' had become a catchphrase of liberation: if capable of flying an Auster or Tiger Moth he would have sky-written it above the sloping green back of Pulau Timur – but contented himself with sending it by Morse during what seemed the empty hours of his nightwatch, only to hear the initials ROTB throatily repeated from some half-asleep operator at Karachi or Mingaladon, a quartet trail of four-letter symbols piped out of electrical contacts by a heart-guided but distant hand. Locked fast in the Devil's Island of conscription, everyone wanted to go home, to drop gun, spanner, morse key, pen or cookhouse spatula and bat like boggery to the nearest bluelined troopship. Inconspicuous chalk marks behind their beds digited the months already served, as well as figures giving the current demob group ready for release, and after a while it looked to him like some magical transposition of formulae for exploding the atoms that held their prison bars in place.

He held himself from the gala of hope and speculation, living too much in the present to imagine going back to Nottingham. Not that hooks didn't exist to draw him there, for he had been married to Pauline nearly a year before leaving England, and she had a kid of his to keep her company while he was away. On the other hand he had spent no more than a few weeks with her, and there had been no real married life between them yet. She was no great letter-writer, and a year apart was too long a time to keep the ropes fast around him. He was unable to make chalk marks at the back of his bed, though knew to a day that ten months of his time abroad was still to be somehow gone through, and that to exhibit these future scars called for a waste of energy and spirit that he couldn't bring himself to spare so easily.

He grew turbulent and black, ready to smash down the peace of this long hut walled up with books because he didn't know the reason for it. The sound of lorries lassoing the MT section with noise, and gangs passing by to the NAAFI, didn't draw him out of it. 'That's wonderful, Brian,' Mimi said when he told her of his fourteen days' leave. 'You haven't had a holiday since you came.' He wondered why she was so happy: she'll miss me after all, as well as me missing her. Yet his suspicions never lasted long, and her response reassured him, gentle and concerned as she lay on the bed and leaned over to kiss him. A blind urge to contrariness took hold of him, a hatred of the death-like placidity that seemed to lurk at the heart of her, and without waiting for the kisses he sat up and pulled her down, pressing the immobility of her mouth against his own to kill the passion in himself in an effort to get at hers.

She drew back, seeing all, he thought, yet giving nothing. 'I'll be away for three bloody weeks,' he shouted. 'Are you bothered or aren't you?' – immediately regretting the explosion of his big mouth. This wasn't the way to go on, her silence and eyes were telling him. What is, then? Christ Almighty, what is? He had to be satisfied with the act of love alone, and it wasn't enough.

'I'm sad as well, Brian.' Her smooth nakedness rubbed against him, dispelled the stabs of his deeper gloom. 'I wish you weren't going.'

'So do I.'

'No you don't. It's good for you to have a rest. You need it. You work too hard, much harder than the others.' Maybe she's right: them fourteen-hour stretches are driving me round the double bend and half-way up the fucking zigzags, though on the other hand it's nothing at all when you come to think on it. 'They run a bus from Muka,' he grinned. 'I'll be able to see you every night at the Boston Lights – if you can spare me a dance.'

'Yes,' she said vaguely, unanswering, a neutrality he would never be able to break down – though he'd never stop trying. She placed her hand in his groin, but he was stone cold, and his black mood returned, filling him with an impulse to smash her for trying a trick like that. 'You got a better idea then?' he asked roughly.

Her hand pulled away. 'Come and see me if you like.' An endless tape, he thought, that wants snipping with scissors then maybe it'll finish and begin to give off the real thing. A wind roughed-up the treetops outside, a nervous agitation that completed nothing. He sat on the edge of the bed and reached for his shirt. 'Don't bleeding well put yoursen out, will yer? If yer don't want me to come, say so.' She gripped him tight, her lips between his shoulderblades before his shirt could swing into place. 'I've got a better idea.'

'I don't give a sod.'

'I'll come out and see you at Muka. We can find a lonely spot on the beach for a picnic. I'll take the morning ferry and then the bus. How do you like that?'

A blinding flash caught her in the face, knocked her against the wall. When the knife fell deeply enough between them all was well. Her small fists struck back, and they were holding each other on the bed, buried under a tree of kisses while the wind moaned outside.

He walked to the billet for his pack. Pete Kirkby and Baker were due out on the same lorry. Baker was a Londoner (his old man a Stock Exchange fluctuator who had made a small fortune), tall with steel-grey eyes, short-sighted under rimless spectacles, fair hair shorn to a crewcut. 'Any sign of the lorry yet?' Kirkby asked.

'It's on the airstrip running races with its shadow to pass the time away,' Brian said. Baker fell back on his charpoy, worn out after a night on watch: 'All I want is sleep. I'm browned off with sending morse night after night.'

'I was up as well,' Kirkby said, stuffing trunks and slippers into his pack; 'took a thousand-group message from some whoring slob at Singapore at four this morning. It was wicked. The bloke there was too shagged to send and I was too wanked to get it. I nearly went up the pole. We didn't finish till six: two solid hours. If this leave hadn't come I'd have fastened myself to a transmitter and switched the power on.'

Baker gathered his aeromodel plans and stowed a supply of balsa strips into his case, hoping to finish a new design in time for a competition. As he looked through the open doors there was a glaze over his eyes that had gone beyond fatigue, a puzzling stare such as might precede a fit of madness and set him running into the breakers for a longer sleep than he really needed. He was undisturbed by a fly that crawled over his knee. Brian felt he had been miscast as a wireless operator: his morse lacked rhythm, leapt from his key-contacts in a way that jangled the ears of operators trying to receive it several hundred miles away. He disliked the discipline of radio procedure, possibly because he'd had too much of similar endurances at the minor public school he often boasted of having been to. He was contemptuous of wireless operating, saying that if you had a natural sense of split-timing and a parrot-sized memory to hold all the rules and pages of Q-signs, then you had reached the limits of your job – which as far as he was concerned made it work for inferior minds since it gave a satisfaction too complete to be valuable or exhilarating. His passion was for a deeper form of life, engines, motor-bicycles, model aeroplanes, something unpredictable in motion and performance to be made out of bits and pieces. According to his story he had been a madman on the dirt-track in England, splitting the silence of Surrey back-lanes on Sunday afternoons with an equally dare-devil girl riding pillion and screaming into his ear for him to do a ton. His low forehead, aquiline nose and thin straight lips gave an impression of a supercilious pride that often drew anger when others in the billet suspected it might be justified, though the haughty look was little more than a mask of control over fires of recklessness burning underneath.

Kirkby folded a wad of redbacks into his wallet, and they went out to the lorry. Baker wore a bright green floral shirt open at the chest and flapping down over Betty Grable shorts, a Christmas tree of cameras and luggage. They sat fifteen minutes on the open back, raging against the dilatory driver who'd vanished behind the cookhouse. 'We'll miss the ferry if he ain't careful,' Kirkby groused. 'We could a made our own way and bin over at Muka hours ago.' Baker launched into a bout of singing in response to Brian's remark that Muka would be paradise without a squeak of morse for fourteen days:

'Oh how I'll miss the morse
Sending it out every day
On eight-and-a-penny pay
On eight-and-a-penny pay
Headphones around my neck
Hanged on the quarterdeck . . .'

He reached into his pack for a white trilby, which he bashed into shape and put on. 'For Christ's sake stop your row,' came a shout from a near-by billet. 'I'm trying to get my head down.'

'Belt up,' Baker railed, 'and get some overseas time in. You pink-kneed ponce.'

'Bugger off,' the voice called back, a little wearier for not having the blazing sun overhead or such a well-developed string of hackles as Baker. 'I've been out here five years.'

'Tell me another,' Baker shouted. 'I was in Bagdad before you were in your dad's bag.'

'Witty bastard' – but he said no more. Baker had been quiet and withdrawn on his arrival at radio school back in England, still unsocial even after eight weeks' squarebashing. Now, his silence seemed to have become a ruse, Brian thought, a tactic of breeding employed when pitched into a bunch of noisy strangers whose language he hardly understood. But he could now harangue and barney like an old sailor when he chose to. The door slammed and wheels skidded in the dust, rolled towards the guardroom. Brian sat down for a smoke, and a big pack landed at his feet, then a small pack and waterbottle, a bush hat without badges, two tins of cigarettes and a couple of Penguin books. While the owner of these belongings began to climb aboard, Brian read a title: *The Ragged Trousered Philanthropists*, and wondered what it could be about.

'Grab hold of that lot and give me a pull up.' The lorry gathered speed, and he was trotting behind. Brian and Eric Baker shot out their hands, tugged until the late arival's body had more weight over the backboard than towards the ground, when he fell safely into his possessions and sat on the wooden plank to open a tin of cigarettes. 'I hope this is the gharry for Muka,' he said, handing them around.

'It is,' Brian told him, accepting. 'Thanks a lot' – shielding a light towards his face. 'You got fourteen days as well?'

'Just about. I'm posted here when I get back. I came up on a plane from Changi this morning. You three in Signals?' He'd be medium in height, Brian saw, bull-like and stocky, and about thirty-five years old. He covered the tufts of his bald head by the bush hat that had landed over Brian's shoe like a hoop-la ring at a fair, wore a pair of khaki slacks, service mosquito boots into which went the bottoms of his trousers, and a white-drill five-dollar shirt – the cheapest possible way to be out of uniform in fact. His rolled-up sleeves showed thick hair, and a chest of it at the open neck of his shirt. On his left arm was tattooed a naked woman. A regular, Brian deduced. Must have been in ten years, and with a tan like that he ain't new to Malaya either. He had a face about to turn florid, red at the cheeks despite his tan, a heavy moustache streaked with grey, and light brown eyes suggesting that he once had sandy hair. Yet beneath all this was an air of youthfulness still, of intelligent and simple living that Brian had noticed in other regulars who existed in a closed world and were easygoing until they became NCOs (he suspected that the one opposite was, yet couldn't be sure, and felt uneasy because of it. Should he address him as Tosh, or not?). He had a narrowness of purpose and a broad humour which came from having no cares in the world – though outside in a civilian street and suit they seemed to be going through life in a dream.

The lorry roared through the village, its swift rush drying sweat patches on every shirt. 'I'm in signals as well,' he said when Kirkby answered him, 'so I suppose I'll be working with you lot when I get back. Knotman's my name, Corporal Knotman to the CO but Len to you lot. I don't believe in discipline and bullshit, stripes or no stripes.'

'I'll believe it when I see it,' Baker said. 'Where will you be working?'

'Telephone exchange. I was a wireless-op once in aircrew, but I lost my stripes when they found they'd got too many of us. They wanted to put me peeling spuds in the cookhouse, but I ended up as a telephonist-erk, a regular in the good old FBI.'

Kirkby took to him: 'What's the FBI?' he grinned.

'Freebooters' Institute. Federation of British Imperialists. Footsore, Ballsed-up, and Inked-out of your fucking paybook. Ten bob a day and all found, including the crabs. I'm dead beat,' he said. 'I was up at four this morning.'

'That makes two of us,' Baker put in. Knotman pulled a bottle of Chinese rice-spirit from his pack. 'Have some of this. It won't rot your guts. It's best whisky but I carry it in this hooch bottle so that I don't have to offer it to bastards I don't like. They think I'm doing them a favour in fact when I don't push it their way, and that makes them begin to like me. But by then it's too late.' Brian took a swig, so did Kirkby. Baker decided to wait a while. 'Too late by then, Shag,' Knotman said. 'Always take what's going and you won't go far wrong. You might have a heart attack in five minutes and be crippled for life. I was weaned on loot.'

'Where you from?' Brian asked, detecting some peculiarity of accent.

'Canada, but I've been in Limey-land eight years, so I reckon I'm the same as you now.' He stuffed the bottle in his bag and sang in a gruff but tuneful voice as they sped along between palm trees and beach:

'Oh you won't go to heaven
On an old Ford car
Cause an old Ford car
Won't go that far'

until Brian, Pete, and even Baker joined in. It was difficult to tell whether Knotman was drunk or just whacked-out – though it might have been a mixture of both plus an armature of back-logged work unwinding in his brain. They followed his words and caught on to fresh verses, roaring loud as the lorry entered Kota Libis and turned in at the pier gates, where turbaned Customs officials stopped looking into bags and cases to see what the wind had brought in:

'Oh you won't go to heaven
On a QDM
Cause the Lord ain't got
No radio gen . . .'

Brian stood by the rail to watch green water tracking towards Muong. Three large junks, heavy with flour sacks and rubber, headed in the same direction, huge patched sails so slow in the water that they seemed not to be moving at all and reminded him of a poem he'd read a few days since about seeing old ships sail like swans asleep. They were like that, he thought, though at the same time resembling swans that had been in a fight and were creeping inch by inch towards the safety of a harbour. Knotman stayed on the lorry, head in hands for a while, then stared back at the long mainland line of each as if uninterested in where he was going.

The boat went between anchored ships with such smooth precision that it seemed to be on train tracks placed invisibly under the water. As it slid towards the pier Brian heaved himself back on to the lorry. Knotman was alive again, sat with beefy arms folded looking at Malays and Chinese going up the gangways with bundles and baskets. 'Christ,' Baker said, 'they're like flies. Thousands of them.'

Knotman's face lost its expression of sleep: 'Ever been on the London subway at eight in the morning? This is as graceful as a Covent Garden ballet compared to that.' Cars packed on deck slowly unwound and the lorry drove cautiously along the pier, headed through the town and took to a wide ramparted boulevard leading by villas on to the coast road. All were bareheaded for fear their hats would blow across the beach and out to sea. The town gone, a series of blue bays stretched beyond. When one was left behind the driver rode his vehicle up the dividing spur before another, and from the short tarmac stretch at the top could be seen other bays and spurs still to be crossed. Then the lorry slid into the steep bay-gully immediately in front, and at the bottom was a shelf of sand between two heaps of rock, with palm trees along the banks of a stream. A Chinese family sunbathed by a bungalow, and on the beach children fled from each other into the water. The blade of sea broadened, narrowed to a sawedge because of tree trunks, disappeared, and the lorry was upward climbing again. 'Marvellous,' Knotman said, passing his bottle around. 'Let's drink to it. Anybody who won't is dead from the neck up. Why didn't you tell me Pulau Timur was this goodlooking?'

'I couldn't get a word in edgeways,' Brian said, handing the bottle to Baker. Marvellous, and he didn't need Knotman to tell him because he'd allus thought so. Who or whatever made this must have had good eyes, wielding his brush over such bays and washing broad streaks of sea around them; and a giant fist to punch the land so that hills came up from oblivion, the same hand throwing jewels along the valleys that turned into temples. Ships sailed from the old kingdom of Barat and anchored in the straits between island and mainland, and a town grew up on the neck of land that was sheltered. Such permanent and colourful scenery, the full depth and meaning of its long life in comparison to his own, the warmth lavished on it by the sky, and the smaller lives he knew to exist in every branch and grass blade that made up the greenery and in blue that denoted the sea, made him think of death and dying. Overwhelming beauty brought overwhelming sorrow. He stared before him, seeing the hills and ocean no longer – only the sentence that had fled from somewhere for refuge in his own mind.

Muka was twelve miles from town, several cream-coloured two-storied buildings set a hundred feet above the rocks and beach. 'There was nothing like this in Kenya,' Knotman said.

'How long were you there?' Brian asked. They were directed to an upper storey in the central block.

'Couple of years.'

'You bin in the jungle?'

'I went hunting once.'

'Bag anything?' Baker inquired.

'Yes; my big toe and a group-captain. Nothing living though. This looks like it.' They climbed the concrete stairway: 'If you slip on this after a few bottles of Tiger Beer you'll break your legs.' They had a billet to themselves, and a Chinese to do their laundry for a dollar a week, as well as someone to make their beds, clean shoes and bring in morning tea for another dollar. These deals settled, they ambled down the rocky path for a swim.

Brian ran into the sea, as if out of the death of the land, to save himself in forests of salt water dragging grittily over his face, falling into it at fifty yards free and releasing his weight against the water until he became a log and felt sand on the bottom scratching along his shoulderblades and spine. It was as far away from Morse Code as it was possible to get, water pressing milkwarm and forceful even at the palms of his hands and trying to get in, so that he hit the surface near to bursting and opened his mouth, burned by the sun that had waited to grip his hair plastered flat and hard. Eyes still closed, he made a guess as to whether he was turned towards sea or land. If I'm facing land Mimi will come and see me. If I'm looking out to sea she'll give me the go-by. He stared at the black sails of a loaded junk entering the straits a mile from the beach, and before he had time to speculate further, Baker made a dive at his legs and took him under. Brian lashed out with fists and surfaced, getting Baker round the waist and pressing him off balance, chin into sternum until his adversary's weight fell from his grasp. Brian held him down, but soon he was up again, fists pounding the malleable surface.

Less than a dozen were at the camp, leaving a free beach most of the time, and good service in the dining-room. 'The lap of luxury,' Brian said to Knotman, who threw back a Penguin book by way of reply: 'Read this while you're here.'

On the second afternoon those in the camp set off for a swim in a mountain pool on the other side of the island. Brian stood up on the lorry, between an urn of lemonade and a box of sandwiches. A long band of yellow beach ran along the northern shore of the island, ending in the jungled prominence of Telebong Head light. Brian searched out some secluded spot in case Mimi should visit him as promised, though he became pessimistic about it as soon as he saw a cove beyond the farthest village, an ideal place with a few rocks on either side and palms set behind.

The lorry climbed steeply beyond Telok Bahang, away from the sea and up a looped road with hillside falling hundreds of feet down to the valley. Clusters of huts lay in clearings by a stream snaking through bushes and speckles of sun. A Chinese woman was gathering wood: she was toothless and bald, her face brown and sexless with age, and she straightened her doubled back to smile as the lorry passed. Brian waved, felt the pendulum of his spirit move between desperate unfulfilled answers and happiness.

The hill blocking their view fell away at the road's next bend, so that before and below was a vista of paddy fields, a sheet of bright dazzling green stretched taut, dotted here and there with the brown patch of a village. A flat plain rolling beyond to the darker green of mangrove swamps ended in a blue haze at the sea-horizon. This also brought happiness, for paddy fields meant people working for food, though the vision of it quickly faded as the lorry changed gear and began to descend.

Half-way towards the plain it pulled into the roadside, where a stream came under a wooden bridge from up the mountain and quarrelled between rocks on its way to the fields. Brian dropped from the lorry, followed the stream up-course and reached a large clean pool held in by a horseshoe of cliff, silver fishes turning under its cool surface. The watershed towered two thousand feet above, and the stream came down through forest and gully, making an entrance into the pool where he was standing. Isolation, until the others came shouting in behind, shooting their naked bodies into the pool, which was quickly filled.

George, a warrant officer up from KL for seven days, also came into their billet. He'd not long since been SWO at Kota Libis, so Brian already knew him as a man who must have reached his rank merely by having been in the air force thirty years – certainly not by bullying or ambitious bum-crawling. He was more like the harmless, kindly, nondescript birdfancier at a branchline ticket-office that British pictures like to show as the typical working man than the usual sort of sergeant-major. Nothing bothered him, and he was so innocuous he didn't even possess a sense of humour – having enlisted to avoid the trivial worries of civilian life, or maybe he had just drifted into uniform with no design whatever. He obviously carried out his routine admin duties with some efficiency, though at Kota Libis he was little in evidence as warrant officer, sitting day after day in his office reading an Edgar Wallace with as much wide-eyed intent as Brian remembered his uncle Doddoe used to scan the racing paper, though in the latter case with narrowed eyes and for only a fraction of the time because Doddoe had somewhat more work to do. 'What does it matter how you live as long as you live in reasonable comfort?' George said one day, taking his socks off before going down to the beach. 'I've got fair pay, grub, clothes and a bed to sleep in. In return I do some work (only a little though, he winked) and lose my independence. You can't have it fairer than that, can you, lad?' He filled the bowl of his large pipe with such complacency that Brian felt like kicking his teeth in. He's dead, the dead bastard, the brainless old bleeder. He's a natural-born slave. 'It don't sound a good life to me,' he said. 'Maybe not,' George answered, unruffled at what Brian saw as the greatest insult, 'but I chose it, didn't I?' Some people 'ud choose prison if they could get a cup of tea, he thought. George was of medium height, bald and pot-bellied and spindly-legged, wore bathing trunks and resembled a white ant grown to a man. He took up his towel and went out, leaving Brian to read. Christ, he thought, he's been in this mob thirty years, and I'm only just twenty. I hope I'm not as dead as he is in thirty years. I wonder if Len Knotman will end up like that? Though I don't suppose so because his time's up in a year, and then he says he's getting the hell out of it back to Canada where he can get a job up north and be a free man again. 'I've learnt to know what freedom means in these last eight years,' Knotman had said to him. 'And the bloke who doesn't learn that, sooner or later, isn't fit to be on the face of the earth, because they're the types that end up as the enemies and persecutors of those who know what freedom means.'

At five o'clock he lay on the beach, a coolness coming invisibly in from greying sea. Baker waded in from a swim, maddened by horseflies spotted on to his legs like currants, skeins of blood running from each as they chewed his flesh by the mouthful, having hovered in wait by the water's edge. 'They're like flying leeches,' Knotman said. 'Ever had a leech on you?' He lay against the rocks, having swum himself out for the day, bush hat on the back of his head though the sun was well down behind the island. 'No, I ain't,' Brian answered, slinging a fag over.

They smoked in silence. Gunong Barat lay to the north, a black aggressive monolith coming out of the mainland twenty-odd miles across the water. Brian wanted to ascend through its wet forests (leeches or no leeches, snakes or tigers or elephants – it didn't matter), to test his strength on its steep incorrigible slopes. Hard labour would be needed, but the claws of endurance would goad him on, turn him into a treadmill of effort as he struggled up. This revelation grew indistinct and gave way to grandiose speculation as to what it would be like to use the distant encircling vision of its eyes from four thousand feet.

'I've thought a long time about trying to climb that mountain over there.'

'What's to stop you?' Knotman said lazily.

'Nothing, I suppose. It wouldn't be easy though. A bloke in the billet came down from Burma the other day and flew over it: he said it's up to its neck in thick jungle.'

'It would be an experience,' Knotman said. 'You can't leave Malaya and not know what the jungle's like.'

'What is it like?' Brian asked.

He laughed: 'Like a woman maybe – deep, dark and hard to know. Dangerous as well if you don't watch your step.'

'It might not seem like that to me,' Brian said, having already told Knotman he was married and seeing no reason to switch the subject so abruptly.

'It did to me. I had eight years solitary – meaning one woman. Then I got out quick.'

'I was talking about Gunong Barat though. Why does it have to be like anything?'

'Because it does. Otherwise it's got no meaning. And everything means something.'

'All right,' Brian said. 'I give in. What does Gunong Barat mean?'

'You mean what does wanting to climb it mean? I read once that you only climb mountains when you've got no ambition, but think you might as well get something out of life. Of course it's different with you: you're just an idealist, meaning you give in to worldly values without dirtying your hands on them.'

'So what? Can't you do it just because you want to?'

'If you like. I expect you can buy a map in Muong. They've got everything taped there. Then you can see what you'll have to cover to get to the top. Can you read a map?'

'Sure.'

'Ask for a week's leave then and shin up. Get Baker and Kirkby to go with you.' The mainland was darker, a solid lowdown horizon more important than the distant skyline of the mountains because it was close and immediate. 'Start thinking about it seriously,' Knotman went on, now encouraging where before he had been diffident. 'The three of you should be able to do it as easily as going for a swim – or taking a pull of whisky.' He passed the bottle: 'A sundowner?'

Knotman was not the wild impulsive drinker he had seemed at first, his boozing having enough method to be a helpful and enjoyable habit. The impression bossed Brian that Knotman had developed, through the jungle of years and circumstance, a sort of calm and order into his existence, a compromise between strange perplexity and wakeful eyes, whereas Brian at the moment saw life as something you bashed into without thought or consideration either for others or for yourself, because he had neither the time nor the intelligence to manage things better. Everybody's different from each other, he thought, and I know for a fact I ain't got the wisdom of Knotman. I wonder whether I'll be cleverer though by the time I'm his age?

Between bouts of swimming, after a fight with the swell of the tide – near to panic on the last hundred yards to his depth – Brian sat on the beach and, joined by Baker, built castles in the sand. Each structure was enclosed by a complex zigzag of exterior moats, and endless tunnels led from one system to another beneath the medieval storybook designs. They sat with the patience and built-in delight of children creating edifices out of sand, using skill to keep lines angular and embankments firm. Before climbing back for tiffin at midday they would watch the tide come in, its advance-guard of foam creeping nearer by the inch to the outer wall of fortifications. The first wall crumbled like bread, Brian feeling a quiet I-told-you-so satisfaction at the unalterable laws of the slow war of attrition between earth and water. Artifice made the contest more exciting: tunnels built out to the water led under the highest towers, so that they collapsed while the tide was still some feet away, a subtle fuse of destruction that gave great delight when it worked cleanly.

Mimi came to see him once during his leave. He hadn't expected her at all, had given her up with bitter disappointment because his holiday was nearly at an end, so that she appeared almost as a disturbance in the calm atmosphere of Muka. But when he saw her standing by the gate in a blue flowered dress, a yellow parasol on her shoulder, holding a straw picnic bag in one hand and waving to him with the other, it was as if excitement punched him under the heart: suddenly filling the gaps of what was an obviously thin existence when she wasn't near by.

They shook hands, laughing because such stilted formality made it seem as if they hadn't seen each other for years. 'You didn't expect me, did you?'

'Too true I didn't. I nearly gave up hope – which means I'm glad to see you.' She explained how late she'd been sleeping after long and heavy nights at the Boston, her serious face more placid than when she sat unspeaking. They stopped at a stall in the village to buy bottles of beer, plantains and oranges. An old Malay passed, driving a bullock cart loaded with coconut husks; he wore sari and sandals, and brown ribs at his chest stuck out like a lesson in anatomical engineering. Brian reached for her hand. The curve of the open and deserted coast, like an ivory boomerang held in the cool blue teeth of the sea, took on a flesh-and-blood feeling of reality now that she was with him. 'Don't you think it's the best scenery you've ever seen?' She walked sedately a few paces off, swivelling the opened parasol on her shoulder so that the shadow of its hood rippled on the road as if taunting their walking feet to come under it out of the sun. 'Yes,' she said, 'it is good' – with a sincerity that for once satisfied him.

They turned on to the beach at Telok Bahang. The high forested hill of Muka rose leftwards, toppled by the white pinnacle of a lighthouse. He led her to the cut-off beach seen from the lorry, over an arm of rocks to a hammock of untouched sand. Mimi looked through his pack as soon as they sat down. 'You naughty boy,' she laughed, 'you didn't bring a swimming suit.'

'Who needs one here?' He pulled off shorts and shirt, felt the sun rush against his flesh like warm water. 'You'll soon be as brown as a Tamil,' she said, looking at him. 'You were fair and white when I first saw you.'

'Well, which do you like best?' unbuttoning the back of her dress.

'Black,' she said. 'I want you to be like a negro. Leave me alone,' she giggled. 'I can manage.' The top part of her dress spread around, one petal fallen from the flower of her. 'I can't get as black as a negro,' he said. 'I would if I could though, to make you happy.'

'I am happy,' she said lazily.

'Happier, then. Maybe I'll rub boot-polish all over me, if that'll satisfy you.'

'I wouldn't like the smell.' She drew Chinese lettering in the sand.

'What are you saying?' he asked.

'It's a poem: "Poppies live best in a blue wind."'

'Funny poem.'

'I read it in a book.'

'What does it mean?'

'It means what it says.'

'What's a blue wind though?'

'What poppies live best in,' she said.

'I don't get it. I'll bet you aren't writing that at all.'

She rubbed it out. 'Yes, I was. Why don't you like it?'

'I do.' He felt foolish and clumsy. 'I don't know what it means, but it sounds good.' They lay close to each other, and he thought it strange, his brown arms around her pale, almost tawny flesh. Her nakedness had no relation to the sun, whereas his had longed for it, taken the full rush of its energy and heat during his year in Malaya and held it like a power for good. His body was lithe – sinewy arms and broad chest tapering to thin loins, and Mimi's body was strangely cool to the touch, sun-rejecting, alert to his caresses and graceful in slow movements of reaction that tore passion out of him. The sea knitted its quiet feet into the sand, withdrew, came back with a slow hiss one tone below the wind, an echo and at the same time a forerunner of its chafing at the treetops behind. He felt locked in a timeless dream of sun, water and sand, held by forest and sky and boulders and the cream-like water they suddenly ran into, away from the enervating sting of the sun and the subtle ache of satisfied loins. He caught her from behind, flattening her breasts in the spread of his fingers. Coconut oil on her hair mixed with salt water, and rubbing his face into it he savoured the whole familiarity of her who lay beneath. In the long moment he dragged her laughing into the foam, and beyond into clear water, swimming back later to eat sandwiches and drink beer. He lit a cigarette, noticing that when he struck a match its flame was invisible because the outside heat was so intense. They slept naked, and when she nipped his thigh to wake him up he leapt after her along the sand, over boulders and into the shade of trees. A livid green snake ran off from them, its body effortlessly curving through leaves and twigs, no visible source of energy carrying it along. Trees like endless columns rose above, shutting out sky from the flowerless jungle. When they ran to the warm sand, a predatory urge came into his loins. She drew him into the shade of a rock, roused again by the blind inconsiderate animal force of his lust, her caresses sluggish until the over-powering crisis came into them, the orgasm beginning in her like the quick pleasure of warmth after the whole body had been unknowingly cold without.

'I'll never leave Malaya,' he said after.

'You mean you love me?'

'You know I do. It's marvellous here.'

The next evening he went back to Kota Libis, had no sooner unloaded his pack than Corporal Williams came to say he was to start operating on the DF frequency in the signals hut. 'Give me time to get back to the bleeding camp,' Brian said, seeing he'd be unable to visit Mimi that night.

'Don't blame *me*,' Williams said, one of those long-standing wireless-op corporals on whom prolonged morse-taking had acted like shellshock: left him with an apologetic face, a permanent stare, and hands that shook as if he'd got palsy. 'A Dakota's coming up from Singapore. Flying Control say you're to listen out for him.'

He picked up his drinking mug and tin of cigarettes, stuffed them in his small pack and walked towards the Signals, dejected and enraged, spoiled by his fortnight of freedom. Hands in pockets, he followed the path through the trees, oblivious to a jumped-up sharp command from the adjutant standing outside the orderly room. 'Airman!' he called again when Brian still headed for the medley of different morse-pitches coming from the Signals. He put his cap on, went over and saluted.

'Why weren't you wearing your cap, airman?'

The sidewalk of the long single-storied hut of the admin block was raised a foot above the soil on which Brian stood. The adjutant had a sardonic look on his face, fixed as if it had been branded there from birth – the only expression in fact that gave it a glimmer of intelligence. He had what Brian assumed (from his reading of mediocre novels) to be finely chiselled features, though there was no denying that drink and a giving-up of life had left them as blotched and pock-marked as the king's-head side of an old coin. He wasn't known for a martinet, was easy-going, almost dead-cush in fact, the more gentlemanly sort of officer who only bothered to pick up a 'crime' when he was bored by the dead days of his regular life; the worst sort in a way because you never knew how to take him, were caught unawares like now when you relaxed your alertness and protective screen of cunning.

He had no answer, yet said: 'With Signals section being so near I didn't think it was necessary, sir' – his voice a calculated blend of defiance, and regret that he had sinned. In a similar situation Kirkby had a knack of looking as if he'd just finished fourteen days' jankers, so was half-pitied and merely told-off for what 'wrong' he had done, but Brian's face and feelings were too friendly with each other to be much help. I'm not fresh into the Air Force from school like some, he cursed. I've done four years' work in a factory already. I'm married and got a kid – though you wouldn't think so the way I let them boss me around.

'What's your name?'

I'll get seven days I suppose. He could hear Baker laughing from the billet window. 'Seaton, sir.'

'Why are you going to the Signals section?'

He'll ask me why I was born next. 'I'm on watch, sir.' It's best to stick it out. As Knotman says: 'If you want to fight them, do it on your own terms. Otherwise you'll lose.'

'Well, look, Seaton, don't let me catch you outside the billet again without your hat being where it's supposed to be.'

He walked away, laughing to himself that he hadn't been

confined to camp for seven to fourteen days. If I was the government I'd nationalize the Air Force and close it down.

He tuned in his receiver, turned the slow-motion dial until, key pressed, the strident whistle of the transmitter crept up on his ear-drums. It rose to a shriek, the strong piercing cry of a soul in torment above the Ironside layer, burning the relays of its earthbound transmitter until he lifted his hand off the key and stopped it. He then tapped out a call to Singapore to test his signals strength. QSA 4— QRK 3. Not bad for half-past six.

A message came from the lumbering Dakota high above the backbone of jungle. In work his bitterness was forgotten, and after the plane landed he amused himself by sending poetry from the Pelican book by his set, each letter going out at fast speed, hot sparks burning the brain of anyone who could read its symbols. Word by word, line by rhythmical line, the whole of 'Kubla Khan' found its way from his key, and he felt exhilarated in knowing that such a poem was filling the jungles and oceans of the Far East, coming, if anyone heard it, from an unknown and unanswerable hand. To send plain language on a distress (or any) frequency was, so the Manual of Persecution said, an offence to be tried by court-martial, but as far as he knew all official stations had either closed down for the night or were too far away to receive it. So 'La Belle Dame Sans Merci' also went singing hundreds of miles out into darkness, perhaps reaching the soul of the man who wrote it and maybe also touching the source of golden fire that sent down these words to him in the first place. Dots and dashes went out at a steady workmanlike speed, all poetic rhythms contained, even in the sending of one word. The mast top of the transmitter high above the trees outside propagated the chirping noises of his morse, as if releasing cages of birds into freedom.

20

After a tea of sausages and beans he raced upstairs to get changed. 'Tek yer bleddy sweat,' the old man called, when his workboots bashing on the wooden stairs caused the wireless to crackle.

Trousers and jacket hung on a chairback: a suit his mother had got second hand for six bob up Alfreton Road, utility blue with faint pin stripes, shining at joints and not a turn-up in sight. But a suit was a suit and there was a tie and white shirt to make him spruce after a day mixing alum and flour at the shitsmelling pastebins – and five bob in his pocket out of the two-pound wage packet he'd given up downstairs. Stripping off boots and overalls, he whistled a wild jig set to the lyrics of a carefree Friday. The double bed under the window he shared with Arthur and Fred, though he as the eldest had charge of the room. In one corner was a cupboard holding his books, a hundred and thirty-seven with a list of titles and authors pinned inside, and LONG LIVE RUSSIA AND STALIN chalked up in Russian on the back of the other door – words of magic made up by him from a Russian grammar asked for at the library a few months back. Opposite the window was a desk knocked together as a special favour by the old man, skilfully botched from packing cases and painted dark brown. Above hung a map of Eastern Europe, its battle-line marked by a band of pencilling. Soon it would be useless, for the grey tide of his constant rubbings-out had edged far towards Poland and Rumania, though in his cupboard was a folded map of Western Europe which would complete the picture of Germany throttled – providing the Yanks and British got cracking with that second front.

He opened the cupboard, proud of his collection of books,

though he'd read few of them. The combined bulk and story of *The Count of Monte-Cristo* and *Les Miserables* had kept his desire for reading away from the rest of the stood-up spines. Nevertheless their existence gave some feeling of refuge from what tempests now and again sprang up (for no reason that *he* could see) in his brain. Most of the books had been stolen from a shop downtown, brought from its endless shelves to the light of day under his shirt, often two or three at a time costing maybe five bob, while in his hand were a pair from the threepenny box he'd pay for at the office with a nondescript starvo look on his face. He acquired them by the simple action of walking in and walking out Saturday after Saturday, bricks for the building of a barricade against something and someone as yet unformulated and nameless. Shelves grew, became classified into Languages, Fiction, and Travel, made a distinguished graphline along their tops as if to hold down the sombre colours of uneven spines. To run his fingers along them would mean washing his hands again before going out, with the risk of marking his white shirt that he was now pulling over his bare chest.

The books hadn't been added to for more than a year, though the mood came easily back in which they had been stolen. Standing in the downstairs department where he couldn't be seen, he had slid each week's choices one by one between the undone buttons of his shirt. The smell of damp paper from row upon row of cellar-stored books was pungent in wet weather almost to the pitch of ammonia, and the coal fire burning in the corner grate of another room through the archway only seemed to make it more intense. He spent half an hour of search and excitement, a bliss in which he was lost, heightened by the stark fact reaching at him now and again that sooner or later he would have to load up and walk with them into the street, and for three hundred yards to the bus stop expect the manager's cold hand to tap him on the shoulder and say: 'Would you mind taking them books out of your shirt and coming with me to the copshop?' He went through the threepenny boxes, the sixpenny tables, the more expensive shelves, marking possibilities for his short list, and hoping other customers walking about wouldn't buy them in the meantime.

There were rare occasions when no books interested him, and once, so firm was the procedure fixed in the ammoniac smell of the shop that he nevertheless came out with a French hymn-book, a Hindustani grammar, and a set of nautical tables, feeling as relieved and happy with his load at the bus stop as if they were books he had wanted to get his hands on for years.

He browsed through the boxes, looking at each title, opening the covers of some, knowing that sooner or later he must slide out the books he wanted – three, and sometimes as many as four or five if they were thin ones – and make off with them. In the far-off days when he paid for the books – no more than threepence each though – he came one Saturday morning with Bert and browsed while his cousin impatiently flipped through the magazine table. Brian took his time, was at the mercy of his title-chasing eyes and page-checking fingers, so that the minutes ran into Bert's brain and needled him to find Brian and say: 'Got owt yet?' 'These two' – he held them up, also picked out a guide to Belgium: 'I'd like this as well, but it's half a dollar.' 'Let's get going when you're ready,' Bert said, 'or we'll miss the picture.' Hold on a bit, Brian was going to say – but his mood broke and he turned: 'Let's scram then.' At the picture-house queue Bert handed him the book he'd wanted but couldn't afford. 'You're my favourite pal,' he said, gripping his shoulders tight. 'Here y'are: I'd do owt for yo'.' Brian was overjoyed, clutched at the small red book, bent its flexible gold-lettered covers and saw its marbled pages. 'Thanks, our Bert. I shan't forget a favour like this.'

He didn't: from that moment he never looked back as he stood by the shelves in the bookshop cellar department. Though feeling as if he were visible to all, since the tremble of hands and knock of knees seemed to give him a luminous shining quality, his fingers nevertheless hooked slyly out to the target his blue eyes fixed on. He stood without courage but with the gamble of a green-eyed cat on his shoulder, set in the circle of irresistible temptation, his fierce and quietly burning purpose to augment the bookshelves in his room while leaving the reading of them to whims of boredom and curiosity. His eyes were lights of panic, though kept quiet by an inner will which made his hands accurate in their sly split-second motion of simple extension and drawing back loaded with a prize towards his shirt. One, two, three – they were safely in, and he walked up the stairs, not thinking about what was hidden between shirtcloth and chest-flesh for fear he would fall top-heavy back and break his neck with guilt crash-bang at the stair bottom. With an abstracted air, as if dazed legitimately by the jewelled sight of so many books, he handed his pair of threepennies to the girl assistant, mumbling 'How much?' 'Sixpence,' she said, and he thanked God at the first whiff of outside fresh air and petrol fumes, letting himself free into the roar and shoulder-knocks of Saturday crowds.

It was too good to last. Not that he became careless, he always had been. It was simply that his luck ran out and he was more ashamed afterwards at the thought of what a loon he must have looked to the girl assistant who saw him stuffing maps and books into his shirt, than for the crime, now revealed because he was caught, of stealing. At the cash desk he asked how much for a couple of mouldy Walter Scotts, and heard her say, the biggest shock he'd had for a long time: 'You'd better take them books from up your jumper.' He did so, silent and white-faced: three books and two cloth-backed maps. 'What's your name and address?' No one was by the cash desk at that moment. He told her, but she didn't write it down. Borstal, Borstal were big words drum-beating against his brain. You'll get sent to Borstal for three years, and not the same one Bert's bin in for the last six months, you can bet, so you'll have no company. He stood. She looked at him. She was thin and bloodless too, in a blue overall, young and old, eighteen and sixty, dying eyes and hands that slid the pile of books away and back on to the table when the manager emerged from a not-too-far-off doorway. Her heart he only knew the value of when she said softly: 'Go on out, and don't ever come in here again.' If the coppers had searched the house and found his book hoard he'd have been up for five years solid, but luckily the girl knew whose side she was on, and afterwards he wondered how much better the world would be if everybody stuck up for each other in that marvellous fashion.

He whistled a tune from 'The Arcadians', getting dressed on a Friday night in the full blood of his sixteen years, not thinking of a criminal life but gazing at his books. The cupboard they stood in was a present from his grandparents when they decided it wouldn't fit into the new abode of the Woodhouse. It still carried a smell of spices: curry and cinnamon, thyme and mustard seed, camomile and sennapods and pepper, not yet killed by the more pungent odours of damp and ageing paper.

White shirt flew on to him like a bird of peace, drawn together at the neck by a blue-dotted tie. He felt spruce and warm in his suit, the garb of a labouring man whose face was pale but muscles hard enough to carry him along with confidence anywhere. He slammed the doors of his bookcase, put on his jacket and ran downstairs. 'Don't be late,' his mother called as he let the back door of the scullery clatter to.

It was spring in the street, late sun coming from the tops of snowclouds, children running in and out of air-raid shelters that blocked any clear view from up to down. The mass of close-knit factories and houses were spread on the steady slope of a hillside, though this was hardly noticeable with feet firm on cobblestones taking him energetically towards his meeting with Pauline. He lit a fag and flicked the match on to a window-sill (a notice within said WREATHS AND CROSSES MADE TO ORDER AT SHORT NOTICE), catching sight of his greased-up quiff that made him look, he laughed, as handsome as the day was long. People were still rolling home from work by the time he hit the boulevard. A toffee paper blew towards him in the wind, fastened itself like a badge on a tree trunk.

She'll be out any minute, he thought, approaching the factory, because the machines were switched off, leaving the high-sided street calm and quiet. It was a long, red-bricked and straight-windowed building, a hundred years old though still in its prime. This sort of workpile had driven a nail of terror into him when he passed it as a child, not knowing what all the noise was about; but he knew now right enough, and wasn't afraid of it, though on nearing any strange enormous factory at full blast he still felt a curious memory of half-fear stir in him at such compacted power that seemed pressing at every window ready to burst out like some fearful God-driven monster. Funny, he thought, how once you got in one it didn't bother you, was peaceful almost because then you were on its side.

He stood by the clocking-out machine, eyed but not bothered by the commissionaire in his Home Guard uniform, a grey-haired old ramrod about seventy wearing a fish-and-chip hat, and smiling at a mirror in his bogy-hole to adjust a row of medal ribbons. England's last hope, Brian grinned, the old chokka. I bet he got them medals mowing down fuzzy-wuzzies. 'Waiting for the girls, I suppose?' he called.

'Waiting for a pal,' Brian responded after a pause. 'Yo' goin' on p'rade, dad?'

''Appen,' the man said, turning huffily away. Brian knew him to be too old for it now, felt a bit sorry he'd spoken. Poor bastard. He wasn't the only one around. Nottingham's Chelsea Pensioners they called them, doing part-time work to eke out their ten bob and joining the Home Guard while there was still time to get themselves a winter suit and topcoat, going to the drill-hall now and again to meet younger pals and listen to lectures, but mostly standing in pubs and swilling beer out of those who'd treat them. I wonder if he'd give a cup o' tea to a deserter? Brian wondered.

He saw Jim Skelton on the stairs: 'Hey up.'

'How do.'

'Where's Pauline and Joan?'

'In t' lavatory dolling up,' Jim said. 'It's tekin' 'em long enough as well.'

'Fag?' Brian offered. 'Fag, mate?' – to the old man.

'I don't mind,' he said. 'Thanks very much.'

'Ta,' Jim said. The three of them lit up. 'It's still 'ard to get 'em,' the old man chipped in, 'even if you've got munney.'

'It is an' all,' Brian said. See all, hear all, say nowt. Eat all, drink all, pay nowt. There were a dozen cartons in the house, hidden in a wooden box under the coal, a present that crept in one night on his cousins' backs. They'd not long since been lifted from a shop up the street, swiped from a shopkeeper who'd told Brian only the night before when he went there on the hunt for tobacco-hungry Seaton that he hadn't a fag in the place. It was true right enough next morning after a visit from Colin and Dave. They'd not only cleared him out of fags, but silk stockings, a bottle of whisky, stacks of grub, cash.

They savoured their cigarettes. 'A couple o' sixteen-year-olds like yo' two ought to be in the Home Guards,' the chokka said. 'Do you the world o' good.' Brian went numb at this, as if somebody had called him bone-idle or a copper's nark. 'That's what yo' think, mate.'

'I'd rather enjoy mysen than shoot a gun,' Jim told him. He was the same height as Brian but stockier, with a broad Tartar face, well rounded dimpled chin, squared teeth and a squashed nose, ginger hair well flattened back from his forehead. He was a mechanic and looked after the girls' sewing machines, saw that the khaki uniforms ran smoothly through so that anyone could get a share of that weekly bonus. Brian, though highly regarded by Jim for his store of books, respected him for his handiness with machines and electricity and the making of traction engines.

The girls were down already, and out of the door before a word was spent between the four of them, spread in a line across the street. 'Where are we going then?' Pauline wanted to know.

'Out,' Brian told her.

'Clever bogger' – she thumped him.

'Leave my mate alone,' Jim said.

'Men,' Joan exclaimed. 'Allus stick together. Where're we goin' anyway? That's what I'd like to know as well.'

Brian hoped he wouldn't be contradicted: 'Up Cherry Orchard.'

'It's too far,' Joan said. 'I don't know what you want to go up there for anyway.'

'I do,' Jim laughed.

'Well you wain't catch me going,' Pauline said decisively. Brian winked at him: we'll go in that direction anyway. 'You can stop that, fawce dog,' Pauline said. 'I saw yer winking, Brian.'

'You want your eyes testing then.'

'You'll get yourn blacked if you aren't careful,' she threw

back. 'He don't half think he's a cleverdick,' Joan said, ganging up with her pal.

'Go and get dive-bombed,' Brian said. 'I only wanted you to come up Cherry Orchard.' Pauline was as tall as Brian: long brown hair spreading back over her buttoned-up dark brown coat, that hid a lighter overall dress he'd glimpsed as she came down the stairs. She had white skin, and large brown eyes that seemed to see everything as a defence against the fact that she saw very little. Jim said she was one of the fastest at her machine and wasn't so dreamy as she appeared, though both agreed that you wouldn't think so to look at her. On some evenings, when left to their own thoughts or emptiness, undisturbed by the lack of talk, they walked arm-in-arm along sunlit lanes and streets that were silent between knocking-off time and dusk. Brian felt her largeness when she was with him, noticed how delicate was the expression of her hands and face when seen against the gracelessness of her general movement. She had a good figure – he knew it well by now – fine pear-shaped breasts, noticeable hips, and legs a bit heavy. It was almost obtrusive – but not quite, for she was just below the stature that could have given her the label of a 'strapping girl'.

She was arm-in-arm with Joan in front, and they went down Ilkeston Road, followed at fifty yards by Brian and Jim. 'They don't seem in a good mood tonight.'

'P'raps they've got the rags on,' Jim laughed.

'I hope not,' Brian said. 'I like Pauline though. She's a good sort, and passionate. How yo' going on with Joan?'

'All right. *She* don't say a deal either. Never says a dicky-bird sometimes all night. I asked her what was wrong once. We'd been to t' pictures, and I thought she was fed up and ready to chuck me. I said: "What's up, duck?" when I was walking her home later. "A penny for your thoughts," I said, and she burst out crying. She never told me what for either. I'd thought she looked a bit funny earlier on when she was in our house 'aving a cup of tea and some toast. When I kissed her good night though, she was ever so passionate; so it blew over and she was as right as rain next day at work.'

Brian saw Jim's courting as a more intense affair than his

own. Not only did Jim work near his sweetheart – often called over to fix the belt on her machine, or to clean and oil it – but she spent most of every evening helping Jim's mother, or sitting with him to guard his sisters and brothers while his parents were at the pictures. Pauline had never been to the Seatons, and neither did Brian have the intimacy of being with her all day at work. They met on many nights of the week, but whereas Jim and Joan had a physical closeness about them like any young couple a year married, Brian and Pauline were still at the hit-and-run stage, would melt away and almost forget each other until the next date because only the need to make love drew them together. He had never asked her to come home and sit in with his mother and father, Fred and Arthur and Margaret and Sammy, as if she belonged there. He envied this state between Joan and the Skeltons, but was somehow unable to build up a similar relationship between himself and Pauline. He spent many evenings at her house, and the two families had at one time known each other, but Pauline had never in any case suggested that she come to his home. Brian thought that maybe she was too shy to ask this, and he used her shyness – if it existed – as a way of preventing her from doing so. The idea of Pauline at home with his father and mother gave him spasms of embarrassment, and he was unable to say whether this was because he thought he would be ashamed or whether it was because he knew Pauline would dislike it and feel out of place. He didn't want his mother and father to know he was courting, wanted to keep his second life a secret from them as if, should they know, it would result in their sharing this love and intimacy and making it less real to him. But when his mother once said: 'I met Mrs Mullinder today and she says you're going out with their Pauline,' he didn't feel at all embarrassed, though he still wouldn't ask Pauline home. 'I go out with her now and again,' he told his mother. 'Well,' she said, 'that's all right. She's a nice gel. Only don't come here though if you get anybody into trouble.' And that was that.

It was getting dark as they passed Radford Station. 'Good,' Brian thought. 'I don't want to see anybody I know' – though no sooner had this crossed his mind than Uncle George came biking over the hill, from Woodhouse, calling as he went by: 'Now then, Brian, you're a bit young to be courting, aren't you?' He put a good face on it, bawling back: 'Ar, I'm doing all right an' all.' Fancy shouting out like that, though he laughed at remembering back to when George had persuaded Vera to introduce him to a young unmarried woman in the yard, and she had sent Brian to tell Alice Dexter she wanted to see her a minute – all to help her stringy brother, blacksmith George. When Alice Dexter came into the house George picked up a newspaper to make her think he'd been reading like a sober educated man, but he'd been unable to read from birth and the paper was upside down. Which caused periodic laughs in the family especially from Seaton because he couldn't read either, and would never have tried to impress anybody that way by pretending he could.

Wind blew across the bare dark stretch of the Cherry Orchard. 'Are you all right, duck?' he said to Pauline. 'Keep well wrapped up.'

'It ain't cold,' she whispered. The others were a merging shadow far to the left, intent on finding their own private hollow in which to snug down. He held her tightly around the waist. 'We'll find a good place.' Stars were pale and liquid-eyed, each as if nervous at not knowing whether it was next to be hidden away. 'It's marvellous out here. It's warm and lonely.'

'It is an' all,' he responded. My grandma used to live over there' – pointed far off into the darkness. 'And my grandad. He was a blacksmith.' An inexplicable pride came at the thought of his grandfather having been a blacksmith. Blacksmith was a word of skill and hardiness: a smith makes things, and black means the toughest sort of work – like when I did that bout of flue-cleaning – the shaping of iron and steel between hammer and anvil, moved by muscle in a subtle mixture of controlled strength.

'Ooooooh!' she drawled out. 'Mek a wish, Brian.'

'What for? Mind that bush.'

'I saw a shooting star.'

'I didn't though' – pulled out of his blacksmith world.

'There's another one, look' – still pointing.

'Yes, I saw that one,' he was glad to own. 'I've made a wish.'
'So've I.'
'What did yo' wish?' he wanted to know.
'I'm not telling you. It don't cum true if you tell anybody.'
'Well,' he teased, 'I shan't tell you what I wished then.'
'I'm not asking you to,' she said, offended. 'Don't if you don't want to.'
'What do you think I am?' he cried, indignant. 'If you wain't tell me I'm not going to tell yo'.'
'Well,' she said, 'if you tell me what yo' wished, mine'll still come true.'
'Mine wain't though,' he reasoned, no thought of self-sacrifice.
'P'raps our wishes was the same,' she ventured. This put him on his guard: 'I bet they worn't.' I didn't wish we could get married, he told himself. It's enough if she did, though I'll bet she'll be wrong. 'You know what mine was though, don't you?' she said, pressing his hand. He did. It leapt across with no words, a shaft of love unseen in the darkness, meeting the wish he had made because no other was possible for him, being with his girl in the middle of the Cherry Orchard in the first darkness of a spring evening. Her words came sweet, into an isolation of something better than he'd ever known, even though it wasn't the first time they'd worked out this desire between them.
'Mine was the same,' he said, seeing the two lines written on the picture in the Nook parlour: 'If you love me as I love you, nothing will ever part us two.' The sentiment quickly vanished because he thought that if he told it to Pauline she might laugh and see him as too sloppy to go out with. Not that he was unhappy at this.
A moon was up, had severed all connexion with the chimney-pots of distant houses, was responsible for the faint luminous gleam that held the humps and hollows and solitary bushes back from the hand of complete darkness. A gentle warm infiltration of visibility overspread from hedge and houses to a vale of Serpent Wood, a vague light giving the impression that the dwindling countryside of the half-mile Cherry Orchard was a vast and untouchable heathland through which no arteries of

life ran. He pulled up a handful of fresh grass to smell. 'I can't see Jim and Joan any more,' she said.

'They're just over there,' he told her. 'They'd hear us if we shouted.' To stop any idea of it he drew her to him, arms fastened around the waist and shoulders of her coat. He caught her mouth, half-open to start some reply to his remark, and felt the moist warm surprise of her lips that closed and hardened to a passionate response, her arms also reinforcing the kisses that she seemed to try and repulse only by increasing the forward pressing of her own. The uneven ground caused him to lurch, and though he kept balance without thinking where to place his feet he succeeded in breaking the force of her kisses, holding her to him and placing his lips on her at such an angle that it was impossible for them to breathe. Both knew the meaning of this manoeuvre; it gave each a chance of proving that the power of greatest love was on their side; for the one who craved breath first bore the lesser love. The closeness of her body and the pressure of her face and lips hardened and sweetened the urgent rod of his loins. He moved his lips over hers, neither taking nor giving breath, prolonging the fleshy meeting with her mouth which was one second dormant and then moving to prove that she loved him with all her strength and was nowhere near losing the contest. He went harder into her face, wanting to lift his head away from her though, and laugh and pull in gusts and lettershapes of pure air, but the sweetness of Pauline, the swell and slight shifting of her lips drew him in so that his kisses, like tears, grew in strength at the feel of her love.

The wind came against them like an outside kiss from the distant curve of the woods (the last leapfrogged obstacle down from the bleak Pennines) and as the pushing within grew at the deep prolonged valley of the kiss, the air and grass and darkness outside pulled away and left them in the grip of an insoluble torment of love. Pauline's hands were at his neck, around under the hair at the back of his head, and she hoped that he would see through her equal torment and relax his wild unfeeling pressure by allowing her to breathe and win because she loved him more. His inner world grew to a blind illuminated space, the inside of a sphere that marked the limit of all pictures in his mind and turned his kiss-breaking into a vision. This was marvellous. He wanted to breathe, but held himself even though the artistry of his kisses suffered, went on through brief seconds of control with each one the reason for further prolongation. His hands roamed up and down her back, from neck to shoulders to take away the drumbeats of his lungs protesting against such obstinacy. I love you, Pauline, I love you. Give in. Start breathing and let me prove it. She pulled him tighter, as if to say that the kiss could go on for another five minutes for all she cared. His knees shook. He moved his head from side to side to keep a further second of breath in him: like swimming under water and hoping to reach a better part of the shore before surfacing. Though her lips were fast closed she swayed also, moaned and tried shaking his head away. He knew that a few more seconds would kill him, for his lungs were barrels of gunpowder and the only vision left in his lighted sphere was that of a curving fuse going into them, with smoke that had travelled along it now close. If he kept on he would die like a man does when he drowns.

She drew her hands away and he wondered what was happening – until her fists came down, and in the crash they made against his spine he heard her taking enormous drinks of breath out of the air. Tears were on her cheeks and he went in this time to a kiss of love in which both could breathe, so that he felt tears springing to his own eyes, but tears of laughter and happiness. They leaned against each other, hands free. 'I love you, Brian,' she said.

They went into a wide hollow and lay down by a bush, dark banks bringing the night closer. The earth felt damp under his hand, and she drew him down to it, spreading kisses like salt on his face as if to recompense them both for his victory of kisses up in the field and bring them back to loving. He tasted the sweetness of her lipstick and opened each button of her coat as he fought back his own kisses into her loving mouth.

They afterwards lay in the dip of the Cherry Orchard with no watch between them to tell what time it was, each smoking a cigarette to give taste and body to the fragrance of their exhaustion and an illusion of comforting warmth to the humid freshness of the night. 'You ought to get yoursen a topcoat,' she said. 'You'll get pneumonia like that, duck.'

He laughed: 'Not me. I've got blood like boiling water. A walking stove.'

'Still,' she said. They walked out of the hollow. 'It must be after nine. I wonder what happened to the others?'

'Gone, I expect. Joan lives at Lenton, don't she?' He felt loosened from the fever, vibrant and sharp against the night air, as much in love with the rustle of bushes and odours of soil and grass as with Pauline. He stopped and drew another kiss from her, gentle and indrawn. 'Well,' she said with a laugh, 'you can never have enough, can you?'

'I can't' – taking her naked hand by the dark shadows of Colliers' Pad. They came to the lights of the main road: 'Mam and dad'll be at the pictures being's it's Friday,' she said. 'I don't expect they'll be back yet.'

'If your dad's in p'raps we'll 'ave a game o' darts. I'm hoping to beat 'im one of these days.'

'You'll never do that: he had too much practice when he was in 'ospital.' He agreed: Ted Mullinder had been bed-bound through an accident at pit. A truck underground had run into his foot and all but crushed it when coming back from the face one day. He'd got off too soon at the skip, thinking the truck had stopped when it hadn't. It was as if a shark had got him, pain leapfrogged to his brain and exploded there, blowing him into a mixed land of black-out and dreams in which he had mistaken his own pain and suffering for somebody else's, then woken up to find with horror that it had been his own. Operation after operation, and now he was a sad asthmatic cripple with a job on top, the only compensation being that he had become the unbeatable champion of the local darts team. On most nights he made his way on two sticks to the John Barleycorn, slung down three pints of mild and got his hand in before a game by going round the clock. Though able to stand, he played from a chair set at the regulation paint mark, preferring to sling his arrows this way because his hospital marksmanship had been built up from a wheel-chair. He was broad-shouldered and dark, kept in life and friendship by sufficient bouts of ironical cheerfulness, buttressed against despair by his wife and four daughters.

Mullinder now sat at the table with his bad leg spread towards the fire while his wife, a tall nutbrown gipsy-like woman, followed Brian and Pauline in with a loaded enamel teapot and set it before him. What a life, Brian observed: waited on like a king. Not that I wish it was me, with that bad foot. Eleven-year-old Maureen took up the other side of the hearth to read a comic. 'Hey-up, Brian,' she called out, no sooner was he in.

'Did you pass your scholarship?' he asked. You could tell she was one of the family all right, her face oval and alive, and even more mischievous because of her age.

'I don't know yet. But I don't care if I pass or not. I'll feel daft in a uniform and all that. I want to go to work when I'm fourteen, not stay till I'm sixteen.'

'Don't be barmy,' Mullinder said. 'You're a lot better off at school. You don't know you're born until you start wok, Maureen Madcap!'

'I'll get mad all right in a bit, our dad. I've told you before not to call me Maureen Madcap.' But from almost crying with shame and shyness she called to Brian: 'Hey, Brian, you know what heppens when you wash too much?'

'What?'

'You get soap rash! Don't you, our dad?'

'Go on,' he called. 'I reckon Maureen Madcap's the name for yo' right enough.'

Mrs Mullinder set Pauline to wash more cups, and put Brian at the supper table facing her husband. 'Tek a couple o' them cheese sandwiches,' she said. 'I hope you don't mind sacs in your tea, but I don't get the sugar ration till tomorrow.'

'That's all right. We've got nowt else but them.' He felt it strange that an issue should be made of it, as if he'd strayed into a higher degree of civilization than he was used to. Tea was tea whether it was dosed with saccharine or sugar. In fact the ration at home was always three weeks in advance because his mother had wheedled it out of the grocer. 'She's clever,' Mr Mullinder laughed when he mentioned it. 'When the war ends she'll have had three weeks for nowt.'

'What's the score on the Russian front these days?' Mullinder asked, teasing Brian's obsession, who took him seriously: 'They'll be in Germany soon. I'm sure they'll get to Berlin before anybody else.'

'Let's hope they stay there,' Mullinder said. 'They want to finish off that lot once and for all this time.'

Brian ripped into a sandwich: 'I'll say.'

'Get my fags out o' my mac pocket, Pauline,' her old man said. Brian liked to see her doing such things, washing-up, slicing bread, paring cheese and spreading butter. He observed the mature sixteen-year-old shape of her body as best he could with so many in the house, saw how attractive it showed when prized out of the voluminous thick coat and clothed only in the blouse and skirt she had worked in by her machine all day. The raw animal sweetness lingering from their love-making in the Cherry Orchard still beat in his loins, and now and again as she passed him at the table he caught a faint odour of her face and skin, of powder and lipstick she lightly used – though her father had told her time and time again not to wear it. He was surprised that no one could twig they had spent the last hour loving each other, felt it should be showing in their eyes and the way they moved.

He ate his food slowly, drank tea, only half-aware of the squabble going on between Maureen and Doris, the eldest daughter who was to be married in a month and seemed to be getting her bellyful of family fights before leaving them off for good. Mullinder switched the news on hopefully, but it didn't get a look in, so with a pit curse – also drowned – he flicked it off again. I don't know how he puts up with this racket, though maybe he likes it – you never know. It's certainly a lively family. If there was an argument like this in our house fists and pots would be flying already. Pauline sat opposite eating her supper. She caught his look and picked up her cup of tea to dispel it. He was overwhelmed by an impossible thought, an outlandish idea that would drag him from all settled notions of work and courting (and freedom that nevertheless existed between the two states) and set him on course so new and head racking, yet in a way perhaps wonderful and good, that he wished the vision of it had never fixed itself like a hot picture-transfer against his skin. Maybe she already is pregnant, he thought, we've done it often enough.

21

Seven hours gone, and seven to go: it was a long watch, two workdays wrapped up in the parcel of one black night. The air in the hut had left off being air and turned to sweat. Talk about dead beat! this is what trade unions is good for, but they're all verboten in this Belsen. He screwed up his eyes so that they opened wide when the pressure of his knuckles lifted, adjusted a few of the dozen dials to get spot-on frequency and tapped out a legible two-letter call-sign KB KB KB – more to fill his own earphones with a companionable noise than drag other and distant operators from their stolen half-burnt slumber. The morse lacked energy, like his eyes and mind. Singapore was silent down the steps of latitude: Saigon, Karachi, Negombo meaningless ghosts beyond the periphery of consciousness. He wrote his call in the log: half-past three, wanting five hours still to be back in camp and under the sluicing cold bite of a shower. Most of all he wanted the bullock-cart of the year to take off its brakes and roll quickly into next week, for he and Knotman had formed a jungle-rescue team and arranged that its initial exercise be an attempt to climb Gunong Barat from the south. He'd done weeks of work, had drafted charts to show how the grub-tins and biscuits would be divided between the six donkey-backs of the team, and had already plotted each night's camping position on a three-inch map he'd spent a week drawing in the Camp Library. 'Planning the trip'll be the easiest part of it,' Knotman said. 'Don't bank on three miles a day. Make it two.' I suppose he should know, Brian thought. Even so we'll do more than two: I could go that far on my head. At Transmitters the wireless mechanic was breathing life into a walkie-talkie, and Brian had more overlapping maps to sketch and trace, and would have to queue in a day or two for injections against typhus and typhoid. Camp monotony was broken, a thing of the past – and as a team ever after they could be called on to trek and search for the survivors of any kite that belly-dived in the north Malayan jungle.

A month ago he had gone by air-sea-rescue pinnace as relief sparks to a buoy-laying scheme off the Barat coast. The pinnace made tracks like a well-polished beetle around tiny jungle islands, while Brian's morse kept a couple of rusty and worn-out naval tugs in touch with Kota Libis. There were few messages to send, and he spent most of the day on deck, reading by the donkey engine. At night the pinnace was moored a few yards out from an island, a half-sphere of grapefruit jungle with no more than six feet of sand for a beach. He did anchor-watch, and looking down in the darkness there was nothing in the sea but grey humps of giant jellyfish, stationary and sinister below the surface as if waiting for a sleep-laden inhabitant of the boat to lose his footing and provide a meal for them. Now and again he swung the leadweight, sounding fathoms to make sure the boat didn't drag its anchor. At seven he watched the sun feeling its way up the jungle of Gunong Barat, showing him at this close range secret valleys and subsidiary hilltops invisible from the camp, and coastal knolls coming almost down to the still night-laden sea. The sun poured yellow fire on to each pinnacle and dyed the greyish villages red as if they were in some nightmare waterless land of iron ore, then hardened to a purple and crimson. Yellow grew out of it, came towards green, until the sun broke through its barrier and slowly turned the water around the pinnace into a sea of blood.

He slung down his pencil, restless from the memory of that fabulous dawn, felt feverish in the dank tobacco-soaked air on which insects seemed content to draw their calories of existence. Kicking open the door he smelled the warm stillness of the tigernight, took up the rifle and walked outside, feeling the tall brittle blades of elephant grass chafing his knees as he made his way slowly towards the far wall of trees. I hope I don't put my foot on a snake, he thought, going slower so as to give any comfortably curled up krait or cobra time to make its getaway.

Half a mile off was an open shed in which an airman armed with a wooden club was set to guard petrol and tools. A few nights ago – Brian reminded himself – the poor sod had seen the face of a full-grown tomcat tiger gimletting from tall grass outside. With no doors to hold it back should the tiger roam around, he nearly curled up and died at the shock, but was able to use the field telephone and explain with garbled obscenity to some officer at the mess that they'd better come and get him before he was chewed to bone and gristle. Half an hour later a jeep of drunken officers roared up the runway firing Stens – by which time the tiger was safe in its hideout jungle.

Maybe I'll meet that tiger: he slid a bullet up the spout. My claws are as sharp as his while I've got this .303 in my fist. The fear livened him and he walked on, though slowly as if a cord were tied to his feet. The grass moved, bent into a hollow. He peered and saw nothing, a shadow of wind perhaps, though his .303 burst against it, sending a hemisphere of deafening noise shaking towards the hills.

Back in the hut he switched the tuning dial from its allotted wavelength to find some music, hoping no plane would choose to send an SOS while he wasn't listening. The needle flickered across graduated readings behind the glass, settled on a station whose music he eventually recognized (able to follow the tune though static made mincemeat of crotchets and semi-quavers), as Bizet's L'Arlésienne Suite. He remembered hearing it first when he was fourteen, alone in the house as it played in the interval of Daudet's play, the same music now wavily crossing the Pacific. The sad melody had haunted him ever since, bringing sharply before his eyes the vision of a sun going down over the flat grey land of the Camargue, where the air is cool and still to the insane cry of someone dying of love.

When the first hearing of the music finished he was in tears, a shameless unfair desecration of his working manhood. It was an evening in summer before the advent of darkness, when children had stopped screaming along the asphalt path by the lavatories, and the group of women who normally gossiped at the yard-end had gone in to give them their teas. No anti-aircraft guns belted away at illusive aeroplanes and no sirens wailed their warning song. It was the dead hour between tea and supper, light and dark, between the end of barking dogs and the start of lad-gangs calling at passing girls from unlit lamp-posts. The feeling of poetry and death was broken as his mother said, having suddenly walked in: 'What's up, Brian? You're never crying, are you?'

'No,' he answered. 'The sun hurt my eyes today when I was out up Trent.'

The same music came to him now, in places distorted or impossible to hear, so that he tried to tune it clearer, using all his skill to bring it free from the murderous inundations of atmospherics. He allied himself to the music, related it to the workings of his own brain. In the enervating damp heat of Malaya both thought and action took place in a kind of haze, and he sensed strongly that his mind could be far deeper and sharper than it was. The only practical way, it seemed, of reaching this occasionally perceived and ideal state in the near future was to get back to England, for he imagined that in a colder and clearer temperature his thoughts and perceptions would deepen and increase.

He glimpsed it now, but vaguely because the music confused him with self-pity, reminding him that no letter from Pauline had come for a fortnight, and no news from Mimi either; and he couldn't envisage a future beyond the dark escarpments of Gunong Barat.

He hadn't seen Mimi for several weeks in fact, and through the hard and alternating watches (increased day-work because bombers patrolled the jungle on square-searches, termed exercise) he pondered on specific reasons for it. The widow, she said, had been told of his visits and threatened to throw her out if he came there again because she didn't like English airmen invading the sacred territory of her house. Or is Mimi making this up to put me off? There was no way of knowing, and brooding gets you nowhere. Sooner or later the good things end, your troubles start. Only for so long can you think the world is a lovely place to be in, until with a couple of mild hits between the eyes it reminds you that you don't count as to whether it's good or not. Some invisible thug takes you by the shoulders and shakes you this way and that, roaring all the time: 'You're alive, you stiffnecked jumped-up bastard. You're alive I'm telling you. And here's summat to let you know it.' You're left tottering, trying to see what's wrong and put things right, when underneath all you want to do is crawl away and sleep while the trouble and bother works itself out – die in other words. I should have known things would go this way with us, but that's the trouble about being slow on the uptake, because I didn't do anything to stop the rot setting in.

Her silence hit him like a double hammerblow of optimism and despair, a carpenter's pendulum to stop you doing anything, yet keep you living. Where do you go from the highest point of passion? To sustain it into love would have meant seeing her more often which, because he was a prisoner, was impossible. He reached the agony of believing that perhaps he had wanted the break to come, because the toil and emotional fight needed to sustain what he may have imagined to be there in the first place was too much for his diminishing energy in the blood-boiling north of Malaya. Maybe she just doesn't want to see me and that's that.

Granted that what the eye didn't see the heart couldn't grieve, he realized he was nevertheless doing the dirty of the rottenest sort on Pauline, thought of her often from his far-removed and new-cut stomping grounds of Kota Libis, knowing that while opportunity offered he hadn't the will to do more or less than accept it. He had neither felt nor heard any angle of moral injury on his silent expeditions through the Patani darkness and swamps to see Mimi, and as long as he didn't wonder whether or not Pauline was playing the same trick on him he hardly thought to explore the unfaithful pointers of his own actions. But he was eventually pushed into considering such a possibility when the idea that Mimi could be betraying *him* crept into his mind. And this was such an enraging idea that he forgot about his injury to Pauline (and maybe hers to him) as soon as it was broached, detesting Mimi for a betrayal he could never have proof of.

Mimi was strange to him because her one-sided character appeared so complete. Her chief trait seemed one of a lassitude so overpowering that his only reaction to it was anger. He saw no way in which they could really and finally meet in love, his immediate dark reason for this being that they were too much strangers to each other for having been born and reared in different parts of the world. I understood Pauline, he told himself, so why shouldn't I get through to Mimi? Still, some women are harder to get to know than others – and don't I know it? – for I was four years with Pauline before we had to run down to the Registry Office and get spliced up. Mimi is too passive, and I want somebody to grind myself to bits on maybe. Don't be a loon: all you want is to shag yourself silly, you know you do; what brains you've got dive overboard as soon as you get a woman hot and undressed in bed. Mimi's doing it on you, and it's looped your vanity in a half-nelson. You thought you were all set to make a go of it, live it up for good perhaps, get married maybe (after you'd ditched Pauline, you foul bastard) and fill her with a few kids. Well, think on it: you'll be back in England in six months and then where will you be with all this humming and aahing? Who knows where I'll be in six months? I could walk away from this wireless-set, tread on a snake outside the door and be dead before I knew where I was. So all that crap about the future wain't wash; except I suppose I'll be back in England soon and loving it up with marvellous understandable Pauline.

Life on the camp was boring between morse and map-making. Twenty-five dollars a week at eight to the pound was only enough to keep him in cigarettes and odd meals at the canteen, so he couldn't dazzle himself with the expensive lights of Pulau Timur more than once a month. No wonder Mimi's fed up with me, he reasoned. If dad could send me a few quid every week – like some blokes get – I'd be able to jazz things up a bit. The poor bogger needs every penny for himself, even though he is at work. I don't expect the couple o' bob a day I allow Pauline would make much difference to my whooping it up either, because she could do with it, as well as the odd food parcel I'm able to post off now and again.

The camp cinema had been six weeks closed because the rickety equipment had given out. It was so old they must have got it from the scrapheap outside some shutdown fleapit. You could go, of course, to the Nanking Talkies in the village, but it was a dead loss hearing Rin-Tin-Tin barking in Chinese and the man on Movietone News ringing his bell in Hindustani three months out of date, and seeing joss-smoke billowing from Buck Jones's ivory-handled guns. So he'd sit in the billet, reading for hour after hour until his concentration snapped and he was ready to argue with anyone who happened to be about. No one believed in God, he found, and most would vote Labour if they were old enough. Getting them to admit a monarchy useless proved easy, and from then on it wanted only half an hour to win them over to a form of communism terrifying in its simplicity. At the apogee of his boredom he found himself possessed by a wild and compelling gift of the gab, would sit on the end of his bed and talk talk talk on any subject that came into his head, spouting without effort and only realizing afterwards that the boys had actually been listening with enjoyment, had been influenced by his voice, laughing when he said something amusing and nodding in agreement when he came out with the extreme breath of revolution. They'll believe anything when they're bored, he saw, exhausted from his peroration, pleased at himself as he fell asleep over his book.

Baker sent paper aeroplanes flying from his bed, happy when they found landing-grounds on somebody's book, letter or face. He captured a large dung-beetle that hovered clumsily around the lights, imprisoned it in a matchbox while searching through his locker for a length of cotton. 'Don't hang it' somebody shouted. 'It looks a strong bastard: make it work.' He tied the cotton to the beetle's back leg and the other end to one of his paper aeroplanes. 'There's no life in the bloody place,' Baker shouted as he released the beetle. With a buzz like the roar of a minute engine it soared through the open door and lost itself in the trees. 'Funny bastard,' a voice said.

Brian was calm, half-way through a novel and wanting to finish it, but Baker was in a hard, useless, destructive mood. Someone put 'Horo Staccato' on the gramophone but Baker ripped it off and skimmed it out of the door so that it shattered against a tree. He then sat by the pile of records and slew the fifty of them after 'Horo Staccato' – looking at each label before committing it to smithereens. No one thought the records good enough to save, being all of tuneless tunes out of the good old days.

He broke the spell, caught sight of the table on which he sometimes spread a mattress and stretched out when he couldn't stay awake. On its surface, reaching from side to side of the hut, was a kettle (that would leave a black ring when lifted), a tin of sugar housing a lucky ant or two, a packet of strong Air Ministry tea, a couple of tin mugs with flex around the handles, and a haversack of bread and cheese. Propped in a corner was a loaded rifle whose meat-skewer bayonet had been used to spit holes in a tin of condensed milk also on the table. There were over a hundred .303 rounds in a floor box, fifty more than the camp armoury knew about, hard cylindrical handouts with lead noses to punctuate or terminate whatever moved outside or in.

The music grew back – or he turned round to it, unwilling to be entirely alone. A thought he considered stupid and out of place came to him: 'I don't want to go up to Gunong Barat. The only place I want to be is Nottingham.' It slid the earth from under him, like the trick when someone flicks the cloth from beneath a tableful of pots without disturbing them, the difference being they are nearer the reality of true-grained wood. With the ground insecure he knew he would still go to Gunong Barat, which, though a self-erected obstacle, had to be crossed nevertheless because he had created it in his own mind as a stepping-stone to the future. In any case, Gunong Barat meant the jungle, a luring and mysterious word that had taunted him all his life from books and comics and cinema, an unknown flimsy word meaning something else, so that it would teach him perhaps whether or not he wanted to enter the real world it sometimes appeared to be screening. Without the expedition there would be no future, only a present, an ocean of darkness behind the thin blue of the day, a circle of bleak horizons dotted by fires burning out their derelict flames.

He remembered an encounter with Mimi one night on his way back from the Egyptian café. She passed him in the darkness, was a few paces ahead before he called her name.

When she turned, his feeling of gladness became one of misery at thinking she may have hoped to pass him unnoticed. 'Where are you off at this time of night?'

Both were shocked at the meeting: 'I'm going home,' she said. 'I felt like walking.' She seemed in a hurry and he went along with her.

'I could do with a stroll as well,' he said, curt and sarcastic, a mood that turned her into a perverse witch, no longer beautiful and withdrawing. Well, he said to himself, you wanted to get to know her, now you have. She's a whore, doing it on you. They walked in silence, he feeling a hopeless awkwardness, unable to speak as if his throat were full of soil.

'I had a hard night,' she told him, walking unconcerned by his side. 'An American ship is in harbour, and I've danced for five hours. We thought the police were going to come, but the Americans just got senseless and took each other back to their ship.'

'I've been in the canteen,' he said, 'playing dominoes.' The turning-off point was reached. A few people were about. A trishaw from the last ferry was taking a drunk back to camp. He wished it were midday and dazzling sun so that the shop-fronts were decked out like open pomegranates, with haircream and razor blades, watches and fountain pens, cameras and cheap shirts, fruits and food and people and traffic. He felt uneasy at being alone in darkness in which you couldn't really be alone, sensing beneath Mimi's nonchalance her deeper uneasiness at being with him. Before he could broach the question she said: 'There isn't a free night this week. Three Dutch ships are coming in and I'll have to work all the time.'

He said nothing, regretting that he was unable to make an immediate answer, though knowing it wouldn't have done much good. Her mind was fixed. Maybe she's fed up only for the time being and we'll be on the old footing in a week or two. His notion that she'd found someone else made him sick with jealousy and disappointment, too confused to ask himself what had eaten into their love. I'd seen it coming, and maybe that was what was wrong. 'I'm busy myself these days,' he said.

'We'll see each other again.' I suppose this is what they call a stiff upper lip, he thought; the stupid bastards. 'I'll let you know when I've got an evening off,' she said, almost tenderly. Maybe she's happy I'm not doing my nut and pasting her all up the road. 'I've been thinking of taking a job at Singapore,' she went on. 'In fact there's a good chance I'll be on my way soon.' This meant little to him: she'd spoken of it months ago, and it might come to nothing. But he said: 'I hope you don't go. I love you too much to let you go as easy as that.'

'I know,' she said slowly. They kissed passionately, then broke away and walked in their different directions.

He swore at the night, at himself, at everything under the night moon, his curses hammering at the stockade that had been built around the limit of his words without him knowing it, even before he was born perhaps. I can't say or do a thing right. Christ, I'd cut my throat if this was the first tart I'd gone out with.

He was hailed from a passing tri-shaw: 'Hey, Brian, you dirty ramrod, where have you been sinning tonight? I didn't see you in the stews of Pulau Timur.' Belt up, he thought, black as thunder. 'If you want a lift get in,' Knotman went on, 'but if you want to walk your feet off your ankles I don't give a Gunong Barat.'

'I heard you the first time.' He relented and sat in the tri-shaw beside him, the padding feet of the coolie clip-clopping along the empty road. 'Been to the Boston Lights?' he asked Knotman through the high power of his whisky breath.

'Not likely. Costs too much. I got me a nice steady girl, Eurasian, nurse at the hospital. Says she loves me and will I marry her? Sure, I say, be glad to when I've made up my mind. You're unjust, she says, you're persistently procrastinating, like Hamlet (she's an intellectual like me: that's why we get on so well). It's hardly fair, she says, the way you use me (reads *The Tatler* as well), we *should* get married, you know. We sit in the Botanical Gardens feeding the monkeys: "I'm rotten," I say to her, shedding tears of blood. "I'm the rottenest melon as ever rolled God's earth; I'm as rotten as they come, so help me bloody God. So you'd better forgive me or I won't be able to marry you; and stop taking my feed bottle away from me like that you sly bitch or I'll sock you on the jaw." I'm finished, she says. You treat me worse than any prostitute from the Boston Lights. You only treat me so badly because you've lost your self-respect. Goes all deep down and perceptive on me, really gets her nails into my inside tripes – metaphysically speaking of course (I've read *The Tatler* as well). I'm going, she says, I'm off. You've hurt me too much – and here's me rubbing my psychological sores because they're giving me hell. But she ups and goes and that's the way life is with a woman. I meet her at the gate. "Where are you off?" I asks. "I was hoping I'd see you again because I forgot to give you the poem I'd written to you." (I'm sobbing now, almost anyway). "I've been working on it a week and have found it very difficult not to give it you before it was finished. But it'd be a terrible shame if we were to part for ever in this flippant fashion, before you know how much I really love you, and without me having shown you the marvellous poem I've been composing for you in my heart these last three months." I charm her – you understand? She listens. "I'm sorry," I said. "True love never runs smooth" (her face has traces of smallpox but I'm crazy about her). "I'd like to hear your poem," she says. So we go back to the seat we were on before. I got out a piece of paper, maybe my will and testament, and made up a poem on the spot, anything to save my broken-down future marriage. I've been divorced after marriage, which was bad enough because it was against my Christian principles, but never split up in an irreparable divorce before marriage, which would be against my pagan principles. So I make up a poem as Miss Prim-and-Proper waits for the beautiful lines to flow – you know, Dante Gabriel Rossetti and all that crap:

> 'I've loved you my darling since birds began to fly
> Since apple-loaves baked in my oven's eye.
> When fires begin you can't put them out
> With anything less than a waterspout' –

well, that was the first verse and it wasn't bad, being made up on the spot, even though I do say so myself. I'm not a Limey so don't expect any false modesty from me. But after three more verses it wasn't so much my education (or lack of it) that began to show as that my upbringing and dirty mind came through, so that, old buddy, I ended up with such a mouthful of barrack-room filth that she fled from me clutching her skirt, and the last thing I saw of my dark little nurse was two tri-shaw wheels going round a corner. I was brokenhearted and still am. I got myself a few drinks to drown my sorrows, because I'm sure I'll never see my living doll again and who can blame her? But out of the rotten carcass came forth sweetness, as they say in *Sanders of the River* – or was it *Das Kapital*? – and I'm going to start writing poetry as a life of penance. I'm going to be a real poet, even though I do say so while I'm as stoned as an iguana. I'm going to be a writer, get spot cash for deep thoughts. So when you see me tomorrow remind me of what I say, because if you don't I'll forget all about it.'

Brian guided him to his billet, tipped him fully dressed on his bed and pulled down the mosquito-net.

When Brian laughed at his own self-pity the bark of a pariah dog made a duet with him. The music ended and so did his sadness, and with a blank mind he walked to the door and booted it open, shivering as cold air blew into his sweat-ridden shirt. I want to get out of this, he said. Another three months and I'll be on the boat, thank God. Five hundred yards towards the airstrip was another similar hut where pal Jack, not having to keep an all-night watch, had spent the last eight hours with his head down; and eastwards black humps of forest rolled up to the highest ridges of Malaya. He pissed a tune against a petrol tin to keep himself company, then went back and slammed the door.

He listened out on frequency: nothing. The whole night sky of South-East Asia was empty of planes as far as he was concerned, but he didn't want to go to sleep. As soon as I get my head down some no-good crippled kite will start belting out an SOS – and then where would all of us be? They'd be dead and I'd be in the glasshouse, but I wouldn't let them down anyway. He called Singapore and got no answer: five o'clock. They're asleep, but I don't want to be, though the only thing that would waken me now is a woman, succulent and willing and fiery, burning for me as much as I would be for her. It doesn't happen unless you get her that way yourself, though I know Pauline was marvellous when I've got the heart to think back clear enough, adept and full of love when both of us were properly wanted. Well, I could read for a while, but what's the use of reading a book? They lull you into a false sense of security, as Len Knotman says.

His head went down on the desk, and in half a minute he was walled-up in sleep.

Morse came marvellous and sudden-quick, a circular saw out of some rip-roaring operator fresh on the job, singing into the earphones still noosed around Brian's neck and waking him. Sunlight cut under the hut door like the flame of a blow-lamp, a knife-glare that swamped his brain and pinned him to the foul interior air. Only the morse was clear, piercing beyond tiredness and cold sweat, and without thought he wrote it in the log, ran fingers through untidy hair as other notes jerked into the mêlée at varying scales and strengths. Stations were tuning up, filling the wavelength with staccato importunate utterings of good morning – as if every operator had smelt sunlight at the same time, or sat at his key only waiting for the first one to tap out his call sign, before taking a running-jump in with his own rhythmical identity.

He fastened the door open. Sun, visible above palmtops, pushed an ache of sleep back into his eyes, flooding warmth over him. Longpoled sparsely-set trees stretched thickly to jungle on mountainsides still purple in morning light, while clouds from seaward cast islands of shadow along the wide black canal of the airstrip, leaving a whiter reflection in paddy fields already shimmering to the south. A Dak revved-up at the control tower, gleaming silver and going slowly along the runway. It gathered speed with a great belly roar, turned and stood as if for a final indraw of breath. A green light from the tower eased it forward, and it was a few feet off the ground by the time it came level with the DF hut, was soon heavy and slow over the sea towards Pulau Timur, then swinging back low over the trees, heavy with supplies for some distant outpost.

It would soon be sending weather messages from along its route, so Brian set sticks over a copy of the *Straits Times* in his outside fireplace and dosed it well with paraffin, putting a match under the kettle so that flames exploded and hid it completely. He spoke by field telephone to the other hut: 'That you, Jack?'

A yawn sounded in his ear: 'Yeh. Making tea?'

'Just put the kettle on. I'll put a mug by for you.'

Jack's voice became clear: 'Thanks, Bri. Be over in five minutes.' He lobbed spit at the fire and watched it do a quick-change act into steam, answered by the kettle throwing water from its spout as if competing against him.

He saw Jack coming along the path, an ex-collier from Abertillery, a slim-built thin-faced youth whose grey eyes had been used all his life to the murk of his home valley and later to the dust and grime of the pitface. Often in the billet he would be lying asleep under his mosquito-net, dead to the world and dreaming maybe of his welcome in the hillsides, yet with his eyes wide open. 'I've always slept like that,' Jack told him, grinning to show his uneven teeth. 'Can't help it, man. My sister back home used to try and make me close them, but couldn't. And I didn't fancy letting her stitch them together every night.' He carried the Sten gun slung high on his shoulder, every inch the bantamweight, dark hair curly at the front and falling on to his brow. He took great delight in the Sten, feeling twice the man as he walked out with it to the DF hut from his own post, advancing at the ready as if a black mamba might uncoil and strike at the grimy toes of his sandals, or a tiger slouch from the higher elephant grass bordering the monsoon ditch. Buying a Box Brownie from his saved pay, he asked Brian to take photos of him holding the Sten like any film star on active service, and both admitted that the reproduction certainly made him look fierce and tough.

Brian slid a mug of tea over, 'Get that in your guts.'

'Get much sleep?' he asked from the radio table.

Jack drank half before he'd speak, lolled in a basket chair near the door and gave a disgruntled reply: 'I would have, only those bloody dogs howled all night. It's enough to send you to chapel. You hear 'em?'

He sipped his tea: strong, sweet and scalding. 'They didn't bother me. I had to be awake anyway.'

'Considerate bastard,' Jack said. 'All for one and one for all. I'd like to have got one of them though. Used its guts for garters I would.' Brian took down a message from the Dakota while Jack grumbled on, phoned it through to flying control. 'I would have taken a shot at them, except that the bastards don't let me have a rifle. Think I'll let fly at the officers, I expect. Not that I wouldn't by mistake though. "Sorry, sir, but my glasses were at the laundry. I'll aim the other way next time." Man, what a life! You should 'ave brought one down with the rifle.'

'Couldn't be bothered' – flicking an ant away from the sugar. 'It was so dark I wouldn't have seen it.' He hacked off slices of bread and cheese: 'Get some o' this. I'm clambed.'

Jack shuffled back to his hut, cursing the air force, God and Winston Churchill. Brian swept up and cleared away the breakfast things, dug a hole fifty yards off to bury the week's tins. Another message rattled in from the far-off Dakota, then Jack was on the phone: 'Listen,' he said, so excited it seemed his head was in the earpiece of the receiver, 'There's a great dog, man, about fifty shakes from your wanking pit. Fetch him down with the rifle. My Sten won't reach or I'd let him have a burst. He's one of the sods that's been keeping me awake all night.'

'Wait for the bang then. See you soon.' Sliding one up the spout he stepped to the door. It was as big as a full-grown Alsatian, and not too far off to be winged at the first crack. He stood perfectly still, its coat was straggly and white, had a long bony head and the noble face of a handsome outcast that didn't know what was in store for it. Its eyes looked as if waiting for something to move in the near-by grass.

A perfect target. Maybe I'll scare it with a shout and get him on the run. He lined foresight and backsight with its right eye and eased on the safety-catch, feeling for the trigger. The dog turned and there was no fear in its gaze, as if it didn't realize that another animal was so close, though Brian knew it saw him, felt its curiosity and quiet inquiring surprise. His finger was on the rounded steel of the trigger, and he visualized it already with a hole battered into its skull, fallen like a piece of floorcloth after the butt had jerked against his shoulder. He brought the gun down.

The dog moved, and with no thoughts left Brian followed it into the grass, leaving the radio to fend for itself. A sudden spurt put the dog out of range. He felt the sun pushing at the back of his neck and impelling him towards the trees. A hundred yards off, the dog leapt into the air: I should have got it then – but when he reached where the dog had jumped, his legs and shorts were ripped by barbed wire concealed in the grass, paining as if burning embers had peppered his flesh. He aimed and fired, but the grass obscured his aim. I'll get it on the dispersal clearing. Stop, he told himself, leave it be, you lousy bastard. Yet he was enjoying the chase, couldn't force himself to draw off.

Concealed roughage below the waving grassblades buckled his ankle now and again and, falling behind, he expected the dog to wheel out of range and reach the safety of the trees. But it stopped from time to time as if sick, hoping perhaps to lie low and be given up. Brian went on, driven by pain in his legs.

The dog veered from the trees, circled back for the hut, so that all he needed to do was wait. Maybe it wanted food. He whistled a tune until it reached the clearing, told himself not to shoot it but was too weary to listen. On his knees he fired, the noise sharp and great, directly connected to the dog that dropped by the hut door. He circled the hut himself, feeling a black end-of-the-world weariness as he dragged himself, after some minutes, towards it.

In spite of the great hole in its head, that he couldn't bear to look at, the dog still twitched. He dragged the limp relaxed body ten yards and dug a hole out of the stony ground, half an hour of feverish hacking and lifting because the sun was up and draining rivers of sweat off him. He pushed the dog into the deep trench and shovelled stones and soil in, hating himself for the rottenness of what he'd done. It was impossible not to think thoughts that wouldn't come to him before but did so now. Christ, I shouldn't have done it. Useless and mad. I ought to have slung a brick and let it go, not shot it like the cruel and wicked bastard I am. At the set another message came from the Dak, its signals fainter so that he listened hard to pull down the five-figure groups. Out of the biting heat his mind grew cool, drew him back a dozen years to a thundery week-end at the Nook, to a walk across cornfields with grandad Merton to look for Gyp who was missing after a fearful kicking for nothing at all. The air was heavy with unshed rain and a cool breeze blew – as they tramped by hedges and over stiles. The picture was not clear, needed an effort even to keep it at this blurred pitch, but he remembered at the end of it finding the dog on the railway line, bloody and curled up after being hit by a train. It was impossible to say who had killed it: Merton, the train, God. Who? The family said Merton, and in this case, in spite of the phone call from Jack, anybody with two eyes would have said Brian had done it. And so would he in their place. But never again, he thought. One dead dog is enough to have to pay for.

At eight-thirty the relief lorry waited at the airstrip, and Kirkby was on his way to take over, a dot seen in the distance as Brian stuffed his haversack with towel and books. Sun scorched his hair and he could smell the sharp stench of sweat from his body when the breeze lifted. Far to the left was the paddy field where the old DF hut had stood, though the flat expanse of rice shoots had no aerials now to break the monotony of it. The Chinese peasant guided his oxen through where they had been, and palm trees on the far edge that had received the full blow of the last monsoon lay like kitchen mops over the water.

Jack came out of his hut and walked in step: 'That was a good shot, man. I watched you bring him down. Smack! Keeled over he did, just like that.'

Brian stopped to light a fag. 'Listen,' he said, filled with rage at his own useless cruelty (A dog's a dog: it's got to live. Even Dave and Colin would admit that): 'That's the last fucking dog I shoot I'll tell you that, mate. In fact it's the last thing I shoot at all. Christ knows why I killed it; I don't.'

'Well,' Jack said, subdued at seeing him in this funny mood, 'all right, comrade, man, don't do it. I suppose it didn't do any good, now you put it like that.'

'Too bleeding right it didn't,' Brian fumed. 'Roll on the boat, that's all I can say. This place is beginning to get on my wick.'

'It's no good letting it get you down,' Jack said. 'We'll be in that steaming jungle next week.'

From watching Baker test his model aeroplane (fuselage and wings were smashed on the second flight, though the engine was saved) Brian saw a letter on his bed bearing a Singapore postmark. It was a note from Mimi, not exactly filled with words of love, but merely saying she was on her way back from Singapore (stopping at KL to visit her parents) to take up her old job at the Boston. Yet because her words were unadorned, his imagination flamed with possibilities, set him cursing at the fact that in only a few days he would be off to climb Gunong Barat. He reflected though that such a life of expectation and promise, enabling him to see Mimi for a few days and then make a trip into the jungle, wasn't such a bad thing. And a couple of months later he would be on the boat, making his way back to Pauline and the kid. He wondered why Mimi had abandoned the idea of Singapore so soon: happen the job hadn't turned out as she'd expected. Or maybe there hadn't been work at all, but she'd gone down on the trot with some boyfriend who'd taken a fancy to her at the Boston – who'd packed her up when his ship left. Then again she could have come back because she missed me. Now you *have* got a touch of the bleeding sun.

That afternoon a dozen from the Signals stood in threes outside the admin office, being told by a sergeant (what they as wireless operators knew already since all information sent to the camp went through them) that they would be demobbed in three months. For some reason the short ratty sergeant gave a lecture on their lack of smartness, threatened them with guard duty, kit inspection and morning parades, which they as wireless operators had so far avoided. Their great dread was that the air force bullshit machine would find its way even into this easy-going outpost of dialectical imperialism. 'I like it the way it is,' Corporal Knotman said to Brian. 'You don't jump when I walk into the room, and I don't jump when any other rattlebox shows his mug. They don't realize that the War's over, and times are no longer what they were.'

'And so' – the sergeant bawled from the veranda, a little man who knew how to have his own way because he in his time had been bullied blind – 'I want to see Signals types look smarter and be a bit more punctual. You were all late for this parade, every manjack of you, by four minutes. Four minutes is a long time in the air force and I want you to know that you must *never* be late again, NEVER! Understand? Not even for ten seconds. Now, another thing – no, I haven't finished with you yet, not by a long way – I was walking through your billet this morning and it was untidy, scruffy in fact. WILL YOU STOP JUMPING AROUND LIKE A LOT OF BLOODY BALLET DANCERS AND HOLD STILL? That's better. The beds weren't made on time and I want you to see that they are.'

'Inferiority complex,' Baker grumbled, his lips hardly moving. 'He's like Hitler. A nazi louse. I wonder where he's left his swastika? "Lost, one swastika in Piccadilly Circus. Reward of half a crown." Blokes like him'll be slammed in the gas-ovens next time.'

The sergeant went on to instruct them about going to England on the troopship: 'You'll wear full webbing equipment, with waterbottle and big pack, also carry a kitbag and rifle. All your surplus possessions can go into *one* deep-sea trunk.' He asked for questions. Brian could feel Baker seething near by, like a doglover whose pet bonzo has just been trodden on in a crowd and is out to set on anybody with two legs. It's understandable: it takes him a month to make such streamlined aeroplanes. Baker's hand shot up: 'What about our suitcases, sergeant?'

He let out a sneering roar: 'Suitcases? who's got *suitcases*?' I wonder if he's married, Brian wondered, and treats his kids like this? Everyone put their hands up, and the majority vote rattled him. 'Now listen to me, you can only take what's on Standing Orders, that is, the equipment provided by the air force. All personal stuff has to go in a deep-sea trunk, crated and made to specifications by some wog chippy in the village. Any airman who wants these specifications can call at the orderly room after the parade, and I'll be glad to see he gets them.'

This hit everyone, for all had suitcases to hold the growing volume of presents stored up since arrival. Brian had a dressing-gown for Pauline, things for the kid. Baker spoke up: 'I'll burn all my equipment. I'm not leaving presents behind.'

The sergeant seemed about to rush back to his office for the Riot Act. 'Who said that?' He leapt from the veranda and came so fast into them that he burst against Baker and knocked him backwards. Baker recovered quickly, squinting down at him with insolent amazement. 'You shouldn't strike an airman, sergeant,' he said gently.

The holy rank awarded by the air force gave way. 'Take him to the guardroom,' he bellowed, jabbing out with his fingers. 'You, you, you as well.'

Baker was dragged off by his mates, Brian unable to decide whether he was acting or in earnest as he struggled violently and called out: 'I'm innocent, I tell you. Innocent!'

22

He remembered how on the long straight street of the housing estate Pauline ditched him one night: 'I don't want to go out with you any more. I've got a date with somebody else tomorrow.' Just like that; and even though they'd been getting on each other's nerves it was still as abrupt as if she'd prodded him with a hatpin or knitting needle.

'Go and get dive-bombed then,' he raged, and walked at a quick pace down the street to catch up Albert Lomax, who had just bid good night to his girl, Dorothy.

'That was quick,' Albert said. 'Has she chucked you?'

'Don't be bleddy funny,' Brian retorted. Then: 'She has, if you want to know. Not that I'm bothered. We've been getting fed up with each other the last week or two.'

'You've been having too much of it, that's what's wrong,' Albert said soberly. 'You've got to lay off now and again, not see owt of each other for a few weeks, then you wain't get so bored.' Exactly what had been in Brian's mind, but neither he nor Pauline were made for the mechanics of sensible separation. Too much passion was involved, and any letting-go would have to come out of hatred, not understanding.

Weekdays had been given to kissing by the back door, or sitting in with old Jack Mullinder over a lugubrious game of darts. Jack was off work now – for good, it looked like – because his foot had broken out again, was giving him jippo he admitted whenever an evening passed with not much more than a snappy word from him now and again. To Brian it was a house of silence compared to what it had been, no fun with poor old Mullinder trying to nurse his pain without going off his head. He felt sorry for him, as if he were his second father dropped into a cleft of hell, and was moved to weeping one night on his long wind home through the black-out. Nothing could be done except take the foot off, the doctors thought, and that's what it seemed like coming to. It was a miserable look-out when you dwelt on it, what with the War and everything.

On dry days of mid-week he walked with Pauline past the Broad Oak to Strelley fields and they lay on his topcoat behind isolated hedges making love again and again into an intimate and speechless lassitude. They were blind in such darkness, unable to see except by the touch of hands against each other, which suited Brian down to the ground though Pauline was sometimes irritated when his solicitude went on too long afterwards. 'I can't help it,' he laughed, 'if my old man was a rabbit. John I was christened, not Brian – Jack Rabbit to my pals.'

'I don't know about a rabbit,' she said, wiping herself, 'but you must a bin born in a boat if you ask me.'

'It's so bleeding dark,' he said, 'I can't see a thing.'

'Stop swearing: wash your mouth out with soap, foulmouth.' The tone and volume of her voice were calmer than the content of her retort, the main fire staying in her eyes, which he could not see. Shocked nevertheless at her reaction to a plain truth, he stood up and took a few paces away as if to make the darkness thicker by being on his own. It certainly was more comfortable, and his rage at her temper went like the matter from a pimple back into his bloodstream and left him calm. But she hadn't finished: You're allus swearing, and you never stop doing it for my sake. I suppose you think it meks you look big.'

The darkness was lit up, as if he had been smacked in the mouth – like his fight the time they first met. He wanted to walk off without turning towards her to do so – impossible because it was a lunar and dangerous landscape they were in, full of limekilns and abandoned pit shafts, wells and outcrop workings where one false step might cripple you for life. So it was better to stay and try argument: 'There's nowt wrong wi' swearing. It's just words like any others.'

'It's what they mean though. You know it is' – not so brittle now she had forced him to argue rather than quarrel. Of course they're different: all words are different. 'They're adjectives I suppose,' he said. 'It's all right if you don't mean 'em to be bad.' His back was to her, determined to avoid a row because she was plainly trying to head him into one. 'Shall we go? I'd like a pint.'

'Yes,' she answered, 'cleverdick' – the word 'adjective' still ringing in her ear. He shook his mac, as if hoping the damp would drop from it. 'We don't want to stay out too long drinking or we wain't see dad before he goes to bed.'

Thank God I'm too young to get married, he told himself, helping her through the hedge. 'Well, I'd better make the best of it as well because I'll be in the army in a year – unless I can dodge out of it.' The sky had cleared: 'A marvellous night,' he said. 'It's a wonder the bombers ain't up, smashing the Jerries.' A year! What a nut to mention it. I'll be eighteen, which is too far off to bother with. It was a mile to the pub and they walked arm-in-arm with only the crunch of their leisurely feet sounding along the lane. When my time comes I'll desert, he thought, rather than leave all this. I'll go on the run in every town round about so's the redcaps wain't know where to find me. There's plenty o' people who'll see me right. Dad for one. Aunt Ada for another. Even old Mullinder'll fill my gob with a meal if ever I need it. I don't expect for a minute it's principle as keeps Colin and Dave out of the army either, so much as not wanting to be bossed about and shouted at like dogs. As it is they keep themselves by night work and spend their nicked dough on women in pubs, having the time of their lives, only dodging back into the black-out shadows when they hear police whistles. They've heard a lot of them in their time, though they never got used to the jitters of them any more than I got used to the bombs and the rattle of anti-aircraft guns. It was so bad once when I went to Aunt Ada's to have tea (they lived off the fat of the land, for there was a ham on the table as fat as our Sammy), that when a whistle sounded from the next backyard they couldn't scatter fast enough. No bump came at the door but the whistling went on, low and frightening as if a thousand coppers had surrounded the Meadows and was closing in, but it turned out that the man next door had joined the air-raid wardens and his snotty-nosed kid had got hold of his whistle while he was upstairs having a Sunday afternoon kip with his missis. Everybody laughed when they knew: Colin and Dave bolting out of the house for fear of the coppers when all it was was a kid blowing on his dad's tin whistle.

'Why don't you talk? You don't say a deal these days.'

'I was thinking.' She offered a penny for them, but he wouldn't mention his deserting cousins to her. Not that he thought she'd give them away, but you never knew whether or not she might as a sort of joke mention them to somebody who would: there was a war on and you couldn't be too careful because walls have ears and all that pack of lies. 'I was just wondering where the planes were off to, that's all.'

'That ain't much: I'd want ha'penny change.' There was disappointment in her voice: 'You never tell me anything' – as if after two years' courting I've got much to keep from her. There was certainly more to his thoughts than he could make into living words, and he often fought battles to try and unroll the pictures and monologues that seemed for ever playing within himself on to his tongue so that he could share them. This happened during the first year they knew each other when, as if inspired, his mind and tongue would now and again unite and he would make jokes or assume the life of some other person to make her laugh – Churchill, Lord Haw Haw, or the Xmas Day Speech. But to try at a time when he didn't feel like it was impossible. 'I suppose you'd like me to tell you a fairy story,' he responded. 'As if you was a school kid.'

'I don't want you to tell me owt,' she said. 'I just want you to talk.' They were level with the Broad Oak, but he was too full of rage to turn in, unwilling to enter such packs of noise and faces while their quarrel was on. And Pauline no longer wanted a drink. 'If I don't feel like talking, I can't talk,' he replied. 'Anyway, we're talking now, aren't we?'

A few feet grew between them, a space of live invisible wires that fused now and again like the flashpan of Dick Turpin's pistol: 'No we aren't talking: we're rowing. We're allus rowing lately, and I tell you I'm fed up on it.'

'It's a lie,' he said, tongue-tied, at her list of truths, 'you know it is.' He was depressed, bitten by an indefinable blind misery.

Maybe she's got the rags on, he thought, and his mood lightened for a moment – until it struck him that she couldn't have. The strong presence of a thousand blacked-out houses of the estate proved itself further by vague noises and smells – petrol, coalsmoke and the vanishing odour of the fish-and-chip van. A gang on a privet corner kicked a tin-can into the road: it ended near Brian and he took great pleasure in booting it back at full speed, for which thanks were shouted. With a laugh he put his arm tight around Pauline and pulled her close. But her mood had deepened and she shoved him off.

'Come on,' he said happily. 'Don't get like that, duck,' and took hold of her again. Had anyone been listening from the shadow of some doorway they would have heard the perfectly aimed smack of an open hand against an unguarded relaxed face followed by a gasp of shock and pain: 'You sod!' They would then have heard a second smack – as hard and resounding as the first – as Brian slammed her back. 'No woman's going to hit me and get away with it,' he called out, for she was already ten yards down and crossing the street to where the Mullinders lived.

At the gate she turned: 'You can clear off, bully.'

'Don't worry: I shall' – and heard the back door slam as he went towards a 16 bus stop.

Christ, what a thing to do. But the week-ends were wonderful because on a Sunday afternoon they made love in comfort. The Mullinders would be out, visiting mothers or aunts at Cinderhill, Mullinder pushed there on a wheel-chair (wife and daughters taking turns at the handle) and making the best of a bad life when meeting any of his pit-mates along the road, braving it with gruff gratitude when one dropped a packet of twenty into his lap. Pauline and Brian were left in the house, it being taken for granted that they would stay together now and maybe even get married when the time came. Brian sensed this but lived so completely in the enjoyable present that it meant little to him. He certainly never thought about getting married – not at seventeen on the four or five quid knocked up on piecework. So he was careful not to get her pregnant, put wise on how to avoid it by a pal at work who said: 'They're only half a dollar a packet, so you want to use 'em. Cost you a lot more than that if you don't.'

'There's nowt like a bit of hearthrug pie,' he said to Albert, walking along in the darkness. 'I'll get none o' that now we've packed each other in. I don't know.' The regret in his voice was plain a mile off: 'It was smashing on Sunday afternoon in her house when there was nobody in. Went at it three or four times. Thanks,' he said, to the offer of a cigarette.

'You'll have to get somebody else then,' he said. 'It's easy done. You ought to come to our club sometime. Lots o' tarts there. It's a Co-op place on Garfield Road. We play darts and draughts and argue politics.'

'Maybe I will,' Brian said, such a club not appearing too silly a place if you could pick up bits o' skirt there. Like a book was all the more interesting if there was a bit of hot love stuff now and again. 'Come up next Wednesday,' Albert said. 'Call for me about seven.' To pass the next mile off they asked each other questions on geography. 'Can you tell me the names of the States of America?'

Brian could, or most of them, and those he couldn't think of were supplied by Albert. When at school he'd been surprised to see in a world gazetteer a reference to the near-by village of Wollaton, and from then on he hunted up maps of Nottingham, eager for larger and larger scales, hungry to find clearer marks of his geographical existence. Later he looked at maps in the headmaster's office which pleased him at seeing for the first time in his life that the streets he ran about in were important enough to be marked on maps that someone as far away as London could easily be gazing at. Then in a downtown bookshop he saw manuals of street-fighting for sale to such as Home Guards – meaning that every street was also marked and no doubt studied because of its military importance now. One such manual was mouldering away in the bookcase at home – forgotten after his first intense study of it.

The geography game didn't quite last the mile, so Albert broke out into his undulating wail of 'The Song of the Steppes', and when Brian joined in – nothing else to do with such a noise so close – it sounded as if the Red Army was swooping from

Matlock Bath and making for Nottingham's centre where the rich spoils lay. Brian wondered how it seemed to those already in bed. The song was long and continuous, coming from nowhere and going into an even darker nowhere, strong only because it was never-ending – like the Red Army columns that had paralysed the Germans at Stalingrad. Brian was out of breath, but barrel-chested Albert went on and on, enjoying the power of his wordless song, staring dead-ahead as he walked and wailed as if the sounds automatically hypnotized his brain to make him continue. Brian had known Albert a few months, met him at Edgeworth's Engineering Ltd in Sneinton, which was his next job after the cardboard-factory. Albert there had shown him how to work a capstan lathe, simple when you knew how; later taught him to set one up which was more difficult; then to sharpen tools, an art Brian hadn't mastered yet. Albert went to night school to learn engineering and maths, wasn't exactly an apprentice but had been promised a good and permanent job by Mr Edgeworth if he showed himself as willing a scholar as a machine-operator. Albert had a flair for setting-up a miller, lathe or drill; could shape metal to any blueprint design, and his skill was always to be relied on; unlike Brian's which occasionally let him down by a sudden flooding in of carelessness.

Albert, almost from birth, had been the handyman in his mother's house, had learned how to mend lamps and fuses after only one shock, how to fix supports into the garden fence to stop it falling, put in a pane of glass or whitewash the attic – because his father had died when he was three. Albert told Brian the same night his mother divulged the secret to him, couldn't wait to get it out, he was so excited. They went into the Wheatsheaf at Bobbers Mill and ordered two pints of mild. 'Sit down, Brian. Mam's just towd me summat I'd never known before. I allus thought dad had died of a bad heart when I was three, but you see, by Christ, you know what did happen?' The previous story had been of Albert's poor dad digging away at his prize allotment garden for all he was worth, shifting heavy clods of spud-soil near beds of multicoloured chrysanths that stood high in the sun like white and yellow pom-pom hats. The picture was that Mr Lomax, having foolishly overdone it when he should have known better, had folded up from a stab in the heart and died on the spot; but it was now revealed to Albert that his dad had really got fed up with life and cut his throat, altering the picture to one of a tormented corpse twisted among the support sticks of his collapsing chrysanthemums. Albert got more pints and drank to it again: 'Just think, the old man committed suicide! I don't know anybody else whose old man killed himself, do you? I wish mam 'ud told me sooner. Fancy leaving it till now.' Brian was glad to see him so happy, and went to get the next round. It explained a lot about Albert's cleverness, and the vivid light in his brown eyes, as if the life that had been forced out of his father had joined with his and made him so much stronger.

Albert sang himself up the slope and over the railway bridge – out of nothing, into nothing – the noise of his primeval voice drowned for a while by the hoot of a pit whistle, but emerging strongly (as if he hadn't heard it) when the hooting stopped as cleanly as if an invisible knife had slewed down it through the black air. He turned off for Radford. 'See yer't wok tomorrer then,' he called to Albert.

No wonder Pauline packed me up, Brian thought, after I cracked her one like that – and me thinking I'd never hit a woman in my life after seeing the way dad knocked mam about when I was a kid and remembering how I hated to see it. I don't know. It's rotten to do owt like that. But if you come to think on it though, dad hit mam for nothing at all, just because she cursed him or said he was a numskull for not being able to read and write, but Pauline gave me a big whack first, before I hit her, and that's a fact. Maybe I shouldn't have hit her anyway, but I'm still not as bad as dad used to be. Anyway maybe it's a lot worse to call someone a numskull who can't read and write than it is to give a bloke a crack across the gob for nothing. It's anybody's toss-up which comes keener; but I still wish I hadn't bumped her.

Bert came home on a week-end pass and Brian went out with him Saturday night to see what they could pick up. Tracks led by nine o'clock to the Langham, Bert lacquered up in khaki battledress and Shippoe's Ale, small for his seventeen years but also drunk by the success of his lies that had joined him up a long while before his time. 'I can't be bothered to desert like Dave and Colin,' he confessed to Brian, a chip on his shoulder at having to justify such action to his disapproving family. Bert had a mind of his own, had the same surviving face as when he was a kid, and Brian didn't think for a second that any Jerry bomb or bullet could put Bert's light out. He was a good shot and adept with foxhole and slit trench, wouldn't starve because he knew how to live off the land, could sleep standing up, march forty miles a day, make a fire in three feet of snow, leap off a lorry with full kit and rifle at thirty miles an hour. 'That's how they train the infantry,' he said. 'You've got to be tough to beat the Jerries, and if you can't beat the Jerries you can't help the reds, can you? Can you though, eh? We was doing street fighting in Newcastle and you know how you get from house to house? You don't go out of one door and into another – like a rent man – you use grenades and blow out the fireplace, then creep through the hole. I enjoyed that. We might be doing it in Berlin soon; you never know though, do you, eh? I hate the cold though, I do. I can stand it, but I hate it. We was on a scheme last January in Yorkshire and had to sleep out, dig holes in the snow to sleep in. Christ, I'm not kidding when I tell you, our Brian, I was so cold I was pissing mysen all night. Couldn't stop. Couldn't hold it. I hate the cold.'

The Langham was crowded but they pushed a way through to the bar: Brian was good at that. 'I can't see her,' Bert said. 'But she swore blind she'd be here at nine. I asked her to bring a pal as well, for yo'. I hope she does.' Brian was jammed front and back, kept his pint at face level above other shoulders, and was able gradually to tilt the jar up so that a wall of ale slid into his mouth. 'How's that tart o' yourn?' Bert asked when Brian shunted a second pint across. 'See much on her lately?' Brian admitted he'd chucked her. 'Looking for somebody else then?' The pub was packed, generating a noise even louder than the machine shop he worked in. It was impossible to hear: 'What?' he bawled, seeing but not hearing the second question. The loudest voice was that of the piano, beating its pathways above smoke and din, where nothing could reach to compete with it. A jaggle of colliers in the corner crashed out into laughter over the antics of their dominoes, a sound like the sudden splintering downfall of a wooden fence.

Bert nudged him, held up the other hand to wave. 'Here they are,' he said, nodding at two young women pushing in from the doorway. Brian got more drinks, two pints and a couple of gin-and-Its, while Bert latched on to the stoutest of the two women, as if, being smaller than Brian, he needed to ally himself to someone hefty in order to strike the right average should everyone be weighed out by pairs as they went into heaven. She must have been well over twenty, married as like as not, a round face and well-permed hair, not much given to powder and rouge but making up for it by the amount of laughter that rolled out of her at everything Bert said – which must have pleased him because it kept a permanent grin on his face, a low burning light which seemed to say: Look what I've landed myself with. She's a rare piece, ain't she? Brian cursed to himself. Her eyes shone, showed by their life that she was having the good time she'd got used to since her husband, you could bet, was going off his head in some snuffed-out hole of Burma or Italy. 'What's your name, duck?' Brian asked.

'Rachel.'

'Down the hatch,' he said. 'That's a Bible name, Rachel, ain't it?' which got him a louder laugh than Bert. He called for two more gins and slid them over before the first ones were finished.

'Steady,' Bert said, thinking Brian might get on all right with gels his own age but that he didn't much know how to treat grown women. If you bought them drinks the second they'd slung one lot down they'd swill 'em off quicker than ever: you had to wait for the hint first, to keep things as slow as you could.

'He's trying to get us drunk,' the other woman said, unable to laugh as heartily as Rachel. 'It'd tek some doing,' Brian retorted. 'What's your name, love?'

A straight answer, as if she didn't mind telling him: 'Edna.'

Bert already had his arm round Rachel's fine middle, like a

kid embracing a jar of sweet biscuits. Edna was small and thin, well made up with rouge and lipstick and looked a year or two older than her pal if the truth were known. She had long curly hair and a well-padded coat – was so thin that Brian thought she might be heading for consumption, though the way she chain-smoked may have helped to keep her that way. Her small features seemed distrustful of the world and of Brian in particular, so that in odd troughs of soberness he wished for the knowledge and familiarity of Pauline. Nevertheless it was good to be in a pub, half-pissed with a grown woman who at last was beginning to smile and give him the glad eye now and again. He held the bridgehead at the bar, passing over gin and beer and cigarettes: soldier Bert was moneyless, and women didn't pay, so money-man lashed out, one half of him not thinking about it and the other half glad to be the fountainhead of so much benevolence. Bert was telling both women that Brian his cousin had a cupboardful of books at home as well as a stack of maps for following up the War, and Brian turned to deny this and make out that Bert was spinning a tale just for the fun of it. 'He says owt to keep the party going,' he told Edna, squeezing her thin waist, but then relaxing his grip for fear he should snap her in two and get hung for murder. Booze was clouding his eyes, and he was glad when Time was bawled because he didn't want to be dead-helpless by the time he got Edna in bed or against a wall, and in any case by ten he'd only that many shillings left, half of which slid away on the last order allowed after towels had been put on.

They linked arms and made their way with 'Roll Out the Barrel' to the bus stop. Bert was half asleep while the bus crawled into town and only woke up loud and clear when Brian tried to kiss Rachel as well as Edna. Bert pushed him away and they poured on to the Slab Square pavement where the bus route ended. Edna lived at Sneinton and Rachel in the Meadows, so the foursome split up.

A cold mist cleared the fumes from Brian's eyes, his body light though more controllable. He kept a tentacle well-placed around Edna's waist as they walked and was not afraid of snapping her in two any more. In fact she gripped tight as well, which made him hope he was in for something good. The streets were empty except for an occasional mob of swaddies making for the NAAFI or YM. They went in a silence of loving expectation past the Robin Hood Arms and turned up Sneinton Dale. He wanted to ask whether she was married and had any kids, but didn't because he sensed she'd get ratty and wouldn't answer. A solitary drunk pushed into them and Brian swung to shove back, but Edna dragged his arm and asked him not to be a fool – which was the most definite thing she'd said all evening. They entered a long street of small houses. 'You live here?'

She stopped by one. 'Just here.'

'Can I come in then?'

'You'd better not. My husband's at home.'

'I can't see any lights on.'

'Wise guy,' she answered, which retort made him wonder how many Yanks she'd been with, and brought up the hope that he wouldn't get a dose of the pox. She leaned by the door and he pressed in for a kiss, whispering: 'Let's go up Colwick Woods.'

'I can't, duck. It's eleven. It's late.' He enjoyed the kisses, for she clung to him and allowed his insistent leg to force hers open. 'It wain't tek long.'

'I'm sorry, love, I've got to go.' But she didn't pull away, though she pushed his hand gently down when it went too close. 'My husband'll come out.'

'I don't care. Come for a stroll to the end of the street.' Someone was walking up the entry but she seemed not to have heard. 'You will if he catches you. Anyway, I'll get it, not you. Stop undoing my coat, it's cold.' They buried themselves into another kiss. The stillness and force of their close-pressed kisses drew a haze over him and he felt himself on the razor's edge of luck, either about to get what he wanted or be sent off alone up the empty street. But he told himself that if he went on trying long enough, even against her quiet entreaties to pack it up, then she would open herself and give in. 'No, don't duck. Stop it, there's a good lad. I'd like to, but I've got to go in now.'

Footsteps sounded again from the entry, of someone soft-treading it out to the street. 'Come on, Edna, we could have been at Colwick while we was chinning.'

'I'm going,' she said, irritated now. 'I've got kids to look after.' A shadow stood by them, silent and oppressive. Brian noticed it, felt it must be that of some neighbour out to see if his kid was on its way back from the fish-and-chip shop, though he cursed himself later that this was the first thing he should think of instead of just running like mad out of it. A stinging hammer of hard knuckles hit him between the shoulder-blades and he swung round, ducking as he did so to avoid number two that missed by an inch. The man, unable to brake, lurched against him.

'Clive!' Edna cried, getting her information out in a fabulous hurry: 'Stop it. Come on in. It worn't owt. I'd only had a drink. He woks at our place.' Brian brought up the full iron strength of his arm into the man's face before he could draw away, then hit him again and pushed him out towards the gutter, impelled to madness by what seemed the savage wreck of his shoulder-blades.

'You dirty bastard,' the man said, and ran back at him. His fist came up and met Brian in the middle of his forehead, making it feel as if the skin had been pushed into his scalp. Words fused with the pain and starlit darkness of his mind: He's winning. He wants to kill me! And with both fists ready he grabbed the man's shirt and felt it rip as he smashed at his face, then rammed out with his shoulders and forced him away from the house-front, hitting out quickly to give more than he got. The man stood in the middle of the street. 'Leave her alone,' he cried, his voice wavering. 'Get off.'

Brian waited with fists raised, though knowing that if he didn't fight any more the man would be willing to let it drop. 'Yo' leave her alone as well, you daft sod. We'd on'y 'ad a drink.'

'Ar,' the man said. 'I know y'ave. I know all about that.'

'Well, I'm telling you,' Brian said. He felt a loon standing with fists raised against fresh air; lowered them and walked off cursing his bad luck, determined not to rub the ache at his forehead until he had turned out of the street and could no longer be seen by the squabbling couple behind.

On Sneinton Boulevard, a wide dark artery of emptiness all

to himself, he burned more with rage than the pain of his indecisive fight, could have pulled God out of the sky and given Him a good thumping – though what's the use when there ain't no God? Belt up, keep calm, then you'll never come to harm. Yes, I know, he thought wrathfully, lighting a fag, and it's no use feeling sorry about Pauline having chucked you either.

PART FOUR

The Jungle

23

At nine o'clock one June morning an open fifteen-hundredweight turned from the camp gates and set the heavy tread of its tyres north along the coast road. The sweat on Brian's face was soon fanned dry by its speed and, one of six, he leaned against the side and took off his bush-hat, felt his short fair hair jerking in the wind. He'd been up since five checking maps, building up the contents of his pack and stowing the compass where it wasn't likely to smash or get wet. Shaded under the palms, the long cookhouse went back to sleep after they had eaten and clobbered out.

He'd thought this day would never come, but now that the powerful rasping lorry engine roared them along towards Gunong Barat he was relaxed, hardly excited at all. Instead, strangely enough when blue and cloud-reflecting paddy fields fanned out richly eastwards, thoughts and memories of Nottingham pushed into his mind and this dwelling on the past damped the intoxication he'd always expected to feel. He was puzzled, but grunted and lit a fag, bending under the backboard to escape the wind. Pauline came to mind: tall and abstracted as she walked along the privet-hedged pavement of the wide street, her pale face given character by a slight thinness after the baby had been born. Everything that happened to Brian since leaving school, the long four years of work and courting, had led to him marrying Pauline and thinking now: I'm spliced, though it's never felt like it should, for even when I slept with her on my odd days of leave it only seemed like getting in a bit of nooky I wasn't entitled to. Even the kid she had ain't made much of a picture to my mind, so why did I marry her? I needn't have done, in one way, and I haven't spent enough married life with her yet to know whether or not I feel good at getting married when I did. Which I suppose is how you're bound to feel when you come to think about it.

The sun's heat, seeming to pierce his skull in spite of the wind, slowly banished the intruding vision, and he was glad to give his eyes up to magic-lantern pictures of Malaya spread all around in colour. They reached the airstrip, and when a plane touched down the lorry belted forward and slung Baker on to the load of packs. 'You louse-bound bastard,' he screamed. 'I suppose he thinks we're just the normal air force cattle. Why the bloody hell did he have to wake us this morning? I was having marvellous dreams, riding down through Kent with a smashing girl on the pillion. There's just no civilization left.'

'Stop your effing griping,' Kirkby growled. 'You get on my wick. Why did you bleddy-well come if you didn't want to?'

'There are stranger things in heaven and earth than are dreamt of in *your* philosophy, Kirkby.' Baker wasn't capable of sneering, but the angle at which he held his head (really a physical defect due to bad eyesight) and the tone of superiority in his voice often angered those who didn't know him, or were unable to match this feeling. 'Listen,' Kirkby called back, 'you'll get this bloody bayonet up *your* bleeding philosophy if you don't sodding-well belt up.'

'You're lucky to be here,' Brian said, 'after we all lied for you the other day.' Baker, with a sane and self-righteous expression, had been marched into the orderly room on a charge of insubordination against the sergeant who'd said they weren't to take suitcases back on the boat. Half the Signals billet filed in behind to perjure themselves and testify that the sergeant had struck Baker first. So he had got off.

The silver, geometrically spaced trees of a rubber estate grew miles back from the roadside and, bursting into open land once more, the stink of putrescent mud assailed them from the banks of a wide, shallow, hardly moving river. The lorry wheels treddled loose planks of a pontoon bridge, and Jack the Welshman hurrah-ed ironically on reaching tarmac. Brown palm-thatched huts of a kampong stood away from the roadside, every turn of which brought them nearer to Gunong Barat, so that by mid-morning its dark green humps climbed up and back to the sharp summit fixed against a mass of white-bellied cloud. 'It looks beautiful, anyway,' Brian called to Knotman. 'I'd never a seen this if I 'adn't left Nottingham.'

'It's all relative though,' Knotman said. 'When I was stationed near London I used to like going round the East End – Whitechapel and Bethnal Green – back along Cable Street. I used to find that inspiring in a strange way. Ever been to Petticoat Lane market? That's beautiful as well. You ought to live in London when you get back. Get a job there.'

'I'd like to. I never wanted to stick in one place. I expect there's lots of small engineering firms in London as 'ud set me on.'

'Sure. You're young. Your wife wouldn't mind a change, would she?'

'Not if I want it,' Brian said. The broad main street of Balik Kubong was drawn by them like a sleeve, and they were back on the open road. Forking left at Penunjok, the lorry nearly scooped off with a petrol pump. 'That bastard wants certifyin',' Kirkby said. Rubber estates grew thicker around, and the lorry switched north along an unpaved road with a small river to the left – recognized from the map as the Sungei Pawan. The road ended sharply at the jungle's edge, as if the surveyors had downed tools and refused to go farther at the sudden dispiriting thickness of the forest. Brian was so glad to leave the lorry he almost fell off: 'He didn't kill us, anyway.'

The taciturn driver spun his lorry around and shot it between the trees, making for the more manoeuvrable spaces of the main road before louder curses got through to him. Brian heaved his pack up, shook it squarely against his shoulders. They were dressed in khaki shirts, slacks tucked in at the ankles to wide-topped mosquito boots, and bush-hats. Each shouldered pack was squared by blanket and cape, and christmas-treed around by a full waterbottle, haversack, kukri and rifle. Brian looked at the jungle, stood in silence a minute or two as if wondering what he was doing there, and why he wanted to enter that towering wall of trees from which only the sound of rushing water emerged in an unfair tit for tat. So that's the jungle: he grinned. Where's all them tropical flowers and Technicolor parrots flitting from tree to tree? What about Tarzan and Martin Rattler, Allan Quatermain and Jungle Jim? Not that I ever believed in all that anyway, at least not after I left school. It was dark green and dull, full of gloom and the uninviting pillars of stark trees.

They advanced in single file up the bed of the stream. Progress was slow, because the six-stone loads made them almost topheavy. Slime-covered rocks underwater often upset their balance, and each on the first days at some time capsized into ice-cold water. Subsidiary hills shouldered to two thousand feet on either side, and the rolling jungle on their slopes looked impossible to penetrate. 'I'd rather be in Kew Gardens,' Baker said, and as if to prove it, slipped and went down into the water like a raft that held up his pack, rifle and hat. Brian levered him out.

Odgeson was supposed to be in charge of the party, a tall, thin, fair-haired dental surgeon not long qualified and looking little older than the other twenty-year-olds. At the first pause for breath Knotman said, his voice firm yet kept in a narrow edge of respect and gentleness, 'If you don't mind, sir, I'll be in charge from now on. I've done this sort of jungle-crawling before. It'll be easier that way.'

Odgeson agreed: 'I was going to suggest it anyway' – pulled the two rings of rank from his shoulder straps and fastened them under the band of his cigarette-case. They went on, each taking turns to be in front and find safe footsteps through the water. Ground rose slowly, and the tree gap stayed wide enough to let in sunlight, so that while they were often ice-cold to the waist, their shirts fastened heavily against them with sweat.

Brian was happy with the exertion, careful to place one foot firmly down before swinging to the other. The pack chafed at his back because all food was in tins, and sharp rims came keen against his bones. Talk flew about, laughter ripping along the canyon of the stream, even Baker finding his feet and spirit after a while. It was a picnic, a climb in the woods for the first hours, and when the stream ballooned into a large clear pool of water they stripped to their tanned skins and waded in.

It was necessary to climb between the trees proper, to outflank a ravine whose sides were sheer for hundreds of feet, a sickle-shaped cleft as narrow as a knife-wound in the mountain slope. Knotman led the way, slung his rifle and drew a razor-edged kukri from its case, parting the bushes for a drag upwards. 'Picnic over,' Jack the Welshman said, second in the file. They struggled through damp soil and undergrowth, lifting into shadows and semi-darkness. Above and all round them on the steep slope grew trees and tangles of bushes. Neither Brian nor anyone but Knotman had ever seen the like, and wondered how they'd get through it. Creepers and climbing plants hung with mosses, and ferns were bound together with long trailers, crossed like webs of rope that some impatient giant had tried making but given up as a bad job. Tall forest trees loomed round about, and the thick massive foliage of their tops made a canopy that seemed to have kept the sky back for thousands of years.

'Why don't somebody put the light on?' Kirkby shouted. It rained, a steady unobtrusive downbeat of water that ate into all they carried. A path was cut slowly through. Loaded like pack mules they found the climb exhausting, and after a few hundred feet each fell into the undergrowth for a rest. Brian pulled clods of red soil from his soaking boots.

'Come on,' Knotman said. 'It'll be dark soon.' With laughter they were on their way, trying to follow the contour and keep the stream parallel, but in reality travelling eyeless since there was no view and even the compass gave no useful aid. Brian took the lead, wielding his kukri at the creepers, one almost strangling him before he saw it. His arms became leaden and unmanageable, as if held into his body by bandaged wounds. 'Have a turn now,' he said to Kirkby. Baker cursed blind in disentangling himself from creepers. They seemed to have it in for him, Brian suggested, and caught at his pack, rifle, arms and legs. He slipped and began rolling, but latched on to a friendlier vine before he went too far down the hillside. Odgeson and Brian pulled him upright – 'like getting a knight in armour on to his horse,' Brian said. 'We need a block-and-tackle for this bleeding job.'

Another hard stretch and they sat down again. It still rained. Brian levered a tin of cigarettes from his pocket, handed them around. Wet soil soaked through his skin, and a stream of water, collected by some hollow and hoarding leaf in the treetop world above, slid down on to the brim of his hat. What a place! As a child (and more recently) he'd imagined the adventure of living beyond all forms of shelter, himself pitted abroad against the vagaries of God's earth, and the abiding sensation had been one of comfort and self-possession, of glorying quietly in his solitude. His long nights alone in the DF hut had given him a forerunning taste of the hermit life, but now that he was wet and chafed under the jungle trees and a long way from shelter or bed, the battle against nature seemed more real. At the same time and in spite of all discomfort, such exposure lit the recesses of his hermit soul with a light that made him feel more equal to himself than he had been before: fag-smoke warmed his lungs, and patterns blown from his lips stayed firm a few seconds in the heavy vaporous air. He sat apart. Hardly anyone spoke, and then in low voices as if trapped in some damp, dusky and endless cathedral. Brian felt dazed, the first spells of exhaustion having worked their way, after so many months of soft life in camp, to the core of his understanding, so that he found the difference between today and yesterday hard to credit.

They descended towards the stream and at half past five made camp on a flat bed of rock where the river dropped into a waterfall as if pouring itself through a funnel, the banks being only a few yards apart. Brian's back ached, half-broken and on fire where the rim of the big pack had rubbed all day into him, and stripping off his shirt uncovered a wide red sore. Two tins of soaked fags were slung into the water, went bobbing their way towards the long drop of the waterfall. 'That'll be less to carry,' he said, aware again of his back, as if a bite had been taken out of it.

'So will that,' Knotman said, putting his cigarette to a bloated leech fixed on a good feed at Baker's shoulder. Shirts and trousers hung over bushes, and more leeches were found: sometimes they didn't drop, but burst, leaving a copious fall of blood on arm or leg. Knotman said they should haul in a stock of wood for the night fire, and a blaze was going by darkfall. 'It'll be a bloody long time before we reach the top at this rate,' Baker said. He stood by the stream, gazing into thick shadowy jungle on the other side. 'What did you expect?' Knotman asked. 'A piece of cake?'

'No,' he shot back; 'a cable railway.'

'You're not in Switzerland,' Odgeson laughed.

'I can't see us reaching the top tomorrow, either,' Knotman said. 'At this rate it'll take three or four days.' Jack had finished eating, was polishing his twelve bore, pulling it through and clearing soil from the barrel. 'I could dig a coalmine under this quicker than we're climbing it.'

'What they ought to do,' Brian said, 'is burn all this down with flamethrowers and grow lettuces. Or build roads so's cars could run over it at sixty miles an hour.' Supper finished, they hung mosquito-nets from overhanging branches and made beds beneath – two beds sleeping two in each. Brian didn't see any reason for two being on guard, but Knotman thought it wise, so nobody argued. 'Two in a bed,' Baker said. 'It's a pansies' paradise.'

'At least you'll get summat out o' this trip then!'

'Balls, Seaton,' he shouted back.

Brian was on guard with Knotman at midnight, sitting on a rock a few yards apart and stilled by a heaviness of unsatisfied sleep. Brian kept his rifle upright and head leaning out for it as he slowly lost consciousness. The crack of a twig came from the opposite bank – so close and overhanging in the darkness he felt he could stretch out his arm and touch it – once he woke up. Knotman had already heard the shrubbery rustling, seen a large cat poised in the low flames of the fire. They aimed at the same time. Brian joyfully let go five shots, glad to have noise in the oppressive darkness filled only by the stream rushing into the suicide dive of the near-by falls. The shots echoed into the surrounding mountain-slopes like God's whips trying to drive away darkness, and presumably the animal they saw slipped unnoticed away. The others didn't stir, and Brian in the silence paraphrased some lines he remembered from Dante's *Hell*, a book he'd collared from the camp library months ago, and had read in fits and starts at the DF hut:

> 'In the midway of this our mortal life,
> I found me in a gloomy wood astray
> Gone from the path direct. And e'en to tell
> It were no easy task, how savage wild
> That forest, how robust and rough its growth . . .
> scarce the ascent
> Began, when, lo! a panther, nimble, light,
> And covered with a speckled skin appeared . . .'

You'd think he'd written it on Gunong Barat, he thought, glad when Kirkby crawled from under the net and told him to get some kip.

After breakfast he sighted bearings on visible hillpoints and plotted them. 'Hey,' he called from a ledge of higher rock. 'You know how far we've come so far?' Nobody guessed. 'One thousand three hundred paltry yards,' he yelled. 'We're a thousand feet above where we set off yesterday.'

'Three more days. It looks as if you're going to be right,' Odgeson said to Knotman who merely nodded and slung on his pack, ready to lead upstream.

A waterfall – two ashen lines on a green limestone cliff – meant another climb up through the jungle to get round it. Some falls twisted like threads of snow down easy slopes and were overcome on all fours, but mostly the sheer cliff was dangerous to scale with such anchoring packs. At times the sores on Brian's back forced their pain into the open, making him lag behind until he could bear weight resting on them again. By the end of the day he had worn down their stings, knew it was only a matter of time before the skin hardened and he didn't notice it any more – like the first time he'd gone with soft hands into the factory. Sweat dripped from his face as he toiled in the rearguard, his whole body – legs and armpits, belly and groin and shoulderblades – caked in salt.

'What's the matter?' Knotman asked, seeing him shift his pack around. 'I've got the galloping singapores,' Brian said. 'The bleeders itch and chafe.'

'I've got 'em as well, only mine are the galloping rangoons.' They sat around and smoked, everyone dwelling on his sores. Jack claimed the galloping hong-kongs, and Odgeson laughed at the idea of being stricken with the galloping penangs. 'I've just got bleeding scabs on my bad back,' Kirkby raged, 'and I wish they'd gallop away.' Hard biscuits and chocolate were handed around, tin mugs dipped at their feet for water.

They sat among boulders in a scattered group, and a small green-fringed bird perched on a bough they all could see. Probably no human being had been there for years, since it wasn't on the way anywhere and nothing grew there that men wanted. Even elephants had disappeared from that particular dent of the mountains. Jack quietly raised his .303, aimed and shot the air wide open. The bird fell on a rock, red mixed with green. 'With my crossbow I shot the albatross,' Brian laughed.

'Fortunately for us,' Baker said, 'it was only some jungle sparrow, otherwise Brian's right: we'd really be in the shit.' Knotman gazed at the bird, stroking the stubble across his chin. 'You'd better go easy on the ammo' – meaning: 'You cruel bastard: you didn't need to shoot it.'

'Every bullet we fire is less to carry,' Jack said, back on his feet. 'This pack's giving me hell.'

'Why did we bring rifles anyway?' Brian thought aloud. 'They weigh an effing ton.'

Odgeson laughed: 'Instinct. Nobody questioned it, did they?'

'Nobody questions bogger all. I wouldn't take a rifle in Sherwood Forest, and this place ain't more dangerous.'

'What about that tiger you saw last night then?' Jack asked.

'That won't no tiger,' Kirkby jeered. 'More like a shadder: yo' lot's a bag o' nerves.'

'It was something big,' Knotman said. 'I saw it, and so did Brian.' Standing to the renewed weight of his pack before starting, Brian wondered whether he had. Noise of twigs and a shadow blacker than those around, then a cascade of bullets chasing it: the obtruding terrors of imagination that might or might not have added up to a tiger. Maybe I was seeing things, though it's hard to believe Knotman was. As long as I didn't wing it, because there was no need.

He sat by one of the two heaped fires during the night, and the few yards of swirling stream held forth a pair of luminous pinheads growing slowly to green eyes then diminishing again. Rushing water had filled his ears for days, was so familiar (like the factory at the yard-end in Radford) that the noise was no longer noticed. Only at certain times – like now when his mind turned fully to wondering what the phosphorescent lights across the stream belonged to – did the sound rush back. From humps of net-protected blanket someone grunted in his sleep: lucky sod – I expect he's a long way out of this, on the back row at the pictures with his juicy young girl. I wish I was dead to the wide and dreaming away. The eyes still shone. Not another tiger, he hoped, and was about to laugh out like a donkey, but instead raised his rifle to fire before he got too terrified to do so. The eyes drifted apart and vanished, and he stared out each one until he had to close and re-focus his own eyes. If the others knew I'd been frightened at a couple of fireflies, he laughed. The trouble is I'm too ready to lift this bleeding rifle when it's not needed, almost as bad as Jack. A bullet never did anybody any good. I'll jump at my own shadow next.

'What's going on?' Baker demanded from the other fire.

'Nothing.' He laid more wood on the embers, and was startled by a dancing scuffle from Baker whose shotgun exploded with a dull roar, the wake of its echo filled with curses. 'What's up?' Brian cried.

'A snake. It just uncoiled near my boot.'

'You want your brains testing.'

'I'm not the only one,' Baker said.

Even though each morning the amount of stuff to be packed diminished because of food eaten, it was hard to fit everything in: blankets, capes, mosquito-nets, food and ammunition lay scattered around waiting to find a place in the packs. It looked as if someone had tipped a dustbin over.

They set off for the third day. No greater distance was spanned, but it was accomplished with less grumbling and exertion. At one place they saw the peak, a scarf of white cloud across its throat, two thousand feet above. 'Tomorrow night,' Knotman said, 'and we'll be up there looking down on where we are now.' Everyone derided this, argued that by the look of it they'd be on top tonight, or early in the morning. Knotman hitched up his pack and went on, whistling to himself a good fifty yards in front.

> 'But when a mountain's foot I reached where closed
> The valley that had pierced my heart with dread,
> I looked aloft and saw his shoulders broad
> Already vested with that planet's beam,
> Who leads all wanderers safe through every way.'

'What's that?' Jack said, catching up.
'Poetry.'
'I thought it was. You like poetry, man?' Baker and Odgeson overtook them: Brian heaved a swig from his waterbottle. 'Sure.' He was bone-tired and exhilarated, caught in the jungle with water that seemed continually pouring through his heart. They tramped on, boots clashing over beds of small stones, stepping carefully across the green-mould rocks. The peak was out of sight. A bend in the stream brought them to the foot of another waterfall. The file became a group, realized it was impossible to scale the cliff, made another file that went into the jungle.

Brian dragged himself up by a bush root, eyes following the slow-lifting pair of mudstained boots in front. Sixteen hundred yards a day was still the average. You'd starve on piecework at sixpence a hundred. Even a bog wouldn't be much cop. We'll go ten times as quick on the way down, though if I do come on another lark like this I wain't carry so much stuff. Eighty pounds is a mug's game, tins of snap chafing my back to boggery when all we need is a load of biscuits and a few mashings o' tea and sugar. Like the Japs: a bundle o' rice and off they went.

Coming out of the jungle the stream had narrowed: large fallen trees laying more often across it had either to be clambered over or crawled underneath. They came to the foot of a waterfalling from the sky itself. It shook down in white streams, scarves gathered at evenly spaced ledges, and was transported with slow-intentioned gentleness into a pool of clear green water. 'Maybe that's the top of the mountain,' Odgeson said hopefully, but it turned out not to be. The watercourse no longer roared, was thinner and more rhythmic in its travelling the higher they climbed. To reach the escarpment top meant another spell among the trees. There were no paths and they kept by instinct to the line of the stream. Brian chopped and hacked until his muscles turned as dead as the wood under his feet. Fallen trees, overgrown with shrubbery and blocking his way, often proved to be no more than huge cylinders of purple soil held into shape by the tree's covering of bark that took longer to decompose: He stepped on to what had once been a tree or log and sank into soft soil. The only sign of life came from a few ants scurrying busily over the leaves or one or two leeches looping towards them like pieces of live bootlace. The whole place stank like a shit-house, Kirkby called on taking over the lead. When they stood still there was no sound but the distant spate of water from the falls or the music of a few birds in the treetops. And when they moved there was only the crashing of six men imposing their momentary will on the primeval forest, a splitting of shrubbery soon lost down the empty valleys. In the flashpan sunlight of a sudden emergence to the stream, an iguana darted into hiding.

On a ledge overlooking the valley they hacked bushes down to make room for a fire and beds. Jack found a huge, beautifully green grasshopper with antennae-like feelers going out from it. Brian edged it away with his boot, but Jack slammed it with the rifle-butt. It still wouldn't move, so Baker came up with the shotgun and blew it to bits. A battery of mess-cans sizzled on the fire: spam, meat and veg, tea, fruit pudding, cheese and biscuits. By seven those not on guard crept under the nets to sleep.

Brian and Knotman took the first two hours, talked in low voices: 'What are you going to do when you get out?'

'Find a job, I expect,' Brian said. 'I don't know what at though. I was on a lathe before I got dragged up: only a couple o' years ago, but it seems a century. Christ, I'll be glad to get back to Pauline though.' This last wish came into the open before he had known she was on his mind, a fervent cry that surprised him in the pause that followed. 'You get your ticket soon, don't you?' he said, to break it.

Knotman reached to the fire for a light. 'At Christmas – just a few months after you. They can get somebody else to guard their played-out Empire then. Not that they won't though: there's one born every minute. They've made use of me for seven years, and now I'm going to do all I can to balls *them* up. Not by way of revenge, mind you: it's just second nature, and I'll enjoy doing it in a light-hearted sort of way.' He spoke in an easy, yet tired voice, giving Brian the impression that maybe it was possible to undermine the British Empire all by himself. 'Sure sure, I volunteered to stay on in the air force' – having expected Brian to point this out – 'but I was crazy, I admit that. I thought the Germans would want keeping under a few more years, but from fighting fascism I found myself helping the fascists out here. All I want to do now is get my hands on some hard work for a change, and if any of the friends I make happen to say they believe in the British Empire I'll be in a good position to tell 'em a few things about it. Not that I'll get all hot and bothered, because they wouldn't believe me if I did. No, I'll drop it like a wise man who knows what he's talking about.'

'You sound like a resistance fighter,' Brian laughed.

'No, I'm just talking. It's so quiet in this jungle.'

'That's what you think,' Baker called from under his net. 'Don't you two bolsheviks know that all's for the best in the best of all possible worlds?'

Dawn was grey, opened to a slow drizzle and the sound of Baker emptying his rifle down the valley, one bullet chasing another into silence while Knotman got up to make a breakfast of steam pudding and milk. An early start was planned against the summit, and waterbottles were dipped in what was left of the Sungei Pawan, because no more would be found until they crossed to watercourses on the far side of the mountain wall.

Breaking away from the stream the undergrowth turned from moist into brittle and thorny, covering each hand and arm with shallow but livid tears in Brian's flesh which seemed to fester while he looked at them. It was no longer a question of conquering the mountain, to look out with pride and exultation from its summit, but only to keep on climbing, stay locked in the treadmill of intentions formed in idle dreamlike hours that had never comprehended the reality of this. What good's it going to do us? he thought. Fuck-all. Crash – his kukri flew at a sapling of thorns, and down it went, held under by his agile boot so that Kirkby following wouldn't be cut with it. They hoped to reach the top by evening and light a fire for all the camp (twenty-five miles off) to see. The thought of this grandiose plan had excited him during the long weeks of preparation, but now that he was close to it his enthusiasm went, tempered to a hidden-away part of him by the long drag up from the coastal lowlands.

Bushes thinned, and for the next five hours they climbed without resting either to talk or drink water. Sweat, helped by the high-up blistering sun, poured out of him like a refugee soul, and after midday they walked into damp forest covering the steep surface of the escarpment – glad for once to enter it because the next clear daylight would come when they broke on to the actual summit. In places the vegetation gave way to grey-humped cliff, which on Knotman's advice they circuited. 'You wouldn't be up to much if you slipped a couple of thousand feet,' he told Baker, who was all for going like a fly over the smooth surface. Then an hour was spent fighting another belt of thorn bushes, a strange misplaced preliminary to a pull-up through more wet forest, clinging to vines and creepers with the tenuous strength of curses and worn-out hands, arched laden backs crawling under fallen tree, boots caught in damp messes of soil. Brian no longer wanted to get to the top for the unparalleled view it would give (higher than any he'd seen) but only because the climbing would end, the expedition be as good as over. That in itself was enough to keep his legs moving. There's no point in climbing a mountain unless there's some purpose behind it, like to make a map, or get food, collect wood or stake out a place to live, he thought, locked in his prison of leaves and branches that remained the same in spite of a continual movement.

Near the end of the afternoon the mountaintop loomed above, a wide door of smooth rock with neither path nor footholds for fully loaded men. 'It's too steep to scale,' Odgeson said, and Brian followed his gaze between mosses and lichen, up and into grey sky. They shed packs and rifles to sit wearily between trees, wedging themselves so as not to slide down the steep ground. Knotman looked done for, smoked a cigarette: 'To get around that cliff could mean another six hours. Even then it might not be possible,' he said. 'We might go round in circles and still find a slice of cliff facing us.'

Brian opened the map. 'We'd have to go south-east for two or three miles. There's a gap there.'

'Count me out,' Baker said. 'It'd take days.'

'I've had my whack,' Kirkby said.

'And me, man,' said Jack.

'Maybe there's still a way from here,' Brian persisted. To get up there seemed important again – now that hopes of being able to were fading. It was loony not to get to the top after struggling so far. Admitted they were all shagged out, but maybe with one last shin-up (an hour at the most) they'd be on that peak and making camp. He lifted Knotman's kukri – feeling let-down by both him and Odgeson who were, after all, supposed to be leading this foray. They were lost in some half-dream of cigarette smoke: 'I'm off to see what I can find,' he said.

Knotman offered him a fag. 'Have a smoke first.'

'When I come back.'

'Suit yourself.'

'You'll be wasting your time.' Baker chipped at the tree-bole with his knife. Its sharp blade, digging with nonchalant dull strikes at the wood, sounded vicious and useless, an acknowledgement of defeat. 'As long as I'm not wasting yourn,' he threw out. 'It's barmy to come all this way and then turn back.'

Knotman listened, sat without interfering. He'd brought them this far and now they could make up their own minds about reaching the top. If they found it collectively important to do so, they'd see a way there – though as far as he was concerned there was no point in taking risks. The three-mile detour was impossible because it would mean perhaps two days without water. 'I'm knackered,' Kirkby said. Jack suggested they bed down for the night and have a bash in the morning: 'Once we're over the summit there'll be plenty of water.'

'I think we can call it off,' Odgeson said, and he was taken up on it: 'Suits me,' Baker agreed quickly. 'I didn't like this picnic from the beginning.'

'Why did you come then?'

'For the experience.' Brian couldn't argue against such an answer, unwilling to admit that his own reasons were felt to be deeper, if more diffuse.

From tracking the contours he edged upwards, tunnelling like a collier through thick undergrowth, clambering over the fallen five-foot girth of trees that blocked his way. There was too much silence, and he wielded his kukri against ironwood to create the rough companionship of noise. Such a tree-filled wilderness put fear into him, and now and again he stopped in his crashed pathway as if to listen for its full effect, looked for ants, leeches, a snake maybe, but could see nothing except the swinging of his own arm when he went on. Kota Libis camp was years away, England a dream before he was born, Pauline walking to the shops on Apsley Lane a dim apparition: maybe since I came up here all the rest of the world's turned to jungle and there's nothing to go back to.

He climbed towards the summit, came by a green rockface blocking his way. He thought, among the claustrophobic desolation of this high jungle, of the waterfalls and pools several miles down towards the plain, of the stream's noise which had seemed so tormenting at the time but which now was remembered as a sort of heaven. Both places mixed before his eyes. He leaned to light a cigarette.

A clump of trees overhung the summit, rag-mops giving him the glad-eye from too far up. Maybe if I edge farther along I'll find a chimney that'll get me through in ten minutes. Above the rag-mops were grey and waterbellied clouds settling in for afternoon and evening. He was determined to reach the summit and, looking along the way he might take, saw a coiled python placed a dozen feet away.

He was protected by a screen of horror, within which a hand went to his shoulder only to find that he had forgotten his rifle.

As he backed away the stripes and diamonds began to move, to perform a colourful oscillation along the ground, over trees and roots; it was bigger than any he'd seen in the snake temples of Pulau Timur or the paddy field at Kota Libis. He went downhill, from tree to tree bole, still watching the snake which wound back into its sluggish coils now that he wasn't too close. His fear of it went, for somehow, being without a rifle, there seemed no need to hurry or panic, and in the shadowy gloom he lost sight of it. Then his fear came back and fled towards the others, no longer feeling alone in the jungle. He didn't mention having seen the python: 'I can't find any way round or up,' he grumbled, before sinking down for a rest, glad that no one retorted: I told you so.

Knotman hitched up his pack and rifle, and the rest followed, threading a way between trees and bushes. A different set of muscles came into play for the descent, and Brian's legs ached and stung as he steadied himself on the steep slope so as not to be slung forward against some hard tree. A slow drizzle fell, and in the dusk Brian and Kirkby spread their blankets into a rough cradle between two bushes, sat down to chew biscuits. Jack rammed a bayonet into a tin of jam and handed it around, but there was no energy to forage among the tins for a more elaborate meal – and no dry wood on which to cook it. 'The sooner we get back to camp now the better,' Kirkby said.

'Maybe they'll rustle up something good at the cookhouse when we do,' Knotman laughed, 'like humming-birds' foreskins on toast, or some such thing.' On their bleak dark four-thousand-foot ledge Brian felt as if the party had shrunk in numbers, they were so isolated and dispirited. He counted them: six, yet wouldn't have been surprised to have seen only two or three, thinking that maybe a fire would have made a bigger crowd out of them. Perched high in the saturated air and mountainous vegetation, miles from the nearest spark of light, he couldn't fight through the steel band of exhaustion towards sleep, was afraid that if he did he would roll off the ledge and perhaps spill against some tree.

He lay all night with a built-in sensation of closed eyes roaming through some demanding wilderness of half-sleep, the trammels of an exhausted mind and body searching for something impossible to find, then grieving over the fact that it might never be found even in a thousand hours of real sleep. The hard curve of rocks and soil under the blankets troubled him distantly, though less than the damp mist coldly moistening his face. Such uneasy rest was a variation on great silences, broken by fire within and a furious crashing of noise that often dragged him half-back to consciousness, as though a force over which he had neither control nor resistance fastened itself at his entrails and sent him into more coughs until the sound of it woke him up. Kirkby grunted and nudged, causing someone else to curse at the dearth of real sleep. Aware of his aching bones he opened his eyes on the offchance of encouraging sleep should he close them again decisively, but then found he had no desire to close them, and lay for what he could have sworn was a long time looking into the silhouettes of bush leaves and humped bodies round about.

It often seemed that dawn was about to appear: when the shape of bush leaves began imperceptibly to change, he kept his eyes closed for as long as he could bear it, imagining that when he opened them the leaves would have taken on colour, and hoping that before he could witness this miracle of change no voice would yell that it was time to get up, or that Baker's buckshot-gun wouldn't start the day like a newly sharpened tin-opener ripping across the dark sky to let in sunlight. But he never slept more than a few minutes (that had nevertheless seemed like hours), so that the leaves before him were still outlined with the same blackness against tree-boles behind.

When day did come it approached like thought: impossible to say from where. Grey light crept out of the fibre of each bush, escaped from thin leaf veins to show bodies sleeping roundabout and tree trunks developing a neutral though positive shade. They rolled blankets in silence, were damp and exhausted, each face showing the bewildering fight of attempted sleep. Baker passed around biscuits spread thickly with jam, hard to get down the throat on a swallow of water.

Mist cleared while they were packing, a curtain drawn from a vast area of north Malaya. Below and far into the distance long bars of white mist were drifting across lesser summits and spurs, breaking up over rice fields and coastal swamps as the sun gained strength. Smaller hills of Gunong Barat reared at them from across the valley whose waterline, hundreds of feet below, was buried deep in the green furrowed jungle.

Loftier mountains, far to the south, formed a low line of blue amorphous summits in the far-off sky. Small villages were dotted about the coast, lay in loops and bends of silver rivers that twisted from the hills towards greener landscapes, mingled with mangrove swamps, and entered the indistinct frontiers of the sea.

'That's a view and a half,' said Jack. 'It's a pity you can't drink it though.' Baker thought it the least they could expect after a four-day climb. Brian had nothing to say, yet when they began filing down into the forest, he held back and was the last to leave. It was too much to grasp in a mere few minutes, impossible to carry away so soon. He wanted to stay until the sight of it drove him down by its familiarity, to sit where he was for a long smoke and look of contemplation at the land spread out below in choicer and more living colours than the most artistically produced map. All this climb, he thought, hearing the others already on the crashing descent, and I've got to leave it. I might never come up here, or any other such mountain, again – which put such a dismal shadow over his heart that the next thing he knew he was ploughing with drawn kukri into the cool gloom and familiar dank smells of the wood.

They came to the brink of a precipice, a thousand-foot sleeve of grey rock on the mountainside blocking the way to water farther west, so they backed up three hundred feet and found a thin ledge with a few bushes and shrubs growing on its surface. Baker pushed his paybook into Brian's hand: 'My will's in there.' Brian shrugged and stuffed it into his shirt pocket: 'Don't blame me if I lose it, you loon.'

Knotman dropped his pack and was feeling a way over, looking like a brigand with unshaven face, dirty clothes, and rifle sticking above his broad shoulders. He spanned the first gap, his legs a pair of compasses about to draw a circle in empty air, hands clutching the rock above. The sky was blank below him for hundreds of feet, a few insecure bushes sprouting occasionally out. Fascinated by such peril, Brian wondered whether it would have been lessened had they talked among themselves and ignored him. Jack threw down his cigarette and leapt forward, even before Knotman's boot-studs had stopped sliding.

He hung from a bush, his boots waving methodically about for a foothold: 'Stay where you are,' he called hoarsely. 'I'll be all right.' Brian already wondered how they'd get down to the plain if Knotman brained or injured himself, and how they'd find him if he fell like a stone into the treetop forest below.

He made footholds, coaxed the fair weight of his body slowly back, his rifle a guiding finger of safety at the ledge he was trying to reach. He stayed still a moment, seemed to relax his efforts as if uncertain whether or not it was worthwhile saving himself. No one spoke, fearing to break the spell of survival: then he gathered strength for a terrific pull-up, and was on the ledge from which he had fallen.

He organized a chain to get the rest of them over. Brian stood with feet spanning two gaps in the rockface, unafraid only because he resisted looking up or down as he reached for packs and rifles passed to him, easing them over his chest to the next pair of hands.

On the other side they sat for a smoke, and Brian unhooked his waterbottle. 'I'd save it,' Knotman said.

Brian opened the map: 'We'll reach water soon.'

'I'll believe it when I see it,' Knotman replied. So he didn't drink, though his throat felt like cracked celluloid.

They went in single file, bushes curving overhead, wet leaves brushing hands that swung at creepers as they skirted the roots of great trees – against which they occasionally crashed if accelerated by weakness and a topheavy load. Brian felt done-for, and crouched under creepers rather than drag energy to his bones and chop them out of the way. The brown whip-like tail of a snake disappeared through the leaves, a sight that cleared his vision and gave back strength. The last thing he wanted was a skinful of poison, so he walked upright. He stayed in the lead to go at his own rate rather than follow someone else's pack, for the more exhausted he grew the quicker became his pace – though never so great that the others were left too far behind. A look of effort marked everyone: they came down with kukris no longer used, and loads bearing no resemblance to the neat shape of a pack. Their shirts were dark with sweat and soil patches, trousers and sleeves torn, faces set hard with tiredness and a week's growth under slouched bush-hats – coming through the tunnels of the forest, fatigued at having climbed a small upshoot of earth on which they were lost like insects.

He turned, to slash at creepers in a new-found strength that kept him ahead, swinging with joy down each bank that lay in his path, until one led him between lips of brown soil that formed the dry bed of a stream. He followed it, stepping over lichen-covered boulders, and soon saw water jerking out of a spring, the beginning of a stream copious enough to sink his tin mug when he threw it in. 'I was ready to do a Rupert Brooke on you,' Baker said, 'in the corner of this foreign field. Brian has my will, so it wouldn't have mattered.'

'We were lucky to find water so soon,' Odgeson thought.

'It was due to my good navigation,' Brian claimed. 'I steered by the sun and had my map open all the way.'

'You couldn't see the sun,' Baker cried, pulling off his boots, 'and the map you drew is no bloody good.'

'You won't be able to get them on again if they're wet,' Knotman said. Baker ignored him: 'I could have steered better with my cock,' he called to Brian.

'If there'd bin a brothel down here I suppose you could.'

Tributaries came in by thorn-covered gullies as they tramped along, unnoticeable until threads of water were elbowed from under bushes by their side. They reached an island in the stream and split up for the even tasks. Baker sat on a rock in his underwear patching his trousers, while Jack and Brian were high up the bank, filling the air with the splinter of branches and dragging wood back to the fire.

It grew dark, and water formed two phosphorescent humps as it dropped into a deep pool at the foot of the cliff face. Fire shadows danced at the bordering wall of the forest a few yards away, and they ate a hot meal, back in the familiar sound of water travelling out of nowhere into nowhere, a stream that hurried by six men locked in the shadows of the forest, mocking the purposelessness of their journey as it passed.

Brian lit a cigarette and lay back, stars like the eyes of fishes set between black tree-shapes towering about. The primeval noise of the water receded into another locker of his mind, leaving his immediate senses in a vacuum of half-consciousness. Then the noise poured back into his brain and ears and he heard Baker say: 'It looks as if Seaton's asleep' – so he pulled off his shirt and swilled himself in the icy water, then, in spite of its sting, fell straight into a deep blank slumber.

Waking early he was glad to be getting out of the forest. Now that there was no such obsessive goal as reaching the peak he felt its spirit imposing too heavily on him, saw the jungle for the desert it was, a dull place because no one of flesh-and-blood lived there. All you could do was burn it down, let daylight and people in; otherwise it was only fabulous and interesting when written about in books for those who would never see it. Still, he'd always be able to say he'd been in the jungle, tell anybody who asked that the best thing was to leave it alone, but that if you had to see it you should get a few thousand feet up and look down on it. He could easily understand how the jungle would drive you crackers if you had to stay there too long; how its great forest-mind could eat you up with the dark grin of possession. He sent a nub-end spinning into the stream, watched it taken to where they would follow.

They descended by the winding defile, taking to jungle at midday to avoid stone-faced waterfall cliffs. The panic flight of tin-footed minuscular fugitives sounded on the foliage roof, a commencing tread of raindrops before the full weight of water crashed on to them, spattering hats and finding a short cut to their skins. Soil and leaves made anchors of their boots as they slithered down, edging back to the stream. Brian shouted through the wall of rain: 'One minute dry; the next drenched.' Baker, only a foot away, heard nothing.

'That was a big piss,' Knotman said when they stood by the stream. Clouds were scattering and shirts steamed on bushes in the returning sun. An Avro 19 droned like a silverfish high overhead towards Burma, and Brian waved in greeting. Brown water swirled at their thighs as they slowly descended, and when the sun burned, Brian's shirt felt pasted to his shoulder-blades, a poultice that increased the aches instead of lessening them. By map and compass they were close to where the lorry had brought them nearly a week ago. A score of tins remained, dragged up and down the mountain for nothing. 'We might as well dump 'em,' Kirkby suggested.

Knotman didn't agree: 'You've a month's rations there, in right-little tight-little England.'

They came out of the jungle. Stubbled, tired, bush-hat pulled down, Brian felt he could have travelled for weeks more, until he reached the dam over the stream and collapsed on to its concrete platform, held there for a minute by a wild saw-toothed cough that left him without breath, sitting still and trying to bring trees and sky back into focus. He watched the others emerge: Jack with his shirtsleeve torn away; Knotman limping because he hadn't had his boots off for days; Odgeson chalk-white and walking carefully as if afraid he might fall, while Kirkby and Baker looked fit by comparison.

Odgeson went to the planter's house and telephoned for a lorry from the camp. They set off four miles to meet it at the main road, a slow straggling file all but done for after the rapid descent. Brian was at the end of his strength, faint itches chafing at various parts of his body where leeches still fed. I don't feel at though I've got enough blood left to keep myself going, never mind them, the greedy bastards. I'm pole-axed, and wish I was in Nottingham out of this blood-sucking sun, back where it's cool and my brain will clear so's I can start to think, pick up the bones of my scattered thoughts. I'll be twenty-one next year, and an old man before I know it.

Packs were swung like corpses on to the waiting lorry, helped by a sergeant who had come up for the ride, the same who had got Baker in trouble outside the Admin hut last week. 'There's a war on,' he told them. 'It started while you were away. We thought you might have got caught up in it.'

'What sort of war?'

'The communists are at it, trying to throw us out of the country and take over. They've killed a lot of people already.'

The lorry drove south along the main road, through villages and rubber plantations, the sea a perfect blue sheet to the right, sky equally blue and empty overhead. A breeze cooled them and took away the heavy smell of soil and sweat. No one spoke. Brian leaned back with eyes closed, wondering at the sergeant's words about a war with the communists in Malaya.

24

Almost every day of his life Brian had heard his mother say she was going to pack up and leave Harold Seaton. But she never had, and on those days when there was no cause to say it, she dwelt on the still-hot embers from other quarrels. Before coming to work this morning Brian had a real set-to with his father. The house had been a boiling sea of sabre-toothed rows this last week because Seaton had been observed by a neighbour drinking in a Lenton pub with a woman he'd knocked-on with before he met Vera: black-haired inscrutable Millie from Travers Row – now long since married herself. Not that such a brazen cheeky-daft outdacious baggage would let anything like that stop her, Vera raved when Seaton came home all fussy and pleased with himself, unsuspecting that a neighbour had got in with a colourful story half an hour ago. In times past, fed up to the teeth and eyeballs with him, the whole family had heard Vera say he could clear off and get another woman for all she cared, but now that there were reasonable grounds for thinking that he might, the house witnessed pitched battles that even made the money quarrels of the dole days look like the pleasant tit-for-tat of a lively courtship.

It gave Brian something to think about during the long hours of watching the dead-slow traversing of his piecework milling machine. He fixed an aluminium elbow into the jig, released the lever, and sent it towards the revolving cutters, making sure that the sudpipe was well aimed against it – otherwise it might seize-up and spray hot metal against his skin. His mother had kept up her tirade for days, even though Seaton had promised faithfully, never to see Millie again. Brian asked his mother to pack it up now, saying it was no use going on and on and keeping the house in misery, but she replied: 'Why should I? He's allus bin a bogger to me, and this is the last thing I'm going to stand for from 'im, especially now yo' lot's growing up.' So Seaton went on being put through the mill, using a rare control and saying nothing because he knew himself to be in the wrong, until this morning when he was dragged into the blackest and most impressive rage Brian had ever seen and threatened to bash Vera's head in. Brian stood between them intending to bash *his* in if he laid a finger on her. 'He thinks you're still a baby and can't stick up for me,' Vera bellowed, half-way between rage and tears. She was triumphant: 'I allus said he'd have to watch his step when you grew up. Now he knows what I mean.' Brian was baffled, caught in a fire of despair, knowing he wouldn't be able to do much if the mad eyes and beefy fists of his father made a move. 'Christ,' he shouted, his voice brittle, 'can't you both act better than this? It's about time you learned more sense.' Maybe they caught the impending crack of his spirit; for the raw feelings of cold and early morning were drawn from all three gradually as tea was mashed and poured out. No one spoke, but twenty minutes later Seaton had been thawed by a fag, and his good morning to Vera was almost cheerful – though it stayed unanswered.

Brian was glad to get away, pedalling his bike along Castle Boulevard, playing the fast and tricky dare-devil between cars and buses to keep his mind blank. Speed brought drops of water to his eyes and cheeks; the spring air was fresh and cold, good because the world was waking up with the buds and blue sky. High above, on a wall of rearing sandstone rock, towered the Castle, an art museum and prison for deserters. It crouched like a spider with the beaten soul of the city in its mouth, a Union Jack fluttering on high. Brian cycled as part of the river of people flowing to work along the traffic artery far below, happier when once he'd passed it by and was already half-way through Canal Street. It seemed that the War was finishing, that soon the world would open for travel like a South Sea pearl. He could save money and go to France or Italy, free because call-up would stop with the battles. Yet perhaps it wouldn't be as good as he imagined: Edgeworth's would lose its War Office contracts and he'd be slung on the dole like his old man had been, unable to get a job anywhere, trapped for life in a queue every Tuesday and Thursday for a few measly bob to starve along on. Starve-along-Cassidy, that's what I'll be. 'Don't believe it though' – an uncluttered stretch of cobbled short-cut allowed him to talk aloud as if before an audience – 'the soldiers'll be back and wain't stand for dole queues any more, government contracts or no. They'll get the reds in and then we'll have plenty of work. Yo' see'f they don't. And not all of Fatguts's spouting about good old England and all that rammel will stop 'em either.'

Cycling into the endless streets of Sneinton made him happy, a spirit retained even when he passed the house by which he'd fought with the husband of that bag Edna, picked up in the Langham last autumn. What a night! His black eye lasted a fortnight, and he only hoped the other bloke's had taken as long to disappear. When Bert came home three months later his side of the story was spilled: Rachel had taken him to bed and he'd had the time of his life, including breakfast on a tray in the morning. Bert had all the luck, though he couldn't but laugh as he skidded into the street on which was Edgeworth's Engineering Ltd.

It was a small firm, one long building of sixty workers, and two side offices at the street-end where a typist drew up the Friday wages. The glass-panelled door took him into a cul-de-sac of waist- and breast-high machines, lit by blue fluorescent gleams from overhead. Belts under the ceiling ran races with each other, pinjoints clicking against motor-driver wheels. Ted Edgeworth, the owner, worked like one of the men, tall and miserable, with long grey hair, dressed in a boiler suit only different from the rest in that it was changed every day instead of once a week. His wife came in often to see him, drove down in a flash car from their bungalow by fresh-aired Thurgarton. Not to help, but to stand by his side while he fiddled with some blueprint or component on his bench at the end of the shop. Their backs were to the workers, but it was safely assumed that she nagged him black and blue over some long-corroding domestic detail because, though no words were heard above the drone and roar, the back of his beanpole neck stayed bright red while she was there. Maybe it's because she caught him with some fancy woman or other a few years back and wain't let him forget it, though that's not likely because Ted is a bit pansyish if anything, the way he puts his hand on your shoulder when explaining a new job. Maybe it is something like that: you never know, what with having such a cat-faced scrag-end of mutton for a wife, and two sons in the army who didn't want to take over the business.

When Mrs Edgeworth stayed away there was Burton the government inspector from Birmingham to give him hell, as like as not. Poor old Ted. Burton was a real Hitler who played on the fact that Ted was a timid old bastard, even though he was a boss, one who couldn't answer back too much because he was salting thousands away out of the fat government contract whose work Burton came every now and again to inspect. He was bigger than Ted, well-built and pan-mouthed, and let himself go into rages about inferior work that Ted was trying to palm off on a government that had had all the money in the world to spend since 1939. Two thousand nuts went one week to a Birmingham gun factory and all of them had been drilled and threaded so much off centre that the guns would have killed our own blokes instead of the Jerries. Burton made a special trip up in his car and saw boxes of them still being blithely turned off on a row of lathes. He pushed by poor flummoxed Ted, stood at the boxes with his battleship jaw fixed on his gauges, and then carried one back to Ted's bench. Even over the noise of machinery you could hear him shouting, and he ended up by knocking – maybe an accident, but nobody ever knew – the whole box of them over the floor. After he'd stalked out and driven off, Ted started screaming at his tool-setters and viewers, but not near enough to get his own back.

Ructions, everywhere you went, though Brian hoped it would get quieter at home after this morning's bust-up. The house was too small and so was the factory: often Brian would load his saddlebag with sandwiches, a bottle of milk and a map and take off into the country, pedalling north through the open fields and scrublands of Sherwood Forest. The smell of tree bark in spring reminded him of his far-off days at the Nook, and of his not-so-distant ramblings over the Cherry Orchard with Pauline. Ructions with her it had been as well, though things had got better lately. Some months after their parting he'd been walking along the open pavement by the Council House lions one Sunday evening with Albert Lomax, and had spotted Pauline talking to a couple of other girls on the steps. Everyone was out in their Slab Square best, perambulating to either get or give the eye: perhaps in an odd moment stopping to hear a few words of admonition from Sally's Army, or soak up a bit of sound advice from some communist speaker, or argue with a Bible-backed old god in a trilby hat – who was so thin you'd think somebody had nicked his ration book.

Pauline waved at Brian's smile as if she were glad to see him. He'd never noticed before how pale she was. You'd think she'd got jaundice by the look of her. He went up the steps, followed by Albert. 'Hey up, duck. How yer gooin' on?'

'All right.'

'You want to come out of the wind or you'll get a cold.' Though it was so long since their quarrel, he still felt affection for her. Her friends stood to one side, made sharp responses to the calls of passing youths. He also felt jealous at the world of time that had fallowed between them, some land of other-occurring days lost and never to be known. Why does it make so much difference? They should have been closer, and he considered it her fault they weren't. 'I feel marvellous,' she said. 'I ain't 'ad a cold for weeks. Where you off?'

'A walk. Where yo'?'

'A walk.' Picking up lads, he thought, like her pals now talking to some – feeling rotten against himself for these unspoken words, because Pauline seemed to have less ebullience and stature than when he had last been with her. 'Do you still go to the Capitol on Sat'day nights?'

'No.' She was absorbed by people moving around the square, as if wanting to be among them and away from this meeting that she had, by a characteristic lapse towards good nature, let herself in for. 'I didn't think you did,' he admitted, now hoping to get her going with him again, 'because I often go there to see if I can spot you.' She didn't, as he wished, take him up on this, and they stood awkwardly. It was a fact that he'd haunted the cinema the last few week-ends to see if she would get off a 7 or 22 and walk slowly towards the queue he stood in – though knowing that such meetings never happpened when expected or encouraged, came only when all thought of them was deep in hiding, like now. Her friends had dismissed the youths, and even Albert was impatient for a walk up Trent. 'How's your dad?' Brian asked, offering a cigarette, which was refused.

'He's dead.'

The beginning of an ironic laugh came, a disbelieving start to a sentence that would have been catastrophic if he hadn't pulled himself up in time: 'You . . .'

'He died about six weeks ago,' she said, his doubt unnoticed. Disbelief withered, was overpowered at what he saw as the residue of grief in her pallid face and the damaged spirit of her slightly glowing eyes. He remembered the exact physical centre of the blow, as if someone had struck him by the left eye, dazed his senses so that he took her arm – which seemed to her a gentle pressure of sorrow. But he shouted angrily: 'Why didn't you let me know?'

She drew back. 'I couldn't very well telephone you, could I, loony?'

'You knew where I lived, didn't you?'

'Well,' she shouted back – and Albert stood amazed at this unexpected blaze-up of a quarrel – 'you knew where *I* lived as well, didn't you?' Which floored him with its logic and quietened him down: 'I'm sorry about your dad, duck, I liked him a lot, you know that.'

'I know you did,' she said, half jeering still, enraged at him starting a row where so many people might hear and notice. 'But don't mek me cry though, will yer?'

'All right then: I was just trying to say how sorry I am.' They stood in the path of a raking wind, and he wondered why she and her pals chose such a perch to flirt with lads. She turned from him, in some deep way insulted, though he couldn't see how. 'You could have called for me,' she said. 'You didn't think I was going to run after you, did you?' He'd never thought that at all, he argued, knowing that to knock at her house and ask if Pauline was in would have been too simple; he preferred to hang around the pictures in the hope of seeing her on the off-chance; and in any case, much of his time had been taken up boozing and gelling with Albert, just as it looked as though hers had been occupied ladding with her pals. There were ten sides to every story, when you came to think about it, but he didn't want to tell her this – and perhaps upset her even further. The fact that Mullinder had died caused an emptiness even of air inside him, leaving nothing for his lungs to draw on. 'Come up to the club next week,' he said, expecting her to swing round and tell him to clear off. 'You'll have a good time,' he added. 'Albert brings his girl as well.'

She turned and smiled: 'If you like. As long as it i'n't on a Wednesday, because I wash my hair that night.'

'Thursday's the night,' he told her, believing again in happiness. 'You look perished, duck: let's go off and get a cup o' tea somewhere.' She ditched her pals and went with him, and had gone to the club every week since. The old times came back, though different. He thought about them as he set the miller spinning, invincible steel teeth biting soft as butter into aluminium castings, gouging out grooves with such exactitude that even Burton wouldn't be able to complain. Sub-drenched splinters spat over the jigs and tray, cleared away every so often with a specially provided handbrush. Pauline had taken to the club like a duck to water, and though they still had violent rows, they usually made up before the good-night kiss. Nowadays there was less of the rough stuff, both of them not so eager to tread on the fine gauze of self-control and descend into thumped-up quarrels. Brian was gentler and more protective, learned to see that her previous tom-lad bouts were only indulged in so as to be like one of the rest. Even so, she sometimes became angry at his continual solicitude, but would have hated him to lose his temper over such resentment and go back to his old retaliatory ways. Their lovemaking was a natural prolongation of calm and seemingly endless walks together, showing that a new stage of tenderness had been reached.

Grandfather Merton saw them arm-in-arm one evening,

copped Brian at it, as he told Vera later, talking to his girl like any love-struck youth as they walked along in the spring dusk. Merton was over seventy, had a lean sardonic face that at one time had reminded Brian of a cross between a strengthened Don Quixote and the head of George V on the back of coins; but Merton was clean-shaven, a blacksmith mixture of both, an upright man in the prime of his old age who still knocked back his seven or eight pints of Shippoe's every day, much to the disgust of Lydia – who thought it time he packed it in a bit, though not daring, even now, to tell him so. Afraid once upon a time of the stick he beat his dogs with, she was, at forty-five, still wary of him lifting the stick he sometimes allowed to accompany him on his walks. Lydia was unmarried, lived at home and, as she told Vera and Ada many a time, 'The old man's still a bogger, leads poor mother such a dance as well that I can't help thinking it'll be a good job when he's out the road.' But Merton had always been gaffer, and would stay that way. 'I'll drink what I bloody-well like,' he said when Mary told him about it. 'As long as you've got enough snap on the table don't try and tell me what I can and can't do.' And knowing how much he liked his ale – and his own way – she didn't mention it again. In any case he was never so drunk that he didn't know what he was doing. During a period when Harold Seaton was amiably disposed towards his in-laws he called there at midday one Sunday and went out with Merton for a drink.

They took a bus to the Admiral Rodney in Wollaton Village, walked back a mile to the Crown under blue sky and fresh-smelling wind, then to the Midland, the White Horse, the Jolly Higglers – the distance between each pub shrinking as they got into Radford – ending at the Gregory with Harold groggy on his feet, fuddled with beer fumes and fag-smoke, wrestling with the earth-pull at the calves of his legs, while Merton stood up tall, sliding a pint into himself now and again between casual called-out remarks to some pal or other. Considering, Seaton thought, what a hard old sod he'd been to his family, it was surprising he was so well liked by all and sundry. Still, Merton worn't a bad owd stick at times, and you couldn't deny as he'd wokked 'ard either. Seaton took him in small doses, enjoyed bumping into him but made sure it didn't happen too often. Even now, over forty himself, he felt too much like a son when with him, and because his own father had been dead twenty years he resented Merton's natural sense of domination.

Seaton liked his beer as much as anybody, which gave him something in common with his father-in-law. A five-pound wage packet made him well off, and on week-end nights he would go out with Vera and let his voice rip on the old songs that he liked, his brown eyes, broad sallow face and black receding hair set against his favourite corner in the Marquis of Lorne. For the first time since getting married he was able to buy a suit – utility and ill-fitting – but one in which he felt compact and proud, boss of himself when away from work. He had money to buy wood and paint and nails, spare parts for his bicycle and wireless set, but these materials for brightening home and life were hard to find because of the War. He made do and did what he could, though considered he got little thanks for it from his wife and five kids. What was the use? A bloke couldn't even have a row with his missis without his son getting up and threatening to bash him. Still, he'll know different some day. He felt grieved that he seemed to get little love from anyone after all he'd done for them this last twenty years: serving two months in jail to pay for the grub he'd got on strap, which had been no picnic either; not to mention his odd-job versatility and force-put cunning in dodging the means-test man.

I reckon Brian thinks a lot o' me though, even after our bit of an argument the other day, because last year he bought me a new set of teeth for nine quid when I'd lost my others being sick down the lavatory after a booze-up. It must a took him a long time to save all that out of his wages, so I don't think we hate each other even if we do have our ups and downs. By God, you can't have everything, you can't. We're lucky to have some work and grub and not get blown to bits, I do know that much. With his labouring spade he spent all day at the bicycle factory loading mountains of brass dust and splinters from the auto shop on to lorries for the scrap trucks over the road. At just turned forty he was stocky and of iron strength and knew he would have flattened Brian in ten seconds if it had come to a smash that morning, though unlike Merton he found it easier to knock his wife about than his children: the idea of fighting with solid hard-working Brian seemed an impossible disaster; while Merton on the other hand had knocked his lads about, but never Mary.

Brian didn't mind meeting his grandfather when walking along Wollaton Road with Pauline, and noted the mischievous wink in his eye: 'Hey up, Nimrod, where are you off to then?'

'A walk.'

Merton looked at Pauline: 'A bit o' courting, eh? I suppose you're off up Cherry Orchard?'

Christ, Brian said to himself, he wain't say the right thing now. 'Maybe,' he grinned.

'What's your name, me duck?' Pauline told him. He'll run me off if I'm not sharp, Brian thought. I'll let me gra'ma know if he does though. 'I wondered if you might be going to Abyssinia,' Merton laughed, turning to Pauline: 'The young bogger used to say that, when he was a kid. If I got on to him and made him wok too 'ard he'd get up and shout: "Bogger you all, I'm off." "Where yer off to?" his Auntie Lydia would say. "Abyssinia," he'd tell us, and run back to Radford. He was a bogger when he was a lad.' Brian wondered how Merton could have invented such a tale on the spur of the moment – then realized it was true, and that while it had been buried deep in him and may have seemed a century ago if he'd remembered it at all, it appeared only a year or two back and as plain as a door to Merton. What else will he come out with? he wondered.

Pauline laughed: 'Well, he's still a bogger, if you ask me.'

'I allus knew he would be,' Merton said, ready to be on his way. 'So long then, Brian. Look after yourselves, both o' yer.'

'He's nice, your grandad,' was Pauline's verdict, as they turned towards the Cherry Orchard to make love in some hump-lipped hollow of the dusk, and be there an hour in silence before piped notes of cuckoos nipped out on the echo from Snakey Wood.

The club was noisy and popular, absorbed those youths and girls from streets round about who snubbed any suggestion of joining a cadet force yet wanted a place to meet friends once a week. Two middle-aged women of the Co-op and Labour Party ran it, organized talks (mostly political) and saw that the evening ended with hot tea and sandwiches. After being at hard work all day a lightness or lack of weight crept into Brian's bones on getting the body back into motion after a twenty-minute sit-down slump at the tea-table, energy recalled by a second wind of fatigue and fought by a cold breeze footballing it down from the Pennines when, having thrown off his heavily greased overalls and had a good swill at the sink, he walked the odd mile to the club.

Frank Varley met him at the school gate, a crafty smile on his lean handsome face. 'Hey, Bri' – he waved a wad of paper from the step-tops – 'have yer seen this one?' He was the penpusher of the gang, worked in an insurance office downtown, and somehow got hold of dirty stories that were given to him, he swore blind, by his brother when home on leave from a Signals battalion at Catterick. Brian inwardly disputed the truth of this, wondered whether or not Horace Varley sat at his typewriter all day making them up, though if he did they were bleddy good and he was on his way to earning big money as a journalist. Somebody started 'em off, and that was a fact. Usually they were a dozen typed sheets of single-spaced narrative, the first one Frank handed around being about a special sort of club in India formed by officers' wives to keep themselves happy while their husbands were away for months at a time. The goings-on described in Frank's black-market tale made everybody's hair curl – the girls' included, for they wouldn't be left out of such exotic reading. Another story described a week's leave spent by a soldier in Rome, and the wad now handed to Brian as he entered the playground concerned, he discovered on stopping in the middle of the yard and not caring that those sitting on the far side knew what froze him, the adventures of a nubile young woman who kept a St Bernard dog. Wind bent the pages back and he made this an excuse to turn round so that no one would witness the slow growth at his groin. The story ended when some man shot the dog because it attacked his little girl, and its mistress died of a broken heart. Brian read it again so that by the time he walked across to the others he need no longer feel ashamed.

He held it up: 'Who's next?'

'Nobody,' Frank said, a grin of triumph. 'They've all read it' – indicating Pauline and Dorothy. Albert was immersed in his *Soviet Weekly*, bringing his squat head up now and again to spout out some marvellous fact about Russia: 'It says here that ten years after the War nobody's going to work more'n forty hours a week.'

'I don't see how that can happen,' Frank said, folding up his sexual proclamation. And the cranky bleeder let the girls see it, Brian cursed. Think o' that. He ought to have more sense.

'It's easy,' Albert argued. 'All you do is round up them bastards as never do a stroke o' work: get 'em in the factories and on the railways.'

'Round up a few penpushers as well,' Brian put in, a punch at Frank. 'All they do day in and day out is copy dirty stories, then come here at night and get a cheap thrill passing 'em round to girls.'

'*He* might,' Pauline said, 'but I don't get a thrill, I can tell you that. It just makes me laugh.'

'I think it's disgusting,' Dorothy said, her round swarthy face flat and angry.

Frank laughed out loud: 'Owd Dolly! You know you liked it.'

Albert set himself square like a boxer: 'Lay off Doll. Nobody likes that sort o' stuff, you penpusher.'

'We can't all work a machine, you know,' Frank recoiled.

'Somebody's got to reckon our wages up,' Pauline said, coming to his defence. 'Not that it would take long to reckon up mine.'

'Don't worry,' Brian said. 'We'll be better off as soon as we've beat the Jerries. We'll get rid of Old Fatguts and vote a socialist government in.'

'You'll still have to work though, won't you?' Dorothy called out sarcastically.

'Shurrup, sharp-shit,' Albert said, as if forgetting she was his sweetheart. 'I don't mind wokkin'.'

'You should wash your mouth out with soap,' she called.

'It don't bother me either,' Brian argued. 'As long as I get paid.'

'I don't see why you've got to 'ave money,' Albert said. 'I reckon you should be able to get all you wanted for nowt. As long as everybody worked, what difference would it make? I read in the *Worker* that it'd be possible for bread to be free in Russia one o' these days. That'd be all right, wouldn't it?'

Everybody thought so. 'It'd tek a long time to come true though,' Pauline added. Shadows lay heavily in the playground, from air-raid shelters to lavatories, gate to cycle-shed. The sky was blue, and starless unless you looked hard for a few seconds. A cold night was driven into the city like a lost traveller wanting warmth, harried on by an officious wind that scaled the wall and played around them. Coats were unobtrusively pulled together and buttoned.

'Suppose it took fifty years?' Brian said. 'That's nowt: the flick of a gnat's left eyelid. As long as we start now. There's enough snap and clo'es and houses for everybody.'

Frank was dubious: 'It'd tek a lot o' doin'.'

'I ain't found anybody at wok as don't want another government,' Brian put in. 'Ave yo', Albert?' No one had. The end of the War was coming, and so were the days of change, a definite thing that everyone felt.

'Our old man wants a new 'un,' Dorothy said. 'There was ructions at our house the other night when Fatguts was belly-aching on the wireless.' Albert spun round with a broad over-powering laugh: 'Oh Christ yes. Go on, tell 'em, love.'

'Well,' she gave him a mischievous look, 'Owd Fatguts was going on and on, and dad ups and brings his grett fist down on the wireless. I thought he was going to bost all the valves. "Tek that," he says. And there was a big crack right across the top, "you old bogger," he says. Mam towd 'im not to be so daft, but when she said that, he hit it again, as if he was going off his loaf, and he kept on hitting it – ever so hard – until Owd Fatguts made as if he was coughing hissen to death and the wireless stopped. 'I don't *'ave* to listen to that bleedin' liar," dad says and mam gets on to him then because he's broke the wireless.

But he just tells her to shurrup and says he'll get a new one next week. He towd me later, when mam was upstairs, that he felt an electric shock when he gave it the last big crack.' Laughter engulfed them, like ice breaking.

'He saved England though, didn't 'e?' Frank Varley called from a few feet away.

'You reckon so?' Brian answered. 'It was him and his gang as turned hosepipes on the hunger marchers before the War.'

'Old Fatguts was saving his own neck,' Albert said, 'not ourn. He didn't give a bogger about us. It was all his bleeding factory-owners he saved, the jumped-up bags like owd Edgeworth who's making a fortune. You can't tell me owt. I've got eyes and I use 'em to read wi'.'

'I can read as well, you know,' Varley retorted. 'I get the *Express* on my way to work every day and I read all of it.'

Albert wasn't in a quarrelling mood, laughed: 'I read three papers every day, Frank, not one, because it's best to get more than one opinion so's nobody can say you're biased. I get the *Worker*, the *Herald* and the *Mirror*. And my old woman gets *Reynolds'* on Sunday so I have a goz at that as well.'

'We'll make you Prime Minister in the next government,' Varley said. 'Then you can boss it over vacant bleeders like us.'

'If I was Prime Minister,' Brian said, 'I'd get rid o' blokes who sit at wok all day typing dirty stories.'

Mrs Dukes walked slowly over from the Infants' door while Albert was reading aloud from his worn-out *Soviet Weekly*. She listened a minute before breaking in, regarding him as one of the most intelligent members of the club: 'I'll get Jack Taylor to come and talk to you in a week or two,' she said at last. 'He's a socialist and you'd like hearing him.'

'He'll have a job to convert us, Mrs Dukes,' Brian laughed, 'because we all are as well.'

'Still,' she said, 'you've got to know more than you know.' And they went in to get their share of tea and sandwiches before splitting up for home.

He stood with Pauline by the back door of the Mullinders, and the end of their quiet evening blazed between them in a battlefire of kisses, bodies pressed close and arms inside each other's open coats. Neither wanted to leave, and time ran by. Pauline's mother was in bed, had left her to a good-night kiss at her own risk. A cat scuffled before the lightless windows, a dog dragged its chain over the stone-cold monotonous paths of the estate gardens, and they were snug in the porch, out of the wind and half asleep against each other, warm and inexhaustible in a bout of long slow kisses. This is love, he said to himself. 'I've never been in love like this, Brian,' she said into his ear.

'What?'

'I must go, and I don't want to. I've got to go in now, duck.'

'Not yet,' he said.

'I don't want to either.'

'Don't yet then: I can't let you go.'

'It's comfortable,' she said. 'I like being here, so close. I hope it's allus marvellous like this.'

'It will be,' he told her. 'I know what you mean. I mean I love you.'

'I shan't go yet,' she answered. Work tomorrow, but so what? Work was the one definite landmark always visible at any moment from the delectable night before, so it didn't matter whether you felt good or bad about it. He'd be able to get up no matter what time he went to bed.

The moon saw him home, following him on a long walk through the utter silence of allotment gardens, a cigarette to keep him warm, the smell and presence of it an added comfort along the same lonely footpath as when he had fled from the Nag's Head clutching a couple of beer-mug handles five hundred years ago, Bert running after him to say it was all right. It is all right an' all, he laughed, blowing out smoke against the damp air. In a few days the War would be over, and there was nothing on God's earth to stop it ending. Then the world would change, at any rate be new to him, because he hadn't been alive long enough to know what the ending of a war was like.

It finished well: wooden forms and bunks were dragged from air-raid shelters and heaped on to bonfires. In the White Horse, a buxom loud-mouthed ear-ringed woman of fifty did a can-can on one of the tables, clattering her shoes among a ring of pint jars to the bashing of the rhythmical piano, cocking her legs up high to show – apart from her fat knees – that her baggy drawers had been made from the gaudy colours of a Union Jack.

Brian, sitting in the pub with Pauline and his parents, drained his pint and joined in the wild release of singing with the rest of the packed room, enjoying the empty thoughtlessness that went like flashpowder among the moving throng and only allowed the arms of the clock to move by the half-hour. Yet at certain moments he stopped singing to take in the dozens of faces, saw them as mere life-shapes with such sad clarity that even the sound they were making left his ears and drew back until he couldn't listen any more. They were wild with excitement because the War had ended, yet the truth of it didn't seem real to him. This was just a booze-up night, more joyous and violent than usual, but what difference would it make to everybody? They would wake up tomorrow with sore heads and see out of their windows the same backyards and line of lavatories, hear the same drone of factory engines. He remembered opening the *Daily Mirror* when just home from work a few days ago, coming to the double pages of the middle and seeing spread out before him something he could never forget: the death pits of Belsen, a scene of horror making a pincer movement through each eye to the middle of his brain. He closed the paper, every other word irrelevant, and the images stamped for ever. But the end of the War meant something, he thought, lifting another pint his father put before him, a lot in fact: backyards and Belsen – and it meant getting rid of both.

But the beer stunned that part of him and, victory or no victory, he was kay-lied. Pauline, his mam and dad, all of them sat at a table roaring their guts out, arms around each other and happy, done for at last by the six-year desert of call-up and rationing, air-raids and martial law. All this was finished and victory had come, victory over that, even more than over the Germans, and what else could he want but to sing out his happiness in the biggest booze-up anybody could remember?

Vera and Seaton had been drinking all day, and Brian helped his father along Eddison Road at firelit midnight. Pauline behind with his mother and the children. Seaton leaned heavily, slurred his words, tried to apologize but clapped hand to mouth to stop his false teeth falling. Brian was flexible on his feet, sober enough to hold himself up as well as his father. 'Come on, dad. Stop draggin' or you'll 'ave *me* down as well.' He turned: 'Y'all right, mam?'

'I've got her,' Pauline said.

'I am, my owd duck,' his mother shouted, riotously plastered. 'I'll mek yer some supper when I get 'ome, my love.'

'Yer'll 'ave a job.' Brian laughed at the earnest tone in her barely controlled voice. He felt love for them both, heavy Seaton who pressed a firm hand on his shoulder to help himself along; his mother happy and light-headed behind; above all for Pauline who, by witnessing how totally they took to a good time, was in a way being as intimate with him as when they were in Strelley Woods together.

The last high flames were belting up from a bonfire at the end of the terrace. Gertie Rowe leapt through them, and her four sisters led all the lads of the street in a fire-dance – a rapid roaring circle around.

Pauline packed the kids off to bed, while Brian saw his father and mother safely snoring between the sheets. He came downstairs, back to Pauline who sat on the rug by the built-up fire in the hearth. 'Feel all right, duck?' she asked.

'Solid,' he said. 'I must have had eight pints.'

She took off her cardigan and threw it over the chair. 'Do you good. Our dad used to like his beer, I do know that. I'd hate to go out with a lad who didn't drink.'

'Well, you'll never be able to grumble at me,' he laughed. 'Not that I'm a big boozer, but I like a sup now and again.' Poor old Mullinder – it was too happy a time not to think of him. Into the world and out of it; out of nothing and into nothing, and that was all there was to it, the beginning and the end of it. He stood by the shelf, looking down at her: long unpermed brown hair falling to her shoulders, breasts low and pointing outwards, full and mature, legs turned back under her. She smoked a Park Drive – as though it didn't belong to her, he thought, or as though she didn't know it was lit – in short inexperienced draws without bothering to take down, a long pause between each as she stared into the fire. He reached back to switch off the light.

In the yard outside footsteps and calls of good night were loud between the street and back doors. Children's voices diminished, and because they were put to bed, dogs rested free from torment by fireworks. Someone clattered his way into a lavatory, and after a few minutes dragged the chain down and slouched his boots out again, rattling his gate and calling good night to a neighbour on the way in. Mester Summers, Brian thought, able to recognize every voice no matter how much drink had gone into it. The yard quietened, and the festival of sound left the flickering fire to itself. 'Are you all right, duck?' he said tenderly.

'Yes. Are you?'

'Yes.' He pushed the chairs back, took cushions from the sofa and placed them on the rug. 'Did you have a good time?'

'I liked it in the pub,' she said. 'A bit o' singing like that does you good, I reckon.'

He sat by her: 'It does, an' all.'

'I ain't 'ad a night out like that since our Betty got married.' She threw her cigarette into the fire, watched it strip off its paper like a coat as if to dive deeper in. They kissed, and lay down on the rug, and knowing that no one would disturb them that night he drew skirt and blouse and underwear from her white and passionately waiting body. Her face glowed from the nearness of the blazing fire, and from the unfamiliarity of allowing her nakedness to be seen by him. She grew towards his caresses, a thoughtless process of kissing that, as he undressed, passed into an act of lovemaking that was slow and marvellous, submerging their closed eyes into a will over which neither thought of having any control. They lay together with no precaution between the final pleasure, into a smooth rhythm of love and a grip of arms to stop them crying out at the climax of it.

They dressed in silence. He went to the back door and stood looking up the yards, suffocating from a deep still-burning fever. He felt a laugh of over-satisfied joy begin in his heart, then caught a full cold draught of the night air which made him think it was about time he took Pauline home. The smell of ash and burnt paper from dead bonfires drifted in from the street, pointing out how silent were the thousands of houses spreading around. It was a good smell, and he savoured all it would ever mean: spring flames of victory and love. The factory dynamos still filled the air with their ominiscient low drone, so all-pervading that unless they were brought to mind by an act of imagination the noise would go unnoticed. The factory hadn't shut down its row! Not for a minute. On it went, through booze-ups and victory fires, never stopping. Work, more than anything, was something good, hitched on to the slow grinding chariot wheels of life that never ceased.

Pauline came to his side, coat on and ready to be walked home. She hadn't once mentioned that her mother would be mad at her having stopped out half the night. Not that either of them thought it mattered any more. They walked up the street arm-in-arm, through many streets, passing deflated bonfires, from some of which a red eye still glowed, potent and hiding its colours. A few months later, victory fires would burn again, red posters in every window, red streamers waving from every child's hand, red in the real victory for which the people had waited like the glowing eyes of the bonfires.

25

He closed the doors early, shutting out the unquestionable superiority of insect life, and the red-soaked sky at dusk that filtered away to blue scrub and forest and a runway flattened to cold sleep. He spun the goniometer like a roulette wheel and it stopped at east, the opposite direction he wanted to take. No aircraft fenced the atmospherics with its morse, and he slouched in the basket-chair, bored and tired, tense at the thought of a dozen empty hours before daylight and relief. It wasn't possible any more to take the occasional potshot at shadows with the rifle, for together with fifty rounds of ammo it had been recalled to the armoury so that if bandits attacked the hut (still the farthest outpost of camp and airstrip) they couldn't capture the wherewithal to knock-off a few planters or swaddies. They'll kill *me*, but as long as they don't get the rifle, that's all that matters. The old man would laugh if he knew I was in such a fix: What did I tell you then, eh? Don't join up, I said, didn't I? And what do you do? You join up, don't yer? If you get shot it'll serve you right. Don't come crying to me with your head in your hands, you bleddy numskull. That's how he'd carry on, and he'd be dead right as well. Still, there are fifty-odd rounds the armoury'll never get back, which I'm holding for when the communists come up and say: 'Stand and deliver: your bullets or your life.' And if they mow me down first they'll be plain enough to find by anyone good at looting. I suppose the old man would say I was daft for climbing Gunong Barat, but there I'd argue, because even though we didn't get to the top I wouldn't have missed it for the world. I weighed a solid hundred and fifty when I went up but only a hundred and thirty now, and no matter how much I scoff (and I feel clambed all the time)

I can't put it back on. So it cost twenty pounds of flesh to find out that Gunong Barat wasn't worth a light.

He saw Mimi the same evening he got back, not having thought of her once during the trip. Both spoke little, moved quickly and blindly into love on her narrow bed. Shuddering at the orgasm he roared like an animal, the jungle bursting out of his soul. It was as though, in this first night asleep, shrubbery entangled itself in his brain, branches and leaves worked their way to the back of his eyes. He burned in a fever, as if next to a fire, plunged like burning iron into a bath of warm water. After the hard earth of the forest it was difficult to sleep. She woke him at midnight: they talked and made love, and he finally slept as if he had no life left.

He walked a few yards out for a piss, into a night still and warm, as if the sky had stopped breathing, it had so many stars around. Anybody hiding in the grass could shoot me while I shake the drops off: the thought turned sweat cold on his back, though he didn't hurry to get inside. And just imagine, he don't know I'm really a friend who'd go into the jungle and help him if he came up and asked me to. All I'd feel is a hot thump at the back of my neck and the next second I'd be dead, listening to the old man say: I told you so.

I could be back in Nottingham earning ten quid a week at the Raleigh instead of wasting time in this hot district, fighting my pals. He fastened the door and listened-out at the set: nothing doing. But on day-watches a dozen four-engined bombers were up patrolling the mountain jungle, wanting DF bearings as fast as they could be sent. It got so hot at times that the relieving operator had to jump into the chair and take over sending without a hello or good-bye.

Rifle or not, the first burst of bullets would rip through the hut and write LONG LIVE STALIN on my bony chest. I wouldn't even have time to rush outside with my hands up and shout: 'Don't fire, comrades. It's me – Brian. I used to listen to your pals spouting outside the Raleigh only a couple of years back, and I used to buy all their pamphlets and ruin my eyes reading 'em.' His hollow laugh ran round the hut and came chewed up back to him. Why did I let myself get into this? I could have deserted or gone to clink like Colin and Dave. I told Knotman: 'I don't want to do anything against the communists.'

'You won't have much choice,' he told me back.

'Maybe I will have. Something might turn up that I can help them with.'

'Don't be crazy and rush into anything you might regret,' Knotman said, taking another pull at his pint of Tiger. 'This whole system will go rotten of its own accord without you risking your neck. It doesn't matter whether the communists win or lose in Malaya: they'll get the whole world sooner or later, peacefully as well. It might not happen in your lifetime, but as Bill Shakespeare said, it's bound to some day. Too bloody right it will. Let's drink to it.'

He set a fire going outside, long wood-smelling flames jumping into the darkness like assegais, swallowing the black kettle resting on a crude arrangement of stones. The fire made a circle of light, the darkness a prison into which he couldn't walk. He realized how illuminated he was against the lit-up backdrop of the hut should some communist happen to be reconnoitring. A stream of bullets aimed at his silhouetted stick-like figure would finish him off, and bang would be gone the rest of his sweet life with Pauline and the kid: all memories destroyed and expectations nullified; present tiredness, boredom, boots warmed by the flames, his sleepless rimless eyes, obliterated.

Long-range annihilation, a decoy to sponge up bullets. Around the hut was a tin-henge circle, a radius of petrol cans threaded by a piece of invisible string, so that anyone creeping in the darkness would send a resonant warning clatter against stony ground. Should this happen Brian saw himself switching off lights and dashing into the elephant grass, gripping a rusty bayonet, where he'd stick it out while the hut was ransacked for ammunition or maybe spare wireless parts – though he found it hard to imagine himself not being shot at and killed before witnessing this dramatic scene of plunder.

Mechanics at the transmitter compound had electrified the wire fence and rigged the fire extinguishers with sulphuric acid. Perhaps they'll get the orderly officer and a couple of sergeants by mistake, because as Knotman says: 'It's them who shout "Charge" and "Up and at 'em, lads" who are your biggest enemies.'

Guards at the camp had been doubled and armed with rifles – instead of a pencil and book to note anyone coming back late from a good time. Several companies of Malayan Police patrolled the area. A few nights ago two of them ventured as far as the hut and knocked at the door, so he mashed some tea and set them a couple of mattresses on the floor for an hour's kip, feeling sorry at their boring walkabout in the jungle darkness. Brian stayed awake at the set, to rouse them at dawn and send them back to camp. He remembered also how the same pair had been drummed out of the Malayan Police a week later for being found asleep near the Transmitter compound: they walked from the camp after the court-martial, dressed again in saris and trilby hats, laughing gaily while lugging cheap suitcases towards the station. If only it could happen to me.

Barbed-wire fences were repaired and patrolled, and road-blocks between ferry and airstrip manned by Malayan and planter volunteers toting clubs and shotguns. The communists issued an ultimatum that all Europeans in Malaya were to scat within a month, and most of the Signals billet wished it could be accepted. Brian was all for it, but Baker replied, calm and studious in such circumstances, that Chinese communists were causing all the trouble, and that if anyone should rule Malaya it should be the Malays. They were already a long way to getting self-government anyway, though of course the Chinese would have to have a hand in it because they outnumbered other races in the peninsula and were the brains of the country. The Chinese communists, Baker went on, reacting as expected to the emergency, were a small minority who wanted to get rid of the British and set up their own dictatorship. If you believe in democracy you've got to do what you can to put down these terrorists.

'You've been reading the wrong newspapers,' Brian told him.

'You haven't been reading any at all,' Baker said.

The kettle boiled, and the ritual mashing of tea passed a bemused hour. He ate bread and sardines, flipped through a

Saturday Evening Post, unable to read any of the stories. Dry-mouthed atmospherics crashed so loud out of the earphones that he wouldn't have heard a tank roaring by, never mind the feeble warning of a tin falling on stone. 'I can't wait to get back to you,' he wrote to Pauline. 'I've finished with this joint, even though I did like it at first. I know when I've had enough. In a way I volunteered to come out here, because I'm sure I could have stayed all my time out in England if I'd put in for it. But even though it's been murder being away from you all this time, I'm still glad I came.' He was going to scrap that paragraph, but left it and went on: 'I feel good at the moment. I wish you was here with me now though. I don't need to tell you what I'd do to you, and I bet you can guess anyway. It's stark wicked not being able to be near you.' He paused to chase a spider that winged across the table – red diamond among hairy legs – which he cornered and flattened with a one-pound hammer after it tipped itself in a suicide dive to the floor. It could have bitten me to death: I won't get back to England if I'm not careful. 'Still, it's only six weeks now, sweetheart, and I'll be on the boat coming home to you. So keep well for me, and look after the young 'un with a few kisses from me. We'll have a smashing time.' The envelope was marked with reciprocating cyphers: BURMA; ITALY; SWALK; Be Undressed and Ready, My Angel; I Trust and Love You; Sealed With A Loving Kiss.

By one, he felt his bones melting, senses falling to death. Sending his call sign to all stations brought no answer, so he spread a mattress over the table and heaved himself on to it, cradled away in seconds to a disintegration of sleep. A metallic hand drew his consciousness together, turned it into a punch-bag and was battering at the fibres of his exhaustion. It began softly and was tolerated, then became like the banging of a drum that he was locked in, increased till it woke him, startled and enraged. He mustered a big voice: 'Who's that?'

His heart bumped and trembled. My number's up, though they didn't shoot first so maybe I can argue, give a few air force secrets away. He looked for something he might use as a weapon. 'Who's that?' he called again.

He picked up the hammer and swung open the door. Light

blinded him and he saw nothing. Then he made out an officer and a sergeant, and slid his hammer back to the table. 'I didn't hear you come up,' he said, observing the dark shadow of a jeep by the aerials. 'I was working on the set.'

They looked around. The NCO, a sawn-off little bastard with a mug like Al Capone, carried a Sten: 'Orderly officer,' he barked as if expecting him to jump to attention and throw a well-ironed ceremonial uniform over his bare chest, oilstained shorts and unlaced slippers.

'Are you the only one here?' the orderly officer said. He was a flying control officer, an enormous red-haired Jew of thirty-odd, more like Goliath than David, with the stature of the proverbial village blacksmith. Brian nodded. 'What are all them tins doing around the hut?' the sergeant demanded. 'I nearly broke my shins on 'em.'

'What tins?' Brian asked, reverting from an intelligent wireless operator to a Radford lout. The orderly officer glanced at his wireless set: 'Any kites around?'

'Not tonight,' Brian said, adding 'sir' when Al Capone gave him a dirty look. 'Where's your rifle?'

'I haven't got one, sir. They called 'em in from outstations in case the bandits should get in and take 'em.'

'I don't suppose you feel very good about that,' the orderly officer said sympathetically.

'I don't mind.'

'Why do you keep the doors closed and locked?' Al Capone said.

'To keep insects out.'

'Gets a bit stuffy, don't it?' Brian kept quiet, while Capone looked the place over as if it were a pigsty he'd stumbled into instead of a brothel. 'Are you all right out here then?' the orderly officer asked.

'Yes, sir.'

'Telephone in order?'

'Yes, sir.'

'Rations sufficient from the cookhouse?'

'Yes, sir. Fine.'

'What did they give you?' He told him: half a tin of milk, some sugar, tea, a loaf and a tin of sardines.

'Enough?'

'Plenty, sir.'

He turned to go: 'If you want anything, phone me at the control tower. I'll be there for the night.'

Brian watched them drive off. It was the first time an orderly officer had thought to call that far from the bar at the officers' mess. Maybe they are bothered whether I get shot after all. Tiredness rushed back, ached into his eyes like creosote. I don't care if all the communists of the world are creeping up on my hut to burn it to the ground, or if all the kites above Malaya are getting sore throats sending SOSs: I'm dead-beat. He lowered the volume of the receiver, stretched out on the bed, and fell into a deep sleep till daylight.

He read every newspaper from front page to last hoping to discover how the 'War' was progressing. A so-called 'State of Emergency' brought in martial law, and he noted with some confusion the fact that he was part of it. Because others in the camp were also mixed up, a civilian education officer came from Singapore to give a lecture on the political situation. He was a thin, dried-out man of middle-age wearing an immaculate flower-blue shirt and beige trousers, a deliberate touch of informality that would endear him more to his khaki-drilled audience. The same talk, called 'British Achievements in Malaya' had been given at every camp along the line, so by the time he reached Kota Libis he was practised and adept in his delivery, the marked set of his jaw and his steel-blue eyes somehow dividing his personality between severity on the one hand, and final disbelief in his own words on the other. Even if what he said didn't seem convincing to himself, he was a gifted enough speaker to make it appear so to the more simple of his listeners. The NAAFI canteen was filled with those who had come to hear him spout on the official view of the Malayan rebellion. And after the station adjutant had spoken a few words by way of introduction the first twenty minutes of his address were an account of how the British had acquired Malaya, how they had rid it of disease and laid a superlative system of communications, pushed back the ravaging waves of the jungle and brought rubber into the country. He then came to the present day.

'War was declared, in a manner of speaking,' he said, 'on June 15th. An emergency meeting of a hundred Perak rubber-estate managers took place at Ipoh, and it was decided then and there to ask Sir Edward Ghent (the High Commissioner, as you all know) to declare a State of Emergency because of widespread outbreaks of lawlessness. For this lawlessness the planters blamed the weakness of civil government, as well as communist political agitators who were also behind the murders that were beginning to sweep the rest of the peninsula.

'It was about this time that the Cornish manager of a tin mine near Ipoh was shot dead while paying his employees, and robbed of two thousand four hundred dollars.' ['And ten thousand people starved that month,' someone near Brian said.] 'The *Straits Times* also reported that three British rubber planters were murdered near Ipoh. They were captured by Chinese communists armed with Sten guns, tied to chairs, and riddled with bullets. All European families were ordered to evacuate the area at once, though only a few would do so. A law was passed securing capital punishment for illegal possession of firearms' ['It's like a law being passed in 1939 making it criminal for the Jerries to have guns,' Brian thought], 'a law which, while necessary from a legal point of view, made little if any difference to the gathering wave of war coming out of the jungle. In such a country as this a few thousand men, resourceful and determined, can hold out for a long time, inflicting far more damage and casualties than they would sustain themselves, at first. Reinforcements come in constantly from South China, moving by secret jungle routes through Indo-China and Siam. British subjects in Malaya are now living under hard and dangerous conditions. Their bungalows – as most of you may well know – are turned into miniature fortresses, outposts on the edge of the jungle, guarded day and night, surrounded with barbed wire and sandbags. The planters carry on their work armed with rifles and sub-machine guns, and these men and their families are showing the usual British obduracy in such difficult circumstances, an obduracy always unexpected by their enemies. The communists had hoped for a concerted rush for the boats at Penang and Singapore, but they were disappointed.

'However, we mustn't underestimate this communist threat to Malaya. They possess a highly efficient, well-organized and strictly disciplined army, moving in battle formation and receiving orders from well-equipped and well-camouflaged headquarters, staffed by experienced officers. Their idea is to strangle Malaya's rubber production, to render the country a dead loss economically, and destroy the conditions of civilization built up patiently by the British during the last hundred and fifty years.

'Effective measures are being taken to meet this menace . . .'

Awkward questions came at the end, such as: 'Since this looked like a popular uprising, wouldn't it be better for the British to clear out before too much blood was shed?' And: 'Would it be so bad to the British economy if Malaya was lost?' The lecturer answered with calmness and intelligence, though some noise came from people at the back of the hall who wanted him to know they weren't convinced. A Scottish cook from Glasgow next to Brian said that his MP was a communist, so wouldn't it be wrong to say that all communists were evil? 'So's mine,' a Londoner said. 'Piratin's his name, and my old man voted for him.' The lecture was brought to a close by a few words on the difference between communists who are elected into power (as in England) and those who try to take a country over by violence against the wishes of the majority (as in Malaya).

Rifles were carried into the billet, locked along a rack with a piece of wire threaded through each trigger-guard. The key to the padlock was kept in a corporal's pocket who happened to be a heavy sleeper so that Brian wondered how quickly they'd get into action if the camp were rushed one dark and peaceful night. 'If he sleeps that deep,' Kirkby said, 'maybe we could nick the key and flog the rifles to the bandits. We could all go on the spree then.'

'If you did that, the best thing you could do,' Baker said, 'would be to make a getaway over the border to Bangkok.'

'In any case,' someone called to Kirkby, 'it'd be stealing' – so that he could only re-state his one rule of existence: 'If you see owt moving, screw it. If you can't screw it, sell it. If you can't sell it, set fire to it.'

Brian showered and changed before going to meet Mimi at the Boston Lights, walked cool and spruced-up towards the camp exit. The first stars were out, and spreading palm tops were still silhouetted against dark blue above. Behind came noises from the camp, and he paused at the grass to light a cigarette while a lorry turned from the gate and raced off to the airstrip. Malayan police were on guard, and a few rickshaws were hanging about for fares to the village. A sudden weird noise grew into the air, like some inspired madman trying to play a tune on a wartime siren. It began from down the road, an alien music dominating the quiet fall of a Malayan sunset. Brian's shoulderblades and the tips of his fingers shivered with an unnatural electric coolness, and the wailing came louder through the tunnel of the trees. Other people stopped to see the advent of this monster that progressed towards them on two hundred marching feet, with the head of a dozen pipers making their instruments squeal and wail as they ate into the head and neck of them. 'They're Ghurkas,' somebody cried. A group of Malays and Chinese stood by the gate and watched them wheel in: men tramping back from the dead, biting out on their dark flowers of music a tune from the underworld. They formed up between the canteen and billets, pipers still playing as the infantry marked time. The final yell of 'Halt' – stopping the rise and fall of their automaton feet like the throw of a switch – seemed to transform the atmosphere of the camp from that of apprehensive gaiety into one of total war.

At the Boston, Brian bought a row of tickets and sat out the dances with Mimi. He got talking about the future and, before he realized his mistake, was too far in to withdraw. 'It'd be easy for me to stay out here, instead of going back to England,' he said across the table – obviously at a time when she didn't want to hear such things, when the tinpot band crashing away close by was determined, it seemed, to override him. Mimi, looking young and pretty and painted up to the nines, pushed her handbag away, then worried it bit by bit back to her stomach, staring straight before her, so that it fell on to her knees: 'It would be the hardest thing for you to do. You talk too nice about it. And you know I don't like it as well.'

'Stop nailing me,' he said, draining his thimble-size whisky. 'I only say what I mean.' Her face was blank with sadness (or was it weariness? he wondered), yet he thought a smile lurked somewhere behind her eyes. I'm getting drunk, he said to himself during a smile of tenderness that brought her hand out to touch his wrist.

She said: 'Maybe you're afraid to go back to England.' The band, after a pause, slonked out another series of foxtrots, debilitating for all and sundry – yet enjoyed – in the heavy sweat of the evening. 'You're dead wrong,' he cried, with such positive conviction that, remembering it later, he wondered whether or not there wasn't some truth in it. She turned her eyes down. 'If I don't know my own mind at twenty I'll never know it,' he said. He called a waiter and asked for two more whiskies, but Mimi insisted on an orange squash. She took only soft drinks whenever their talk got 'serious' – whereas he went to the other extreme of whisky, the result being that while his seriousness tended to become more erratic on the loosening fire induced, Mimi grew more and more into her melancholic fatalistic self – leaving them in the end at emotional loggerheads. At the same time he suspected that no mere earthly decision, such as the one they were trying to solve now, was really vital to her life, which seemed to work on a level where decisions were left – and trusted – to look after themselves, whether you scorched yourself with rice whisky or sat through them with an iced squash. He sensed all this, and the foregone conclusions it implied, yet in the packed dance hall, facing her and having his head pounded out of shape with smash-hits murdered by the Boston Lights Brainwashers, he wasn't so sure he didn't want to spend the rest of his life in the fabulous sunlight of Malaya. 'Our demob group was called before the CO today, and quizzed about staying on in the air force another two years. I could always accept.'

'No you couldn't,' she said. 'You don't belong in a uniform. I know something about you after all this time.' Maybe she did, at that. The CO asked if he'd any complaints to make against the air force now that he was (in a month) about to leave. 'None, sir,' he answered. Who'd be such a loon as to say he had? 'Well,' the CO went on, a set speech made to everybody, 'we need all the trained men we can get in Malaya at this difficult time, and according to the signals officer you're one of his best wireless operators. Would you like to stay an extra two years?' This question wasn't unexpected either: Baker had been in before him and came out with a look of insult on his livid face. So Brian had his answer, a telegram already worded in his brain: 'No, sir' – a pause – 'I wouldn't.' The CO's face, dead but for the handlebar moustache, registered the 'I wouldn't'. 'You can go then, Seaton,' he rapped out.

'If I signed on,' he said to Mimi, 'I might be able to help the communists.'

She smiled: 'They don't want much help at the moment.'

'They might in a few months. You never know.'

'Nearly everybody's on their side in Malaya,' she said.

'I hope they win then. They've even got their own radio station, haven't they? They try to jam our WT channels with a transmitter. I was told to get a bearing on it yesterday so that our planes could track it down and bomb it, but I didn't get a very accurate one. Far from it,' he laughed.

'This war's nothing to do with you,' she said. 'You should get out as quickly as you can.'

'Not much it ain't. I was dragged into the air force against my will and now they want me to fight the communists. I'm no mug. I've learned a thing or two in my life. They can fight their wars themselves.' She touched him with her foot: two Chinese were listening from the next table. They turned to their own talk, and he called the waiter for more drinks.

'As I was saying,' he peeled off another day's pay. 'I can stay in Malaya if I like.' She looked hard at him, and he knew that for a change he was more puzzling to her than she had ever been to him, that she wanted him to act and not involve her in the complex machinery of his decisions. 'If I decide to stay in Malaya, we can get married.'

'You can't marry me. You never could, and you know it.'

The whisky, music, voices and moving colour around their

table, a circular light of agonized intimacy created by the opposite poles of their personality (light and dark for him; dark and light for her) mixed into a flood that he bent his head nearer the table to avoid. 'You're wrong,' he cried. 'For Christ's sake you're wrong, because I'd like that more than anything.'

She reminded him of something he'd never told her and didn't know she knew: 'You've got a wife and child waiting for you in England,' and the shock was so great that no quick lie came to his rescue. He sat with mouth closed and a grim stare in his eyes. 'You thought I didn't know!' He was surprised at her treating as flippant a piece of deception that a Radford woman might have choked him for. 'I've known for months. I happened to be dancing one night with someone from Kota Libis who told me all about you. I thought you knew I knew. You never bothered to tell me you were married, out of kindness, I imagined.'

'That's true,' he said, a little too quickly, though sensing that the river of gaiety looped around them by the dance hall was coming to the end of its tether, about to lay down its head and die – except that there was no diminution in the machine-like power of the band. Mimi's motionless expression was one of unhappiness, and he felt miserable and guilty that he hadn't kept his trap shut – or at least hadn't opened it in the right way – and spent the six tickets on spinning themselves off their feet.

He pulled her into the perspiring drink-smelling mix-up of the dance floor, giving in to the honky-tonk jazz of the Boston Stumpers. Her hands rested lightly, as if she were a taxi-dancer approached for the first time. His movements while dancing were those of some sailor who had never taken lessons, and he used the same erratic and exaggerated steps for all rhythms. Yet their bodies moved together and he drew her slowly to him. With a sudden movement she clung firmly, as if some inner vision frightened her. 'Brian,' she faltered, 'don't go, will you?'

'No.' They pressed warmly together, close to the dark night of each other. His arm was so far around her waist that his fingers touched the under part of her breast. Noise and music were forgotten, stranded in a world they had sidestepped from, its fabricated rhythms alien and unmatched compared to the swaying cut-off warmth of themselves. He felt the shape and benefit of her body, thighs intertwining at each step, shoulders and breasts against him. 'I love you,' he said. 'I feel as though I've lived with you years, for a life.'

'Don't say that. It's not finished yet, is it?'

He kissed her closed eyes: 'What are you crying for?' – misery back and making a lump of stone in his guts, impossible to get rid of because space for it had been there since birth, it seemed. Her forehead creased and lips twisted into a childlike ugliness that she tried to hide. A haze of noise and whisky defeated him, turned easily back the sudden though matter-of-fact intrusions of traffic and ships' hooters from beyond the world of the Boston Lights. Into it came Knotman, framed at the far door with his gorgeous bint – a black flower, smiling as they pushed a pathway to the bar. Mimi and Brian went into another dance, and were drawn tightly to each other: 'You're making me dizzy,' she protested. 'I'll be sick.'

'Save it for the ferry. Are you going back with me?'

'You know I am.'

They were cheerful by the end of the dance, stayed on for another. 'You're thinner than when I first knew you,' she said. 'Your bones are sticking out.'

'That's your fault; you're like a magnet and they're trying to get at you.'

'You're crazy,' she laughed. 'It's impossible.'

'Crazy,' he said, 'like a blind, three-legged blackclock.'

'What's a blackclock?'

'A cockroach. An English shit-beetle.'

'Do they have them in England as well?'

'Sure they do. They have snakes in England, jungle and wild animals and mountains. Cities and swamps and big rivers. You look as if you don't believe me? Well, I can't prove it this minute, but it's true, right enough.'

'If it is, why do you want to stay in Malaya?'

'Because' – even if you don't have an answer, make one up, a lie being better than no answer at all. If as a kid his brothers or cousins had asked: What is the biggest town in Australia? he'd rather have said Paris than I don't know. 'Because I love you.'

But still the tears came, for no lie could stop them, nor even the truth, since what he had said was certainly somewhere between both. 'When I was told you had a wife in England I didn't believe it. I thought the man was lying or having me on. But now you've told me as well it must be true.' He winced at the delayed action of her trick, unable to answer the cunning of a fine ruse played as much against herself as him.

'I'm sorry,' he said, but it was too late. He had lifted her from a passive sort of contentment, and understood that she couldn't forgive him. 'I'll stay,' he said. 'I want to. I can't do anything else,' and while they were dancing he imagined them living in some house like a Chinese widow's, on the edge of the Patani swamps, where bullfrogs and night noises rolled an extinguishing carpet over her senses, an oblivious rest for them both from the strident thump and blare of the band that was beginning to send him off his nut.

The next morning those who had been on the Gunong Barat expedition were awakened at five o'clock. The hand of a police sergeant from the guardroom shook Brian out of the death-cells of sleep, lifted the millstone of exhaustion from his head. He'd been home with Mimi and stayed till two, had run the gauntlet of road-blocks between the village and camp, thankful at reaching his bed with no marks of buckshot on him. It was a feat of tracking, often on all fours by beach and footpath to avoid the groups of Malays who sat smoking and telling tales to each other, alerted for any bandit gang of whom Brian might have been one. It's getting worse, he had told himself. If I don't get shot by mistake they'll report me to the guardhouse for being out without a pass. I feel like a Chetnik freedom-fighter; or I would with a gun to blaze back with if they tried owt.

'Get up,' the sergeant said. 'Out of that wanking pit. There's a job for you jungle lads to do.'

'What's going off?' Brian suspected a practical joke. 'It's still dark.'

'A plane's crashed and you've got to go after it.' He stirred Kirkby, Baker, Jack and a boy from Cheshire. 'Come on, get yer hands off it. The ship's going down.'

Brian sat up, but made no move to get out of bed, while Knotman walked along the billet already dressed: 'Get weaving. We've got to help those poor bastards down. They're fixing lorries and wireless gear at the MT section.' Brian pulled his trousers on: 'Why did the daft bastards have to crash at a time like this? I've never felt so knackered in my life.'

'I suppose you're getting as much of it in as you can,' Knotman said, 'before they drag you screaming down to that boat at Singapore.'

'I wish that was what they was waking me up for this morning.'

Knotman threw him a fag. 'I'll go over to Signals in a bit and find out where it pancaked.'

The sergeant returned: 'Look sharp. Get over to the cook-house and they'll give you some breakfast and rations.'

'How long do they expect us to be away?' Baker wanted to know.

'How do I know, laddie?' the sergeant cried. 'I'll get God on the blower and find out, if it means that much to you.'

'It does,' Baker said. 'We're on the boat in a couple of weeks.'

'GET WEAVING!' he shouted. 'Or you'll be over the wall for fifty-six days, never mind on the bloody boat.' They went down the steps and walked off through the palm trees to a leisurely meal, still finding time to hang around in the billet afterwards. Brian was impatient. 'They're fixing the radio,' Knotman explained. 'I got on to the DF hut and the plane ducked thirty miles south, they think.'

'In the meantime,' Brian said, 'the poor bastards are hanging in the trees bleeding to death.' He lifted a Bible from the locker of the next bed, opened it and put his finger on a random verse to find what the future held, a trick he'd seen in a film a few nights ago: 'And they cut off his head, and stripped off his armour, and sent into the land of the Philistines round about, to publish it in the house of their idols, and among the people.' Among the people. What people? A loony game. I can't make head or tail of it, and in any case I'm not superstitious. His filled pack lay tilted by the bed, this time weighing no more than forty pounds. He was also to collect a medium-range TR, if the mechanics could get it working before they left, for it was the only one at the camp. He flicked open the Bible, again thrust his finger on to a verse: 'And they cut off his head . . .' It kept opening at the same place because the binding was faulty and would open there till the cows came home – unless he deliberately avoided it, which somehow he didn't want to do because the more he read it the more some hidden truth seemed to lurk at the heart of it. He half-understood its meaning by the time the driver poked his head in and bawled out that they were ready to go.

26

On his first leave from squarebashing Brian had got into Nottingham at eight of an evening, having taken most of the day to travel from the back-end of Gloucestershire. Reaching the wide green flatlands of the Trent beyond Brum, he felt so much excitement that he couldn't eat the sandwiches and cake dashed out for at the last stop. Cows were dotted by peaceful and diminished streams and sunlight still burned into the packed corridor, and he felt himself being channelled nearer to Nottingham with every circling clatter of the wheels. The excitement in him was not so much at seeing Pauline as at the sensation in his stomach of being lost once more in the vast familiar spider's web of Nottingham and all the comfortable meaning of it.

After a hello cup of tea with mam and dad in Radford he hopped a couple of buses to see Pauline on the estate out at Aspley. Perhaps by some fluke the house would be empty and they'd be able to love each other on the settee or roll about in one of the made beds upstairs; or if not that, then happen they could go for a walk beyond the Broad Oak and snug down in some dry field of sweet summer grasses.

Everybody was in, at supper, as if they'd been waiting specially to greet him after his first ten weeks drilling like a brainless ragbag for his king and country. You never got what you hoped for, so he might have known it would be like this. Mrs Mullinder poured him tea in the pint-sized mug that used to be old Mullinder's favourite – a gesture indicating that Brian was already part of the tribal loot. Fourteen-year-old Maureen sat reading *Oracle* by the fire, all selfconscious with her small high bosom and trace of lipstick, her face the spit-image of Pauline's when he'd started courting her at fifteen. They're a good-looking family, he thought, though feeling uneasy at the mother's gaze and the comparative silence in spite of the fact that there were five people in the room. 'You look a bit as if you've had a hard time in the air force,' Betty said with a sly grin. 'Do you get good grub?'

'Not bad. Sometimes it's pigswill though.' Pauline didn't say much either, face half-hidden by her hair as she opened a tin of fruit on the other side of the table. However, he was too involved eating his way through the still-lavish supper to let the atmosphere disturb him. Not that he expected them to put the flags out.

Afterwards he suggested a walk. 'You'd better tell him while you've got the chance,' he remembered Mrs Mullinder saying. 'And come to some arrangements.'

She broke it on Coventry Lane: 'I'm having a baby.'

They stopped by a gate, leaned on it so that he could take the shock. Even going into the air force hadn't wrenched the nuts-and-bolts of his world as loose as this piece of information. The picture of his life was shaken, sent spinning like an iron Catherine-wheel in front of his eyes. He closed them tight, knew that this wasn't the way to take such news, so opened them on green fields rolling up to the tree-trunked bastion of Catstone Wood, a mist-green spearblade of sky above which, he realized through his shock, was coloured by the sun going down. 'Roll on,' he muttered with a long-drawn whistle of breath. 'This is a stunner.'

'That's nowt to what I said when I found out, I can tell you,' she retorted, pale and firm-lipped. She was half a stranger after ten weeks' absence, and he felt this wasn't a good way to get to know her again. He remembered how Joan and Jim had got married: it began a mere three months ago by Joan telling Jim that she was pregnant, and by the time she was able to say it was a false alarm they were engaged and didn't think it worth the fuss and bother to put off the tentative wedding date already fixed. Jim told Brian at the time that being engaged made people look up to you, treat you with more respect, like an adult at last. But Brian didn't feel he needed that sort of respect, though wondered whether Pauline had taken a tip from Joan and was only saying she was pregnant to get him on the tramline to matrimony.

'Mam caught me being sick one morning and I said I had a bilious bout, but when it went on for a week she made me go to the doctor's with her. I already knew though in a way, because I'd missed a period. I kept hoping it wasn't true, that's all.' She smiled, and he saw she wasn't concerned – like Joan had plainly been – to trick him into an engagement.

'It's a sod, i'n't?' he said, half-smiling back. He didn't know whether to laugh or cry, was gripped by a hotaches of the heart and brain.

'It is, if you look at it in that way,' she answered. They walked arm-in-arm along the blue blackness of the lane, a cold wind blowing into their faces. His next statement came almost without thought – at least he had wondered whether or not to say it, and decided he would before too much consideration stopped him: 'We'll think about getting married.'

'Do you want to?' she asked, in a dead-level inconsequential voice. He squeezed her arm: 'I do, if you want to know. If you'll 'ave me, that is.'

She laughed: 'Maybe it's a case of having to!'

'We've been going out with each other long enough.'

'In a way though I'm sorry it had to be a bit of a force-put. I don't like *having* to, if you see what I mean.'

He was offended. 'Why not then?'

'Oh I don't know. It would have been better the other way.'

'I suppose it would.'

'Not that I want to get married in church or anything like that,' she said. 'It's old-fashioned now. As long as you're married, what does it matter?'

'That's a good job,' he agreed, 'though I don't expect it'll make your mam and Betty very happy.'

'Well it's us that matter, duck, i'n't it? Not many people bother wi' church nowadays.'

'They don't,' he said. 'We should be in the Broad Oak knocking it back now, celebrating. It's supposed to be good when two people get engaged.' He was fighting away from the part of himself that felt bear-trapped, leg-caught and pulled into the earthpits of responsibility.

'I'd love to have a drink, but I can't face it just now.'

'Neither can I in a way' – glad that she also felt the same mixed sensation of it all.

'Maybe tomorrow,' he said. 'Though I don't see the need for much hurry.'

'Well, we can't dawdle either, can we?'

'I'll see to everything, don't worry. Get special leave and all that.'

'As long as you aren't backing out,' she said, a half-serious caution to see how he'd take it.

'I would if I wanted to,' he said firmly. 'But I won't want to. I love you too much, you know that.'

'As long as I know,' she taunted.

'Well, I've told you,' he cried. 'I've been telling you for a long time.'

'I know you have, duck.'

'You never look as though you believe me though.'

'What do you expect? We both go as far as we can' – this reference to the just-revealed fact that she was having a baby quietened his shock and he held her close: 'Don't let's get mad, love.'

'I've been worrying myself blind these last three weeks. Mam's been on to me as well.'

'Why didn't you write and tell me?' he shouted in the darkness. 'I'd a been out o' that camp like a shot. Nobody could have stopped me.'

'Well, I don't know. I thought it wouldn't be the best thing, to write and tell you it in a letter. Mam said so as well when I told her.'

'You thought I'd run away and never show my face?' he laughed.

Her hard knuckles thumped into his ribs: 'No, you leary swine. But you can clear off now if you want to because I can soon have the baby and keep it myself without your 'elp. In fact that's what mam said. "Don't get married if you don't like him. But if you can, it'd be better." So I don't care how much trouble it is, it ain't that much of a force-put. I didn't want to get married as early as this, no more than yo' did. So I'm not going to marry you just because I'm having a baby. I can allus live at home and stay at work.'

He rubbed the pain out of his bones: her outbursts were the more abrupt and fiery in proportion to her at times angelic calmness. 'You want to keep your temper. I was only having a joke.'

'All right,' she said, 'but you ought to be nice to me sometimes.'

'I often am' – he tried to hit off the correct ratio of his good nature – 'but I come home on leave, rush straight to see you all the way from Gloucestershire and this is what you meet me with. You think it i'n't a shock for me as well?'

'I know it is, but I couldn't break it any other way, could I? I'm glad you've come though. It feels better for me now.'

They drew into a long kiss by the hedge, stopped only when a car drove by and fixed them in its headlights before turning off at the Balloon Houses. 'I don't feel bad about having a baby,' she said. 'I'm sure I'll like it, and that it'll be all right.'

'It sounds OK to me. I suppose we let ourselves in for it.' He was filled with joy and dread. The first shock had shown the future as a confused black ocean, which had lost much of its alarm however in the last half hour because a feeling of having gained some enormous happiness had gradually come into him. They crossed the main road, arms locked around each other, and walked into a wood on the far side.

The day before Brian was due back in Gloucestershire Bert swung up in the yard, resplendent in beret and battledress and a couple of campaign ribbons won from the last push over the Rhine. He was quartered in Trieste and had travelled across Europe on a forty-hour journey of wooden seats to get himself – so he joked to Harold Seaton – an earful of Radford, a gutful of Shippoe's and an armful of fat tart.

They went out to walk part of the way together: Brian to see Pauline at Aspley, Bert to call on his brother at near-by Cinderhill. It was a dry, baking summer, seemingly endless because it had been on almost a week, and they swapped opinions on life in uniform, Brian disliking his incarceration mainly for a reason as yet unspoken to Bert, and Bert enjoying his experience because he had a marvellous time not having to worry where the next meal or shilling came from. 'I might even sign on an extra three years,' he said, 'instead of coming out at Christmas. In fact I'm sure I shall.'

'What do you want to do that for?' Brian asked. 'There's plenty o'wok.'

'I like it better than wok,' Bert told him.

Over a sandstone wall lay a cemetery, cool grass waving and flowers spread on many graves, colours of snow and blood and mustard against marble. It was Sunday morning, and some people tended stones and urns, busying themselves with hedge-clippers and watering-cans. Brian said to his cousin: 'I'm signing on as well in a way, only for life. I'm getting married.'

Both stopped walking. Bert took his arm and stared: 'You're not.'

'I am. To Pauline. Don't you think we've been courting long enough?'

'Come off it.'

'What do you mean "Come off it"?' He wanted more reaction than this, so little not indicating whether Bert thought him a fool or a grown-up, a madcap or a restless layabout who was getting spliced for want of anything new to do, or a shade of every reason. But he underestimated Bert, who looked at him slyly, shut one eye and demanded: 'She's having a kid?' – at the same time offering a fag from a ten-pack to mollify such outrightness in case he was wide of the mark.

Brian's first thought was to say no, she bloody-well wasn't, but who knew how much it would show by the time they were able to get married? And in any case when she had the kid it would be calculated in simple-finger arithmetic (digit by digit backdated), so that it was better to be thought trapped now than be seen to have been a frightened liar then.

'She's pregnant,' he said, 'and we're getting married.'

They walked on, out of step now and Bert looking in at him as if to find a trace of lying on his face. 'But you'll be done for,' he raved suddenly. 'You'll be hooked, finished, skewered and knackered. Why don't you do a bunk?'

'Because I don't want to. I'd never be able to see her again.'

'Come off it. Sign on, get sent overseas, cut your throat, hang yourself. For Christ's sake, you're only eighteen.'

'I'll be nineteen next year,' he grinned. Bert was grieved: 'I know, sure Brian. You'll be twenty-one soon as well, and we'll give you the key to the bleeding door: can't you wait even that long? It's batchy to get married at eighteen. Think of all the fun you can still have. Running after all the women your eyes hook on to. I know it wain't suit yo' to get married, I do an' all. You ain't that sort. You're too much of a sod, like I am.'

'I know,' Brian said, 'but I love her, you see. You think I'm trapped just because she's having a kid? Well, what you lose on the swings you gain on the roundabouts. If I didn't love her I might think twice about it.'

'You've got to think twenty times about whether you love a tart or not.' Brian had thought a hundred times, and knew his mind by now on that subject anyway. Pauline was having a baby, and because he loved her they were going to get married. There was no need to ask himself what he would have done if he hadn't loved her, if she'd been little more than a casual acquaintance. 'What's made you get sloppy all of a sudden?' Bert demanded.

He turned on him, fists clenched and ready to be raised: 'I'm not bloody-well sloppy, so don't come it. I'm just doing what I want to do and what I think is right, and I'm not asking yo' whether it's good for me or not, because I know it is because I want it.'

'Well,' Bert said, 'if that's the way you feel. All right, all right. Let me be best man then.' They shook on it and Bert seemed to think it a good idea Brian was getting married by the time they got around to changing the subject.

The cornfield was being subtly reduced in size. A combine-harvester came towards them, went on by, and passed before they were half-way across on their slow walk. The area of high corn seemed no smaller than before, and already the machine was a red beetle turning again towards the far side of the sloping field, its engine noise filling the autumn evening like the leisured omniscient growling of an invisible mastodon. A few bristles of withered corn lay over the path, like heads at which the big chop of the machine had suffered disappointment.

He reached for her hand as they ambled towards the shrub-covered hillside, a rising gradient of amber bracken. He frowned with concern at her slight limp: 'Does your foot still hurt, love?'

'It aches across the top.'

'We wain't walk far then,' he promised, squeezing her hand tighter, hoping her foot would stop hurting if they ceased to think about it. He fastened the polished buttons of his overcoat, smiled at her long brown hair tied by a piece of ribbon, and noticed the strength in her calm smooth face, her pouting lips, shining forehead – a face resting for the moment from make-up because she had said: 'You don't mind me letting my hair down now and again, do you?' Not that she had ever been much addicted to the alchemy of powders and lipsticks. The fresh smell of mown corn sharpened his regret that this would be their last night together for a few months, and he smiled to hide his anguish: 'I suppose we should make the best of this evening.'

She pressed his hand: 'It worn't a very long leave, was it?'

'Long enough to get married in.'

It was an'all.

'You don't regret it, do you?' A tractor passed slowly, pulling a dray loaded with the systematic droppings of the combine-harvester. The young driver had a sleeve of his shirt torn, and a farmhand on top of the sacks smiled as they passed.

'We're young, so everybody told me at work. But I think it best to get married young.'

'So do I,' he laughed. 'More times for being in bed together.' They'd been married two weeks ago, both families (and the friends of both) crowding the vestibule of the downtown registrar, and packing into the Trafalgar later for a noisy reception.

'Have you enjoyed this fortnight?'

She detected in his voice a sickness at heart simply because he was trying to hide it, at a time when they could hide nothing from each other. 'It's been marvellous,' she answered. Her stomach was beginning to show, a slight pushing from under her voluminous coat.

'I'll be in Birmingham this time tomorrow, on my way back.'

'I wish I was going with you. It's not very nice being left behind.'

'I know. I shan't enjoy it either.' She asked why not, knowing the answer, yet still wanting to hear it. 'Because you won't be with me,' he told her. 'I often think of packing the air force in. Walking out. They'd never find me. We could live in another town.'

'Don't do that,' she said. 'You've only got two years to do. It'll be all over then.'

'I might have to go abroad.'

'But you'll soon be back.' He wondered how she could say these things with such an expression of surety, see two years as being but a feminine small wisdom-tooth of time, a nothing that to him looked like a vast ocean with no opposite shore visible. Her love must be deeper than mine, calm and everlasting, if this seems such a normal hurdle to get over before our proper lives start.

But she'll have something to keep her company while I'm away. 'Shall we go along here?' – pointing to where the footpath forked, through a meadow and up a hill.

'To the left,' he said, not knowing why. Walking before him she hummed a tune. There was a low, grass-covered bank on one side and blackberry bushes on the other. The sound of birds and the combine-harvester working below were hardly noticed now, and the sun, soon to fall behind the hill, lay a pale yellow light over the fields. A breeze carried white fluff from seedpods of rose-bay, some settling on to his grey uniform.

'You'll be a snowmaiden as well,' he cried, her coat spotted white.

'Tell me another. I'm a married woman now!' She stopped by a bush: 'What are these blue flowers called?'

'I don't know,' he teased.

'Yes you do. You should anyway. You're the one who's allus

telling me about living all that time in the country at your grandma's when you was a kid.'

He knelt to look: 'Harebells, I think.'

'I thought they came in April?' she said.

'Bluebells do, but these don't. Where did you go to school?' Three blue heads hung half-concealed under the low leaves of a bush before some ferns. 'Faith, Hope, and Charity's what they look like,' she pronounced, brushing her fingers across them.

'And hope stays still,' he said, when one didn't move.

She touched it, made it sway with the others: 'Easy, you see.' They sat on the bank and she emptied soil from her shoes. 'I don't want to go home tonight, do you?'

'It'd be nippy,' he said, 'kipping out in the fields. It's nearly October. You'll be better off in bed wi'me, duck.'

'You're allus on about *that*,' she cried. 'We shouldn't do it so much now I'm pregnant.'

'Hark at who's talking!' He laughed, walked to a bush and picked a cluster of blackberries, then went to another until he had gathered a handful. 'What are you doing?' she called out, unable to see. He came back: 'Open your mouth.'

'What for?' She picked the juiciest to eat, until a pang of conscience showed in her eyes, and made her feed him some. 'I had a few already, when I was collecting 'em.' Hands empty, they looked at the vulnerable tenderness behind each other's eyes: 'Why have I got to go off tomorrow? It's useless and crazy.' She couldn't reply, but held him and took his kisses.

They walked on, becoming more and more white from rosebay. It even settled on the blackberries, had to be blown off before they could eat them. They found raspberries also, and pink juice ran like blood to his hands: when they kissed he joked about tasting raspberry flavour: 'I thought it was your lipstick,' he said, taking her arm so that she faced him. He saw the tremor of her mouth and they kissed passionately. 'I love you,' she said. 'Darling Brian, I love you' – almost inaudibly. 'I love you, sweetheart' – such committing words no longer unreal or out of place, not scoffed at as they might have been had either used them a while back. He supposed such words were only embarrassing when the meaning of them had been forgotten or wasn't known; when spoken with reason their sounds were as intense and sexual as the kisses that flowered at the same time.

Voices along the path made them stand apart. 'Let's walk on up the hill,' he said, nodding to show the direction. 'There's plenty of bushes where we wain't be seen.' She hesitated. 'It'll be all right.'

They threaded a way up through brambles, Brian in front when the path narrowed. Pauline seemed happier now, humming softly, dignified in her walk, as if heavier than she yet was. The fortnight since getting married had been spent at Pauline's: he lived there as one of the family, and their room overlooked the back garden. Their names were down on the council housing list, but nothing would be ready, they realized, until years after he'd come out of the air force. So on his demob they planned to get rooms downtown so as to be on their own.

'We'll sit here.' He spread his overcoat and took off his tunic.

'Don't get a cold, duck, will you?'

'It ain't winter yet,' he said, embarrassed that she should show concern that he would hardly have noticed before they were married.

'Well,' she said, 'I don't want you to catch cold.'

He put his hand on her stomach: 'You want to worry about that little bogger in there, not me.'

'He's warm enough,' she said. They lay with arms around each other. He raised his head, saw a man walking along the footpath below, and wondered whether he could see them. 'What's up, duck?'

'Nothing' – bending again to kiss her. I'll be off tomorrow – a fact that kept hammering at him, wouldn't let him live out the last few hours with her in peace. It had been in his mind all day, and now they lay silently together it became more painful. Back to prison. I'm free now: I should just piss off and desert. It'd be a few days before they missed me. I wain't see her for another three months, studying my guts out at radio school to be jumped-up wireless operator. It's a wonder I passed the aptitude tests for it. His hand touched her swollen breasts and he kissed each of her closed eyelids: the whole of her vision, all that she had seen and would ever see, was beating in the delicate hump under the thin white lids of flesh. And completely in her is a kid I can't bear to leave as well. We ought to make the most of these few hours – but he couldn't speak. There's a time when you can't do anything but kiss; and the trouble is that you've got no bleeding say as to when it will be.

She clung to him: he'll be off tomorrow, and the fact tormented her, keeping her close to tears the more she thought of it. I shan't see him for a long while, and she felt afraid of being without him, even though both families looked up to her now and would keep her company. It's getting dark already, and we'll have to go soon. 'Brian, when do you think your next leave'll be?'

'Near Christmas.' He raised his head and saw two men walking through the meadow, maybe poachers, though it was hardly dark enough for that, and he was uneasy at the thought that they might be seen. It'd be good to do it out here.

She placed her fingers on his cheek and kissed him. Maybe he will, but I don't know whether it'll be all right, though in one way it would be nice, far from people and houses and on our own. He returned the kiss and suddenly there were tears in her throat and she tightened her arms around him. He won't she thought, so maybe he doesn't love me any more.

His arms were cold and he sat up to reach his jacket. A mist was creeping among the far fields, sun descending like a deserter, skulking behind the trees where grey clouds merged. She opened her hand and patted the ground: 'It's damp. You should be more careful.'

He stood. We can't do it here. 'It's autumn already,' he said. A tree branch swayed near by and he looked hard but saw nothing, helped her up, thinking maybe it was the prospect of parting that made them such clumsy and hesitant lovers. He lifted his overcoat and put it on. 'Look at that mist over there,' she pointed as they walked slowly down. Their attention was caught and suspended by a strange silence. Everything was still and quiet.

'It's funny,' he said, puzzled by it.

'It's the harvest machine that's stopped,' she guessed.

At the foot of the hill they turned for a moment to look into the sun. Why didn't we? he wondered. It would have been good. The sun was blood-red and misshapen behind the thin trunks of a clump of trees some distance off, and it looked like a premature medal commemorating the winter that was on its way. A sombre crimson light flushed the meadows on either side of the copse.

She wrote once a week, and he worked hard training for his sparks badge, an attainment which would mean more pay and the satisfaction of having a real trade the first time in his life. Daytime went quickly at class, drawing and describing super-heterodyne circuits and transmitter units, studying Ohm's Law and WT procedure, stepping up week by week to higher speeds of morse practice and teleprinter operating, to culminate later in outstation exercises. He enjoyed the drawing-in of knowledge and skill, which more than made up for what little parade-ground bullshit there was.

But the long evenings were a yoke that crushed him into a broody silence, so physically strong as he sat by himself in the NAAFI that he grew to feel the resemblance they must have borne to those he had seen his father suffer during the long empty dole days before the War, steeped in vicious bouts of frustration because he felt he could do nothing about the situation he had let himself fall into. It was a naked agony he couldn't throw off for weeks after his return from Nottingham. He wrote two letters to Pauline's one, and was so impatient and disappointed at the inadequacy of hers that he raged and often pulled himself back from screwing them up. But the occasional letter, which was written on impulse and not in answer to one of his, gave out the warm glow of her love in a quickening real sense that his long and thought-out ones rarely achieved. A few words juxtaposed in an unconscious and original way immediately flooded him with the totality of their so-far ecstatic love, drew him right back and painfully into it.

He tried studying, dissected the symbols and diagrams in his notebooks, knowing that if he passed his exams at over sixty per cent he would qualify for more pay, but their pages were too complex to assimilate without further help from an instructor.

As the dark frosts of winter came, the unheated billets at night meant sitting permanently in a sub-zero bath of stale air, because for some reason all deliveries of coal to airmen's billets had ceased. So with a couple of ex-Merchant Navy roughnecks and an ex-Borstal boy from Glasgow, Brian went on foraging expeditions. They crept silently around with high stockpiles of coal near the well-warmed officers' quarters, loading sacks and returning black as bandits to set a red fire blazing – to the benefit also of the timid or lazy – in the pot-bellied stove.

Now and again he went out alone into the white-covered frost fields of a Gloucestershire night and made his way overland to the village, where he threw down a few pints of rough cider and scorched himself by the lavish fire, despite resentful stares from the locals who felt themselves deprived of its flames by his presence – a mere scab of an airman from the camp which they must have regarded as a blight on the surface of their fair county unless they were tradesmen or shopkeepers. Drunk and impervious to the cold, he would weave back to camp, falling like a sack on his bed to be pulled from sleep next morning by the thick imperative rope of reveille at half-past six.

As Christmas and his next leave approached he lived with the healthy sound of an express train passing through a station on one of whose platforms he would be waiting. The clean heavy rhythm of its wheels followed him into sleep at night during the last few days, its wheels regular and cleanly solid, evenly beating out a series of V's, and in the middle of the series of one V coming too quickly on the tail of another and breaking the rhythm slightly – a thrilling and realistic dovetailing of sound. Then the end of the train vanished, the noise dragged into a tunnel, and the wind played on the back of his head – because some thoughtless bastard had left the billet window open.

There was a black fog all over the country and the train took five hours to reach Derby. It was crowded, and with a dozen others he found refuge in a luggage wagon, where they spread themselves over sacks, greatcoats tightened in the bitter cold. He reached Nottingham at midnight, a deserted woebegone station slabbed-out on either side of the tracks as he made his loaded way, ticket in teeth, towards the rising steps marked Exit.

He took a taxi that purred its swift way through the dead roads of town to Canning Circus, a crest of the tarmac wave then sweeping gently beyond the valley of the Lean and along the wide, well-lighted, familiar road to where the Mullinders lived.

His mother-in-law let him in, stood by the stairfoot door saying she'd get straight back to bed because of the cold, and see him in the morning.

'Is Pauline OK?' he wanted to know.

'Yes,' she said, clicking the door to and on her way up.

She must have been too fast asleep to hear him rattling at the door, and only woke up while he was undressing. It was a plain room, with yellow walls of orange stippling decorated last by Mullinder in a burst of energy on some long-lost creative week-end, whose memory he had taken to the grave with his bad foot. Apart from the bed there was a wardrobe, dressing-table and two chairs, with lino on the floor, and a cupboard in the corner holding Brian's books. 'I didn't think you'd be in till tomorrow,' she said, when he laid his cold face by her, close in an embrace of kisses. 'Get in quick, duck, or you'll freeze.'

'Why didn't you have a fire?'

'I didn't need it,' she said. 'It's warm enough in bed. I filled a hot waterbottle.'

'Well, you wain't want one any more – not for the next fortnight anyway – because you've got me. So sling it out.'

She looked well, an hour of sleep blurring her eyes. 'How are you feeling, love?'

'Fine,' she said. 'I go to the clinic every week now. I've got varicose veins, and the doctor says I've got to have something done about them. I'm going to have the baby at home. It should be here in two or three weeks, though I wouldn't be surprised if it came tomorrow, the way it feels at times.'

'If anything happens while I'm here I'll get an extension.'

'I'd like that. That'd be smashing.' He remembered the form that had been passed to all in his class at radio school only a week ago, giving a list of overseas postings and asking for preferences, though not guaranteeing that your choice would be met. The list had so dazzled him during the ten minutes the paper was in his hand (bringing back geography-book memories of fantastic tropical islands and a half-drunken childhood desire to go to them) that he had put an option down for a posting to Japan. He had not filled in the attached application which asked you to state any reason why you might not want to be sent overseas. I'm a nut case, he thought. Maybe I could stay in England, being married and Pauline about to have a kid. But for some unfathomable reason he had left it blank, never knowing what had induced him to do so, neither questioning nor regretting it, except to wonder why he had been sent to Malaya and not Japan.

27

A couple of fifteen-hundredweight lorries stood by the camp gates, the bursting roar of their engines suggesting that when they finally debouched they would drag the rest of the camp with them. A drop in the noise, and the first one set off at a dangerous speed towards the village, ignored the policeman's stop-signal at the crossroads and made for the flat monotonous belt of the Patani swamps.

Before the Dakota was pulled into a belly-dive by some concealed magnet of jungle-soil its wireless operator had scraped out an SOS – ending his message by the continual buzz of a QTG so that its position was fixed with reasonable accuracy by the wideawake operators in the DF huts at Kota Libis and Singapore. No message pip-squeaked out of the plane's emergency-set after the crash, so it was uncertain whether anyone had survived. The DF bearings, plotted on Mercator's North Malaya, crossed on uninhabited terrain of dense forest, between Kedah and Perak.

Brian sat in the first lorry – the wire grid of the earphones chafing his recent haircut – and listened wearily to the crackling of atmospherics that seemed to be holding boxing-matches on the doorsteps of his ear-drums. In some unexplainable way such noise confined against his ears seemed to blur the distant detail of thin trees and kampong huts set beside the paddy fields on spindly legs. So he put the phones back a little to take in and enjoy the landscape flying by, the wide spaces of hot blue flat lands gently floating in the distance, a sight that made him dread entering the dark forests of the mountains where lurked the dead blood of injured men. The straight road in front, with a ditch and line of thin high trees on either side, looked like a tropically lit version of a Dutch picture he remembered from school a long time ago.

His call-sign crept over in slow morse, preambling a short message giving the position of the army screen moving north from Taiping. He tore off the paper and passed it to Odgeson – who pencilled an acknowledgement for sending back. It seemed like a game, an aptitude test of co-ordination in which groups one and two converge on number three which has deliberately lost itself in the mountains. He pushed the bakelite from one ear and said: 'I expect the bandits are picking up all my morse. It should be coded. Not that I mind: they're welcome to it.'

Baker lit two fags under cover of his shirt and passed him one: 'Don't worry, the aircrew's already dead.'

'Dead or not, we'll have to stay in that that jungle till we've found 'em. Maybe weeks.' The wind snatched smoke across his face, forced his eyes open. He looked through the cellophane window into the driver's seat, above which the dashboard needle shivered around sixty. The paddy fields were green, shoots high, lush and cool-looking, untilled parts reflecting white clouds that hid the blue and green ridges towards which they turned at the next crossroads. The second lorry was a hundred yards behind, and Knotman waved a greeting, clenched his fist in the communist salute for a lark and a laugh.

So much windstream came over the lorry that Brian's cigarette soon warmed his skin, so he spat it on to the blurred tarmac river of the road. The lorry slowed down and sweat broke from his face, was rubbed dry into his hair. Beyond a village, the undulating and narrow road went through a rubber estate, where a solitary tapper passed with yoked jerry-cans from tree to tree like some sober advertisement in one of the trade magazines Brian had often flipped through in the camp library. The manager's bungalow was fortified with sandbags and barbed-wire, and from a rise in the lane a Malayan controlled the approaches with a machine-gun.

Morse. It set up impulses in the brain and got his pencil writing a message from the army platoon to say that their lorry had broken down, and he swore while the last words came through in the knowledge that such a delay would keep them out longer than necessary. Odgeson gave him a QSL and map reference: 'We'll wait for them there. I hope it won't be for too long though.'

'I wish I was on the boat,' he said to Baker, 'instead of on this jaunt.'

Baker laughed: 'It serves us right for getting mixed up in that Gunong Barat business. I shouldn't have let you persuade me to go.' His drawn face had lost its inborn English colour and had turned to the first layer of a leathery tan. He'd been on a slow and lonesome booze-up in the NAAFI last night that intensified his usual couldn't-care-less mood. As the time drew nearer to demob, he drank more and more and took to smoking, while engine manuals and motor-bike catalogues lay dusty and forgotten in his locker. 'I'd rather be in a brothel,' he said, 'than in this four-wheeled oven.'

'You soon will be. Or back in London with your girl. Do you think your motor-bike'll have gone rusty and dropped to bits?'

Being so weary he took him seriously: 'I don't know, Brian. My brother promised to look after it, so it should be in good enough condition. Not that he's a very good mechanic, but he keeps his promises.' Odgeson looked up keenly from map to road, his pinkish, oval-shaped face seeming to Brian that it must in some way resemble those of the aircrew they were out to rescue. But the vision of them – college-educated perhaps, certainly skilled to the point of nonchalance and jauntiness – was switched in a second to the foresight of them dead and mangled in the great forks of high, superstrong forest giants. Or maybe wounded, alive and waiting, waiting, being drained of life like a punctured egg-timer.

The lorry was steadier around the curves, with number two only fifty yards behind on the shaded road of the foothills. Brian listened out for the other calls from the army, his eyes half-closed at the soporific easy-going purr of the lorry-engine, while Odgeson worked on a time-and-position message for transmission to Kota Libis. They stopped at the occasional road-block to make a hasty declaration of their mission: 'This must be heavy bandit country,' Baker said. 'All we need is an ambush at the next turning and the only boat we'll be on is Noah's Ark going to heaven.'

Brian called him a pessimist, yet who could be sure now that Baker had mentioned it? Reports in the *Straits Times* backed him up; no pitched battle was ever fought, but the communists picked off isolated police posts, hamlets and estate managers' bungalows, were marvels at guerilla warfare. Forty miles north of Singapore, he had read, ten of them wearing jungle-green and armed with Stens dragged two brothers from a house, shot one dead and left the other so terrified he didn't get the coppers for a couple of days. Another time at Menkatab, forty attacked a police station, cut the phone wires and peppered the joint for hours before making off. They really mean business, he thought, and who can blame them?

The sun was well up, the heat a draughtsman drawing islands of sweat on his shirt. Baker mopped himself dry: 'Why don't you put your hat on?' Brian said. 'You'll go down with sunstroke if you aren't careful.'

'I couldn't care less,' he retorted. 'If I do, maybe they'll invalid me back to camp, raving my guts off on a shutter – telling them where they can put the tinpot air force.'

At the next collection of brown huts Odgeson looked at his watch: 'We should be there in ten minutes.'

'I wouldn't need sunstroke to tell 'em that,' Brian said.

'You'd never tell them at all. You wouldn't know how.'

'Don't worry: I would.'

'You're just a sheep like the rest. You'll go back on the boat, get a job and settle down, and look back on Malaya as the most glorious time of your life.'

'You've got me wrong.'

'I've seen that album full of photos.'

'So what? I want to show my family what it was like. Anyway, what's making you so destructive?' Fantastic sugar-lumps of hillocks, sprouting mops of trees with bears of creeper half-covering purple patches of their cliff face, grew back into the hills, reared up two or three hundred feet into a ghostly local and temporary mist that seemed to mask them off as private property. 'A hangover,' Baker answered.

'Keep it to yourself then. You can take a turn at these atmospherics in a bit. That'll get rid of it for you.'

At the next bend of the gravel track both lorries drew up among the trees. A Malay woman stood in the doorway of a near-by hut and pointed with a smile into the mountainside as they sprang down to flex their legs. Nine rifles were piled by a tree, and the woman came out with a branch of pink bananas that they made up a kitty to buy.

Brian sent a message to Kota Libis saying they had reached the point of rendezvous and were now waiting for the army before lifting themselves into the hills – then handed the set over to Baker. He scouted the shrubbery to amass wood for a tea fire. The flames were obstinate at first, brought smoke from the sap-ends of each stick or drew back from the mossy life of damp pieces, but by absorbed and dexterous application that took him a few minutes away from the worrying reality of his unexpected journey, he succeeded in creating a firm wall of flame. While Odgeson and Knotman were debating how and when to make their next move, he passed around cans of his own black mash.

Looking up he wondered where the plane lay, for there was no tell-tale indentation, no Siberian meteoric crater or tadpole tail of wreckage to show where it might have struck its silver snout. A couple of invisible bearings had crossed in the heavy waves of jungle – or were supposed to have, because who could tell how accurate they had been? He was pulled out of his speculations by the sound of an old Ford car – the original, it looked like – put-putting to a halt by the hut. A Malay police officer, dapper and smart in clean khaki, got down and asked Odgeson what he intended to do. Odgeson said his idea was to set off as soon as possible and look for the plane. The police officer smiled brilliantly and replied that, yes, a plane had crashed up there – pointing into the jungle with his rattan – because people in the village had heard it during the night. Of course, he added, no one could guarantee there weren't bandits in the area. 'We won't be able to hang around much longer though,' Odgeson said. The police officer agreed that it might not be wise to wait too long, though they should be careful not to take too many risks. With a final smile of approval at the way the world was run, he got into his car and drove off, accompanied by his saried attendant who toted a machine-gun. The car rattled down the road, shook hands with a corner, and was out of sight.

Brian swilled his can in the stream and stamped on the fire, and the Malay woman stacked his surplus wood by her hut as if sensing they would leave before another round of tea was called for; but Odgeson and Knotman conferring by the lorries were a picture of stalemate: no word had come from the army, and they had been waiting more than an hour. Knotman suggested humping it with a couple of others into the mountain, but Odgeson still thought it better to wait till the army came.

'It's about time somebody went up there though,' Brian said to Baker as they stood by the radio. 'We've got rifles, and we're experienced jungle-bashers. I don't like to think of them poor bastards snuffing it one by one.' He flipped through his pay-book: 'Here, I've still got your will you gen me at Gunong Barat. You'd better tek it, because if I get up there and want to mash some tea I might get a fire going with it.' Baker accepted, absentmindedly set it under the wireless, safe from wind and rain. The others were restless, scuffled with a mess-tin: 'I'm Arsenal,' one cried. 'I'm Piccadilly Hotspurs,' called another. Baker clicked out the army call-sign, but was unanswered, as if no ethereal dots and dashes could penetrate the isolating tree-glutted mountains that ranged three-quarters around.

Odgeson decided to act: 'Get your rifles. We'll make two parties, four in each. The drivers can stay with the lorries.' Knotman opened the map to discuss routes and times of meeting. 'I don't like the idea of only me and my mate being left here,' a driver said morosely.

'Neither do we like the idea of going up there,' he was told. Baker received a long-awaited message from the army: they'd been ambushed a few miles south and their lorry was out of action. However, they'd split forces and a couple of sections were coming up on foot. So the drivers were satisfied, and the rest didn't mind going into the jungle with the army so close. A king-size Dakota flew north-east across the vast sea of sky, then reappeared at a lower height. It circled twice, went into a dip behind the mountains and roared down over them from the peak, preceded by a wavering belly-shadow. 'He's in on it too,' Knotman said. 'It'll be a big do by the look of it, though they'd have done better sending an Auster or a helicopter.' Brian was part of Odgeson's patrol, Baker and Cheshire, a teleprinter operator, making up the four of them.

Both groups took to a track bordered by waving blades of elephant grass, pliable as bayonets that soon drew them from each other's sight. Brian shared a walkie-talkie with Baker, also lugging a rifle and fifty rounds, a kukri, food, groundsheet and blanket. Odgeson had the privilege of a first-aid kit, for use until any cracked-up flyer could be transported to a better-equipped blood-wagon waiting at the bottom of the hill, for which possibility each party (never to be far apart) packed a collapsible stretcher. 'A small but well-organized expedition' – I expect is what they're saying to themselves back at camp, the CO and Adj flicking their handlebar moustaches and thumping each other pally-like on the shoulder as they stick pins in maps spread on the table to mark the slow progress of my duffed-up and aching legs.

Even so, it's marvellous how at times my thoughts are as clean as stars on a dark night. Maybe when I get back to England where there's clarifying frost and snow, I'll be able to see things intelligent and stark, read a lot and learn to use big words and know what they mean so that Pauline will say: 'Hark at him! Swallowed a dictionary!' whenever I come out with one.

A matter of fifty yards and they swung into the jungle, brushing aside creepers in an initial burst of exuberance at being on the move. It was marvellous, marvellous, and a jolly efficient show the CO would be saying, yet the time was midday and they had been shaken to life at five, which was seven hours ago. So how little energy can you have when it takes a day's work to get started? The idea stabbed his resistance at the beginning: they were to shin-up with all speed to the crest or ridge, descend by different routes, lunge up again at another angle until someone caught sight of the plane or any shot-out component of it, making crazy red-pencilled zigzags on the map like wounded flies.

Stumbling over trees in a well-spaced single-file, chopping at creepers that could not be booted down, Brian was already exhausted. Little was visible through the dim shadows of giant trees and, constantly freeing his rifle from some stray creeper, he climbed automatically, peering ahead and to left and right in the hope that some part of the plane would show itself. Blisters began at his heels, sore spots that grew fat on the aqua-vitae of his life, that soon from the movement and constriction of his boots burst into the covering of woollen sock, stuck there until he pulled them loose during a pause. Which was unwise, he discovered on setting out again, for the soreness took on a new lease of torment against him – that nevertheless had to be lived with.

At two in the afternoon Odgeson signalled a rest and they collapsed against trees to rip open tins of meat, snap at biscuits and bars of chocolate. 'What I'd like to know,' Brian called to the others, 'is who's coming up to rescue us?' After a ten-minute smoke they went on, and in another ten minutes it seemed as if they hadn't rested at all.

If I stopped and lay down I wouldn't get up again. Even the thought of those poor wounded bastards can't make me go quicker. All I want to do is sleep. Why didn't they crash in swamp or sea? They'd have been back safe now without this godless grind. Maybe we'll find them soon and zoom off to camp. Christ, though what if we couldn't even hope for that, if we were flying from the Japs in war with no place to go, or if we were communists running before the Grenadier Guards? In that case we'd soon be out of it, one way or another. He pulled off his boots: one blister had turned white, puffed out like a growth of dirty flour over his skin and hurt more now, as if the air were infectious and gathered it more quickly than the wool. A heavy inappropriate plane roared along the level of the hill, then lifted and flew back at a less dangerous height.

They climbed through bushes and between threatening trees, drying up one dark patch of sweat only to have another painted there as if with a wet brush while they weren't looking. It seemed to Brian after a while that should he for some reason stop climbing, his legs would go on making the same pedalling ache of ascent, out of control like a puppet with St Vitus's Dance. By six they were on the crest, marked on the map as three thousand feet. 'We've done wonders,' Odgeson said.

'We ought to get the VC for this,' Cheshire grinned.

'They could stuff it,' said Baker.

'Let's find them bastards,' Brian said, 'and get out of it.'

They began the descent, slithering on an altered compass bearing. Since Gunong Barat they had developed an instinctive feeling for the shape of the earth under its great wadding of ponderous trees, sensed like ants in the gloom of thistle-strewn hillocks the easy climbs or pitfalls of a quick descent long before they were seen or felt by the feet. To Brian the smell, humidity, quality of travail, the intense silence of desperation felt whenever they paused to rest, seemed now like home and second nature, an acknowledged fight on the earth connected to a lesser known and felt contest in the jungle deep within himself, a matching that in spite of his exhaustion made the trip seem necessary and even preordained.

At dusk, his eyes lost their sharp vision – as if he needed glasses to make leaves and the hats of the others clear again. They watched the sun settting over Pulau Timur, the length of the distant island settling into the sea like a silent deserted raft. Clouds above were spearheads pointing down the sea, so vividly red that it looked as if, while they stared, a tremendous sausage of blood had just burst over the island's black hills and rolled a lava of sunset into its concealed valleys.

By seven it was too dark to go on searching, and Baker worked on the radio to make contact with Knotman's party (the others sitting around as if, in the dark forest, he were trying to get through to some listening God for instructions) until Knotman answered: 'That you, Baker? As if I didn't know. We haven't seen anything yet, so we'll bed down for the night. Went up to the north ridge and looked into the next valley. So now we're half-way to the bottom again. Did you see the sunset over Pulau Timur? It looked like the end of the world from this side. We contacted the army an hour ago, and they'll stay with us tonight, moving in your direction in the morning. I think we're about a mile away, but you can't tell in this.'

Brian spread his groundsheet and blanket in the undergrowth and drifted along tunnels of weird dreams, emerged into the dazzling half-light and half-dark of a snowstorm, heavy white flakes falling thickly around and chilling him to the bone as he fought against it. When the storm stopped the fields were white over, the sky a milk blue, low and still threatening. But the snow-covered fields, in spite of his shivering, felt good to be in.

He opened his eyes to wonder where he was, and the warm smell of the jungle told him. Someone else was awake, sitting with hands clasped around his knees near by. Hoping it was almost dawn Brian looked at his watch: four-thirty, its luminous hand glowed. He felt for his rifle, and cursed to realize it was the first thing he thought of. I should throw it away. 'How long do you guess this search'll go on?'

'It depends on our luck,' Odgeson said. 'We could be kept knocking around for a fortnight.'

Brian lit a cigarette, and threw one over: 'It's a long time to be slogging around in this.'

'We'll be relieved in a few days,' Odgeson guessed. 'Somebody else will take over.'

'Not that I couldn't go on for weeks. It's funny the way I feel in two minds about it.' Like everything, he added to himself.

'I suppose we all do,' Odgeson said. Their cigarettes glowed in the darkness, red flies helicoptering on the warm buoyancy of their thoughts. Odgeson fell asleep but Brian smoked half a tin of cigarettes before it got light.

At six Knotman came through on the radio: the two parties would descend and make contact with the jeeps in a couple of hours. Another jungle-rescue unit had been flown up from Singapore and would join the search. Odgeson acknowledged and they set off.

After a sweet breakfast of canned milk, and the sun's warm penetration to his rheumatic bones, Brian felt renewed. Yet in the first hour he was plunged to the senile age of ninety. He felt weak and nondescript, was already fed up with the zigzag futility of the trip. Scabs were forming in his armpits, sore from the sweat of continual movement, and now the same mechanical ascendancy over the chafing pain had to be won as over the blisters on his feet the previous day. The six days on Gunong Barat seemed by comparison an easy-going romp in which he had held out fine against the rigours of jungle travel, even though he'd lugged twice the weight on his donkey-back. 'I can't see why they didn't hold us in the village until the planes had spotted something,' he called out at the first rest, as if to make it a subject of general discussion.

'It isn't always easy to see things in the jungle, as you know,' Odgeson answered, 'even from the air. In any case I imagine the CO knows what he's doing. We don't have all his headaches do we?'

'I suppose the CO and his pals couldn't wait to start moving pins about on the maps,' Brian said.

Cheshire stood up with mock pride: 'It's the first time I've been a pin on a map.'

'I don't suppose it'll be the last time,' Baker retorted. 'You're a regular, aren't you, you poor sod?' – which brought no answer.

'It'll be the last time for me though,' Brian affirmed.

'You can never be sure about that,' Odgeson said in a tone of resentment, as if they were blaming him for their hardship.

'I can.' Brian felt a sudden hatred of Odgeson who, he realized, would never forget whose side he was on.

'That remains to be seen, Seaton.'

'It don't.' Blind obstinacy brought the words out, as well as the conviction that what he said would come to pass. Even no backing from Baker or Cheshire could not weaken his words: I'm on my own, he thought, and don't need help from anyone. 'We ain't been told to write ON ACTIVE SERVICE on our letters for nothing, and we ain't lugging rifles this time to fire at shadows or fireflies.'

Odgeson saw what was wrong. 'I'm not interested in discussing politics. All I want is to get these chaps out of that plane. In other words, while we're up here you'll do as I tell you to do.'

'All I said,' Brian said, 'was that this was the last time I'm going to be a pin on a bloody map. And I mean it. And nobody's going to stop me saying what I feel.'

'All right, so you've said it. But if you say it once more you'll be on a charge when we get back to camp. I don't care how near the boat you are.'

Brian was the last to move, looked through the trees over the three of them forming the bottom loop of a letter S – Odgeson leading. We argue and the slob throws his rank, but I've got something to throw at him in my hand: I could put a bullet into his sanctimonious mug and nobody would be much the wiser. I can't think of any better reason for carrying this lead-heavy rifle and fifty shells. You've got a mouth to speak with and good cause for opening it, and even when what you say's got nothing to do with tearing your guts out to find that aircrew, you still get told to wrap-up. You might as well be in the grave if you don't open your trap.

Baker had taken the lead, but everyone at the same time saw an enormous wound in a tree before them, bleached by some meteorscoop from the sky. The uppers of the tree were ripped down, flayed open and back like the rough parting on a doll's head long after Christmas. Brian's heart beat heavily, and a slice of steel was nicked into sudden glinting light by the sun. Their troubles seemed over. 'It's trying to send morse to us,' he thought. Under the dark shed of the trees the hillside flattened, became more varied instead of the common up or down, and they followed a ploughed lane of cracked twigs and creepers, snapped so that sap and juice still stained the white ends and were sticky to the touch. A shallow trench of iron-coloured upturned soil started and finished after a few yards, and embedded in a bank was the battered and clawed-at nacelle of an aircraft engine. It lay well into the clay, as if it had been shot dead before swallowing the hard bite of earth it had gone mad for and crashed down from the sky to get. They stood amazed and awed in spite of having expected eventually to find something like it, at seeing a piece of marvellous engineering planted in the middle of this primeval smell. 'Now where's the rest of it?' Odgeson wondered.

'Scattered all over the mountain,' Baker said. 'We'll have to sweat blood for every piece.' Brian was past caring: 'What can you do, O what can you do, but ride to your death on a kangaroo?'

'You're right: the bits that count can be miles away,' Odgeson said to Baker. They separated, split four ways like a signpost and agreed to meet at given whistle-signals.

Brian was alone and liked it, walked from the nacelle with a feeling of ease as if taking a stroll on a quiet afternoon. The landscape was different, humid and arduous still when he had to clamber up a bank, yet being beyond the sight and sound of the group was an immense relief. The jungle appeared less alien, and he felt that it was somehow tamed for him, that he was beginning to understand even the harmlessness and maybe necessity of it. Voluminous leafage moved back to his advance, and the underfoot smell had a richness of decay that no longer held a threat of fever, equal to fresh air since the wind was still and it took away his incentive to peer up through the tall trunks for a pinprick glimpse of the sky. Water dripped slowly down a rockface and, finding no stream bed, he churned the soil into a red mud that hung on to his boots like manacles – much as he'd sought to enjoy every street pool with his wellington boots as a small boy.

After a quick smoke he swung himself under and over creepers, going up another bank until, reaching leveller ground at the top, he saw someone staring from between parted leaves. It was a white face below short black hair, gaunt yet with the sort of calm experience and gentleness that became ferocious when roused for no plain reason. Brian also noticed that he wore a green shirt, before sliding to lower ground with the intention of taking cover by a tree. But the man was already leaping, a kris poised.

An overwhelming grenade of sick fear burst in his stomach, yet within this cloud he felt himself struggling free of his pack and shouting wildly, hoping the others weren't too far off, in a long high meant-to-be everlasting yell that carried little distance through the trees and undergrowth. His pack rolled, and while discarding he had considered the wisdom of hanging on to it; he only now knew this feeling to have been reasonable when he saw his rifle sliding away at the same time.

He reached level earth, fear and hysteria in every extremity of his limbs. Yet he felt himself existing in different zones of consciousness, waiting and watching his chance instead of backing away on the chance of escaping the deathly feel of the blade. The tree, soil, bushes and smell of the jungle, the dank fatigue-memory of the fruitless search, became locked in his senses. The man grunted (the daft bastard thinks we're going to hurt him. Why?) and the split-second in which the kris stayed poised was a long enough time in the soundless trees to make him pleasantly surprised at taking in so much detail – a lightning speed of animal assessment extracted from his unwritten nightmare journal of afterwards.

The wavy blade of the kris was rusty, as if it had been left uncovered in jungle rain, though it was grey near the edge to show it had lately been sharpened. I'm finished, he thought – a short message flashed by the enemy part of himself – I'm going to be killed. He shouted out in terror, catching the man's emotion who breathed heavily and grunted as he struck. His hands went out, as if the fires of survival had set themselves alight in his brain.

Both sprang together: his arms sped with uncanny precision towards the blade – an old ruse of unarmed combat taught him by Arthur Eddison at the cardboard-factory years ago. He fastened both wrist and elbow of the wiry arm gripping the kris, and pressed them with all strength away and backwards. Terrified that the trick had worked, the sweat of control poured from him and he fought as much to keep up his determination to carry it through as to vanquish the actual danger.

He fixed his eyes on what was visible of the blade, that stayed so long in place that he had a desire to laugh at the possibility of it being glued there, resisting this weakness because it would rob him of strength. The man grunted and kicked, swayed the trapped arm and struck out with the one still free, but Brian ignored the smashing of his ankles, and the kris didn't stay long enough in place for the man to think of trying to reach it by the blade-end. The more Brian ground his teeth and pressed, the easier it became to make his attacker drop the kris. It seemed a stupid task, as if the man's arm would break, because all the brute force of his labouring days was behind the pressure and he knew that no one could stand it for long. He wanted to laugh and let the arm go, tell the man to blow town and not be so bleeding daft. The kris slid into the leaves and he pushed the man back, rammed like lightning with his fist and boot, then drew away. His fear returned now and, gasping and stumbling against his pack and rifle, he watched the man free himself from the bush and search among the undergrowth.

Brian picked up the rifle: he's a nutcase and might try something else, but if he does I'll bash him over the skull with this. I'll plaster his loaf all over the trees. Why did he want to come for me like that? He drew back the bolt, slotted it in, a mechanical noise whose significance he only realized as its clear echo died away, retrieving a picture of a dog by his DF hut lying like a length of rag and floorcloth with a hole in its head. The Chinese dropped the kris, stayed a dozen yards off with lifted hands, close enough for Brian to see the left side of his lips twitching on an otherwise hard and resigned face. What's he put his hands up for? Why don't he get running? He drew back the catch to safety, unwilling to press the trigger by accident and be brought up for murder: that's a charge Odgeson wain't be able to put me on. The silence grew: Brian shifted his stance, cracked twigs.

'Get moving,' he said, half afraid the man might be crazy and make another rush. 'Piss off' – threatening to kill him should he refuse.

Words as if spoken by another person deep in his own mind told him he was a bandit, though Brian repressed the thought as being the safest thing for the man before him, and for himself. Maybe he doesn't understand English: 'Scoot, for – ' But the man lost his bewilderment and neutral face of capture, turned and leapt along the level of the jungle, scrambling away fast. Brian stood, still and frozen, then his hand shook, and he held the rifle between his legs while he leaned against a tree to light a cigarette. A plane droned overhead, but he was too shaken to look, could only stare at the soil and undergrowth. The war in Malaya and all he'd heard of it seemed to have no relevance in this forest foreclosed with darkness and humidity, and he told himself that maybe the man had a hut and garden near by and thought he was someone who had plundered it last week, so had been waiting in ambush for him to come back.

Weakened by legs that seemed turned to rubber, and a sensation of chaos and death – he sure wanted to kill me by the look on his mug – he made his way towards where he had parted from the others. Maybe the man had been a bandit, but Brian threw the idea away, then drew it back and hung on to it as though, should this be true, it might turn out to mark some saving of his sanity, to be the salvation of his soul in some unpredictable manner. In any case he wouldn't have been a bandit but a communist. There was a difference – that much he easily saw. The picture that crossed his mind was of a gloomy autumnal dinner-hour opposite the factory canteen a few years back during the War, a composite memorial of many dinner-hours spent in that way. A communist speaker stood talking about the Soviet Union bleeding to death in the good fight against the German nazis and Italian fascists, saying it was time Britain and America started that second front now, when a voice from the crowd heckled: 'Why aren't yo' in the army, mate?' But somebody capped the heckler with: 'Why aren't yo'?' – which stopped his gallop with even bigger laughs.

Brian leaned against a tree screaming with laughter, a mad humorous rage tearing itself out: 'And I let him go! Odgeson and all you bastards, I let him go because he was a comrade! I didn't kill him because he was a man.' The certain knowledge that he had been a bandit was a fist that made him lie down in the soil, curl up and go on laughing, separate from himself yet unable to look on, roaring at the outcome of his own safety no matter what the man had been. The bastard though, I should a pulled the rifle up to my shoulder and pinned him to the soil with a bullet like he would have done to me with his kris if I'd given him half the chance. He smoked a cigarette: I'd better get back and see if the others have found the plane. But if any clever bastard says to me: 'Why aren't yo' in the army?' I'll give him the biggest mouthful he's ever heard. He walked on, quiet in his tracking for fear that other bandits were about, and that if there was a next time he might not be so lucky. Stone-cold with horror, he suddenly recognized the nacelle where he had parted from the rest, an aluminium case holding a complex aero engine whose image vividly recalled the click of the safety-catch a few minutes before. He bounded up the bank, beyond the sinister machine-product towards where he hoped the others would be. Without forethought he fired off rounds into the treetops and sky, let fly half a dozen rapid shots at what ghosts and remnants of his conscripted mind the sight of the communist had let loose. He emptied the magazine, lobbing the rest more carefully at manufactured shadows between the trees, each round buried into some distant invisible soil or trunk after a heyday crack that seemed powerful enough to scare and weal the whole range of mountains. 'What did you do in the War, dad?' 'I caught a communist and let him go.' 'What did you do that for then?' 'Because he was a man.' And not everybody'll look at me gone-out, 'Brian, my lad, I'm proud o' you,' the old man would say.

Calmer now, though still bright-eyed (I feel like a paper lantern, all hollow and lit up) he made his way along the hillside. Odgeson, Baker and Cheshire walked a few paces in front, making so much noise they didn't hear him trailing them. 'Hey,' he shouted. 'Seen owt yet?'

They gathered into a group. 'We heard some shooting over there, so we're heading for it in case it's Knotman's mob.'

'It was me,' he said, lighting a cigarette. 'A bloke came for me, a bandit I suppose, because he bolted when he saw I'd got a rifle. I didn't hit him though.'

'It sounded like a machine-gun,' Cheshire said. 'You must a been cross-eyed not to bring him down.'

Odgeson looked serious: 'We'd better stay close and watch out. There aren't enough stretchers for all of us.'

'Knotman shouldn't be too far away, with the army,' Baker called from behind. 'Shall I get them on the blower?'

Odgeson thought not. 'They won't be listening anyway, so let's get moving and not have so many questions.'

'He's coming out of his shell on this trip,' Brian said to Baker as they trekked on. 'These pally bastards allus turn out to be the worst.'

Baker was close behind and replied: 'My old man says that in the Great War they used to shoot about ten officers a month. The Germans got the rest of them.'

'It didn't mek much difference,' Brian said. 'They kept scraping 'em up from somewhere.'

'The reason the War ended though was because they were running out of officers, not because they didn't have enough bods like us. I've been to a public school, Brian, but I'm just a slave like you are.'

'Belt up,' Brian said.

'That's no argument.'

'It's an answer though. I might be a slave this minute but I'm going to stop being one soon.'

'Only because they're letting you go.'

'That ain't what I mean. I don't care if it takes five years: I'm going to stop being a slave.'

'Close up,' Odgeson shouted back. 'Here's some more of the plane.'

'It's like a jig-saw puzzle,' Cheshire said. 'Three-and-six from Woolworths.'

'You'll never stop being a slave to something,' Baker said.

A tail elevator of shining aluminium lay in their path like a gate barring their way to an abundant and well-cultivated smallholding. They stepped over it one by one, as if afraid to damage it and have to pay the farmer for its repair: Baker had the sense to kick it flat. Brian took the radio from him: 'I didn't try and hit that bandit I saw back there. I fired plenty, but hoped I wouldn't get him.'

'I wouldn't be able to stop myself,' Baker replied, not believing. A clearing had been brewed out of the jungle by the main wreck of the plane: it had come to rest against the far end of a plateau, a cigar-shaped fuselage, a priceless accomplishment hanging dead and derelict half-way down between the trees, pieces of wing and wood and glittering fabric scattered all around. It was inaccessible without ropes, ten or fifteen feet up, looking like the victim of an unsuccessful attempt to decorate a Christmas tree. They stood fifty yards off, speechless after having searched for what seemed like weeks. The fuselage was scattered with rips along its frame where branches had impeded its clumsy uncalled-for descent, some foliage seeming to grow out of the plane itself as if it had been there far longer than forty hours. There was no movement, noise, or cries of life from it. On the underbelly by the pilot's cabin, as though some great hand had given it a nosebleeder, was a broad crimson mark, dried and hardly noticeable in the first look. 'O Christ,' Brian said, unloading the radio.

'What a way to die.' Baker slung down his pack.

'Poor bastards,' said Cheshire. My stomach's hard, but my heart's as sick as a dog's – Brian felt, while Odgeson blew his guts out on the jungle-rescue whistle, hoping to reach Knotman and the army. Its dull throat-notes filled the air, low and warbling, the sort of alarm-noise that during the War sent Colin and Dave scurrying from their fireside cups of tea into the backyard and cold November streets to avoid the coppers they imagined after them. When Odgeson had no breath left he asked Brian to have a go.

It was accepted, and he flexed his lungs so that both God and the Devil would hear, only to be startled by the solid lead-heavy crack of what seemed a tree bough, as though the plane had weighed sufficiently and long enough to snap one down. Baker ducked, as if, Brian thought, the whistle unblown between his lips, the bough was right above their heads and threatening to fall. Another sharp crack revealed this and the first as rifle shots – now they were all down, pressed into the undergrowth as, from the direction of the plane, in the thick bush under its stranded body, leapt a wide-toothed saw of bullets, flying close around, burning into tree bark or burying their noses into soft clammy soil. It wasn't difficult to find cover: Brian moved back, dragging the wireless-set to shield his face towards a length of tree trunk that kept his guts secure, though he felt his feet exposed at the mixture of twigs, leaves and random bullets scattering about them like the butt-end of a typhoon thunderstorm. The incredible noise numbed him with a feeling of helplessness, as if the bullets came from such an army that it was no use fighting back, like an uneven rattling against the palings of hell that left only the impulse to press hands to each ear. 'It's the army,' Cheshire said. 'The bastards think we're bandits. Hey!' he shouted. 'It's us. Nark it, for Christ's sake!'

Odgeson and Baker were sending bullets across the clearing

in the general line of fire, though this was difficult to pin down, for after the first rush it seemed more scattered and spasmodic. 'The army can't be that far off,' Odgeson yelled. 'They're bound to hear this racket.'

Brian pressed a clip into his magazine, raised himself to line foresight and backsight through the undergrowth, settled for a hefty yard-wide monster of a tree and let fly – harmlessly. I'd better hold back, he thought. The others'll have nowt left in a bit. Fear and sickness grew into him and he lowered his head, an image flashed from his first life of when he had been in gangfights, each manoeuvring warrior-band hurling showers of stones and bottletops through the blue sky above tips or field. Though every missile was dangerous and shunned as if it carried death he had stayed fixed on the ground to be held with the rest of them, whether or not he had been frightened of injury at that particular hour.

In such danger he lived on two levels, one of fear, and one of not taking the fear seriously so that the situation seemed a harmless though perhaps foolish kind of game. He looked up, lifted his rifle to fire but could see no one, peered a while at the thick enclosing foliage in the half-darkness of the jungle. There were neither faces nor movement around the wrecked plane, though bullets still came at an uneven rate from it. In a one-second reflection Brian reasoned that maybe the bandits had difficulty in seeing them as well, though as if to call him liar and point out that this was no game, a bullet went too close to Odgeson's elbow as he was lifting for a cool aim. He swore with shock and the rifle jumped from his hands as if a charge of electricity had gone through it, wounding him so that all he could do, and did, was get the whistle up to his mouth and use what extra strength had been given his lungs due to the incapacitated arm – blowing so that the noise rose even above a renewed burst of firing.

Brian did not want to lift his head and be killed, but when he forgot for a few seconds that to be killed was possible he drew the butt into his shoulder and failed to see anything worth aiming at. Maybe the bastard that got away from me is busy letting us have it from over there: though when he did press out a trio on rapid he had no desire to kill or wound because the sense that they were caught in some kind of game was still with him. They want to kill us though, he thought with bitterness, firing into the bushes so that for once at least he had as much chance as Cheshire of stopping someone's gallop for good. Bullets came back. They're rich in ammunition, he surmised, as they smacked into the iron trees or came fizzing so uncomfortably close that the dam of fear broke and pushed his face into the now sweet-smelling soil.

Baker had finished his ammo and was rifling Odgeson's pack for more clips. The noise, according to each bullet's often accidental trajectory, varied from the snap of giant dead branches to the hollow receding echo singing on a last journey down the mountainside, from the savage and vicious clout against a tree to the dull burial in a pillow of soil; and amid all this was the low moan of Odgeson's whistle signalling for help. Brian filled in the gaps of their firing, making his own noise for survival though he knew that his bullets were having no effect, and hoped that no one would notice that they weren't.

He laughed, a shattering loud cry that the others were too busy to bother about: I'm making a present for Mimi, he thought. A good-bye gift in not shooting to kill maybe someone who, for all I know, is the old boy-friend she had at high school in Singapore. He lay on the damp earth of the forest, some yards from a rampart of covering tree trunk, reloading with fresh clips dragged out of his pack. His refusal to get caught up in trying to kill the communists (who were clearly wanting to slaughter them for a rich haul in rifles and wireless gear) held him from the advantages of rage and excitement that might have given him the semblance of courage. As it was the level of fear stayed with him, burning his face and eyes and causing his guts to creak like the timbers of an old battleship.

When the other two blazed away he bent his head down, coughing and choking into wet leaves, bringing up phlegm and hurling it from his bone-dry throat, having recalled for him his father's mad roar that: 'God? God is a bastard. Bastard God' – though the words did nothing to ease his fear and he pushed them out of his mind to lift himself and take aim once more, at nothing. If they charge, he realized, they'll finish us off. They know there's only four of us, so why are they messing about? If they show themselves in a charge I'll wing a few and no mistake, though that wain't do any good to why I'm lying here – which is not to fire at my pals. He laughed, and Cheshire stared at him, a brief glance of incredulity before returning to his skilful defence.

The surprise marked on the coin of his face sent a memory back to Brian as he too simulated an angry few rounds rapid, a memory of some chargehand from the Raleigh recounting how his father had behaved with bravery and foolhardiness during the War (that's a laugh: what's all this pot-shotting if it ain't a war?) one blacked-out midnight when a German bomber had machine-gunned the factory. Harold Seaton had stood in the main wide road of the works looking into the sky and cursing as the Jerry plane let rip on its second time round, while his pals from the sheltering doorways yelled for him to come in and not to be a bleddy fool. But Harold had stayed there working while the bullets sped like the patter of tiny clogged feet running for their lives around and by him, the first and last time he had shown a remarkable calmness in a situation in which it would have been natural and useful to have scattered in four directions – whereas a misplaced word from someone at home would have sent him into a black and uncontrolled fury. Still, he'd got guts, Brian remembered, so maybe some of 'em have been passed on to me here, and I'll use 'em not to fire at the bandit-communists in spite of the fact that in one way my fingers are itching to.

Baker seemed cool enough, knew himself to be calm, what's more, and enjoyed knowing it, firing as accurately as he was able and not bothering about the risk. He'll get the VC, the daft bastard, though Brian saw as well that Baker's lips were turned down in anger as he took aim and fired, though in anger at who or what Brian refused to imagine. He listened now and again for answering signals from Knotman or the army, but heard nothing: a dim surging whistle in the distance turned out to be an echo of Odgeson's still strong blasts. He caught himself laughing at the idea of them making a charge towards the wreckage – the bravest and most desperate military operation he could imagine. The end of it struck him like a cheap picture in a chewing-gum packet for future generations of children, number one in the series before real-life depictions came through: Odgeson or any officer-commanding leading them to the razor's edge point of success, then turning round and panic-roaring to them in the thick of it: 'Run for your lives! Every man for himself!'

Brian's head was low, feeling for another clip. There were four or five still left and, sliding the bolt in, he saw a large red ant – head, body and feelers out on a private patrol of its own – walk cautiously from a leaf on to his hand. It stopped to smell and reconnoitre this new earth of hairs and skin, took a few more paces into the unmapped interior until the grimy nail of Brian's finger flicked it back on to more familiar earth. 'Get to where it's safe, you ginger-haired bastard.'

Another whistle sounded through the trees, away to the left, and the noise against them seemed to relax because of it, though both Cheshire and Baker fired rapidly into some movement now discernible beneath the plane, and Odgeson never stopped blasting his whistle. He was pale, wearing a look of deathlike exhaustion as if about to keel over. 'They're beating it,' Brian called to him. 'The others must be close.' He aimed at the trees, at nothing, an erratic blade of fire to help with the impression of patriotic or devoted noise that still covered the hillside like a sliding roof. 'If you've got any more slugs left,' Cheshire called, 'I'll 'ave 'em. My bleeders are about finished.'

'I want 'em for mysen,' Brian said. 'Keep your nut down: they're still here.'

'I suppose them army crumbs are going to spoil all this for us.' There was a sudden silence, as if the bandits had abandoned the wreckage. Then another burst came to prove that some remained: the loony bastards'll get killed if they don't scram quick. 'I'll be glad when I'm out of this lot,' he called to Baker, lifting himself to fire high into the trees.

'Don't waste them,' Baker said. 'They haven't gone yet: I can see one moving.'

'I'm not.' Their firing was filled and renewed by the first of the army, seasoned and competent in jungle-green as they came through the trees, cautiously blazing away. Brian laughed: 'We'll be back in camp today, after we've cleared this lot up,' he called to Baker. 'I'll be glad an' all.'

'Me too,' Baker said. 'I wish I was . . .' He exposed himself too soon, and an explosion switched his face around, as though an insect had flown into his eye and taken him by surprise with its powerful sting. He lifted one hand to coax it out, then fell back, revealing that he had no face left.

Down through the jungle and wearied to death Brian thought back to nearly two years ago when Baker had been alive on the troopship leaving England, and Brian had stood alone by the rail, watching the dockside with its huge sheds and Martian spatula-footed cranes get farther away as the water of mid-stream eddied and churned around them. Tugs heaved it clear and clouds of gulls squealed in fancy flight at the prospect of swill and scraps, and a group of soldiers down the rail were trying to hit them with sharp crossbow bolts of white spit. Brian smiled at their near misses, wondering whether his aim would be any better, but not bothering to try because there were other things to look at. Bilious clouds were stacked over the Isle of Wight, as stationary and important as if they were part of an urgent stockpile waiting to be transported to some mythical D-Day beach. Before them on the blue water was a derrick-laden top-heavy American ship, and Brian took his hat off to stop the sudden wind flinging it over the side as a titbit for the gulls. Water foamed into salt-white patches below the stern and at the gentle rocking of the ship he hoped he wouldn't heave his guts up at the open sea – his first time out on any ocean – recalling how as sick as a dog he'd been the whole twenty-seven miles to Worksop where he was evacuated in 1939, leaving his pale-faced bile between Newstead and the Trent, between pit-scars of the Derbyshire hills and the stately halls of the Dukeries. They drifted by the *Queen Mary*, left it behind and came towards the green banks of the Isle of Wight, a turreted manor showing itself between the trees. Up Southampton Water, sheds and cranes packed the blue skyline of the quays, ships of all sorts scattered over the blue water, some with funnels smoking thinly like a tailor-made, others in a full steam of thick twist. Marvellous, I'm glad to be leavng England even though the old man did say I was a bloody fool and wanted my brains testing for not getting out of it, and even though Pauline might never forgive me if she thought I'd had a chance of not getting sent over on compassionate grounds. Not that I'm sure I could have got out of it anyway; though if I get broken-hearted to be going, I hope it won't be till I'm a thousand miles away and can't swim back. He winced at a thump on his shoulder and, trying not to turn at it said: 'I can tell that's you, Baker, you bastard.' But he did turn, and Baker leaned towards him like the Tower of Pisa, standing on tiptoe to make himself six inches taller instead of three. 'Are you glad to be off?' he asked, coming to his normal height. 'You bet,' Brian said. 'I've allus wanted to do a bunk from England and see other countries. For as long as I can remember.' Excited gangs stood all over the ship, pointing out the sights. 'They're glad anyway,' Baker said. He squinted at Brian through his rimless glasses: 'It's my first time as well. The old man's been promising me a holiday in Switzerland since the end of the War, but it hasn't turned up so far.' They watched a Beaufighter take a running torpedo-drop at target boards in the Solent, its underbelly roaring across flattened greenish water. 'I write to a girl in Switzerland, so I'd like to go there for sentimental reasons,' Baker said. 'I'd never get sentimental about a country,' Brian scoffed. 'In some ways I wouldn't care if I never saw this joint again.' The ship swung slowly east and along Spithead towards Portsmouth. A surfaced submarine passed, then a destroyer, each dipping their flags. 'I thought you were married though,' Baker said. 'That's hard luck. All I'm leaving behind is my motor-bike.' Brian lit a cigarette, flipped the dead match into a drain at his feet. The moving tide slapped against the ship. Someone farther along pointed out the warships *Ramillies* and *Malaya* at Portsmouth, and the coastal forts built against Napoleon. 'That word "Malaya" seems familiar,' Baker laughed. 'Or will soon, I expect,' Brian said, looking up from the hypnotic rush of sea passing the ship's waterline. Baker observed with calm superciliousness the coast going by:

'England
This syphilitic isle
This seat of majesty
This lump of excrement.'

'As long as you don't include Nottingham in that,' Brian said. 'You haughty bastard.'

'Patriotism,' Baker sneered.

'If you think I'm patriotic,' Brian said, 'you've got another thought coming. I'm hungry. Let's go down and see if we can't snatch summat to eat.'

28

His mother had written to let Brian know that Merton's collection of prize horseshoes was to be divided among the family, and that she had put one by for when he came back. 'You can nail it up on your door as soon as you and Pauline get a council house,' she added. The horseshoe again set him thinking of the picture in his grandmother's parlour, of the girl holding a bunch of flowers and saying to the youth by her side: 'If you love me as I love you, Nothing can ever part us two' – which, pleasurably brooding on his living with Pauline, was how he felt about her. On the last day of his embarkation leave they had walked beyond Strelley Church, lingered between Cossal and Kimberley wherein one part of the earth had been ripped open, and the humps and hollows they had often made love in while courting were scraped to the grey bones of a lunar landscape. To the left of undiscovered coal was a grey-pencilled wood surrounded by black upturned soil and, scattered beyond, a patrol of trees silhouetted their branches like half-opened fans. From behind came the thud of engines and the sigh of slave-driven cranes, while at their feet were dark upended rows of rich loam, heavy and wet yet light on some crests where it had dried in the wind, miniature mountain-ranges still flecked with snow, a whiteness reminding him, in the clear cool air, of the milk of babies – and the fact that they had to walk back home so that Pauline could feed Bernard.

He shivered to think of it, and as the last notes of an unnecessary message from Saigon died away he thought of the death of his grandfather. He heard about it from his mother and aunts, how Merton one morning took a stick and walked past the Cherry Orchard to see whether there was still anything left of the wheatfield and Serpent's Wood. It was an uncertain spring, clouds hurriedly dividing the empire of the sky after a fine start to the morning, a biting wind worrying grass and hedge leaves already clumsy with rain that had pelted down in the night. The hollow tree in which Brian had often played now lay across a ditch with branches scattered around, to be collected as firewood by kids from near-by pre-fabs. The navvies had been laid off because of bad weather, and the trackway of a projected road was deserted, odd planks to one side see-sawed over cement bags, heaps of rammel pointing to grey sky. Even in such weather it was good to walk and smell fresh wind that had come over the fields from Trowel and Bramcote – though these deserted trenches and half-built houses made the land look like a battlefield up for GOC's inspection: a wilderness. By the wood a fine rain began spitting on the leaves, so with a snort of contempt he turned back, walking along puddle-holed footpaths as fresh gusts rammed the bare trees, easing up only to let down heavier drops of rain. 'Didn't expect this bleddy lot,' he muttered, stooping as he walked, coat collar pulled-up, though his shoulders and legs were already wet.

He stamped into the house, was enveloped in a comforting and familiar smell of steam pudding and sausages bursting their skins in the oven pan. 'Where yer bin?' Mary cried, seeing his hair and face soaked. 'You'll get yer death o'code, going out in such weather.' She poked at the coalfire: 'Come on, get out o'them trousers and 'ave a warm.'

He hung his jacket by the door and loosened his braces: 'Don't bloody-well fuss. I only went to see the new road they're pushing through. I wun't a gone if I'd a known it'd a pissed like this.' He stripped to his vest and rubbed head and arms vigorously. 'I'll get yer a cup o'tea wi' a drop o'whisky in it,' she said. 'That'll set you up, if I know yer.'

After dinner he went to bed and slept till tea-time; but came down feeling heavy and still anchored to an unfamiliar exhaustion.

'Gorrout tasty?' he asked from the fire, sneezing into his great spotted handkerchief. He ate chicken legs and broth, but stayed listless well into the evening.

'I don't know,' she said. 'You shun't a gone out in that rain.' Lydia was home for tea: 'Let me get you some Aspros, dad. It wain't tek a minute, from Warrener's.'

'Shut your rattle,' he said to them, and trod his way slowly up the creaking stairs to bed.

'He's a nasty-tempered owd bogger,' Lydia said. 'I don't think anybody in this house has ever had a civil word from him.'

'And no more you bleddy-well will either,' Merton said, suddenly back for his boots. 'If yer've got owt to say you want to tell it to my face.' He stood tall and erect by the mantelshelf, his face swarthy and well lined, his head a bristle of white hairs. 'People are only trying to be good to you,' Lydia spoke out, knowing herself to be in the right.

'I'll bring you a drink up soon,' Mary said, 'and some Aspros.'

'Ah, all right then,' he said, and went up. Sleep didn't come easily. He tossed and sweated and grumbled all night and in the morning, when he couldn't get out of bed, felt angry and ashamed, unable to remember when he had last been pinned there by illness. Years ago as a girl Vera remembered him sleeping awkwardly on two chairs before the fire when he was ill, so uncomfortable that the minute he was able to get up he would do so, stagger out to feed the pigs or get in some coal, breaking himself back into life. Illness was cowardice and weakness, and no man ever let it drive him to bed if he had any guts about him. But here he was gutless and without strength, and grieving that everyone witnessed it. When Mary said she thought he should have a doctor his answer was: 'What do *I* want a bleddy doctor for?'

'Because you aren't well. You know you're not.'

He leaned up: 'If you bring a doctor up them stairs I'll chuck 'im out o'that winder if it takes all my strength.' George came back from work at the cycle factory: 'What's all this then, dad: Don't you think it's about time you got better?' Merton thought so. 'We'll get a doctor to you then,' George said. 'Do as you blooddy-well like,' Merton grunted, pulled back into sleep.

The doctor said they shouldn't have waited so long. Merton

had a severe chill. 'Get that stuff from the chemist and see he takes it. I'll call in tomorrow.'

The weather kept damp and cold, and despite a banked-up pit-fire in the bedroom, Merton stayed down. When Mary came in with bottles of medicine he mustered strength to throw them one by one out of the window; they landed on the kennel and caused the contemporary Gyp to rattle into the open and prepare to sell itself dearly. 'That's nowt but bottled piss,' he said to the empty room. He fell to the floor, and only with tremendous effort reached the bed.

The cold deepened and gripped him in the vice of double pneumonia. The house was silent for a week, and they began to wonder whether he'd get over it – asking the question of themselves at first, but not to each other. George and Lydia, at any rate, remembered the hard times he had given them, the peremptory flames of his volatile temper. Yet talking to each other late one night they had to admit that they had at times been boggers and deserved it – though their wondering whether or not he would get better was still less interested than Mary's. In turn they sat with him and talked, told him what news or gossip came from town or factory or coalmine, reassured him that the chickens and garden were being well looked after. Everyone met by George and Lydia on the street – round the district and even in Nottingham – asked about Merton with great concern and weren't slow in saying what a good bloke he was and how he'd worked all his life for the good of his family and how much of a crying shame it'd be if owt 'appened to such a fine outstanding chap. Well, Lydia said to herself, in one way nobody can deny all that. 'But he'll be all right, ma,' she cried. 'He's as strong as nails.'

'But he's a good age, you know.'

He couldn't listen long to their talk. Something inside stoked up the fires of his coughing, weakened him so that he lay back stiffly in sleep after a dose of medicine he no longer had strength to sling away. Mary exhausted herself caring for him, wept downstairs in the kitchen while the others were at work and wondered however he could possibly get better from such a black and wicked cough. The rotten weather had worn them all out, frozen their guts on short rations and the wet cold misery of snow and ice. Now the weather had broken, and brought this.

The doctor said it was touch and go. But this winter had killed thousands and would kill more, though it was having a hard job with Merton. He slept easier one day, and Mary thanked God he was getting better. 'He's peaceful,' she said to George and Lydia when they came home for tea. 'He'll be all right, mother,' George said. Lydia went out later to the pictures. Mary dozed by the fire, her face wrinkled and tired, her white hair falling down. George sat at the table playing patience, a sheet of uncompleted football coupons held down by a bottle of ink and a wooden-handled pen.

In the pitch dark bedroom Merton slept, moaning when a spark shot off the tight ball of his lived life and wheeled towards his eyes, spinning away and buried in a universe of impenetrable blackness that in some ways he wanted to enter but didn't because he knew he'd never come out of it. Then there was a light growing ahead that he tried to reach, something desirable that he sensed he could live within – though not in his lifetime. The pain seemed intent on forcing him to some course of action, but at the same time made him so weak and wish for such complete and everlasting sleep that he couldn't take any. The light he saw was hardly a light, more a speck of lighter darkness which wasn't so dark as the other mass of atmosphere. In spite of the prison he was locked in he reached up to his eyes and felt tears, and knew what they were. He thought of Mary down in the kitchen: 'How are you feeling?' she had asked. 'A lot better,' he had told her. He thought of Oliver who had been killed in the war, sensed that he might be about to go, and suddenly the spark of light expanded and blinded him when he fell into it. Maybe I was on his mind as well, Brian thought, as he stopped to take down a call-sign from Singapore.

He rode in a tri-shaw almost the whole way to the widow's house, walking the last hundred yards silently through the bushes and climbing into Mimi's room like a bandit. She took a few days off from the Boston Lights on the excuse of a cold, and they lay in bed smoking and talking the dark hours away, drinking the bottle of whisky he usually managed to bring in his back pocket. The many hours were sweet, yet when he wasn't there he wanted them to end and reach the day when with kit packed he could feel the slow train move under him on the first mile to Singapore. He wanted to rush away, because he felt ill. It was nothing he could say was eating any particular part of his body, but a slow omnivorous corrosion attacking equally his physical and mental self, so that if the lingering leave-taking of Malaya lasted many more weeks he would walk to the door of the sick quarters and say, 'For Christ's sake, I'm whacked and finished and can't stand up any more.' Nothing serious, he laughed, watching the dawn soak itself over the palm tops from the door of his DF hut – only hypochondria or whatever it's called, or maybe just plain sickness of the sort that this pox-etten country is drenched with. As soon as that boat gets into the Mediterranean Sea I'll feel fine, quick-minded and strong again like I've always been.

Malaya was a battlefield whose values had no part of reality, wasn't life to him any more, and he had to get away by taking a slow boat to England. He hoped the communists would get Malaya, though he had no more wish to help them at the moment than he had to fight them, having dreamed the bad dream that maybe the same one who had escaped him on the mountain had later circuited back to the acid drop of an aeroplane and taken the fatal potshot at Baker. If anybody was to blame though, it was, as far as he could see, the government who had seen to it that they were dragged up and bundled like unthinking sackbags to do guard-duty in worn-out parts of the British Empire. Maybe the government's fed up and weary and don't know what it's doing. He could believe that anyway, having long hours to ponder on such things during empty and interminable nightwatches. But the communists aren't weary and that's a fact, never will be either because they've got an up-and-coming vision that our side can never have any more. They used to spout outside the factory – and still do, according to Pauline's letters – which is more than the conservatives dare do, because a lot of the communists are working-men like ourselves and know what's what. They'd got the kitty right enough – the whole works of his brain and heart spinning – bells, lemons, keys – back and forth like jackpots on a fruit machine. I didn't much know what I was doing when I let that bloke go, though I'm glad I did what I did, no matter what happened. Only underneath my mind did I really know what I was doing, but that was enough and good and marvellous, because when things occur like that, it must be what I'd do anyway if I had the brains to calculate things properly like sums.

Out of the confusion of his brain grew the tangible and valid fact that between now and England he would have the human warmth of Mimi to help him stay sane and solid. It would end soon and they knew it, so saw each other as often as possible. He went quickly through the trees to the widow's house (BEYOND THIS POINT OUT OF BOUNDS TO ALLIED FORCES) even when the widow was there, silently making his blindfold way up the veranda and along to the unlocked window behind which Mimi waited. They lay naked together in bed, Mimi with her long-black hair down and her warm well-appointed breasts flattening against him, whispering softly, and both, even in the bliss of love, making no more noise than could be covered by night sounds of Malaya from the bushes and trees outside.

Often they were conscious of having dead time on their hands, lying in bed in the half-darkness, talking softly because the widow was in her room not far off, and because there was little to say since time was shortening before that big three-funnelled flag-bedecked boat rolled into the straits and narrows of Singapore and he tottered up its gangplank loaded to his forehead.

I wish I'd realized what I was doing when I let that bloke go. I'd still have made him scoot; but if only I'd done it cold and intentionally. He felt as if he'd been tricked and laughed at, not knowing how the trick worked or when it began to work or what had caused it to begin ticking away inside him. He had an idea though that it all began before he was born, certainly at a time when he was powerless to know or do anything about it. But he couldn't come to any conclusion, maybe not wanting to, because it might tell him that after all he could blame no one for the trick that had been played on him except himself.

They heard the widow walking about her house, then silence. 'She'll start sewing now,' Mimi whispered, turning her warm body towards him. 'You'll hear the machine. It'll go on for hours, I think.'

'It's funny,' he said, 'me not having seen the old woman. She's been our guardian angel in one way.'

'She has.'

'What's she like? You never say anything about her.'

'There isn't much I can tell. I think she knows you come to stay with me now, but she doesn't mention anything. We've never talked about you, but I just know she knows. Anyway we won't speak much. Sometimes I give her American dollar-bills so that she can exchange them for me into Malayan money, and she doesn't give me as good a rate as the black-market. Still, it doesn't matter. She is kind, and often she gives me rice or soup, sometimes tea when I come in late and she is still sewing or reading. When I can't pay my rent, she doesn't bother me.'

'Sounds a good woman.'

'She's generous, but very careful with her money. I saw her shopping once at the market, and when she buys eggs she takes a bowl, fills it at the market tap, and tests the eggs in front of the stall-holder's eyes. They don't altogether like her, but she gets good eggs. Another thing, she goes shopping with her abacus frame and says: "I want that, how much is it?" Tack-tack go her beads. "And how much is this?" Tack-tack-tack. "And that?" Tack-tack. "Well," she says, tack-tack-tack-tack, "that will be so much, won't it?" "Yes," he says, knowing that he can't even put on an extra cent.'

Brian reached out and lit cigarettes for them: 'Is she happy, or what?'

'I think so. Why shouldn't she be? She shares in a rubber-estate, among other things.' Smoke blew across his face. 'She has relatives in Pulau Timur.'

'Why does she live alone though? Chinese grandmothers usually live with their families, don't they?'

'She wants to live alone. I don't know why.'

'She's got you in the house.'

'We don't see each other much.'

'Not to mention me,' he laughed. 'I wonder if she'll be lonely when I've gone? To tell you the truth I used to make up stories as to what she was. I imagined she was some sort of communist agent or other, getting information, or recruiting people for the cause, a sort of commissar for north Malaya, wreaking havoc among the British occupying-power.'

She laughed. 'How silly you are!'

'Well, you've got to have something to do at the DF hut, or you go off your head waiting for the boat to roll on.' The brief and hidden mention of his departure struck them both into a momentary silence. 'Mimi,' he said, 'just before we got caught in that ambush up in the mountains I captured a bandit, a Chinese.' The story came out, as he'd known it would before he left her. 'I let him go,' he said, 'because I couldn't kill him. And later in the ambush I didn't aim for anything. I fired where nothing could be hurt. It took some doing, but I held back. I did it.' He talked on, and she listened with such interest that neither approval nor disapproval was written on her face. She sat on the bed, a cigarette smouldering from her hand.

'Why?' she said at the end of it. 'Why?'

He was angry that she hadn't understood. 'Because that's how I wanted it to be,' he said. 'I just thought I'd tell you, that's all. Don't you get it?'

The last fortnight dragged its slow length along like a chain-and-ball ankle crossing a wide high gorge by a six-inch bridge – with Brian all of a sweat that it might never get him to the other side. The camp lapsed into its state of sordid demoralized siege, and he was always glad to escape from it. Barbed-wire was rolled out along the boundaries, sandbags filled and erected at vulnerable places, extra guards mounted until it seemed that only half the camp slept in the night. There was even talk that the privileged members of the Signals section were to be drummed into filling sandbags. The final indignity, many said, conscription within conscription – unable to believe it could happen.

And so Merton had died, and he remembered it again, how

he had taken to the earth with so little resentment after nearly four-score years of staying in life like a fire that matched the glowing coals of his forge. His wife went six months later, drifted off into an afternoon sleep and never woke up. By which time Brian was already in Malaya, in distance even beyond their wildest dreams of Abyssinia, the limits of the fantastic world they had laughingly taunted him with on those far-off rainy evenings as a kid. When he read *Kubla Khan* or the *Blessed Damozel* and other anthological bits and pieces in the bottom-nightwatch of the DF hut, the mood cast over him equalled that tranquil dream recalled from a long way back, the mirrored image of a winter's childhood when, one peaceful afternoon, he sat looking out of the window at another fire reflected, as if it were held up by some beneficent god for him to see as proof that there were possibilities of comfort even beyond the warmth of his own house. What had fired off this barbed harpoon, sent it zigzagging back on a tenuous line of cord, may have been his night-long reading of the poems, but it was the first time he realized that he had a past, and had not evolved out of a dream. He could say: 'I remember that time walking across the Cherry Orchard ten years ago and meeting Alma Arlington,' ten years being no longer a meaningless massive chunk of time, but something that could be dissected and sorted out, and called a past. In a week he would be on that boat, going back in a way to join himself up with the past, and the idea of it was one alternately of fear and distaste, as well as one similar to the feeling that came over him when reading the poems. Neverthe-less little of the past was yet visible; and neither had he much vision of the future, but at least he knew that both existed. 'This time in Malaya is a big slice out of my life,' he said to Knotman over a table crowded with bottles in a Muong bar. 'Maybe it seems like that now,' Knotman argued, 'but I'm telling you, you'll look back on it in ten years and it'll seem like a dream that lasted a few days.' 'Well I can't imagine that,' Brian said. 'You will' – Knotman filled their glasses.'

Those from the Signals billet were rounded up with clerks, cooks, drivers and orderlies to fill sandbags. Brian had no confidence in what they were being made to fortify, believing that sooner or later, even if they built a stone wall ten yards high, the whole lot would crumble. But he worked hard and for a long time and, though not particularly tired, knew he was in a fever. Sometimes he spoke a word out loud to isolate the sound of his own voice, and once when he got an exact image of it, had to thrust it away for fear of running insanely towards the sea. Surrounded by many people, he felt entirely alone, worked within the clearly defined circle of his own actions. They had been on the go since seven, with only two breaks, and he dug at the sand mechanically, sometimes getting a light shovel that slewed against the embankment, at others finding the load so heavy that some had to be tipped off. His throat ached for a drink of water, a walk under shady trees to spend a few minutes away from filling sandbags. Those farther along the embankment had the worst of the job since they were in sight of the guardhouse and had to keep on working, unable to skive off for a drink now and again, as he had done. The sentries were monuments of perspiration. 'What did you say?' Kirkby demanded. 'Nothing,' Brian replied; 'I must have been thinking aloud.'

Down by the long huts a man walked out of the showerhouse, a white towel around his lobster body, slopping his feet along in wet sandals and whistling a Malay love-song popular on Radio Timur. It was an image of clarity, but when it vanished the aches came back into the bones of Brian's chest.

The whole thing won't last much longer, he thought, seeing, even more vividly than Baker's death, the vision of the aeroplane hanging dead between the trees like an enlarged piece of carcass in a butcher's shop. It was clearer in his eye than the face of the communist he had let loose and the ambush later, something he had dreamed around more than once, seeing the plane hanging between tall buildings – a dead whale blocking streets, and suspended also in Serpent Wood where he used to play in the past that was no longer an unrememberable dream, its broad fuselage tied between trees above the small brook he spent hours trying to dam and divert until, in the dream, the plane fell to the soil and caused him to wake up.

He felt better, his head no longer a battleground. Each spade of sand seemed lighter in weight, and he no longer pitied either the sentries or himself, but enjoyed the hard manual work because the feeling for it had come back into his bones after so long cloistered at the DF hut. Elated and happy, he paused in digging and looked around at the others, saw how much they had slowed down in their exhaustion. The sun didn't feel harsh to him, trees looked green and cool from a distance, as if even out in the space where he worked they sent some benefit of shade and hidden moisture.

Told to go, he walked off alone through the trees, towards the latrine for a drink and a swill, afterwards to the billet to pick up his eating irons for dinner. The latrine was near the beach and a Malay fisherman walked by with a long netpole on his shoulder, and over the two-mile water he saw a straggle of grey and black ships in Muong Harbour, and beyond that the colourful line of waterfront buildings looking, he thought, like a row of posh kids' toys on a window-sill. He stood by the barbed-wire, hunger and thirst momentarily forgotten, wondering what he was doing inside this fortress, when so many ships were over there ready to scatter like funnelled and smoking waterbeetles to all parts of the earth. I call myself communist, and yet I'm slave-laboured into building these sandbag ramparts to keep them out.

'You're not a communist, Brian,' Knotman had said when they got talking politics the other night. 'Not from what I know of you anyway.' 'Well I'm not part of this system, I'll tell you that.' 'I don't blame you,' Knotman went on, 'because I don't think anybody would be in their right mind, but most of the world isn't in its right mind, though I expect it will be one day.' 'What do you think I am then?' Brian asked. 'You might be a socialist when you've read more and know a bit about it.' 'Hitler was a socialist,' Brian laughed, 'a national socialist, and I don't want anything to do with a nut like him.' 'He wasn't a socialist,' Knotman informed him patiently, 'he only said he was to deceive the working man. He was sucking up to big business, and they used him to rob the Jews and stamp on the working man eventually. They fell for it as well. No, if you're anything you're a socialist-anarchist.' 'Maybe,' Brian admitted, but he knew that all men were brothers and that the wealth of the world should be pooled and divided fairly among those who worked, doctors and labourers, architects and mechanics. That's what those on the other side of the sandbags feel, and even though they might not, as Knotman averred, be true socialists, he was still building up sandbags to keep them out. At least, my eyes have been opened. All I've got to do now is learn to see with them, and when one person sees, maybe the next one will as well. 'It's a matter of time,' Knotman said, 'before the world unites, not only the workers either. It's taking the long way round to get there at the moment,' he laughed, 'but that's a thing that often happens.' 'Don't you think you should do something about it though, to help it?' Brian persisted. 'Yes, but no more than you can without being untrue to yourself. History is on our side, so just bide your time: you won't even know when to act; the first thing you know you'll be acting – and in the right way.' Brian found these words unsatisfactory to his nature, because in the jungle the communists had acted and he'd seen it with his own eyes, felt their bullets spinning and travelling around him.

He met Mimi at the Egyptian Café the evening before his train left. They sat by the trellis work, next door to crickets and bullfrogs: 'Every café has a café of insects and animals around it,' he laughed, spinning the miniature glass of neat gutrot round in the palm of his hand. He shivered at the coldness of the meeting, thinking how much better it would have been had they, through some accurate and supersensitive whim, decided half an hour ago to stand each other up – for old times' sake.

She wore neither lipstick nor make-up, had her hair tied back to show for the first time how long she'd been letting it grow in the last few weeks. 'I didn't want to come,' she said, 'but I couldn't help it.'

'Neither could I,' he said. 'I feel a rotter, a black-headed no-good bastard.'

'Why?' – her dark eyes opening wide.

'Because I'm leaving you when I don't want to. There's a boat waiting to take me eight thousand miles and I'm not dead keen on going the same way.'

'That's silly.'

'It isn't. I don't want to go. But I've got no willpower not to go. I want to stay here with you. But I know I shan't. I'm going to do something I don't want to do.'

'Everybody has to do that sometime or other. It won't be the first time for you either. Nor the last.'

'No,' he said, sending a hot needle of whisky down his thoat. 'It won't, now you come to mention it. Far from it. But I've never felt it as keen as this on any of the other times.' Insects spun like needlepoints through the doors and lattices of the ramshackle café, gathered in clouds around strings of bare light-bulbs. Tables around them were loaded with drinks and noisy jokes: the café had at least one fight a month, every second payday, often being put out of bounds, or closed down for a time. 'I've got to go soon,' she said softly, hoping he wouldn't make her stay, 'to get the next ferry. I'm supposed to be working, and if I don't go I'll lose my job.'

'I'll send you them books.' No tremor came into either voice, though he felt a sea of hopelessness pressing against his throat. 'That'll be nice,' she said, 'if you mean it.'

'Of course I do. I'll write as well – letters now and again on a Woolworths writing-pad. Who knows what I'll do? I might even come back in a year – or ten or fifteen years – walk into the Boston Lights and have a couple of dances with you before you know who I am.'

'You won't,' she said.

'I don't suppose so'

'You'll never leave England again. You'll be too busy working, and enjoying yourself.'

'Well,' he laughed, 'you can't do both.'

She stood up: 'I'll get a tri-shaw to the ferry.'

They walked to the door, looked for a moment at the dim lines and lights of the road that penetrated the heart-shaped shadows like spears and arrows denoting love, yet with no initials. He held her hand, kissed her on eyes and lips, felt the kiss returned and her hand go around him. 'Good-bye, Mimi. Look after yourself.' She hesitated, then turned back to him: 'What you told me the other night, about up in the jungle, you were brave. I understood. It was marvellous. You were right not to shoot at them.'

He watched her walk to the nearest rickshaw, saw the dim shadow of her light body bend and set itself in the seat. The feet of the man gathered speed between its shafts, soon beyond the range at which Brian, watching from the doorway, could hear. In place of it another and louder sound, stranger to him yet too real as soon as it was felt, swept over him, a sea from the back of his throat as he turned and walked in the opposite direction.

All day the train took him through familiar landscapes, leaping at first like a straightlined arrow between rice fields and by the edges of swamps, then towards mountains, twisting and turning like the illustrations of alternating-current theories on the blackboard at the radio school. The beautiful names of the country were lit up in the store-rooms of his memory: KEDAH, KELANTAN, PERAK, TRENGGANU, PAHANG, SELANGOR, NEGRI SEMBILAN – rhythmed out to the thudding self-assurance of steam-driven wheels, an antidote and agreeable opposite to deep jungle rolling beneath waterclouds on mountaintops, and fortified bungalows on village outskirts. The clean, beautifully rounded train wheels were taking him towards Kuala Lumpur in the evening, the big city from which the sun would sink at half past seven, just as it had twenty-four hours earlier beyond Pulau Timur, when he had watched it from the billet door before going off to see Mimi.

The passing jungle absorbed him, made his mind as blank as if he were drinking water from a stream he wasn't sure he would see again, so that it was only when he turned his eyes back to the carriage and noticed his webbing and pack straps spilling over the rack and swinging from the regular kick of the train that the fact of his having left Mimi for good rushed into him. Now that the journey had begun he couldn't get out of the country quick enough, yet his good-bye to her numbed him, rendered him unable to dissect to the bare bones an anguish he knew was useless but that stayed much of the journey with him. Towards dusk however the previous fire had left little for his pain to grip on, and Mimi was almost as far apart from him as Pauline had been when he had first danced with Mimi at the

Boston Lights over a year ago. As the train drew near to Kuala Lumpur he felt he had seen the last of her and of Malaya, and sensed the doors of its vivid beauty closing themselves in the immense distance and depth of mountains behind. He sat motionless, apart from the others of the demob party, gave himself up to the grief of a slow half-sweet amputation that grew to hard misery because he did not know to what exactly he was saying good-bye, and hadn't yet realized the vastness of the other part of his life still to be lived.

At Kuala Lumpur they gathered their kit to cross the dismal platforms towards the night train for Singapore. A transport sergeant stopped Brian and demanded to know where his rifle was. 'I haven't got one.'

'Sergeant, when you address me,' came the barked refrain.

'Sergeant,' he said.

'No one is allowed to travel on the night train without a rifle,' he stipulated. The group of them stood around, awaiting the issue. 'I don't care whether I get on the train or not,' Brian said. 'You dead-gut, you gestapo-eyed gett, you flap-mouthed effing scumpot.'

'You what?' – the fierce face was stuck towards him, smelling of sweat and carbolic soap and sucked-out fags. 'Listen,' he said, 'for your information the train going down last night got machine-gunned.'

'We had to hand our rifles in at Kota Libis, sergeant.'

'They'd no bloody right then. You'd better wait here till I see what's to be done with you.' He marched to the head of the platform and conferred with an officer. 'We'll miss the blinding boat now,' Jack cursed. 'I can see it.'

'They can stuff their rifles,' Brian said. 'Next time, I turn mine against that fuckpig – if he's on the train and we get ambushed he'd better watch out. By Christ I mean it. Still, if I don't get him maybe the bandits will – one of these days.'

'No such luck,' Kirkby said. 'It's poor bastards like Baker who stop it first. They never get the right ones.'

'Workers of the world unite!' Jack shouted. 'Let's get on that bloody train.'

The sergeant didn't look like coming back, so Brian loaded

his kit aboard, followed by the others. Each secured a bunk, debouched again to besiege an ice-cream trolley for the night's supplies.

The train set out, rattling away into the darkness of the wastelands. Brian undressed and climbed into his top bunk, pulling the sheet over him. Some of the others were already asleep, empty ice-cream cartons rolling about the gangway, knocking from side to side like worn-out bobbins at a cotton mill, the ones that had often poured from the backs of lorries on the tips, far away in a half-forgotten world. Sleep seemed impossible, and he lay on his back staring at the ceiling a few inches above his forehead. I'd rather be in bed at home, he thought, with Pauline, and soon will be. I'll get off the troopship in three weeks and get demobbed the next day, will take a flying train down to Nottingham and a taxi to Aspley and – where will we be that night? Will it be the Barleycorn or the Beacon for a good drink of mild, a laugh and a long talk, a few kisses when we think nobody's looking?

I'll see mam and dad as well. Look, dad, I'm back, I'm out of jail, finished, free, paid-up and ready for a hard job at the factory. Pauline, go and buy me a couple of pairs of overalls, an old jacket and a mashcan, a good pair of boots to keep the suds and steel-shavings out. What number bus do I need to get there spot on at half-past seven every morning? Don't try and tell me; I was born knowing it. Do you still work in the same shop, dad, carting steel rammel away on that barrow from them auto machines? Is that big bloke with a cauliflower nose still your shop-steward and does he bring the *Worker* in still every day? Tell him to put me down for the union as well. It'll be good to meet my old school pals again, back from their own jail sentences by now, I should think: Jim Skelton and Albert, Colin and Dave. Bert as well, when the loon gets finished with the further three years he had after all signed on for. He'd go sometime and see Ada and his Uncle Doddoe, get a plate of stew and slab of cake, and listen to Doddoe's nostalgic curses as he recounted his new adventures as a gaffer down the newly nationalized pit, or told of hair-raising escapades on his recently acquired high-powered motor-bike.

I'll bump into other pals as I charge across to the canteen for my dinner. Or maybe I wain't bother with the canteen but will go home to mam's, round the corner and up the street, along the yards and clobbering into the back door. 'Hey up, mam,' I'll shout from the lavatories: ''Ave yer mashed?' 'Ay, Brian, my owd duck,' she'll shout: 'I 'ave an' all.' And at night I'll get on the bus back to Pauline, out with the charging mass into fog or sleet (or maybe sunshine if I'm lucky, though Malaya's spoilt me for life in that way) smelling the fresh warmth of our room a mile before I get to it, the smell of her powder and kisses as I put my arm around her by the door and pinch her in the right places, dodging out of her way before she tries to crack me one. Over my snap I'll maybe tell her about the paint and wallpaper I'm thinking of buying, because somebody's got to get the house fixed up now that Mullinder's a long time gone, and I'll be just the bloke for that. I remember the cistern in the bathroom was going rusty before I left and I'm sure nobody's done much to it, so I'll start on that first. After tea I'll be out in the dark rainsoaked streets, passing the beer-offs and fish-and-chip shops with a fag at the slope, smarmed up in my best and heading for the pub to play darts and sup pints with Johnny and Ernie and Arthur, Nan and the rest of them. I'll spend a night or two helping the union, you can bet, because somebody's got to do it, and I feel I'm just the bloke for a thing like that. I'll get to know what's what as well, pull a few more books into the house to see what makes the world tick, maybe read some of those I nicked years ago. I ain't let the bastards grind me down in the air force, and I wain't let them get a look in at grinding me down outside; in fact if I 'ave owt to do with it the boot'll be on the other foot.

His thought swung from this to a vivid and agreeable picture flashed back from the forgotten train journey when on his way into Nottingham for his embarkation leave. He stood in the corridor kneeing his pack and kitbag towards the door, and as the train rolled over the Trent he saw below on its banks a youth and girl casually looking up at the bridge, his arm over her shoulder as if they had left off kissing to see the train over, and would kiss again as soon as it was out of sight.

While the train rattled him down through Malaya he couldn't get to sleep so thought mainly of Pauline and the long-since-gone aura of their courting days which he hoped would come back to them a while when he got demobbed and home. A daylight yet dim picture of the Cherry Orchard (now covered in houses, she had written) came back to him, bringing with it a stronger feeling of Pauline than any other scene from Nottingham. He smelt the damp soil and grass blades at the end of a summer day when they had wandered there after meeting at the factory, remembered touching the ground before spreading his mac in one of the hollows for them to lie on when dusk came to hide them from anybody's view. He smelt her body as he opened her coat, as she lay beneath him, sometimes guiding his hand in the urgency of her desire, and the great feeling of loving completeness with which they went on embracing each other afterwards, and then the smell of smoke commingling from their cigarettes and mixing with the odours of soil and darkness. This vision was strong and weak, came to him like beautiful music pianoed from some distant broadcasting station thousands of miles across the empty and landless ocean, indistinct and varying in loudness, from booming to nothing, but with the thread for ever kept whole in the mind that was attuned to it.

Turning through the jungle the train sloughed off tunnels like a magic snake and sent its woodsparks into the limitless air of the tiger night. His pillow was heavy as lead from sweat, the sheets cold. There seemed to be no ventilation, and he felt as if he were being killed by a nightmare, a storm of past and present rolling loose, unhinged by the transition taking place. He told himself that Malaya was already left behind, that in the morning when it was light he would be off the peninsula and in the catchnet of Singapore. The long dream of sunshine was behind him; jungle mountains were fur-backed sleeping monsters taking their rightful place in the past. He had made his last foray into the jungle – the Malayan jungle, anyway – and sent his final rhythmical morse phrases into the last blood-flecked sunset over Pulau Timur. Yet there was a feeling of heartbreak about leaving it all.

In the morning, he thought, as he fell off at last towards sleep, the boat will roll from Singapore, and I suppose there'll be a Highland band playing bagpipes as we draw away. Looking back, and looking forwards, he somehow felt he had the key to the door, especially when next year's birthday seemed already near enough for his hand to reach. (If you lived to be twenty, twenty-one or twenty-two – or a year older than you were at the moment, till your next birthday in fact – then you were immortal and indestructible.) And with the key to the door all you need do now, he smiled with an irony that made his heart constrict, was flex your labouring muscles to open it; though I wouldn't be surprised if that doesn't take more than half as long again.